P9-ECT-400

"Filled with multiple subplots, intense emotions, sizzling sex, and action galore."   —*ParaNormal Romance*

"Holly's Midnight saga is one of the best historical urban romantic fantasies written today . . . *Saving Midnight* transports readers to a romantic fantasy alternate depression era that is bloody great."   —*The Best Reviews*

COURTING MIDNIGHT

"There is mystery, adventure, and lots of hot sex. Fans of vampire, werewolf, and shape-shifter romances can savor this one."
            —*Romantic Times*

"A wonderful blend of emotional depth and explicit sensuality—it's just what I always hope for in an erotic romance. The result is a rewarding experience for any reader who prefers a high level of heat in her romance reading."   —*The Romance Reader*

"A wonderful . . . supernatural romance."
            —*ParaNormal Romance*

"A torrid paranormal historical tale that will thrill fans."
            —*Midwest Book Review*

HUNTING MIDNIGHT

"Sets the standards on erotica-meets-paranormal . . . Will have you making a wish for a man with a little wolf in him."
            —*Rendezvous*

"Amazing . . . Red-hot to the wall."   —*The Best Reviews*

"A roller-coaster ride of hot passion, danger, magick, and true love."   —*Historical Romance Club*

CATCHING MIDNIGHT

"A marvelously gripping mix of passion, sensuality, paranormal settings, betrayal, and triumph . . . Dazzling . . . A sensual feast."   —*Midwest Book Review continued . . .*

BEYOND SEDUCTION

ANGEL AT DAWN

EMMA HOLLY

BERKLEY SENSATION, NEW YORK

THE BERKLEY PUBLISHING GROUP
Published by the Penguin Group
Penguin Group (USA) Inc.
375 Hudson Street, New York, New York 10014, USA
Penguin Group (Canada), 90 Eglinton Avenue East, Suite 700, Toronto, Ontario M4P 2Y3, Canada
(a division of Pearson Penguin Canada Inc.)
Penguin Books Ltd., 80 Strand, London WC2R 0RL, England
Penguin Group Ireland, 25 St. Stephen's Green, Dublin 2, Ireland (a division of Penguin Books Ltd.)
Penguin Group (Australia), 250 Camberwell Road, Camberwell, Victoria 3124, Australia
(a division of Pearson Australia Group Pty. Ltd.)
Penguin Books India Pvt. Ltd., 11 Community Centre, Panchsheel Park, New Delhi—110 017, India
Penguin Group (NZ), 67 Apollo Drive, Rosedale, North Shore 0632, New Zealand
(a division of Pearson New Zealand Ltd.)
Penguin Books (South Africa) (Pty.) Ltd., 24 Sturdee Avenue, Rosebank, Johannesburg 2196,
South Africa

Penguin Books Ltd., Registered Offices: 80 Strand, London WC2R 0RL, England

ANGEL AT DAWN

A Berkley Sensation Book / published by arrangement with the author

PRINTING HISTORY
Berkley Sensation mass-market edition / January 2011

Copyright © 2011 by Emma Holly.
Excerpt from *Nightshade* by Michelle Rowen copyright © by Michelle Rouillard.
Cover art: "Couple" by Jon Bradley/Getty Images; "Building" by SuperStock.
Cover design by Leslie Worrell.
Interior text design by Laura K. Corless.

ISBN: 978-0-425-23965-0

BERKLEY® SENSATION
Berkley Sensation Books are published by The Berkley Publishing Group,
a division of Penguin Group (USA) Inc.,
375 Hudson Street, New York, New York 10014.
BERKLEY® SENSATION and the "B" design are trademarks of Penguin Group (USA) Inc.

PRINTED IN THE UNITED STATES OF AMERICA

10   9   8   7   6   5   4   3   2   1

THE VIEWING LIST

On the Waterfront
Rebel Without a Cause

I WAS A TEEN-AGE VAMPIRE
(page 309)

One

1956

Two Forks, Texas was a long way from Hollywood.

Grace's boss, up-and-coming director/producer Naomi Wei, had informed her the name of the town was "North Fork" back in the thirties. Why they changed the *North* to *Two* was anybody's guess. Maybe so visitors would think they'd actually find someone to eat with in this deadsville burg.

Grace grinned to herself as she turned the two-tone, pink and cream Plymouth Fury off the minuscule main drag. The urge to floor the V-8 past the Dairy Queen was almost irresistible. Although Miss Wei had disappointed Grace by not buying a convertible, Grace had once pushed the boatlike car to an impressive 120 miles per hour.

Miss Wei might be eccentric, but she knew her horsepower.

The road Grace had turned into wasn't as well paved as the two-lane that cut through town. As sprays of gravel hit the custom whitewalls, Grace's employer stirred sleepily in the passenger seat. Because Miss Wei had been anxious to reach their destination, they'd gotten an earlier start than usual for them: at least an hour before dusk. Miss Wei had immediately sank into a doze, bundled like Greta Garbo in her long powder blue silk scarf and her glamorous cat's-eye sunglasses.

"Thank God," she said now, tipping up the glasses to take in the lollipop red shards of sunset that were melting on the horizon.

Miss Wei was not, by any stretch of the imagination, a day person.

"We're close," Grace told her, as always enjoying the moment when her boss woke up. From their first encounter in the greasy spoon where Grace had been waitressing, she'd liked Miss Wei's company—in large part because she was the sort of take-charge woman Grace wanted to be someday. "The cat at the Texaco said the Durand Ranch is a mile west on the turnoff."

"The *cat*?" Miss Wei repeated, her perfectly painted mouth pursing with her smile.

Grace never got over how youthful her employer looked—her face unlined, her figure trim—and never mind she claimed to be old enough to be Grace's mother.

"*Cat* is what the kids say," Grace informed her.

Miss Wei laughed softly. "As if you weren't a kid yourself."

Grace's fingers tightened on the white steering wheel. At twenty-four and counting, she was hardly that. Sometimes she felt as if the sands in her hourglass were perpetually running out.

"Fine," Miss Wei teased with her uncanny ability to read expressions. "You're a woman of immense maturity and intelligence. Why else would I hire you?"

"Because I work for peanuts?"

"As I recall, I gave you a raise last week."

Because she had, Grace smiled to herself. The increase in pay had been generous.

"I'm worth it," she said blithely.

"You might be," Miss Wei conceded in the same airy tone.

She seemed happy tonight, her short hair ruffling in the wind from the open window, her dark eyes sparkling for the challenge in front of them. Filmmaking might be difficult for women, but the "old boys" at the studios never intimidated her.

"You're sure Mr. Durand is expecting us?" Grace asked.

"If he's not, he should be," Miss Wei answered, which wasn't exactly a yes.

But it was too late to worry, because the Durand Ranch's wooden gate arched over the road ahead like an image from a John Ford Western. The ground here was dusty. Flat as a pancake, too, with scruffy-looking grass a herd of dieting cattle could have starved on. An oil derrick poked up in the distance, black as night against the still faintly rosy sky. Its presence suggested Mr. Durand could afford extra feed for his hungry cows.

"Longhorns," Miss Wei said. "Christian raises Longhorn cattle. He's one of the last holdouts. They're hardy," she added when Grace lifted her brows at her. "Shorthorns and Herefords need too much pampering out here."

"I didn't know you were interested in ranching."

"I'm not. But it pays to know your quarry."

Slowing as they got closer—because who knew if this Texas boy kept shotguns—Grace pointed the car toward a low-slung adobe house.

"Try the barns," Miss Wei corrected. "Unless I miss my guess, Christian is in that one over there."

The barns were a collection of worn-looking plank buildings. Grace parked in the rutted dirt beside the one Miss Wei had waved her arm at. Grace was wearing flats for driving, but her soles still sank into the dry earth as she got out. The wide double doors of the barn stood open. Caged bulbs were strung along the rafters to light the big space inside, though Grace wouldn't have said they lit it well. If someone was in there, she couldn't pick them out from the shadows yet.

Miss Wei came around the front grill of the Fury and laid her cool hand on Grace's sleeve. "Just let me do the talking. Christian Durand . . . owes me his life, you could say."

For some reason, this request increased Grace's nervousness. She dried damp palms on her white pedal pushers, allowing her petite yet formidable employer to stride into the cavernous structure ahead of her. Grace followed more sedately and looked around.

Without question, this barn was a male domain. No cows resided between its walls, only a collection of automobiles of varying vintages and states of repair. Her mood improving, Grace spotted a 1950 Buick in the process of having its body "chopped" to reduce wind drag. The Harley-Davidson leaning on a hay bale also looked promising. Ever since Marlon Brando starred in *The Wild One*, motorcycles were big with kids.

Maybe her boss was on to something with this harebrained scheme.

"Christian," Miss Wei called out. "It's Naomi Wei. I've come to talk in person."

Grace heard the clank of a wrench hitting the barn's dirt floor.

She saw the man then, or his bottom half anyway. He was bent over the engine of a glossy all-black, two-seater, convertible Thunderbird. If the car hadn't made Grace's mouth water, the man in those Levi's certainly would have. The metal-caged bulb above him shone a literal spotlight on his well-formed behind. His legs were long and strong looking, their finer qualities only heightened by the cowboy boots he was sporting.

He stretched farther into the engine, exposing two tantalizing dimples at the top of his hindquarters. Grace's mouth did its best to go desert dry. Maybe he sensed her attention, because he spoke. His voice was dark and smooth, with just a hint of a Texas twang.

"Told you on the phone I wasn't interested. All dozen times you called."

"You never heard me out," Miss Wei said.

Mr. Durand straightened, braced his arms on the side of the open hood, then slammed it down with a bang. Grace's heart began to beat faster as she took in how broad his shoulders were. A snug-fitting and oddly spotless white T-shirt clung to his tapered back, making very clear the fact that he didn't have an ounce of fat on him . . . exactly the way she liked her men, to be truthful. Despite Mr. Durand's leanness, the muscles under that clean white cotton rippled with contained power. His hair was long enough to need tying back, and just as black and shiny as the finish on his car. His hair would have to be cut, of course; leading men couldn't run around looking like Indian braves. For herself, however, Grace liked the ponytail.

As if to warn her how much she liked it, her panties dampened in a hot, quick rush—a tad embarrassing, she thought. If Mr. Durand looked this good from the front, she might be in trouble. No matter how handsome the actor, Grace prided herself on always behaving professionally.

"I'm not an actor," he said, still not turning to her employer. "And if I were, I wouldn't star in no damn flick called *I Was a Teen-Age Vampire*."

"It's bound to make heaps of money."

"I don't need money," he snapped.

"You owe me, Christian."

"I don't owe you shit, *Naomi*."

It wasn't so much his language as his unabashed hostility that had Grace sucking in her breath. The sound wasn't loud, but Mr. Durand spun around like lightning on hearing it.

He was facing her then, and his eyes went wide. Grace's heart slammed into her ribs, but he seemed more shocked than she was. Knowing pretty well how she looked, she was used to men reacting to the sight of her. This man's response took the cake from them all. His head jerked back like someone had popped a knuckle sandwich into his chin.

He bit out a word she thought meant *shit* in German.

"Well," Miss Wei purred, her gaze shifting back and forth between them. "Isn't this interesting?"

Grace's brain recovered enough to realize that Mr. Durand's face was movie-star gorgeous, which probably accounted for why her pulse was pounding like a jackhammer. Oh, he didn't resemble James Dean or Marlon Brando, but he had their can't-take-your-eyes-off-him charisma. She judged him about Dean's age, early twenties or thereabouts, a little lined from working outdoors but still young enough to pass for eighteen. His coffee dark eyes smoldered with hypnotizing hints of gold. His lips were thin, it was true, but a girl could slice her heart on those high cheekbones. Even his arms were sexy, the muscles graceful as they hung loosely at his sides. And, by golly, he was *tall*—six feet and change, she was willing to bet. Neither the recently departed Dean nor the still-rising Brando could pretend that.

Best of all, from the toes of his cowboy boots to the dashing widow's peak of his hair, Christian Durand screamed *dangerous*.

"You're right, boss," Grace said, before she could worry how it would sound. "Every red-blooded American female *is* guaranteed to sigh over him."

Christian couldn't wrench his attention from the woman who'd traipsed uninvited into his barn with Nim Wei. She was the spitting image of his Grace, lost to him for—*Christ*—nearly five centuries. This female was a little older, but every year had given her a blessing. Her face had character to go with its prettiness: a shadow to make her glow shine brighter, a stubbornness to her peach-soft jaw.

Her tidy outfit of pedal pushers and crisp white blouse was ridiculous, of course, a girl playing dress-up as someone far more serious and less sensual than she was. Her figure was precisely the sweet temptation he remembered: a buxom, narrow-hipped torso set atop a pair of showgirl's legs. This woman's hair was shorter than Grace's, waving only to her shoulders, though it *was* the same deep, dark red.

Movie actress hair, he supposed. Had to come in Technicolor.

Vampire that he was, with all the knee-jerk responses that went with that, he'd started hardening the instant he saw her. *Hardening* wasn't the word for what he was doing now. Running his eyes up and down her very warm-blooded beauty had his prick screaming for mercy inside his jeans.

It didn't care that she couldn't be his lost beloved. It was chomping at the bit to burn down this barn with her. On the bare floor right in front of him sounded fine, with his pike shoved up her pussy as far as it would go. He winced as his cock struggled harder against his fly, but the erotic images wouldn't stop. It had been too long since he'd cut loose with a woman. He had too little trouble imagining this one's ankles around his ears.

"This is Grace," Nim Wei said in that insinuating voice of hers. As distracted as he was, he marveled that he made out the words at all. "She's my close personal assistant. If you agree to star in my movie, you'll be seeing her every day."

The girl seemed startled by her employer's promise, but she stuck out her hand gamely.

"Grace Michaels," she said. "I'm very pleased to meet you, Mr. Durand."

The name belatedly registered.

"*Grace?*" he repeated, abruptly hoarse. His normally cool palm turned fiery where she clasped it.

"Michaels. But please call me Grace if you like."

He couldn't release her hand. Her name was Grace, and her eyes were as clear and green as a peridot. All the times he'd stared into them rushed back like yesterday. He remembered these very fingers touching him with such kindness he'd feared he'd cry, remembered the way her spectral energy could tingle straight up his cock. The nerves there were tingling now—jangling, really, like a telephone ringing off the hook. Grace wasn't a ghost anymore. She was as solid as the ground under him. Lord help him, if she brushed against him, his dick was going to erupt.

"Christian," he said, having to push his name past the constriction inside his throat. "My name is Christian. Please call me that."

"Christian," she agreed nervously.

When she attempted to tug her hand back, his fangs punched down from his gums, reacting precisely as if she were prey fleeing. Her accelerated pulse was lub-dubbing in his ears, a siren song he wasn't certain he could resist. Alarmed by his out-of-control responses, he let her go and stepped back.

Grace massaged her palm as if he'd hurt it.

"So?" Nim Wei said to him.

He looked at her, and he had no idea what she was asking. He wasn't even certain what he felt. However it had happened, this seemed to be Grace, the same Grace who'd promised him forever and then abandoned him in his darkest hour. His face flashed hot and then icy. Did he hate her? Did he love her? Did he simply want to fuck her without stopping for the next ten years?

The painful surge of blood to his groin told him the answer to that was affirmative.

"Christian?" Nim Wei said, her lithe little arms folded. "Are you going to help me make this flick or not?"

She doesn't know, he thought. *Not who Grace was. Not what she means to me. All she knows is that her assistant has my cylinders running hot.*

Grace couldn't have remembered Nim Wei, either, or she wouldn't have been trotting after her like a faithful girl Friday. Hell, the prissy sweater she'd tied around her shoulders was the same shade of powder blue as Nim Wei's scarf. The witch of Florence was Grace's goddamned mentor, as if Nim Wei weren't responsible for half the trouble that befell them both back then.

All of which boiled down to Grace not remembering him.

He stared into her wide green eyes, his immortal heart contracting in his chest with an emotion very much like terror. She wasn't putting on an act. He saw no recognition in her expression. She *was* flushed; attracted, unless he was mistaken, and embarrassed because of it, but only in the way—how had she put it?—any red-blooded American girl might be.

He didn't understand what it meant. Had she been reincarnated like that crazy Bridey Murphy from the bestselling book? Could people come back looking just as they had before?

Without realizing it, he'd folded his arms in an echo of Nim Wei's posture. He caught a flash from Grace's mind of how he looked with his biceps bulging in the white T-shirt. That definitely didn't lower his blood pressure. When Grace extended her hand to touch his bare forearm, her fingers were trembling.

"We'd both consider it a favor if you'd agree," she said. "Miss Wei needs an ace in the hole to break out of making B movies."

"And you think I'd be your ace."

"Oh, *absolutely*," Grace breathed, her enthusiasm momentarily teenagerlike. "I know you're inexperienced, but we could coach you. A person's presence is what matters for most films. Acting is something plenty of folks can learn."

"And *you* could coach me," he said.

Grace shot an uncertain glance at her boss before turning back to him. "We both could. Or we could hire someone. Whatever you're comfortable with."

Despite feeling more discomposed than he had in four centuries, despite loving the peaceful life he'd built for himself out here, Christian sensed a rare canary-eating grin rising up in him. Love Grace or loathe her, he couldn't hate the prospect of having her at his beck and call.

As the grin spread across his face, threatening to bare his fangs, Grace tensed warily back from him.

"*You* coach me," he said firmly, "and we might have a deal."

"She'd be delighted to!" Nim Wei exclaimed before Grace could speak. "Now why don't we drive to that two-bit town of yours and all have a drink on it."

How much he disliked her answering for Grace dismayed him. After all this time, and certainly considering the way Grace had broken her promises, he shouldn't have felt protective. His shoulders began to ache with the tension gathering there.

"Would you excuse us, Grace?" he said, his gaze locked firmly on Nim Wei's, where he suspected it was safer. He noticed idly that the bitch queen had cut her hair. Because the black locks didn't or wouldn't curl, the feathery cut was boyish, giving the vampiress a disconcertingly modern look. Modern or not, he bet she was as devious as ever. "Your boss and I have a thing or two to sort out."

He took his old nemesis by her deceptively slender elbow, pulling her to the shadowed privacy of his workbench—far enough that Grace's human ears wouldn't hear. He wasn't consciously showing off his strength, but he knew he'd done so when Nim Wei rubbed her arm.

"Someone's been eating their spinach," she observed dryly.

"You're not the only master vampire here." He'd lowered his voice in order not to sound petulant. Nim Wei smirked anyway. They both knew physical strength was probably the only arena where he could match her—maybe the least important in an age that had advanced so far beyond hand-to-hand combat. Christian was relatively new to his elder status. Nim Wei had been queen among their kind for millennia. Add to that her mystic bent, and he doubted her drawing his long-lost lover into her orbit was a coincidence. Why Nim Wei had drawn Grace was a better question. She'd always been able to sense and pluck the strands of Fate for her convenience, including when she wasn't aware of it.

Not inclined to help her become aware, he shielded his thoughts from her.

"You shouldn't be offering that girl on a platter like she's your possession."

Nim Wei's perfect black eyebrows rose. "Nonsense. Grace adores me. And rightly so. I saved her from a fate worse than death—or almost. You've no idea what indignities human waitresses put up with. Besides, don't you want me offering her to you?"

Christian ordered his fingers to release the edge of the worktable, where they were threatening to crush the wood to sawdust. It was an effort to speak coolly. "If I wanted her, I wouldn't need your help."

Nim Wei's smile exposed a quicksilver flash of fang. "Don't be so sure. Grace already idolizes me. Imagine if I bit her. I doubt even your red-blooded manliness could override my thrall."

His hand blurred up to grip her neck so swiftly that his better judgment took a moment to catch up. He might as

well have throttled a statue. Unruffled by his attack, Nim
Wei's marble white fingers stroked the bones of his wrist.

"Temper, temper," she scolded as he eased his hold and
let go. "Really, Christian, this is a wonderful opportunity
I'm offering you. A bit of a challenge to ameliorate your
boredom."

"I'm not bored."

"A little birdie told me you resigned from X-Section."

"Senator McCarthy's witch hunts soured me on spying.
Let the humans search under their own beds for Commu-
nists."

She nodded knowingly. "You want to run your life, to
shape it without answering to anyone. I remember being
that age."

Christian glanced past his maker. Grace was hunkered
down beside his Harley, her fingers trailing curiously along
the chrome tailpipe. Hers was a human posture: slightly
awkward and off balance, but it seemed beautiful all the
same. Her hair glowed like blood where the uncertain
light touched it. His ribs tightened with discomfort. Could
she be the symbol of what he wanted? A future such as
mortals dreamed of when they reached adulthood? He
snorted at the ludicrous concept. He was 496. He was never
going to have two-point-five children and a rancher in the
suburbs.

"I gave you this existence," Nim Wei reminded him.
"Without me, even the worms who ate you would be dust
by now."

"You seem to forget the less than idyllic circumstances
of my change, the way you helped my father destroy my
life until I had nowhere else to turn."

"You're the one who craved the sort of vengeance only
an *upyr* could mete out. Got it, too, as I recall. In any case,
if I worried about every vampire who harbored a grudge
against me, I'd never ask for favors."

"God forbid," he muttered.

Nim Wei slapped his upper arm, the sting a bit too sharp to be friendly. "However little you like to acknowledge it, you're my get: a city vampire. Moldering out here among the cows won't ever be enough for you."

"I like the quiet."

"Please. You can be quiet when you're dead. You know as well as I do the question isn't how many years we *can* live; it's how many we *want* to. Time has weight, Christian. I can see yours weighing on you."

"And this is your answer? To make some idiot movie about vampires?"

She shrugged, a fey gold amusement glinting out from under her down-swept lashes. "It's entertaining to hide among the humans, to beat them at their own games."

"Some victory that is when you're making up the rules."

"I'm only cheating a little."

"If one of your subjects wanted to do this, you'd never permit it."

"Maybe I need to express myself."

She threw this off like a joke, but he didn't doubt it was true. Though she excelled at hiding her true nature from mortal eyes, she'd always had a flamboyant streak. Considering the newly prosperous humans around her were so busy "expressing" themselves by buying yellow refrigerators and green bathtubs, why should she be immune?

"Come on," she said coaxingly. "It can't hurt to share a drink with the two of us. Grace is adorable when she's tipsy. Makes her cheeks all yummy and pink."

The growl that trickled from his throat was as dark as it was unplanned. Normally, he gave nothing of his interior life away. Laughing, Nim Wei poked his chest with a pink-frosted fingernail.

"Take your motorcycle," she advised. "Grace will love watching your big strong thighs straddle that. Especially if you have one of those biker jackets with the zippers all over it."

She turned away before he could form his curse into words.

"Grace," she called. "Start the car. Christian has agreed to hear out our pitch."

The primal roar of Christian's motorcycle led Grace through the town of Two Forks. The Fury's headlights, their only illumination once they left the main street behind, lit up their mounted guide. Something in the way his strong young body leaned into the turns, in how his booted foot strafed the loose dirt for balance, had Grace swallowing hard. She didn't doubt Christian could sit a horse—or whatever the proper term was—but watching him maneuver that growling monster around the curves made him seem both an ancient and modern beast.

A centaur, she thought, whose lower half was a big machine.

That image was more suggestive than she'd intended. Blushing, she squirmed in the driver's seat.

"Handy he rides so well," Miss Wei observed above the rush of the September wind. Her slender hand held her scarf in place. "Almost makes one think he was born to play Joe Pryor."

"Yes," Grace agreed, then cleared her froggy throat. "We won't have to hire a stunt double for those scenes."

Christian's thighs bunched as he turned into a flat, dusty parking lot. His butt clenched, too, but Grace tore her eyes from that before she clipped the rear of someone's parked Ford pickup. It was cool now that dark had fallen, but her sweaty hands nearly slipped on the steering wheel. She had to pull herself together, and she had to do it now.

She'd met handsome men before, plenty of them in LA. Betraying an interest wasn't compatible with being taken seriously—hard enough for females at the best of times. In this case, she saw a reason for prejudice. How could you appear authoritative if you behaved like a love-starved fan? Grace didn't need to be vulnerable, not in any part of her life. Watching her mother abandon all integrity to appease her father had taught Grace that hard lesson.

The reminder issued, she parked the car and got out.

Christian had led them to a rustic bar called Buck's on the edge of town. It didn't look like much to her, but it must have been a popular watering hole. Vehicles as old as the pickup she'd parked next to filled the slots near the door. Christian waited there for them, tall and expressionless, while twangy hillbilly music spit through the cracks in the worn building. He was tall enough that the hems of his jeans weren't rolled up.

"Charming place," Miss Wei observed as they reached him.

"You're the one who wanted a drink." Christian's gaze slid to Grace's and locked there. Though the look he gave her was neither friendly nor flirtatious, heat cruised through her like a Russian rocket. His eyes were thick-lashed and dark—unreadable, she would say. His thin lips tightened as if he disapproved of her in some way.

Grace's panties redampened, which they really should not have done.

"Thank you," she said, her voice too breathy as he held the door for her.

Inside, the drinking spot was dark, swirling with tobacco smoke, and stuck in a style that harkened back to when Two Forks had still been *North*. Yellowed WPA posters hung on the walls, reminders of a depression that had been wiped out by the prosperous aftermath of the last world war. Unimpressed by the improvement, a Lone Star beer sign flickered moodily behind the bar.

At Christian's approach, two men vacated a booth: *his* booth, apparently. Young though he was, Christian must have been a big wheel in Two Forks. The bartender walked over almost before they sat down.

Grace didn't know if it was better or worse that Christian had placed himself across from Miss Wei and her. She wouldn't have wanted to sit next to him, but he really was too good-looking to confront comfortably.

"Mr. Durand," the bartender said, his manner as respectful as if Christian were a much older man. "What can I get you and your guests tonight?"

Christian narrowed his eyes at Grace. "You sure you're old enough to drink?"

"You're asking *me* that?" Grace retorted in surprise, because he looked younger than she did.

"Grace is under the impression that she's a twenty-four-year-old crone," Miss Wei put in helpfully.

Christian grunted. "Even if she were, she wouldn't stay one hanging around you."

This sounded like an insult, but Grace wasn't sure to whom. When she glanced at her employer, Miss Wei was pursing her mouth in some sort of tease at their terse companion. Concluding her boss could take care of herself, Grace turned to the bartender.

"I'll have a beer," she said firmly. "Whatever's cold."

"The usual," Christian said, "and the same for *Naomi* here."

The currents between the pair were making her uneasy, which might have explained why she spoke less cautiously than normal when the glasses were set down.

"*Wine* is your usual?" she exclaimed.

Christian raised one eyebrow. "You have some objection?"

"Beer would be better. Or bourbon with branch water."

"Better for what?"

She refused to let his tone cow her. "Better for your image. It's fine to be sensitive. James Dean proved girls go for that, but you don't want to take it too far. I'm afraid we'll have to cut your hair as well. Your clothes are fine, and the motorcycle's great, but if you had one of those black leather biker jackets to wear with it, that would be wonderful."

For some reason, Miss Wei snickered into her wine.

Whatever the joke, Christian didn't share her amusement. "I didn't realize you were going to be *coaching* me on how to pull on my pants."

"It's just how the game is played," Grace said, leaning forward earnestly. If Christian didn't get this, they'd be stuck in the mud right here. "All the studios manage their stars' images. You'll be an artist, sure, but moviegoers want a fantasy they can latch onto. Men have to be *men*. I don't mean to insult you. You really are close to our ideal."

"How nice to hear," Christian drawled icily.

He'd leaned back as she leaned forward, his body screaming annoyance even as his face remained studiously blank. Grace would have been grateful for Miss Wei's aid, but her employer seemed content to leave the talking to her. Determined not to disappoint her, Grace drew a bolstering breath.

"Take Vivian Lavelle," she said, "the actress we cast to star opposite you. She's been playing juvenile characters for years. Fresh-faced. Puppies and gingham bows. Now that she's eighteen, she wants to make the transition to adult roles."

"Don't tell me she'll be tossing back bourbon, too."

Grace laughed in spite of her nerves. "No, but we did arrange for her to be seen dating older leading men. If you act like a grown-up, it's easier to be considered one."

"And you arranged this."

Grace shrugged. "We called the actors' agents to set it up. It makes the older men seem younger. Everyone benefits."

"My God," Christian murmured. "Since when have *you* been this cynical?"

Grace didn't understand his emphasis, only that it made her feel defensive. "It's not cynical; it's pragmatic. It's—"

"—how the game is played," he finished. With long, agile fingers, he turned his wineglass slowly on the table. His gaze was fastened on hers again. Hot-faced beneath the scrutiny, Grace couldn't keep her hand from creeping up to her hair. Its waves were smooth already, but she hadn't felt this self-conscious since her days of being the perpetual new girl at school.

"It isn't a bad game," Miss Wei said into the pause. "In fact, making movies is exhilarating. All those people sitting in the dark, staring up at you on the screen. They're in the cup of your palm, Christian, caught up in the story you're telling. That's a power so basic most of us have forgotten how magical it can be."

"Most of *us*," Christian repeated, thankfully shifting his attention away from Grace.

"Everyone needs to leave a mark," Miss Wei said softly. "Maybe everyone deserves to."

Christian's dark eyes glittered and then turned down.

The small reaction humanized him. Prickly though he might be, he was like any young person: wondering what he'd been born for, why it mattered that he drew breath. The ability to see into people's hearts and know what they longed for was one of the gifts Grace most admired in her employer. Though she'd never be anyone's doormat, Miss Wei was a truly generous soul.

"Jesus," Christian said for no reason she could think of, his startled gaze jerking up to hers. "That's some bill of goods she sold you."

"What?" Grace asked, wondering where she'd lost track of this conversation. Her confusion increased when Miss Wei rose.

"I think we should go now," she said. "Christian needs more time to consider our proposal."

Grace gawped at her. They'd barely started in on convincing him. It wasn't like her mentor to cut short a pitch. That was too close to taking no for an answer.

"Now," Miss Wei said, laying her hand rather firmly on Grace's shoulder.

Grace got up as Christian slouched back on his bench and snorted derisively. "Better hurry. Before your house of cards collapses."

Miss Wei had been guiding Grace away, but Christian's comment stiffened and turned her back. "There is no house of cards. You're the one who invaded Grace's privacy. I'm simply protecting her."

Christian's sneer of response held more layers than Grace could see any basis for.

"Good night," she said, because it seemed like one of them ought to be polite. "I hope you consider taking the role. I think you'd be swell in it."

Christian's eyes darkened dangerously. As she followed her employer out of the bar, Grace had the sensation that his gaze was boring into her neck.

Miss Wei didn't say a word, not in apology or explanation, until they pulled into the spanking-new Best Western where they'd booked rooms. Per Miss Wei's request, their accommodations were at opposite ends of the roadside motel. Though it wasn't Grace's place to judge, she imagined the separation was due to her employer's fondness for picking up strange men. Shared walls might have made that fondness a little too obvious.

Not leaving the car just yet, Miss Wei turned to her on the front seat. Grace expected her to explain her recent behavior, but that wasn't what happened.

"Do you trust me, Grace?" Miss Wei asked.

"Of course I do!" she exclaimed.

"I'd like you to look into my eyes," she said. "I'd like you to think about the reasons you know you can rely on me."

Grace blinked in surprise. The light from the motel sign cast a glow across Miss Wei's face. Her features were so perfect, so smooth and unblemished, that they seemed unreal. Dizziness whirled through Grace as golden sparks appeared to spiral upward from the depths of Miss Wei's black eyes. With a wistfulness Grace couldn't fathom, her employer brushed Grace's left cheek with cool knuckles.

"I hope I'm not going to regret this."

"Regret what?" Grace asked, the question slurred.

Miss Wei put her hands on either side of Grace's temples. "If Christian wants you, he should have to figure you out just like any man. So . . . your thoughts are your own, my friend, and your will. No one can violate them, not even me. As I speak these words, so may they come to be."

Grace shook herself. She had the impression she'd missed something. "Are you okay, boss?"

"Fine," she said. "Why don't you pop the trunk, and we'll get our bags? We'll tackle our future movie star tomorrow."

Two

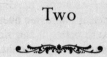

Unable to lie abed while their business remained unsettled, Grace got up bright and early—well, ten-ish, anyway—and drove back to Christian's ranch. The endless sky was clear as crystal, the temperature milder than she expected for Texas. Willing to use her sex appeal within reason, she wore a dress today: a pretty Dior knockoff with a full skirt and petticoats. The fitted bodice showed off her bust, and the flowered fabric's green background made her hair redder—something men seemed to appreciate.

Confident she looked her best, Grace knocked briskly on the adobe house's wide Spanish door.

Her calm was ruined by it taking three tries for anyone to answer. When someone did, it was a trim older man with a sun-lined face.

"Can I help you, miss?" he asked, his drawl twice as thick as Christian's.

Grace held her spine as straight as she could, the precious

document she carried clutched close against her waist. "I'm here to see Mr. Durand. We have business to discuss."

The older man chuckled. "Haven't been doing business with him long, have you, honey? Not if you're coming here at this hour."

Christian's gatekeeper wasn't moving out of the doorway, and he didn't appear impressed by her feminine wiles. Grace wished she were better at batting her lashes, but it was too late to fix that now.

"Perhaps I could leave a message. If he's busy with a cow."

The older man frowned like he was going to turn her away. Luckily, Christian appeared in the shadowy hall behind him. Grace's stomach did an unsettling flip. He was dressed only in his blue jeans. Both his torso and feet were bare. He didn't have a lot of hair on his chest, just a thin veil of black over steely muscles and olive skin. The way that hair narrowed to a line and dove past his navel seemed too personal to stare at.

"It's all right," he said, sounding as sleepy as if he'd just then rolled out of bed. "I'll talk to her."

His guard dog seemed surprised to hear this. "You sure?"

Christian rubbed his palms up and down his face, causing interesting muscles to shift in his arms and chest. His biceps displayed veins Grace wasn't familiar with. "I'm sure. Go check on the barbwire in the east pasture."

The older man opened his mouth, shut it, then shot Grace a warning look. "Don't you overstay your welcome, gal."

"Cross my heart," Grace promised, which earned her a harder stare than before.

Sadly, Christian's manners weren't any better than his companion's. Grace surmised he must be a night person like Nim Wei.

"Suppose you want coffee," he muttered.

He turned, treating her to his fine back view, and padded on long pale feet into a large, viga-beamed kitchen. She would have said it was decorated in "frontier" style, except the cabinets looked like they really might date back to those days. He had the usual appliances, though their color was hard to identify. The room was as dim as the entryway, probably because every shade in the place was pulled.

"Was that man your father?" Grace asked as she followed.

"Roy? Hardly. Though I suppose he acts like one now and then." He scratched his bare chest, then seemed to remember what he'd come here for—or at least he sort of remembered. He tried three doors before finding the coffee mugs. He took one down like it was heavy. "Roy usually keeps coffee brewed on the stove."

Grace could tell he did. Even from where she stood, the pot smelled undrinkable. Deciding politeness was the better part of valor, Grace took a seat at the stainless steel and splatter-patterned Formica table. She didn't ask if Christian wanted to don a shirt. As absentminded as he was acting, he might disappear for good.

"I thought we could talk some more," she said. "About you starring in our film."

"Right." He set a mug half full of ink before her, then glanced unsurely toward the big Frigidaire.

"I *would* like cream," she prompted, "and sugar if you have it."

This resulted in more searching and banging of cabinets, but at last Christian unearthed the items she'd requested. He dropped down, with apparent relief, into the vinyl chair opposite hers.

"Don't cook much," he said gruffly.

Because this seemed a reluctant apology, Grace found herself smiling. "I brought the script." She pushed the clipped stack of pages across the table. "I thought reading it might help you make up your mind."

He took it, blinked a few times, and looked up at her. Grace had to brace against the heart-stopping handsomeness of his face.

"Your name is on the front page," he said.

When he mentioned this, Grace flushed the hardest yet, the rush of vibrant color sweeping up her forehead. Nim Wei was right about her blushes being yummy. Though it was too early for his responses to be at full strength, his gums itched in reaction. If it hadn't been daytime, he'd have been flashing fang. Gritting his still-normal teeth, he focused on her answer.

"I reworked the screenplay," she said, "so Miss Wei said I should share credit. Film is a visual medium, and the first version was too long and talky. Also, there was too much on-the-nose dialogue."

"On the nose?"

"That means characters say exactly what they're thinking."

"And that's wrong?"

"It's not wrong; it's just boring. For example, suppose your character, Joe, walks up to his gang and says, 'Charlie, I'm mad as hell because I think you're trying to take over. Why don't we rumble?' It's more interesting for the audience if Joe picks a fight over something else, and they can guess why he's doing it on the basis of actions that came before. Even if Joe and Charlie don't fight, the audience will know Joe's angry because he's showing it on his face. They're more involved if they're helping puzzle out the story. Plus, it's more like real life. People rarely tell the truth about themselves straight out. Half the time, they don't even know what it is."

Enthusiasm had carried her through this speech, her

blood close to her skin for different reasons now. Grace had changed from the Grace he knew, if indeed he'd ever known her. She gave thought to this movie stuff. It was important to her. Unnerved, he felt the metal frame of his chair dig into his shoulder blades.

"I'm not in the habit of putting my emotions on display."

"But that's perfect!" Grace responded. "You show and hide them at the same time. Acting in a movie isn't like being in a play onstage, where you have to play to the farthest rows. The camera picks up every facial twitch and flicker. Every expression can be smaller. Look at you now, if you doubt you're expressive."

Christian's eyes went unnaturally wide. "Now?"

"You've leaned away from me in your chair. Your hands are pressing the table hard enough that your fingertips have gone white. You're not comfortable with me, and your body says your guard is up. That's exactly the sort of reaction Miss Wei and I want to catch on film. In fact, that guardedness you're automatically demonstrating is the core of Joe Pryor's character."

For a moment, Christian's brain was jarred clear of thought. It shocked him that she saw so much, that he'd lost his usual blank face in front of her. Needing to distract himself as much as her, he tapped the stack of paper in front of him.

"You really think my reading this script will convince me to work with you?"

"Well, it isn't Tolstoy, but I figured once you saw it was a story young people could relate to, you'd want to be part of it."

Clearly, she thought of him as a "young person"— younger than she was, apparently. Christian laughed under his breath. "There really isn't anything inside you that knows who I am, is there?"

Grace's brow furrowed. "I've always thought the best way for people to know you is to show them what you can do."

This struck him as the rationale of someone who *didn't* want anyone getting close. "Don't you think any number of real actors would appreciate this opportunity more than me?"

"We auditioned them. By the hundreds. A few were all right, but none were magical. You're magical, Mr. Durand. You have that mysterious something inside you the big ones have, that special spark no one can take their eyes off of."

"Christian," he reminded her absently.

They'd leaned toward each other with their forearms on the table, and she'd reached out to cover his hand. Realizing this, her fingers tensed as she prepared to withdraw. Then she stopped. He watched her throat move with a swallow.

"Christian, then. You did imply you wanted to work with me."

Her fingers felt like ice to his vampire senses, no small accomplishment for a warm-blooded being. He didn't have to read her to know she didn't truly want to flirt; she was simply willing to for her job. Feeling abruptly cooler himself, he pulled his hand out from under hers.

"I did express that interest, but not because I wanted to take advantage of you against your will."

"Of course," she said, fighting a stammer. "Forgive me. I didn't mean to suggest you did."

He suspected they both were lying, which possibly proved her point about on-the-nose dialogue. He turned his head to the doorway, cursing softly in *Schwyzerdütsch*. He asked himself what would be so wrong about taking advantage. Given what she'd done to him, no matter if she didn't remember, didn't she deserve it? *He* certainly deserved something. Needed it, if it came to that.

His legs were sprawled beneath the little eat-in table, his bare feet so close to hers he couldn't help but register her heat. He wanted to tug at his jeans, his now huge erection uncomfortable. He gripped the table's molded steel edge instead.

"I'll read the script," he said, harsh and low. "Come back tonight at nine. I'll give you my answer then."

Grace pushed awkwardly from her chair, the slight human imperfections in her movements unacceptably appealing. "Of course. I'm sorry for dropping in unannounced. I'll return later."

"Grace." His voice stopped her at the kitchen doorway. When she turned, he feared his heart would pound through his chest. The hesitance in her expression, the lush beauty of her features, were exactly as he remembered.

"Yes?" she asked breathily.

He was nearly breathy himself. "When you come back tonight? Be sure you come alone."

Despite his piled-up years, Christian hadn't read ten pages before he saw what Grace meant about this being a story young people could relate to. *I Was a Teen-Age Vampire* was operatic, with a generous ladling of high school angst. Its central characters were teenagers, the few adults little more than mustache-twirling obstacles to the young people's seemingly just desires. The villain was Joe Pryor's father, who locked horns with his son in a classic intergenerational struggle. Age versus youth. Corruption versus ideals. The plot couldn't have been heavier-handed if he'd written it himself when he was Joe's age.

He finished the tale in half an hour, with the back of his neck tingling. When he reached the scene where Joe's power-hungry father slew one of his friends, Christian gasped audibly. The dead boy was called Matthew, and though it wasn't spelled out, he might have been romantically involved with another gang member named Philip. Matthaus and Philippe had been Christian's friends when he was mortal—a difference of a few letters. They'd died not at his father's hand, but certainly at his behest.

Substitute a band of Swiss mercenaries for a motorcycle gang, and it sure looked like Grace was stealing pages from his past.

"Christ," Christian said and flipped faster to the end.

When Roy returned at noon for lunch, Christian was still slumped in the kitchen chair, his hands feathering slowly across the first page of Grace's script. The sun that snuck past the edges of the window shades wasn't strong enough to burn him, only to make him drunk. His thoughts were so sluggish they could have been waterlogged. The effect was pleasant if dangerous: an opium dream for vampires.

Roy gave him a look that said he knew what he'd been doing and didn't approve. He strode past Christian with a grunt, retrieving a sandwich and a beer from the Frigidaire. Roy didn't cook any more than Christian did. A woman from town delivered supplies to them every couple days. Roy unwrapped his sandwich, cracked the beer, then took a pull from it. Almost as familiar with Roy's rhythms as he was with his own, Christian knew he'd be saying his piece any moment now.

"Didn't feel like sleeping today?" Roy asked.

"Couldn't," Christian returned.

"You know you shouldn't sit up like this. It makes you blue. Who was that gal anyway?"

"Someone from my past."

Roy thunked his Lone Star on the counter. "How can that be? She was a kid."

Though human, Roy was—thanks to a brief and involuntary stint as a vampire during the depression—a lot older than he looked. It was one of the reasons he and Christian had fallen in together. The associates Roy used to have would have expected him to be dead by now.

"I can't explain it," Christian said, his voice thick from

sun exposure. "But I'm sure she's someone I was involved with when I was mortal."

"That was a long time ago."

"Yes." Christian shook himself and sat straighter. "She's working with Nim Wei on that vampire film. Evidently, Grace is responsible for the script." He patted the cover, just barely touching it with his palms. "There are details in here, parallels to experiences from my life, that I don't think she could have invented by accident."

Roy spoke around a bite of sandwich. "You think those two are running a scam on you?"

"I don't know. If they are, I'm not sensing it."

"So you reckon this is some sort of reincarnation deal? That this gal has a past life swimming up in her unconscious?"

It seemed like more than that to Christian, but all he could do was shrug. Roy leaned back into the counter.

"Well," he said in his deceptively lazy drawl, "I know I owe your illustrious queen. She did turn me mostly human again. The thing is, I wouldn't put anything past her. Besides which, casting a vampire in a vampire movie is a pretty damn big risk. How does she know she won't blow the lid off y'all's secret existence?"

"I believe the risk is part of the appeal for her."

"Hmph," Roy said, his final comment for the time being. He finished his lunch in silence, then patted Christian's shoulder.

The touch sparked Christian's recall of another man, one he hadn't thought of in a while. Hans had been a father figure to him, gruff and protective much like Roy could be. Christian's real father had arranged to have Hans murdered, by that sneaking bastard Lavaux. He'd died bleeding in the mud beside some nameless Italian stream. Hans's last words rose up in Christian's mind. *Sorry, son,* he'd rasped. *Wanted . . . to stay with you longer.*

"Get some sleep," Roy advised, drowning out the whisper of memory. "You can't afford not to be sharp around Nim Wei."

"Right." Christian looked up to meet Roy's Texas sky blue eyes. "You tell Sam McCrory I agreed to give him his loan?"

"Yep," Roy said. "Though I think your terms are too easy."

Christian pushed to his feet, suppressing an urge to groan. "I don't mind folks feeling grateful, so long as it's not sticking in their craw."

The locals' aptitude for turning a blind eye had enabled Christian to settle in here—for nearly two decades now. He'd bought the land around the river that had bumped North Fork up to *Two*. Many lifetimes' worth of mercenary fees had kept the town on its shaky feet through the dust-bowl years. In return, the people hereabouts ignored his oddities. That meant more to him than they'd ever know. Christian almost felt he belonged here. For a man like him, *almost* belonging was a big deal.

He took Grace's script as he sought his light-proof fall-out shelter under the house. Roy might read the screenplay or he might not, but that wasn't why he carried it away. As smart as it would be to keep his distance from this project, Christian couldn't release the thing. Grace had touched these pages. Grace had created them. He couldn't have left them sitting on that table any more than he could forget what she'd meant to him.

Grace had hoped she and Miss Wei could discuss developments when she woke up. They often strategized how to recruit this or that professional to a film. The great Wade Matthews, their director of photography, was a prime example. His expertise was crucial for shooting in the newly popular wide-screen format. The main reason he'd agreed to work for an up-till-now B director was because they'd hired a young man he was sweet on to head wardrobe.

Grace had collected the useful gossip while playing wallflower at a Hollywood party. Moving from town to town as a kid, having to hide the details of her home life, hadn't prepared her to be the toast of any gathering. In this case, her social awkwardness had been an asset. Once guests established she wasn't an actress and only had the vague title "assistant," she'd become invisible to them. Nothing could have made eavesdropping easier.

Afterward, Miss Wei had complimented her on her initiative.

It seemed unlikely any such praise would be coming her way tonight. Miss Wei emerged from her motel room in a mood Grace recognized: restless, distracted, and about to go on the prowl.

Her strapless red and black sheath dress left no doubt as to what she'd be prowling for.

"Are you sure you won't have dinner with me?" Grace asked once she'd given her the short version of her news. "Viv Lavelle is going to get a complex if her director's waist is that much tinier than hers."

Miss Wei didn't laugh the way she normally would have. Her gaze settled on Grace briefly. "You'll be fine with Christian. He knows better than to harm one of my people."

The idea that he might have harmed her otherwise wasn't reassuring, but Grace shut her mouth and nodded.

"Good," Miss Wei said, her attention sliding off toward the county road. "I have faith you'll seal the deal tonight."

She strode off into the darkness, in her pointy-toed stilettos. Grace didn't offer to drive her where she was going. She'd long since learned not to interfere with her boss's quirks. No injury—that Grace could tell—ever came to Miss Wei from her adventures. Plus, her little feet must have been made of steel. Grace had no other explanation for how she could walk so fast in those heels.

She ate dinner by herself in the Best Western's diner, jotting notes on her napkin and fending off leering invitations from a pair of traveling salesmen.

They reminded her of her father, past their prime but fueled with liquor to dull their awareness that they weren't— and maybe never had been—Don Juans. She ignored them until they left, telling herself she knew lots of males who didn't behave like them. Their brilliant DP, for one, was a sweetheart, the sort of kind, calm figure who made the whole crew happy to come to work. Some of the actors they'd cast as gang members were nice, too. They'd treated Grace with respect even before they realized she was more than Miss Wei's gopher.

Men aren't evil, she assured herself. Very few actually went home and beat their families. Sometimes their hormones and their insecurities just ran away with them.

Grace didn't know about Christian Durand's hormones, though he certainly didn't seem insecure. He was the take-no-prisoners kind of male those traveling salesmen likely wished they could be.

Sighing, she let the tired waitress clear her plates. Her bracelet watch jingled as she checked it. She couldn't put this off any longer. It was time to go see Christian.

At five past eight Christian told Roy he wouldn't need him anymore that evening. After some debate, he decided the living room was the best place to talk to Grace. In case she was hungry, he set out a plate of cheese and crackers. Lighting the fire would ensure her human limbs didn't take a chill. A bottle of wine seemed civil, as did the nice crystal.

When he started wondering if he should dash to town and grab a bunch of flowers, he cursed himself.

"Grace is not your girlfriend," he hissed between his teeth.

She wasn't his lover, either. Or the guardian angel he'd taken her for when she'd first appeared to his mortal self. Guardian angels didn't jump ship when their drowning charges needed them most of all.

Just barely, he refrained from tossing the crackers out. He did pour a glass of wine for himself. To hell with waiting for his guest, and to hell with her idea of a manly drink. Red wine was the only alcohol he could drink—not that it affected him like it did humans. The inebriation caused by tossing back a glass was as fleeting as the breeze from a butterfly.

He poured a second glass and forced himself to sip it. He was calm—not *guarded* as Grace put it—just collected and decisive. He checked his glamour, once, in the hall mirror. He wasn't glowing, wasn't nervous-looking or marble pale. He'd been passing for human for centuries. No specter from his past was going to rob him of that skill now.

He recognized her car from a mile away, then her footsteps coming to his door. Though he knew she'd knock, her brisk triple rap turned his palms sweaty.

You are *an idiot teenager,* he reproved himself.

Once he'd wiped his hands on his jeans, he went to answer it.

"I've decided to say yes," he announced. That settled, he held the door and stepped back.

"Oh." Grace took a moment to gape at him. "I . . . I guess I can throw away my napkin." She smiled when his eyebrows rose, pulling a folded square from her purse and jiggling it like a flag. "I was writing down more arguments at dinner. It's a shame you agreed already. Some of them were good."

This might have been a joke, but Christian hadn't had his sense of humor as long as his other gifts.

"Come in," he said, deciding to ignore it. "I opened some wine for you."

She hesitated just a moment, and her heart rate sped up. The hint of female caution thrilled him. His cock began to thicken and the roots of his fangs to burn. Her fear of him was an aphrodisiac, the smallest taste of the punishment she deserved.

"I shouldn't stay long," she said, "but if you have any questions, I'll answer them as well as I can."

Unable to speak, he gestured her to the living room. As if one half of him warred with the other, he was suddenly—abysmally—glad that he'd lit the fire. She was dressed as she'd been that morning, in a sleeveless, green flower-skirted dress. The thing was perfectly respectable for her day and age. The bodice came to her throat while the hem floated inches below her knees. Her heels were no different than he'd seen on thousands of women. Perversely, the effect of the outfit on *her* turned his cool blood molten. She was so damned female he could have screamed.

She sat on the couch with her knees and feet nervously together, though she tried to look confident. Every inch of his skin abuzz, Christian poured a glass of wine and handed it to her silently. Grace sipped it and set it down next to the crackers.

Then she stole what was left of his reason by wetting her wine red lips.

He sat down carefully next to her, the part of him that had lit the fire not wanting her to become alarmed. That would have been a bit too exciting for the predator in him.

She saw something in his expression, maybe the intensity he was trying to hide. "Christian?"

He pressed the pad of his longest finger to the seam of her mouth. "Don't speak."

"Don't sp—"

He covered her lips with his, gently molding the contrasting surfaces together. His mouth was cool and narrow, hers pillowy and warm, but the differences between them didn't prevent them from fusing into one. She gasped when he licked her lushness, and her hands fluttered to his chest. Though her pulse was racing like a wild thing, she wasn't pushing him away.

She trusted him—or wanted him—enough to let him do this.

Abruptly, he was so happy he couldn't remember when he'd last felt this good. Not since he was human, he suspected. Well-being washed over him in a tidal wave. He forgot everything but the simple pleasure of being with her again.

"Grace," he murmured and turned his head to go deeper in.

Her tongue met his tentatively, wet and warm and small. Struggling not to let his desires run away with him, he slid his arms around her, pushing her gently back on the cushions. Their moves were a dance he didn't have to think about. He pushed, she fell, and their limbs made familiar places for each other. She uttered an unsure sound but not an objection. The couch was firm; it was her delicious body that gave for him. She was the one who let her thighs part, her full skirt and its petticoats frothing around his hips. He remembered the times she'd been no more to him than a ghost, when they'd been grateful for the meagerest brush of sensation. Tonight, her unchanging physicality was like catnip. He wanted to push his hips into the inviting cradle at the top of her legs, wanted to rub his aching erection over the place that was made for it. He knew she wasn't ready, but he could make her. He slid his hand under her petticoats . . .

"Christian—"

"Shh." He kissed her more deeply, using all his centuries of practice at seduction. Happily, she wasn't immune. Her arms tightened wonderfully on his back. There were nylons under her dress, attached to her undergarments by small garters. He found the place between the elastic struts where bare, warm skin smoothed around her thighs. Grace shivered and squirmed as he caressed it.

"*Christian.*"

He could smell how wet she was, could hear how his name was almost a moan. Her heat beat up at him in tantalizing pulses. Fighting impatience, he twisted his hand under dampened silk and into her creamy folds. Her clit was his goal, ripe and swollen, perfect for rolling and rubbing between dexterous fingers. Her lips tore away from his to catch her breath. Her timing was better than she knew. She missed his fangs sliding down by seconds.

He didn't think he could have stopped them. How badly he wanted to bite her had him panting, though he did manage to keep his fingers hard at their work.

"Oh, God," she moaned, her throat and hips both arching. Her eyes were screwed shut, her hands curling into fists at the small of his back where the muscles of his ass began. The pressure she exerted stirred sensations deep inside him, making him want to drive her up the wall as far as she could go. Maybe he'd succeeded quicker than he expected. When he teased one finger into the first drenched inch of her vagina, her groan was tormented.

She reacted as if she'd never been touched like this before, as if how good it felt came as a surprise to her. He buried his fangy mouth in her beautiful outspread hair, shifting to the side to straddle one of her sprawled thighs. He couldn't *not* push himself against her, though he tried to prevent his strength from doing injury.

The hand that wasn't squeezing her pussy cradled the back of her head.

"Go over for me," he whispered into her ear. "I want to feel you spill in my hand."

He remembered what she liked, even after all this time. How she loved when he pinched the soft skin of her clitoris and pumped it over the little rod. How the sound of his hastened breathing could make her tighten on his finger. How she'd come all the harder if he kept her waiting. Each rediscovery dragged him closer to losing his own control, but he was damned if he'd go before her. He could do the things she liked better than he had as a man. He was quicker, stronger, and more precise. He could sense the slightest increase in her excitement and immediately build on it.

Though his balls throbbed with a painful pressure, he backed off strategically.

"Christian," she gasped. Her left knee was up, bracketing his hip as her body bucked against his. She was strong for a human, and her writhing felt incredibly good. Her curves were the ideal combination of firm and soft. Pleasure drew a helpless cry from his throat.

Soon, he began to promise, hoping to slow her down. Before he could, she captured his mouth again.

She cut herself on his fangs the moment she kissed him.

She didn't seem to notice, but Christian couldn't hold back a moan. If her fear was an aphrodisiac, this was worse. When his kind took blood, it was always orgasmic. He only had to suck the little cuts she'd made, and she'd come.

He worked a second finger into her instead. To his surprise, he encountered more of a barrier than tightness. Realizing what it meant, his cock went as hard as stone. *Upyr* lungs weren't supposed to heave like his were.

"Oh, God," she repeated, lurching up to him. The squelching sound her pussy made sent fire blazing through his nerves. As if to issue a warning, pre-ejaculate trickled from his cock.

"Do it, Chris," she urged. "Push me over the edge."

No one had ever called him that. The nickname shocked him, aroused him—though he had no idea why that was. With a grunt, he shoved his groin closer to her thigh, strafing against her as fast and rough as he dared. Unable to wait for her to do it, he took her mouth himself. The longing noises he was making should have scared him. Way past caring, he brought her to the precipice with his fingers, then pulled hard on her bleeding mouth.

Her climactic cry was hoarse, but no more than his was. Her copper-cherry taste exploded on his tongue, almost overwhelming him. Fearing the reaction might make him drink too deep, he wrenched his head back, shooting hard inside the clasp of his jeans. For all his powers, he couldn't delay his ejaculation or cut it short once it had begun. The floodgates had been broken, and the pent-up tide was spuming.

He came longer than she did, collapsing atop her to find her hands hesitantly stroking him through his Western shirt. After a moment, she squirmed underneath his weight. That was all it took for his cock to swell hopefully, though it seemed her intent wasn't to kick-start a second lap.

"Mr. Durand," she said. "Do you think you could . . . remove your fingers from where they are?"

He removed them, maybe not graciously. He hadn't forgotten what he'd found when he put them there.

"You're a virgin," he accused, poised above her on his elbows. Grace's cheeks went pink, but he still forced his fangs back into his gums.

"You say that like there's something wrong with it."

It wasn't wrong, precisely; it just seemed illogical. He remembered taking her virginity. Admittedly, that Grace had been different from this one—a past life or whatever. All he knew for sure was that trying to figure it out had his brain aching.

"You're twenty-four," he said stubbornly. "And Nim Wei's protégée."

Grace sucked an angry breath, her voluptuous breasts rising to his chest. "Miss Wei's hobbies are her concern."

Christian snorted. "I suppose that's one term for them." Calming slightly, though he wasn't certain he wanted to, he peered into Grace's eyes. "You really don't remember doing this before."

"If I'd done it before, I wouldn't be saying no to you now. Or maybe I would. Maybe if I were experienced, this would be old hat."

"Sex will *never* be old hat with me."

"Well, I'll have to take your word on that, won't I?" She huffed as she shoved ineffectually at his chest. "Please get off me, Mr. Durand. I want to go back to the motel."

He knew he ought to move, but he couldn't. Determined to get through to her, he took her face in his hands. "I want you to remember, Grace. I want you to remember us."

He knew he meant it, even if he wasn't clear on his motives. His will pushed from him in a concentrated thrust.

"I'm not likely to forget," Grace snapped. "What you did just now was pretty dramatic."

His mouth fell open. He'd pushed his full thrall at her, and it had no effect at all. To his dismay, he couldn't read her thoughts, either, though he tried hard enough for beads of sweat to pop on his brow.

"What did she do to you?" he burst out.

"What did who do?"

"Nim . . . Naomi. Your precious boss. She locked me out of your head."

Grace seemed to lose all patience with him at once. She squirmed out from under his slackened muscles to stand and glare down at him from beside the couch. "I think *you're* out of your head, Mr. Durand. You probably shouldn't drink before you have guests."

"Christian," he retorted as he sat up. "And I promise you, I'm not drunk!"

Sadly, he was impaired in another way. The heat in his eyes warned him they were close to glowing, and that his glamour wasn't up to concealing it.

He pushed to his feet and turned away from her, muttering imprecations under his breath. Vampire emissions tended to evaporate quickly, but his had been so copious the front of his Levi's were dark with it. He looked like the youth she thought him, overexcited by a grope session in a car. Though he couldn't hear Grace's thoughts, he sensed her indecision. Should she stay? Should she go? Was this crazy person worth humoring to accomplish her boss's goal?

When she laid her hand lightly on his back, he knew which side she'd come down on.

"Christian," she said. "I hope what happened between us doesn't change your mind about starring in our film."

"You really are a professional."

The air shifted as she stiffened. "I refuse to take that as an insult."

He wasn't sure he'd meant it as one. He'd been known to be pragmatic. "I gave my word," he said gruffly. "It's not *my* way to be forsworn."

Her brow was furrowed when he turned to her. She didn't realize it was *her* honor he'd impugned.

"That's good to know," she said unsurely. "Someone from Miss Wei's staff will be in touch about the contracts. You should hire an agent if you want to be sure they're fair."

He could only sigh when she shut the front door behind her. The fire crackled in the silence, tiny creaks issuing from the couch as its springs recovered from their combined weight. Gloom settled over him. Vampire or not, Christian suspected he'd bitten off more than he could chew with this job.

Grace's hands were shaking too badly to slide the key into the ignition. She'd parked by the barn where she'd first met Christian, and now she was glad for it. She didn't want him seeing her like this from his front windows.

"Shoot," she said as the key dropped from her trembling fingers and hit the floor. She picked it up and then sat blankly.

She wished she were certain her tremors were caused by fear, but everything Christian did had been exciting, from that first soft kiss to the final grind of his hips when he had his orgasm. Though she wasn't an authority, she sensed he was very practiced. She'd loved the sure way he touched her, the building intensity of pleasures. Her embarrassment hadn't mattered, or her inexperience.

She'd wanted him, as she never had any man before.

With the sense that she was in trouble, she dropped her brow to the steering wheel. Even his aggression had excited her. She knew if he'd pushed just a bit more insistently, she'd have let him make love to her.

"Stupid," she muttered, feeling her traitorous body twitch hard at that idea.

She wanted him inside her, that thick, warm length he'd rubbed so urgently against her. It seemed to her that she knew exactly how he would feel. How far he'd reach. How hard he'd thrust. The way his beautiful face would twist and darken as his arousal rose. His grunts had sounded so familiar, as if she'd heard them countless times in her dreams. She just *knew* the skin of his penis would be silky.

"Jeepers," Grace swore to herself. The nerves between her legs were actually on the verge of spasming again.

Rather than let them, she shoved the key where it belonged and started up the Fury. She was leaving, no arguments. Christian was too young and pretty to have outgrown acting like a Lothario. He'd break her heart without even trying. However stupid Grace might be, she wasn't stupid enough for that. She was going important places. No Tom, Dick, *or* Christian could stand in the way of that.

She drove with her molars grinding, willfully ignoring how each rotation of the tires tightened her ribs more. She felt like an elephant was sitting on her chest, like her heart was bleeding already. *Turn around,* it was urging. *Go back to him.*

The tears began as she hit the two-lane, two long trickles that cooled in the breeze from the cracked window. She swiped them angrily from her cheeks. There was absolutely no point in missing something she'd never had, something she suspected didn't exist.

True love was for the movies. In real life, people had to count on themselves.

Three

Christian's plane had taxied to a stop by the time Grace drove Miss Wei's Fury onto the oil-stained tarmac. The private airstrip was in Pasadena, a drive from their house in the Palisades—not that it mattered. LA's infamous traffic had been thin enough not to slow her down. Grace glanced at her bracelet watch, a gift from her employer. Clever charms hung from its links: a clapper board, a megaphone, and a film camera. Each year on the anniversary of her hiring, Miss Wei gave her a new one. Grace jingled it out of habit. She was actually a little early. It was ten till midnight: the witching hour.

Four years of working for Miss Wei had inured Grace to nocturnal assignments. Nonetheless, she pulled her sweater closer against a shiver as two men in navy jumpsuits rolled a set of steps up to the small chartered jet. They must have been strong as well as used to the task, because they pushed the ramp into place like it was nothing. The windows of the plane glowed gold into the darkness, and she saw two shadows moving inside, probably Christian and his man Roy. Her breathing quickened. Feeling more comfortable not staring, she shifted her gaze away. The logo on the tail fin was unfamiliar, a leaping wolf with toothy jaws agape. "FC Air" she thought the lettering said.

The *thunk* of the plane door opening dragged her eyes forward. Christian was emerging, a spring in his long lean legs as he descended the rolling stairs. He wore a Western jacket with his jeans tonight, plus a white button-down and string tie. As he moved, the shirt stretched taut across the muscles of his chest, but it was his dirt-colored cowboy hat that tipped her pulse into overdrive. He seemed quintessentially male to her, closer to the earth than the average man, more present in his body. His movements conveyed a coiled energy, as if the power that fueled him couldn't be contained by his flesh. Seeing him like this, so confident and alert, confirmed her earlier assumption that he was a night owl.

When his gaze zeroed in on hers, her throat tightened. Rather than let him guess what he'd done to her, she popped the trunk and stepped out. She worked to make her voice calm.

"You're right on time," she said.

He was in front of her sooner than she expected, as if he had the power to travel in the blink of an eye. Also unexpected was the way he took her hand. He didn't shake it, just clasped it between his own. Even shadowed by the brim of his hat, his coffee eyes seemed to gleam.

"Grace," he said in his dark, smooth voice, sounding almost glad to see her again.

The feel of his fingers—so long, so cool—caused a hard, quick pulse to flicker between her legs. She remembered those fingers stroking her a bit too well. Maybe he did, too. He cleared his throat and let go. Grace had the sensation that Roy's arrival saved them both from embarrassment.

"Nice moon," the older man observed, tipping his head back to take it in. It was a huge, back-rocked crescent, its edges glowing cinematically through what was probably a thin veil of smog.

"Yes," Grace agreed. "You can stow the luggage in the trunk." Her eyes rounded at the number of bags the two airline employees were swiftly setting on the ground. She wouldn't have pegged Christian as a clotheshorse. "The backseat, too, if you need it."

Christian must have guessed her thoughts. "Roy tends to pack the kitchen sink when we travel."

"Ha," Roy retorted, swinging two bags in. "Some of us appreciate our creature comforts."

Christian's grin surprised her, not only because it was very white, but because it expressed such fondness for his companion. She wouldn't have guessed the laconic cowboy liked anyone that much. "We'll take whatever doesn't fit," put in one of the jumpsuits. "All part of FC Air's door-to-door service."

"Do you have a card?" Grace asked, impressed by their professionalism. "My boss might want to hire you sometime."

The jumpsuits laughed as if she'd said something funny. Interestingly, their teeth were as brilliant as Christian's. Whatever toothpaste they all were using, Grace wanted stock in it.

"Your boss knows how to reach us," said the taller of the men. "Whether she has what it takes to hire us remains to be seen."

"We should go," Christian said, before Grace could ask what he meant by this.

"Of course." Grace tried to conceal her flustered state. "You must be tired from traveling."

Without so much as a grunt of acknowledgment, Christian claimed the front seat next to her. When he wedged his shoulders across the corner to get comfortable, his legs were a good deal longer than Miss Wei's. Grace's nerves twitched hotly as his knee bumped her thigh. More than a little rattled, she sent up a prayer that she wouldn't stall the engine on the first try. Thankfully, the V-8 came through for her. Her relief sighed out as the car roared to life.

"Miss Wei leased a bungalow for you at the Chateau Marmont," she informed her passengers, once they were safely on the nearly empty Hollywood Freeway.

"A bungalow?"

The growling question in Christian's voice ran through her in a long shiver. "It's a little house on the hotel grounds. The Chateau is known for its discretion. Lots of big stars stay there when they want to keep what they're up to quiet. Humphrey Bogart. Lauren Bacall. Which isn't to suggest you have anything to hide."

Christian laughed through his nose and slouched lower. "The thought never crossed my mind."

Grace glanced at him. His long arms were stretched along the window and the back of the seat, creating a blatant come-get-me sprawl. The camera wasn't the only thing that was going to eat him up. Grace returned her eyes to the road but not soon enough. Her temperature had taken a noticeable tick upward.

"I think you'll find the bungalow comfortable," she continued, hoping her flush didn't show. "It has two bedrooms and a kitchen. The fridge is stocked with staples, and there's maid service. Oh, I rented a projector, too. You might want to watch the movies I left for you." That conversational gambit exhausted, Grace's fingers tensed on the steering wheel. When she checked the rearview mirror, Roy was staring out the side window, clearly not planning to chime in. "Miss Wei tells me you're having someone drive your car up here."

"And my Harley."

"Good." Grace swallowed. "That's good. And naturally I'll be available to drive you wherever you need till then."

"Jack of all trades, are you?" This time Durand didn't growl; he purred, causing little hairs on her arms to rise.

"That's me," she said too brightly, fixing her attention on the taillights in front of her. "I've scheduled an appointment for you at four tomorrow, with the manager of Mattson's. I know you brought your own clothes, but we'll want to make sure you have the right things for parties and dealing with the press. Then, at six, the hairstylist from the film will start working on your new look."

"You expect me to shop for clothes for *two hours*?"

"However long you like," Grace said, her hands shifting nervously. "I'm sure the manager will make it go quickly."

"You're coming," Christian said, low and dark. "And that's not a question. You'll stay through the whole damn thing."

"Of course. I'm sure Miss Wei would want me to . . . oversee your makeover."

Christian snorted and looked out the front window. He was not a Chatty Charlie, that was for sure. They drove in silence, the light traffic whooshing by them on either side. The towering palms that lined the highway stood silvered by moonlight. Determined not to miss their exit, Grace began watching the signs for West Hollywood. Her skin was all over goose bumps with her awareness of the man beside her. To make matters worse, Christian kept stealing looks at her and frowning, as if unsatisfied with her profile.

"You grip that wheel any tighter, Grace, and your fingers are going to snap."

She didn't see him move, but suddenly his big hand was on top of hers on the steering wheel. She jumped so badly the car swerved out of their lane.

"Please," she gasped once her lungs recovered. "Don't touch me while I'm driving."

Christian pulled his hand back and stared at her. "Fine. I won't touch you while you're driving. I was only trying to calm you down."

"Well, you didn't." Grace knew she sounded as truculent as he did, but she couldn't help herself. She tucked her perfectly brushed hair behind her ear. "I'd also appreciate it if you'd stop staring at me like I've grown horns."

Christian jerked away and muttered something she probably didn't want to hear. When she snuck a look at him, his jaw was clenched, his eyes gone narrow on the road ahead. Grace blew out a breath and told her nerves to settle.

"Welcome to LA," his man Roy laughed softly from the backseat.

Christian's temper was still simmering as Grace pulled up to the small bungalow. Heavy greenery surrounded it, and its windows looked well curtained, but Nim Wei's consideration wasn't counting for much right then. The queen had spelled Grace so well he couldn't calm her with his touch, which—despite what Grace apparently believed—was all he had meant to do.

That he'd made the attempt very close to midnight, when his powers were at their height, told him he still couldn't outmatch his maker when it came to her thralls.

Seeing Grace didn't intend to get out or even turn off the engine, Christian schooled his face to its usual coolness and went to help Roy retrieve their bags. Despite his desire not to repeat previous mistakes, he couldn't quite stop himself from pausing outside her door. She cranked down her window and looked up at him warily. He could see her better than a human would have in full daylight: the hectic flush on her cheekbones, the tremor she tried to hide by rolling her soft lips between her teeth. The only way to restrain his craving to lay his palm on her face was to curl his hand into a tight fist.

This urge to be kind to his betrayer was a pattern he was damn well going to break.

"I'll pick you up tomorrow," she said. "Around three thirty."

"Fine," he agreed, though inside he was groaning at the idea. He was out of practice for waking that early. He almost turned to go, but one more impulse took hold of him. Her elbow was braced on the open window, and his hand found its way right beside that warmth. "You'll be all right tonight? Driving home?"

"Of course I will. I'm used to keeping Miss Wei's hours."

She'd already given him the key to the bungalow. Fingering it in his pocket, Christian stepped away from the car.

"Good night," Grace said. "Good night, Mr. Blunt."

Roy lifted his hand as she reversed neatly out of the drive.

"Sure is a good-looking gal," he observed. "And polite. Not that you got a close acquaintance with the niceties."

"You have something you want to say, Roy?"

"Only that she has you twisted six ways to Sunday."

"Get bent," Christian said—rather mildly, by his standards.

Roy chuckled and hefted a pair of bags. "Well," he said. "You gonna open the door for your human slave?"

Christian chose a curse with a bit more heat. "You watch it, old man. I can make you one anytime."

The surprise that awaited them inside made Christian glad Grace had driven off. The door opened onto a cozy, softly lit living room. Built-in bookshelves lined the wall to either side of the fireplace. The furniture was comfortably worn, the rugs were faded, and the parquet floor had gone pale in places from foot traffic. A bulky TV cabinet filled one corner, along with the motion picture projector Grace had mentioned. *Rebel Without a Cause* sat atop a stack of film cans—his viewing homework, Christian presumed. That exotic accessory aside, the bungalow looked more home than hotel, complete with knickknacks and old paintings.

None of this was what had him stiffening in shock.

A very attractive young human woman sat in one of the leather wing chairs reading a magazine. What really made her presence noteworthy was that she was dressed in her underthings. Her boned black lace corset, which her slender figure hardly needed, lifted palm-size breasts into tempting mounds. She rose calmly as they entered and set down her *Women's Wear Daily*, only teetering slightly on her four-inch heels. She was champagne blonde—not naturally, he didn't think—and her face was painted exquisitely. Under the makeup, her expression was almost as serene as one of his own kind. Despite her slightness, she bore more than a small resemblance to Marilyn Monroe.

"Jayzus," Roy breathed, which didn't cause her to bat an eye.

"Hello," she said in an appealing contralto. "You must be Christian. I'm Nicky from the service."

"From the service," Christian repeated, his brain too slow to make sense of this.

"Snacks R Us." She handed him a card. "Welcome to the twentieth century."

Christian looked down at the silver-embossed red rectangle. The lettering did indeed say "Snacks R Us," plus "all employees fully bonded."

Whatever "bonded" meant to mortals, he knew what it signified to *upyr*. "You've been bitten and thralled. You can't tell other humans who you work for."

Nicky stroked her tanned human neck, drawing his attention not only to its length but to the faint gold glow of a vampire's mark. "One of Miss Wei's senior people runs the agency. You can have a different human every evening, or you can request a favorite. I'm also to tell you that you're free to hunt in the city as long as you don't kill or cause trouble. Sex is extra," she added, "but none of us at the service are averse to that."

He could tell she wasn't averse. Her pupils had swelled while she was speaking. Now she dropped her lashes and waited, her hands clasped servilely in front of her. Christian swallowed the saliva that had pooled in his mouth, his fangs half erect already. He knew he ought to accept this offer. He was hungry. He hadn't fed off anyone since he'd met Grace three nights ago. Hunting would take time in a city he didn't know. Somehow, though, these good reasons didn't end up in his answer.

"This is all very efficient, but I prefer to find my own meals."

"As you wish." Nicky's disappointment was apparent but controlled. She hesitated, then pulled a fogged-up silver pen from her cleavage. "Perhaps you'd allow me to write my direct phone number on the card? You can call me, or anyone at the service, anytime if you change your mind."

Numbly, Christian returned the card to her. Nicky jotted down her information, handed it back, and smiled brilliantly. "I do hope you'll change your mind, Mr. Durand. Thralled or not, I really enjoy my job."

Her hand trailed down his shirtfront as she sashayed by him, the tips of her fingers glancing off his tumescent cock. Male that he was, Christian turned to watch her pause at the door. A long red trench coat hung from the tree beside it. Nicky slung the garment over her shoulder but didn't put it on. As coy and pretty as any starlet, she turned just her face to him.

"My driver's waiting at the gate. Feel free to stop me before I get there."

Christian didn't stop her, though he did admire the jiggle of her ass in the black panties. As he shut the door, he and Roy let out matching sighs. He suspected they both were wondering if Nicky was going to stroll across the hotel grounds in her underwear.

"Wow," Roy said. "You sure you want to send her away? I'm thinking she wasn't lying about relishing her work."

"I'm thinking I don't need the bitch queen finding more ways to get her hooks into me."

"Maybe you could consider it as using one hook to distract you from the other."

The other hook was Grace, of course. Though Roy's words were too on the mark for comfort, Christian had to laugh at his wistfulness. "Maybe I should see if they deliver snacks for humans."

"Don't think I wouldn't," Roy said. "I might seem old to you, but I ain't too old for that."

Snickering at his own wit, Roy wandered into the kitchen to check the Frigidaire. He opened it and leaned in.

"Well, *I* won't starve," he said dryly.

Christian was sure Roy meant well, but his patience abruptly snapped. He was a vampire, for God's sake. A predator to his bones. He didn't need to be spoon-fed—or jollied out of bad moods.

"I'm going out," he said. "I'll be back by daylight."

He waited just long enough to see Roy's startled expression. Then he was off and whooshing through the Chateau Marmont's sloping, tree-shaded grounds. Grace's allure didn't matter. The world was filled to bursting with warm and easily willing women. All Christian had to do was pick one.

Christian snarled in his sleep as a rough hand shook his shoulder. It *couldn't* be time to get up. Every one of his limbs was lead.

"It's three fifteen," Roy informed him, "and that starchy gal is bound to be early. Don't make me douse you with ice water."

"*Scheisse*," Christian hissed as he forced himself to sit up. His upper lip curled automatically, a reaction Roy wasn't feeling kind enough to ignore.

"Pull in your fangs, boy. The queen bitch sent you a care package."

Christian rubbed his face and groaned. He barely remembered stumbling in here at dawn. He'd had quite a run last night, down Sunset Boulevard and south along the coast, where he'd watched the waves crash beneath the cliffs at Point Vicente Lighthouse.

After an hour, the sound had almost calmed him.

"Put this on," Roy ordered, tossing him a small container. "This'll keep you from weaving around today like a drunk."

Christian stared at the object his reflexes had caught for him. "*Coppertone?*"

"Sunscreen is what they call it. It increases the amount of time you can be out without smoking. There's six more like it in the basket. The note says don't be stingy when you smear it on." Roy snapped his fingers to shock Christian's drooping eyes back open. "Ticktock, son. Fourteen minutes and counting."

Christian pushed on shaky legs from the bed. Luckily for him, vampires didn't need to shower or shave. Their energy threw off things like sweat. His jeans were where he'd dropped them, kept clean and soft as velvet by the same magic. He would have sat down again after he'd zipped them, but Roy was still standing there. With all he'd seen over the years, Christian in his glowing, glamour-free skin altogether didn't mean much to Roy.

"Why don't you get that water?" Christian suggested. "I'm thirsty."

"Didn't you feed?" Roy burst out in amazement. "You were gone all night!"

"I was getting the lay of the land. I'm not going to start hunting before I know where I stand."

Roy opened his mouth, then gave up and shook his head. "You get a move on, and I'll pretend I believe that."

Grace had been having strange dreams all morning. She often did when she worked Miss Wei's eccentric schedule; the shift in hours did something to her brain. Of the two dreams that she remembered, one was about ripe red raspberries, which she'd been crushing against her body but not eating. In the other, someone she knew repeated, "The river's flowing. Why aren't you jumping in?"

The voice had been so clear, so distinctive, that it seemed to echo through her guesthouse bedroom after her eyes opened. The clock on her bedside table said it was two thirty that afternoon, barely time to shower and dress and do all she had to before she drove back to the Chateau.

Whenever possible, she liked to be five minutes early for appointments.

Her body didn't want to cooperate with her preference. She felt slow and dreamy as she washed up and got ready. Were those her green eyes in the bathroom mirror, so slumberous and sensual? She was used to looking bright and eager, to feeling businesslike and prepared. She couldn't bear to put on the sensible trousers she'd laid out for herself last night. A pale pink dress she rarely wore called to her. A band of cashmere trimmed its low neckline and cinch belt, practically inviting caresses where she was most female. Though acceptable for a cocktail party, the dress was unsuitable day wear.

She put in on anyway, frowning at her reflection as she settled the belling skirt over petticoats.

If she'd wanted to wear a dress, she should have chosen her fake Chanel. Its long knee-restricting skirt sent exactly the message this afternoon required.

"Too late," she told herself as she grabbed her keys.

In the car, the new singer Elvis Presley was all over the

radio, crooning for some bobby-soxer to love him tenderly. After futilely switching stations, Grace snapped the music off. She didn't mind the song; she just didn't need to be thinking about loving someone herself.

Elvis's hair was all right, though. Maybe minus some of the grease. She'd mention him as a possible model to the stylist. A duck's ass cut seemed like it would suit Christian. If the girls flipped half as hard over him as they did for Elvis the Pelvis, their whole production would be in clover.

Grace pulled up at her destination without remembering how she'd got there.

Christian's bungalow appeared unkempt by daylight. The evergreens overgrew the windows like movie monsters trying to get in. She made a mental note to call the hotel management again. This time she'd be sterner. Miss Wei's guests, for whom she frequently leased this bungalow, deserved well-kept landscaping.

As she lifted her hand to knock, Christian opened the front door. His long, thick-lashed eyes were sleepy, but that was no surprise. Grace wet her lips and tried not to picture them gazing at her from a pillow.

"I'm ready," he said grimly, settling his cowboy hat low on his forehead.

Grace couldn't help smiling. "It's not a firing squad. Just a few additions to your wardrobe."

"And a haircut."

"Are you Samson? All your strength's in your ponytail?"

She reached around his neck to tug it, emboldened by the fact that he seemed to be enjoying her humor.

She had no warning. One moment Christian was inside the door and she was out, and the next she was inside, too. He'd lifted her over the threshold, and now his front was pressed full length against her, backing her into the wall of the entryway. He bore into her as heavily as if he were on top of her on a bed. Her thighs couldn't hold him off. He pushed his strong legs between them, bending his knees so that the thick length of his erection found the soft, hot ache of her sex.

Grace gasped and struggled, but his hands had trapped her elbows where her dress's sleeves left off. His fingers were hard as steel.

"I'll show you my strength," he said.

He rolled his pelvis against her like a stripper. The ungiving bulge of his cock managed to part her folds even through all the petticoats.

Grace sucked in her breath for a different reason. Her fingers clutched the back of his brown jacket. God, his shoulders were broad. She wanted to stroke them, to measure every firm inch of them with her palms. Heat flooded from her core as he rocked again and groaned softly. His head dropped closer, allowing his mouth to drag a burning tingle up the side of her neck.

He was panting, light and quick, and that might have gotten her worst of all. What he was doing wasn't only arousing her.

He drew her earlobe between his teeth, the tiny sting of pressure unimaginably sexy. "Did you wear this dress for me?" he whispered. "Did you wonder what I'd think of you all in pink?"

Lost in sensation, she shivered and arched and slid her hands to the bare skin beneath his tied-back hair. Christian shuddered, then retreated far enough to peer into her eyes.

"Grace," he said, and it was like he *knew* her, like her name was one he'd said many times before. She realized she'd had a similar impression when he clasped her hand outside the plane last night. What was he doing to her? And why was she letting him?

"I'm sorry," she said, her voice breathy. Belatedly, she dropped her hands from his neck and pressed them flat to the wall. "I shouldn't be doing this."

"Fuck *shouldn't*." He kissed her with abrupt abandon, his tongue reaching deeply, sleekly into her mouth.

She didn't stop him. Couldn't stop him. She made a sound like a kitten crying. All she wanted, truly wanted down to her soul, was that he'd never stop doing this. His kiss was wet and indescribably hungry, almost overpowering her ability to answer it. When she tried to, he groaned again, the rumble resonating in his chest as his head changed angles to delve deeper. The muscles of his thighs were shifting, pushing her off the floor until her weight hung on the ridge of his cock. She hadn't known a man could do that, had never been held by one this strong. Each protracted thrust of his hips pushed her closer to climax, the rise of her pleasure as inexorable as it was intense.

Christian must have sensed it. His breath came faster, and something moved in his mouth, something smooth and long that made him jerk with unexpected violence when her tongue brushed it. His arms tightened on her back like a vise. Grace had the feeling something irreversible was about to happen.

"Christian," Roy said from the living room. "Let the gal do her job."

Grace had forgotten Roy was around. To her slightly shamed disappointment, Christian wrenched his mouth off hers. For just a moment, his eyes were dazed. *He'd look like this if he were in love*, she thought. When the softness cleared, he began to glare.

"Maybe this *is* her job," he said, low and gravelly. "To torment me for her boss."

"It is not!" Incensed, Grace shoved at him until he took one step back. "You keep your hands to yourself."

"You touched me first."

"I was teasing," she huffed, smoothing her skirt down where it belonged. "Being friendly. It wasn't an invitation to maul me."

"Maul you!" The faintest wash of pink swept up Christian's attractively hollow cheeks. By contrast, his lips were pressed whitely together. Amazingly, he didn't prize them open to argue more. His jaw ticked like he was longing to.

"Kids," Roy broke in from behind them. "I believe you have an appointment you need to keep."

Grace was too angry and upset to agree. She stomped out to the car alone, trusting Christian would follow when he was ready.

When he did, it should have gratified her that he couldn't sit easily, that a flashlight-size hump was pushing out the front of his Levi's. Sadly, all his condition did was make her squirm restlessly. There was simply no mistaking the substantiality of his manliness.

"Drive," he said once he'd shut the door. "I'd like to get this day over with."

Grace drove, doing her level best not to dwell on how very much she wanted to reach over and squeeze his crotch.

Mattson's wasn't one of Nim Wei's vampire-run firms. It was a regular human business, with human employees. Once there, Christian was peered at, measured all over with tailor's tape, and alternately clucked and cooed over by the store's manager.

What seemed like hundreds of garments were thrust at him through the curtain in the dressing room. Trying them on was a tiresome process when forced to restrict himself to more or less human speed. His one consolation was that Grace's poker-stiff spine gradually unbent. Doing her job relaxed her, a fact for which he was grateful. It wasn't to his advantage to have her stay mad at him, no matter what he eventually decided to do with her.

Christian was in front of the central mirror, resignedly presenting the latest outfit, when the painfully stylish manager had an epiphany.

"Black," he declared to his assistant, one hand tapping

at his lips. "Or navy. Take all the things I put in the 'yes' pile and pull them off the racks in those colors. Neckties, too," he added, snapping his fingers to speed his subordinate up.

He turned a marginally less peremptory look to Christian. "Don't wear the ties unless you absolutely have to. I mean, if your mother dies, all right. Otherwise, they don't exactly scream *rebel*. Stick to silk shirts with the collar open. One button. No cotton. No light colors." He squinted at the Stetson Christian was still wearing. "I don't suppose I could convince you to lose that monstrosity."

"Miss Wei likes the hat," Grace broke in as Christian's neck stiffened. "She thinks it's part of his signature. Because he's from Texas."

The manager looked unsurely from Grace to him. "It's *brown*."

"It's him, Damon," Grace insisted. "It's a real man's hat that a real man has worn. If he didn't have it, he'd just be another pretty-faced young actor."

Christian was no more a real Texan than he was a young man. All the same, he was glad to hang on to his headgear. Given his aura's preserving powers, he'd had to work to get it this broken-in. Childishly, perhaps, he smirked at the clothier.

"Fine," the manager surrendered. "Far be it from me to second-guess a beautiful woman."

"They're the ones who'll be buying tickets," Grace said pragmatically. "Though, of course, we appreciate your expertise. Christian looks great in your selections. As always, you've got the eye."

"And you, Miss Michaels," the flattered manager simpered back, "are always welcome to borrow it."

The rest of their transaction unfolded smoothly. Now that the manager had decided what Christian ought to purchase, all that remained was totaling the damage.

"Send the bill to Miss Wei," Grace said, giving Christian a start.

They were at the front counter, and Grace was scribbling on a store notepad. The motion of her hand, the way she bit her lip in concentration, momentarily enchanted him. She wasn't his Grace then, but she attracted him all the same. She was a modern woman, more so than the female from Snacks R Us. Her own thoughts ran through her head, her own private dreams. Christian was a part of them, but not romantically, not if he accepted her earlier reaction as genuine. That made him shake his head. He hardly knew how to find his place in this scheme of things.

"Here," Grace said, handing the manager what she'd written. "When your staff has finished the alterations, this address will take delivery."

Christian felt uncustomarily off balance as they exited the store, as if *he'd* been bought and paid for. The sun hadn't set. Even with his hat and despite the thin layer of car exhaust, it was bright out for him. Eyes stinging, he slipped his aviator sunglasses on. At least he wasn't woozy. The Coppertone had done its job on that front.

"Naomi doesn't have to buy my clothes," he said.

Grace's brows lifted. "You don't need to be insulted. They're already in the budget."

She'd parked by the curb in front of the store, where the car was doing its impression of a flamingo. He was too sluggish to reach the driver's door before she opened it for herself. Annoyed by his urge to play gentleman, he circled around to his side. The relief of sitting down was almost too great. If he wasn't careful, he was going to drop off in front of her.

"You can sleep if you want," she said. "I'll wake you when we get to the hairstylist."

He shook his head and said nothing. Her concern, mild though it was, bothered him. He was no green-behind-the-ears fledgling. He could stay awake for one damn day. Shrugging, Grace pulled onto a street of ticky-tacky shops and squat palm trees. Women in too-tight clothes sauntered the sidewalks self-consciously, seemingly waiting for someone important to notice them. Hollywood was supposed to be glamorous, but Christian didn't see it. Even at night, with the neon lit, it looked tawdry and fake to him, a stage set with the paint showing.

"It's the dreams that make it sparkle," Grace said, responding to some expression he should have been hiding. "Dreams draw people here—the chance to do something big, to step *inside* of a fantasy."

"That isn't what drew you here."

She looked at him, maybe as surprised as he was by his certainty. "I wanted to pull the strings, to create the fantasy."

Christian thought about that. He liked that she'd answered him, maybe more than he should. Having a lucky insight was no substitute for being able to read her thoughts.

"Did Naomi really say my hat was my signature?"

The warmth of Grace's laugh startled him. "No," she said, shooting him a quick grin. "You just looked like you'd had enough."

"That man kept saying my legs were skinny." Christian nearly blushed at how sulky this complaint came out.

"They aren't," Grace assured him. "They just seem that way because they're long and your shoulders are very broad by comparison."

Now he had to fight a flush of pleasure. He was being ridiculous. He knew there was nothing wrong with his body. The nature of the change from mortal to immortal shifted any human's genes to their ideal. He was the most aesthetic version of himself. The vainest vampire in the world shouldn't need better.

Christian reckoned a simple haircut couldn't be worse than what he'd just gone through. Initially, his expectation appeared correct. The stylist, whose name was Sandy, was seeing them in the basement of her house in Los Feliz. She was a thirtyish young woman with a pleasant manner and gentle hands. She didn't chatter like the clothing shop manager, simply sat him in the salon chair and turned his face back and forth.

She'd outfitted her cellar like a small beauty shop, down to the easy-wipe Formica counters and tri-fold mirrors. Catching sight of himself reminded him to dim his looks with his glamour. He didn't want Sandy too dazzled to do her job.

"Wow," she said after a minute of considering him. "You and Viv are going to look crazy in a two shot."

Christian assumed this was a good thing.

Grace sat on the counter in front of him, her elbow on her knee and her fist pushing at her chin. "I was thinking Elvis with a bit less Brylcreem and maybe not so much flop."

"Oh, I don't know." The stylist trailed one nail in a swooping motion across his brow. "A flop might bring out his vulnerability." She laughed when Christian's head jerked back. "Don't think you've got any of that, tough guy?"

"He's *very* manly," Grace concurred. "You should have seen him bristling at Damon."

"That super-priss from Mattson's? I wish I had!"

At this, both women broke into giggles.

Christian hadn't heard Grace do that in half a millennium. In spite of his irritation at being the butt of their joke, a thrill of heat coursed dangerously up his thighs. The stupid part of him wanted to make her giggle like that for him.

Preferably while rolling around in bed.

"I'm right here, ladies," he said acerbically. "No need to talk around me like I've gone deaf."

"Sorry," Sandy said, swallowing a last snigger. She walked behind him to undo the tie that held back his hair. She spread its length across his shoulders with a professional purse to her lips. "Hm. Nice and thick."

"And *black*," Grace couldn't resist adding. "It'll match all his new silk shirts."

"Ha-ha," Christian responded. "So glad I could amuse you."

He was glowering, but she wasn't afraid. Her eyes sparkled with mischief as they met his. She looked so alive, so happy, that he wanted to kiss her again, to seize her knees and push them wide under that full pink skirt. The need he felt to please her was far too strong. His grip tightened on the salon chair's arms, threatening to snap them. As if she couldn't help herself, Grace's gaze slid tellingly to his lap. What she found there painted her cheeks bright red. His nostrils flared at her deliciously rising scent, but at least she'd stopped grinning. Maybe she suspected how close he was to "mauling" her again. She slid off the counter as if it had burned her.

"I'll just . . . get out of your way," she said to Sandy.

"I don't need that much room," Sandy said. Evidently oblivious to the undercurrents, she swirled a vinyl cape around him. "Why don't you grab another chair and sit close?"

"Yes," Christian drawled, enjoying having rattled his antagonist. "Samson that I am, I might need my Delilah to hold my hand."

Considering the bumps they'd hit along the way, this had been a surprisingly pleasant day. Grace had worked with Sandy on Miss Wei's films before, and they'd always gotten along. The work the stylist had done for *It Came from Venus* had been stellar. Joining her in ribbing Christian had made him seem less intimidating. Christian himself had been a better sport than Grace expected. She didn't know many men who'd have tolerated being led around like he was today.

In addition to which, she had to confess she enjoyed when he got angry—like poking a tiger until it bared its teeth.

With a tiny, inexplicable shiver at the idea of Christian's teeth, Grace shut off the car and turned to him. It was dark, and they were back at his bungalow. The light above the door shone through the windshield, falling full on his handsome face. Sandy had outdone herself. With his dark locks shorn, Christian looked an entirely different man—the opposite of Samson, to be truthful. Hard as it was to credit, he was even more seductive.

If he guessed what she was thinking, it didn't please him. The corners of his mouth turned down.

"It's just a haircut," he said coolly.

"I know." She fought a smile for what a haughty grouch he was. "I just can't stop staring. You've been transformed."

His eyebrows beetled the slightest bit. "Transformed."

"You look . . . suaver now, I think."

Christians brows went up as subtly as they'd drawn down. "So before I looked like a hick?"

"No," Grace laughed. "Maybe a bit old-fashioned, like you didn't quite belong in this time. Now you could walk into any LA hotspot and be the talk of the town."

Christian was staring at her very strangely, his straight and narrow mouth gaping open while something like consternation wrinkled his high forehead.

"What did I say?" she asked.

His expression went as blank as if he'd wiped it clean with a cloth.

"What?" she repeated.

"If you're toying with me . . ."

His voice was smoke pushing through his throat. Her shoulders tensed at the implied threat, even if she didn't understand why he was making it. She couldn't stop herself from shrinking back, but as she did, he leaned closer.

This didn't frighten her half as much as it should.

"Christian." Her hand came up to brace against his

chest, which was hard as iron beneath her palm. He'd backed her all the way to the Fury's door. She couldn't retreat any farther, and some reckless part of her was glad. Seen from inches away, the glint in his eyes caused both dizziness and heat to swirl inside her.

"It's still in there somewhere," he said.

"What's still in where?"

She was breathing too quickly, while he didn't seem to need air at all.

"The truth," he said so softly she barely heard.

"The tr—"

His silken lips brushed hers, silencing her as a tingling shudder ran down her spine.

"The truth about what you did to me."

He pulled away, slowly, his eyes never leaving hers. She wondered if he'd really said what she thought, because it didn't make sense to her. Her skin was pulsing, every cell wishing he'd come back. Then time seemed to run at a different speed. He was outside the car, closing the door firmly.

"Wait!" she gasped as he stepped away.

He hesitated, then leaned down to her open window.

Take me, she wanted to say, her chest aching with a longing too huge to understand. *Take me now and don't let me go again.*

That, of course, didn't make any more sense than him.

"The read-through," she said. "Of the script. It's tomorrow night at eight at Miss Wei's house."

His dark, cool gaze traveled down her body, a flush seeming to follow the path it touched. In contrast to that heat, her nipples were icy pebbles under her bodice. Grace saw his fingers clamp the edge of the door.

"I'll be there," he said tightly.

Four

Christian very stubbornly hadn't done his homework. *Rebel Without a Cause* remained unwatched in its can, as did *On the Waterfront* and *A Place in the Sun*. If Nim Wei had been an idiot to cast him, that was her problem. He would come to her read-through just as ignorant as she'd found him.

He pulled on one of his new midnight blue silk shirts, but that was only because they were comfortable. The black knife-pleat trousers went better with it than jeans, so he wore those, too. His reflection in the closet mirror rather startled him, as if—after five hundred years—he truly could become someone new.

"Sharp," Roy observed from the open doorway into his room. "You should have cut your hair years ago. You look like a real twenty-year-old now."

Christian grimaced and undid the top button on his collar. That priss from the shop was right. One button was the correct amount to leave open.

Roy made a humming noise. "What time is Grace picking you up?"

"She's not. I'm going to run there. Stretch my legs."

"Nervous?"

"Of course I'm not," he said.

Roy's head was down, but he was smiling like he knew something Christian didn't. He turned away before Christian could get angry.

"Break a leg," Roy threw over his shoulder. "I won't wait up."

Nim Wei looked around her spacious Spanish-style dining room and felt a warm glow of satisfaction spread through her icy veins. Grace was circling the long dark table, laying out bound copies of the script. Each was as neat as her pedal pushers and sweater set. In the four years since they'd met, Grace had proved an unexpected blessing. Nim Wei never would have guessed that having someone to share her quest, someone she could help as much as she was helped by, would add such savor to daily life. With Grace beside her, her dream falling into place meant more than ever.

Her immortal heart actually skipped when Grace glanced up and smiled at her. Nim Wei loved that this little mortal had no fear of her.

"Viv called," Grace said. "From her date. She's going to be a few minutes late."

"That's all right." Feeling expansive, Nim Wei waved the concern away. "People will want some time to chat anyway. You know the boys never settle down right away."

She could hear them now in the other wing, joking and scuffling with each other as they cleaned up for the evening. The younger members of the cast, at least the main characters, had been staying at Nim Wei's big 1930s house. She wanted them to be comfortable with each other, so they'd resemble real friends on-screen. *Teen-Age Vampire* was going to be important—not Oscar worthy, maybe, but more than another monsters versus mortals B movie. As good as *Rebel*, she was hoping, the sort of film people remembered.

Grace surprised her by breaking into a laugh. "You're nervous. I don't think I've ever seen you wring your hands like that."

Nim Wei looked down at the offending digits and laughed herself—perhaps a bit shakily. "I don't think I have, either."

"It's going to be fine, boss. Carmela has beer and snacks and coffee, and Wade is bringing his recording equipment. We'll both take notes, and you and Wade can fine-tune the shooting script all night if you want to."

"Right," Nim Wei said, blowing out a breath. "Wade Matthews is the best director of photography in the business. He's not going to let this train racket off the rails."

"Neither are you." Grace propped her hip on the table's end. "And neither am I. We'll do our best, and it's darn well going to be enough."

Nim Wei had to blink a sudden burn from her eyes. She suspected she would have hugged Grace if that had been her style. Queens didn't hug people, though, not even when they were disguised as directors.

"Christian had better not be late," she said instead. "He's the weak link in all of this."

"He'll be fine," Grace assured her, probably because she had no idea how many different kinds of trouble Christian could stir up. "You know the boys are bound to love him. All that guy's guy coolness. They'll be vying for his attention in no time."

Nim Wei was counting on it . . . and a lot more besides.

Nim Wei's house was an ivy-covered Spanish Revival mansion with a red clay–tiled roof. It sat on grounds as flat as if they'd been bulldozed, which were softened by rioting bougainvillea and emerald grass. Lemons the size of grapefruits weighted the well-kept trees. The crowning glory was the stunning view of the blue Pacific from the bluff the property bordered. Taken altogether, it was the sort of house humans pictured when they dreamed of California and movie stars: expensive and plush and just the teeniest bit wild.

Fresh from his run, Christian took a moment to catch his breath in the handsome cobble-lined courtyard. Laughter issued in bursts from the open windows, as if a party were under way. The laughter was accompanied by the music mortals had lately dubbed "rock and roll." Christian thought he recognized Bill Haley and the Comets. Apparently, "around the clock" was the only way to have fun.

As he stood there, letting the driving beats push against his skin, Christian's incisors began to pulse in time. He could smell Grace among the others, could pick out her soft laughter. He buttoned his new black jacket over a sudden heaviness at his groin. He really should have stopped to eat before coming here.

But maybe the discomfort would keep his complaints against her uppermost in his mind. That, he thought, was desirable.

Preferring not to announce himself, he opened the door and walked in.

He found Grace in the living room off the entryway. She was dancing with a loose-hipped, freckle-faced, sandy-haired human boy. He was holding her by the hands while they bounced and twisted from side to side. Showgirl legs notwithstanding, Grace looked a lot more awkward than her companion.

"Shake it, Grace," another young man called from the sidelines. "You're almost loosening up."

Grace dissolved into laughter and stopped dancing, both palms rising to her flushed cheeks. Christian could tell the attention simultaneously pleased and embarrassed her.

"Oh, hey, man," said the boy she'd been gyrating with. "Looks like our star has arrived."

Someone shut off the record player, and everyone turned to him. Six young men were scattered around the large, sleekly furnished room, plus an older man and woman seated on a long white couch. Cautious by habit, Christian took a quick survey of their minds. A few of those present hid resentment, but most were just curious. He tried to thaw the ice he knew had crackled over his own features.

"I play Charlie," said Grace's dancing partner, offering his hand to pump Christian's. "The big boss lady has us sticking to our characters' names, so I guess you'd be Joe. Over by the bar, sucking back those beers, are Philip and Matthew."

Two gawky but good-looking human males waved sketchily at him. Their snug white T-shirts and peg-legged black jeans made them seem even skinnier than they were. Their gleaming greaser haircuts were very like what Christian himself sported.

Satisfied their presence had been noted, Charlie indicated the older couple on the white couch. "These are Mr. and Mrs. Reed, your movie girlfriend's uncaring parents."

"We prefer *ineffectual*," laughed the man. He had a voice like someone who'd performed Shakespeare, his elocution too formal to have been what he was born with.

Charlie bowed to him with overdone and teasing respect, then chopped his hand one at a time at the last trio. "Bonehead, Growler, and Mace, your muscle-bound mortal enemies."

These three boys were indeed more physically formidable than the others. Sandy the stylist must have been at them, too. They had matching clean-cut "Joe College" haircuts, not a look generally associated with villains. Christian began to see how the factions were supposed to shape up within the film. The conformists weren't to be trusted. The rebels were the heroes.

Only Christian wasn't dressed as his character.

He couldn't tell how deeply the trio had taken their intended alliances to heart. Each came forward to shake his hand and, while all seemed to feel a compulsion to test the strength of his grip, only Bonehead could be counted among the actors who resented his presence.

"Rockin' boots," said the one called Growler, his vocal tones as deep as his character's name implied.

"Thank you," was all Christian could think to say.

"Your dad couldn't make it," Mace put in. "Hot date with a starlet. Naomi's going to tar his ass when she finds out."

The sense that he'd dropped into a rabbit hole seized Christian. Adrenaline jetted into his bloodstream, as if his dead father truly were about to show up. For just a second, he felt his old nausea and helplessness. He reminded himself he wasn't vulnerable to Gregori's abuse—and hadn't been for some time.

"That's too bad," he said as calmly as he could. "I'd have liked to meet everyone."

"We all hate you, of course," Charlie said blithely. "You're a regular Lana Turner at Schwab's Drugstore."

Christian was vaguely familiar with the story of the female star's serendipitous discovery. "I don't look as good in a sweater," he said, deadpan.

The boys laughed louder than he expected, and with more good humor. Surprisingly, they all seemed willing to like him, or at least to give him a chance. This was a reception Christian wasn't used to, not without employing his thrall.

"You must have killed your screen test," said the gawky black-haired boy who played Matthew.

Christian was pretty sure *killed* was good and not murderous. He opened his mouth to admit Nim Wei hadn't asked for a test. Grace stopped him by coming over to squeeze his arm. "Would you like something to drink, Christian? Miss Wei keeps a well-stocked bar."

"Just water," he said. "If she's got bottled."

Grace went to get it. She was wearing snug calf-length pants tonight, and her long, curved legs were spectacular from the rear.

"Oh, yeah," Charlie murmured beside his shoulder. "We've all been drooling over that dolly."

Christian jerked his head around to the boy, his upper lip twitching with his instinct to issue a fangy threat. Did this nosebleed think Grace was anywhere near his league? That he could crack a few jokes and dance with her like a monkey, and she would simply fall in his lap?

Oblivious to his danger, which meant Christian's glamour must have remained in place, Charlie met Christian's gaze and grinned. "No joy on that front so far. She's either Mormon or very shy."

An assortment of objections fought to spit out of Christian's mouth, none of them an appropriate response to Charlie's man-to-man friendliness.

"Sorry, sorry," Nim Wei broke in, thankfully saving him. Christian tried to remember if he'd ever heard her say she was sorry for anything. "Wade and I got to talking camera angles and lost track of time."

The queen of all the world's city vampires had entered her living room accompanied by another man. A tiny shiver tripped across Christian's shoulders. The man was in his early forties, with black-rimmed glasses and smiling light gray eyes. Though professorial in dress, he was tall and trim and stood like a fighter with his arms relaxed. His gaze traveled the room until it found Christian, at which point his smile broadened.

"Oh, good," Nim Wei said. "You made it."

Christian was so caught up in staring at the queen's companion that he didn't immediately realize she was speaking to him. She beckoned with one small hand.

"Come meet Wade Matthews, our cinematographer."

Christian's knees were unusually stiff as he crossed the black-and-white geometric carpet. Something was happening. He felt eerily like he had when he first met Grace in his barn. Wade Matthews took his right hand and squeezed it, his left coming up to brace Christian's elbow. The grip

was more a welcome than a mere greeting: the gesture
of a man who was both self-assured and warmhearted.
His eyes held Christian's with an openness few humans
practiced—and even fewer *upyr*. The love that radiated out
from his presence actually caused Christian to catch his
breath.

"So good to finally meet you," Wade Matthews said,
his hand still enclosing Christian's. He had a tenor's voice
with a smoker's rasp. "I hope you're not worried about this
being your first movie. Everyone on this project is wonderful. We're all committed to making sure your performance
is right up there with the rest."

The greenest fledgling couldn't have missed the ripple
of emotion that ran around the room. When the cinematographer claimed they were wonderful—obviously believ-
ing it—every cast member longed to be as good as he said,
not just in talent but in kindness. Christian's mouth fell
open at the strength of the effect. Wade was human. He had
no thrall, no artificially intensified charisma. He made his
colleagues want to be better by simple virtue of his faith in
them.

"Thank you," Christian said, his eyes blinking rapidly
in surprise. "I appreciate all the help I can get."

Wade laughed and slapped his shoulder with the flat of
his palm. Christian experienced a strange doubling of perceptions. Instead of a hand, a leather gauntlet hit the sleeve
of his mail hauberk. No longer gray, sherry brown eyes met
his. They looked at him from a younger face—a more serious face, if it came to that. From underneath those half-
forgotten features, a new confidence shone. *I know who I
am*, it said. *If I don't judge you, why should you judge me?*

Matthaus, Christian's brain whispered.

Wade was moving away to speak to the others. He had a
word for each, a friendly touch or a smile. He didn't seem
to have the least idea that he was Christian's slain friend
reborn.

If, in truth, he was Matthaus. Christian shook himself. He was getting too emotional, not thinking objectively. Seeing ghosts around every corner was not his goal.

"What time is it?" Nim Wei asked. "Shouldn't Viv have arrived by now?"

Grace glanced down at her wrist. "Sheesh," she said. "I forgot to put on my watch."

"Unheard of!" Philip exclaimed, his manner as flirtatious as Charlie's. "Of course that means none of us was even one minute late."

"Nice try," Nim Wei said with surprisingly little ire for someone used to her subjects jumping at a snap of her white fingers. She began herding the group toward the dining room. "We'll start without her. Grace can read Mary."

Wade Matthews took one end of the table, where a reel-to-reel tape recorder sat. Its presence made the read-through seem more official than Christian had anticipated.

"That seat's empty," Wade assured him, possibly mistaking his hesitation for bashfulness.

Christian took the chair he'd indicated. A second later, Charlie grabbed the one next to him.

"No," Nim Wei said when Mace tried to sit across from the pair of them. "You stay on the other end with Bonehead and Growler."

Grace was helping Wade get his microphone situated, effectively drawing Christian's eyes from the seating change. Grace's sweater set was a soft spring green Lana Turner couldn't have filled out better. Against it, her deep red hair glowed like an autumn maple, and her eyes were as bright as gems. Recognizing that he was staring, Christian wrenched his gaze down to the dark tabletop.

"Wait until you get a load of Vivian Lavelle," Charlie said under cover of the general noise. "She's grown up since *The Little Forresters*."

"I don't believe I've seen that film," Christian said.

Charlie gawped at him. "Oh, come *on*. The Christmas

movie? My dad plays it every year. Trust me, you don't want to have three older sisters and watch that scene where Viv's dog dies."

"Her dog dies?" Christian asked, wondering why this was considered festive.

"*Tears*," Charlie said. "Shooting in buckets from little Viv's big brown eyes."

"And your sisters cry as well, I presume?"

"No," Charlie laughed. "I do. Every damn time. My sisters never let me hear the end of it."

He laughed so hard Christian couldn't help but smile, despite the foreignness of the concept of people letting their emotions run amok like that.

"All right. Settle down," Nim Wei said. Everyone straightened and shifted their attention to the head of the table, where their director stood in petite Napoleonic glory. Her smile seemed genuine enough, her manner authoritative but not regal. The smiles that turned to her seemed real, too—excited, respectful . . . and not the least fearful. Christian realized he didn't see her mark on a single neck. Nim Wei hadn't bitten or thralled her cast. They were following her of their own free will.

Christian sat back with a jolt in his chair. He looked at Grace, whom Nim Wei most definitely had bespelled. Probably assuming he was nervous, she smiled at him reassuringly.

"As some of you know," Nim Wei began, "movies shoot their scenes out of order. Tonight may be your only chance to get a feel for the story as a whole before we're done filming. Don't worry about getting everything perfect. It's likely there will be script changes, especially if lines don't read the way we expect. If you stumble, please keep going. This is a read-through, not an audition for the Actors' Studio. Everybody dig?"

"Yes, Naomi," the table said in near unison.

* * *

I *Was a Teen-Age Vampire* began without dialogue. In a calm and businesslike manner, Grace described the opening sequence. A motorcycle gang, led by Christian's movie father, roared into the town of Haileyville bent on extortion. The boys provided predictable engine noises as the gang surrounded, attacked, and finally bit a hapless shopkeeper. Grace remained undistracted by the chomping sound Bonehead made, though she did smile slightly. With an inward sigh, Christian added one more male to the list of those interested in her.

"George still isn't here?" Nim Wei asked, looking around as the scene ended. No one seemed to want to answer.

"Date," Philip said after a small pause.

Nim Wei's expression cooled to one Christian found more familiar. "Very well. Growler, you read with Christian now."

Christian's heart gave an uncomfortable thump as he realized he was up. His character Joe Pryor's name was scattered over the next pages. His voice cracked unexpectedly on the second word, but he soon managed to warm up. It was only when he listened to what Growler was doing that he sensed he was in trouble.

Christian could read his lines like a human would. He knew how mortals intonated, could guess where they'd stumble or rush ahead. Growler, however, was achieving something on a different order—and for a character who wasn't his.

When Growler told his son that attending high school with a bunch of humans was a waste of time, Christian believed every sneer. Growler wasn't forcing the emotions; he was simply being the role, as naturally as if it were a skin he'd slipped on.

"Go ahead," Wade encouraged when Christian momentarily fell silent. "You're doing fine."

Except he wasn't. The further they progressed, the more

he knew it. These little humans were *good*. They acted
from the inside, not the surface. Worst of all, they didn't
seem to be trying. Christian's stomach began to clench.
Any second, someone was going to laugh at him—which
wasn't a situation he should have cared about.

His nerves were coiled so tightly that when the front
door burst open, at least a quarter of his muscles twitched.

"*God*," said a mellifluous female voice from the entryway. "That was *endless*. Someone fetch me a drink."

Matthew jumped up, suggesting at least one male wasn't
homed in on Grace. "Martini?"

"Please," responded the newcomer as she sauntered into
the dining room, tugging off short black gloves.

She didn't look old enough to drink. Her face was ach-
ingly innocent, with smooth skin poured over cheekbones
that were still soft with youth. Her dark eyes were huge
and thick-lashed, her mouth pouting with the rosy bow of
a five-year-old. Christian had been expecting a blonde in
ringlets, but Vivian Lavelle was a wavy-haired, shoulder-
length brunette. With a studied negligence that turned a
casual gesture dramatic, she tossed her smart black coat
onto one of the empty chairs. A curve-skimming knitted
dress in hunter green was revealed. From what he could
see of her figure, it was as softly rounded as the rest of her.

The term "child-woman" might have been invented for
this female.

"I tried to get here on time," she said to Nim Wei,
accepting her drink from Matthew without a word of
thanks. "The old fart kept wanting to tell 'one more story.'"

Nim Wei accepted this with a shrug. "You didn't miss
much. Charlie, scoot over and let Viv sit next to Christian."

Though Viv's thoughts weren't the easiest to read,
Christian was certain she'd been aware of him all along.
Nonetheless, she pretended to be noticing him just then.

"Well, lookie here," she said, turning slightly to tip her

head at him. "We finally meet the cock of the walk. Naomi said you were pretty."

"Be nice, Viv," Grace interjected. "Christian is new to this."

Viv rolled her eyes and flounced into the chair Charlie had vacated. A faint flush stained her cheeks as she sat, so perhaps she wasn't quite as outrageous as she was trying to appear.

"I enjoyed your work in *The Little Forresters*," Christian said politely.

"Fuck *The Little Forresters*," Viv snapped back. Once she saw he was startled, she tossed back her cocktail, grimaced, then bared small white teeth in a sweet and utterly unconvincing smile. "Please don't mention that film in my presence."

The rest of the cast were concealing grins. Christian concluded he wasn't the first to step on this particular trip-wire. Not about to dance to the tune of some human brat, he regarded her calmly.

"I'll mention if I want to," he said with equally insincere pleasantness.

Viv's dove-soft jaw fell open as her director laughed. Nim Wei stopped when Viv stared at her, aggrieved.

"Well," the queen said, not exactly repentant, "now that you've established who's the cock of the walk, perhaps we could continue our read-through?"

Viv closed her mouth and tugged down her dress's sleeves. The motion covered a flash of silver on one slim wrist.

"*I'm* ready," the littlest Forrester said darkly.

Five

Grace could have warned Christian Viv would retaliate for his failure to apply his lips to her derriere. The former child star had a taste for screen idol–style fawning.

Grace hid her amusement by bending over her script. With brisk, irritated motions, Viv flipped through her copy to catch up. She stopped when she reached the scene where her character, Mary, was breakfasting with her parents prior to her first day at Haileyville High School. Rolling her shoulders like an athlete, she cleared her throat.

Grace couldn't doubt that Christian was in for it.

Normally, Viv wouldn't have pulled out all the stops for a read-through. Since Christian had pricked her pride, however, she was determined to show him up. With a single—and believable—quaver in her voice, she became shy Mary. The actors who played her parents were perfect foils, their stage backgrounds making them sound fake even as they strove for sincerity.

"Do *try* to be outgoing," Mrs. Reed advised with a fruity maternal kindness no one on earth would have bought. "Not like at your last school. When I was your age, I was the belle of two classes."

"She was," Mr. Reed agreed. "The prettiest cheerleader any of us had seen."

Viv-as-Mary jerked her head in a downcast nod. "May I be excused?" she mumbled.

Grace could have laughed with pleasure at how convincing she was. The famous little Forrester tears thickened each soft word. All around the table, Grace spotted eyes dewing. Anyone who'd ever felt like an outcast—which, for some reason, included a lot of actors—was touched by Mary's fragility. Christian was surveying the faces, too, though his expression seemed more aghast than moved. Grace could practically hear him wondering if *he* was expected to affect his audience this way.

She looked down before he could catch her staring. As his gaze returned to his script, she saw his shoulders draw in slightly. Guilt for her humor sent a small twinge through her—but surely Christian was a big boy.

Viv didn't give away that she knew she had him; she was too good a thespian. Instead, she let herself disappear into her performance. Grace knew she was watching a tour de force, and hoped Viv could re-create this when cameras rolled. The girl was never overdone or self-conscious. She spoke as if the words came from inside her and not the page.

Grace had no problem admitting they sounded better than she'd written them.

To her delight, the other actors began to come up to Viv's level. Good to start with, inspired by her example, they hit their lines more gently, the rhythm of their exchanges unfolding like real people talking. Their awareness of what was happening hummed palpably through them. They felt the promise of what this film could become.

Only Christian grew tenser as pages turned.

Despite her wariness of his pull on her, Grace was tempted to pat his white-knuckled hand, which he'd clenched on the table close to his chest. Christian wasn't as bad as he thought—certainly no worse than most of the actors who'd auditioned to play Joe. For a beginner, he was darn good. Nothing in his performance jumped out as awful. He sounded smart and articulate. Grace hadn't had to scribble one note to simplify his lines. As for his inexperience, he had his face to make up for that—that beautiful, coolly brooding visage that looked like something interesting was going on behind it even when it was still. With a face like his, brilliant acting was optional.

Grace looked down the table toward Miss Wei, searching for a cue as to whether she ought to intervene.

Her boss looked back, smiling gently and giving a tiny shake of her head. Miss Wei's expressions could be subtle, but Grace thought she was pleased by Christian's dilemma. Maybe she figured Viv putting him on notice would benefit them in the long run.

They'd arrived at the first big confrontation between Joe Pryor and his father. The gang members—with Growler still standing in for George Pryor—did a good job of conveying the frenetic energy of the fight in Reed's drugstore. It was here that the split between the boys who liked George's violent leadership and those who preferred Joe's compassion became irreversible.

They were breathing harder as they finished, caught up in their playacting. Grace tried to ignore the fact that Christian-as-Joe was not. She had her usual role of reading stage directions where no dialogue occurred. Now Joe and Mary were escaping into the woods following the fight. *Mary stumbles,* she read, *not for the first time, to judge by the bloody scratches all over her. Joe picks her up and carries her in his arms. His fangs are down, his face tormented. Joe knows his father attacked hers as a means of*

*punishing him for his defiance. Joe's rage over that, and
his own culpability, hasn't calmed. Worse, Mary's blood is
arousing him. It seems wrong that he wants to feed on this
injured girl who's become so dear to him.*

Grace recited these bits with half her attention, the
rest of her focus on Christian's state. From the corner of
her eye, she noticed Charlie glancing around Viv at him.
By this time, Christian was completely hunched over his
script, one hand hiding the right side of his face. Charlie
looked sympathetic, but also a bit concerned. Charlie was
among the sharpest of *Teen-Age Vampire*'s young actors.
Grace suspected he'd been hoping for better from their
male lead.

Her own palms dampened for Christian's sake. The
scene that came next was one of the script's most emotional. Joe and Mary were taking shelter in an abandoned
boxcar, sharing their hopes and fears regarding each other
for the first time. Christian's inexperience was bound to
show here as nowhere else. If he didn't pull himself together, Viv was going to total him.

"You're a vampire," Viv accused in Mary's tremulous
tones.

"I am," Christian acknowledged, utterly wooden. "But
I'm trying to be a good man."

"Oh, for God's sake," Bonehead burst out from the other
end of the table. "My dog acts better than that!"

"Hush," Miss Wei scolded. "Give Christian a chance to
find his sea legs."

"But he's terrible," Bonehead protested. He lowered his
voice in an attempt to sound more reasonable. "You can't
do this to the rest of us. We've *worked* to get where we are."

Grace's boss turned her coolest look on him. "Rex," she
said, which was Bonehead's real name. "If you were half
as handsome as Christian, you could get away with being
terrible, too."

Bonehead's face paled with hurt and anger. He drew a

sharp, loud breath—about to say something unforgivable, Grace feared.

"Stop," she said, jumping up from her chair. Though confrontation wasn't an approach she enjoyed, this argument was undermining more than one actor's confidence. "You can yell at me if you want, but neither of you are helping. Rex, it's true Christian doesn't have your experience, but both Miss Wei and I know he has promise. Sometimes being a good actor means being a team player."

"Well said," Mr. Reed put in pompously.

Viv let out the first note of a derisive laugh.

"Not a word," Grace instructed, jabbing her finger at the young actress.

Viv innocently batted her eyelashes. "As you wish, headmistress. May we continue now?"

Grace sat down with her knees trembling. Wade patted her arm in support. From the DP's other side, Christian looked at her, his expression unreadable. His putting up such strong shields didn't strike Grace as a good sign. Maybe he didn't appreciate her sticking her nose in on his behalf. She wiped palms that had gone slippery along her thighs. She didn't know whether to be annoyed or relieved that Miss Wei didn't seem unhappy.

If her boss was playing one of her chess games, Grace was going to be angry.

Christian wished the queen had fired him. Then he wouldn't have had to go on. He knew he sounded like a robot as he explained the film's somewhat specious facts of vampire life to Mary, telling her he was a "born" vampire and thus could walk in the sun. "Made" vampires like the rest of the gang could not, which meant Joe and his father were princes among their kind. They didn't have to kill when they fed. His father simply enjoyed it.

"He likes to catch one victim for the whole gang. Then

the human's blood can be drained. There was a girl at the house tonight . . ."

Grace's pencil scratched something on her copy of the script, distracting him from Mary's response. No doubt Grace was making note of the fact that he was a moron. He couldn't believe she'd felt compelled to leap up and defend him.

"Did you hurt her?" Viv-as-Mary asked for the second time.

"I stood by," Christian read numbly. "Oh, God, I stood by."

This came out so leaden Christian's neck grew hot. He was getting worse by the second.

"Perhaps with a *smidge* more feeling," Nim Wei suggested from the head of the table.

Viv touched his arm. His incompetence hadn't thrown her. She was looking up at him as if she were Mary, with her schoolgirl's heart shining in her eyes. She wanted him to deny he was any less than she'd dreamed, wanted to throw caution to the winds and love him without reserve. For two endless seconds, Christian couldn't see anything but her. Grace had gazed at him like that, once upon a time. He tore his eyes away and back to the page.

I need you to believe I can change, it said beneath his character's name. *If you have faith in me, maybe I'll find the strength.*

An uncustomary sweat prickled on his scalp, joining the heat sizzling on his skin. Wasn't this what he'd hoped Grace would give him? The strength not to turn into a soulless killer like his father? His mouth was dry, his tongue so thick it felt like it blocked his throat. He couldn't say the speech. He couldn't *do* this. It was too much to ask.

He pushed too fast to his feet, causing the humans who were looking at him to blink in confusion.

"I'm sorry," he said, the apology as hoarse as he'd feared. "I shouldn't have taken this job."

"Christian," Grace said soothingly. He couldn't look at her. He strode from the dining room with his cool face gone fiery, all his focus on not blurring out of there.

Once outside, he almost crashed into an older man who was walking up to the door.

"Watch where you're going!" the stranger snapped.

Christian ignored him. It didn't matter who he was. He crossed the cobbles of the courtyard with hair-ruffling haste. The breeze was cool, the night scented by the ocean and fresh-cut grass. He didn't want to be calmed by either. He wanted to get out of there.

Or he thought he did.

His feet led him to a light in the darkness, a guest cottage at the edge of Nim Wei's grounds.

"*Scheisse*," he cursed to himself. He knew exactly where he had ended up.

The older actor who played George Pryor stormed into the dining room in full bluster. He'd done a lot of Westerns, and he was good at it.

"Who the hell was that?" he demanded. "The guy nearly ran me down."

"That was your son," Bonehead drawled. "Our would-be star."

"Good riddance, if you ask me," Viv huffed.

"Be fair," Charlie said. "He was doing all right until you two started in on him."

Viv tossed her head. "If he can't take a little pressure, he shouldn't—"

"Why did you begin without me?" George interrupted, looking around, perplexed. "You said the read-through was at nine thirty."

Grace blew out a sound of annoyance her boss couldn't fail to hear. She'd specifically told Grace she needn't call

George about the time. For whatever reason, Miss Wei had
wanted Christian's movie father to be tardy.

"Did I?" Miss Wei asked now. "I *am* sorry. I must have
been mixed up." She met Grace's disbelieving stare without a shred of remorse. "Well?" Her hands made little
shooing motions. "Go after Christian. We can't have our
leading man throwing in the towel."

It took all Grace's strength not to favor her employer
with a few choice words. She would have if they hadn't had
enough drama already. Grace couldn't help but think Miss
Wei had created this situation on purpose. That, however,
wasn't their most immediate crisis.

"You're underestimating him," she said softly but point-
edly to Viv. "Christian brought out something special in
you tonight. That alone ought to earn him your patience."

"I need an equal," Viv protested, drawing back in hurt
at the scold. "Someone I can play off of."

"You'll get one," Grace promised, meaning it thor-
oughly. If it was the last thing she did, she'd drag Christian
up to par for this movie.

For the last four years Grace had been living in Miss
Wei's cozy one-bedroom, ivy-draped guesthouse. Only her
knowledge that the cottage wasn't really hers kept it from
feeling a hundred percent her home. It was closer to one
than any place she'd inhabited, including the many houses
she'd grown up in.

Having an abusive, alcoholic father, whose control
wasn't always what it should be, had meant moving around
a lot.

Logic said she should check the bluff first for Christian.
Most people who were upset would have stalked there to
stare at the waves. Ignoring the reasonable choice, Grace
turned her steps toward the cottage. The air was nippy as

it blew around her. She was grateful for the Windbreaker Charlie had lent her.

What French people called a frisson ran through her when she spotted Christian on her doorstep, exactly where logic said he shouldn't be. The harsh security light flooded down on him. His head was bent, and he appeared to be contemplating her doorknob.

If clothes were all it took to change a man, Christian was a chameleon. He looked dangerously elegant in his dark silk shirt and trousers, the outfit exaggerating both his height and leanness. Grace heaved a private sigh at how exactly he matched the type of man she preferred—muscled and spare and effortlessly graceful. His new short haircut gleamed in the light, the curve of bangs over his forehead just as tempting as promised. Grace wanted to run her fingers through those silky locks, to smooth her hands around his skull on the way to the rest of his gorgeousness. His rear was as appealing in black trousers as it had in been jeans, its taut, high curves screaming to be stroked.

Grace forced her fingers to uncurl from her palms. These weren't appropriate thoughts right now.

"Someone smashed your glass," Christian said a second before turning his head to her. "They locked up again when they left."

Drawn into sharp lines by the light and shadow, Christian's face was beautiful but weary. Grace's chest ached with her longing to comfort him. Belatedly, his words registered.

"Someone broke in?"

Shrugging, he reached through the shattered diamond-shaped pane to open the door from inside.

"Careful," she cautioned. "Miss Wei will never forgive me if you get cut."

He looked at her with studied blankness, and his voice came out the same way. "I'm fine. I don't sense anyone in there now."

"Well, get behind me," Grace said, hefting one of the rocks that lay in the flower bed beside the landing. In a pinch, she could bash someone's head with it.

Christian surprised her by laughing, the sound doing warm and squirmy things to her insides. Like a mirage, a dimple appeared briefly on one cheek. "Grace, I work on a ranch, not in an accounting firm. And, wringing wet, you weigh half what I do."

Grace doubted that was true, but it was nice of him to say. "I'm not letting you go in there unarmed."

Shaking his head, Christian pulled the rock from her hands. "There," he said. "Now I'm armed."

While she gaped, he walked in ahead of her to stand, unmoving, in the center of her dark living room. He was listening, and so she listened along with him. She heard the distant susurration of waves beneath the bluff and the nearer rustling of greenery outside the windows. The faucet in her kitchen sink was dripping. She had to jiggle it just so to shut it off. She realized her initial surge of fear had faded. Though it flew in the face of too many experiences to count, Christian's strong male presence made her feel safe.

"I can't smell who it was," he said after half a minute. "Maybe you should turn on the light and see if anything's missing."

Grace bit back the impulse to ask if he thought he was a bloodhound. After the evening he'd had, he probably wasn't in the mood for teasing. She flipped on the light switch and glanced around. Except for the rock Christian had set down on the carpet and the shards of glass just inside the door, everything looked normal.

The Chinese throw pillows on her couch were in the same disarray as this morning. *Peyton Place*, her most recent read-it-with-breakfast book, still lay shamefully facedown and open on the layer of magazines under which her coffee table was buried. The mess momentarily embarrassed her. Some of those *Hollywood Reporter*s were weeks old.

Out of habit—and *not* because she wanted to avoid drawing her guest's attention to the clutter—she glanced at the half-moon table beside her door. On it, she kept a celadon bowl where she tossed her keys and other assorted items from her pockets.

"My watch!" she exclaimed.

Christian was instantly by her side, one hand lightly circling her elbow. Grace fought the little shiver this stirred in her. Strictly speaking, she should hardly have felt his touch through the Windbreaker.

"I think I dropped it there last night," she said, pointing at the dish. "It was a gift from Miss Wei. The bracelet has little movie-related charms. She gives me a new one for each anniversary of my hiring."

Christian muttered something that sounded like, *You mean she likes to decorate your slave chain.*

"What?"

He waved his hand. "I saw you wearing it earlier." His delectably thin lips pursed. "Why would a thief steal just that?"

"I don't know. Maybe I'm mistaken, and I put the watch somewhere else. Maybe you scared off whoever broke in before they could take more."

She was looking up at him as his dark eyes narrowed, squinting into a distance she couldn't see. "No one else was here when I arrived."

"You're sure?"

"Completely."

His gaze shifted to hers, and her muscles tensed as if in expectation of a blow. The tension wasn't precisely fear. His fingers fanned her elbow.

"You found me pretty quickly after I left."

Tingles ran up Grace's arm from the point he idly caressed, but she kept her answer calm all the same. "Just a hunch. I thought you might have seen the light above my door. It's always on at night."

"I *knew* you lived here." His voice had dropped an octave. "I had no trouble tracking your essence."

This was as strange a claim as saying he could smell an intruder. Then again, actors often were eccentric. Perhaps Christian was better suited to being one than he knew. Grace told herself not to comment as he leaned close enough to brush her cheek with his silken hair. She could smell *him* then, a whiff of fragrance like sidewalks washed clean by a hard rain. He inhaled, slowly, beside her neck, filling his lungs as if he were savoring her. His next words came out a smoky purr.

"I could never forget how you—"

And then he straightened, both hands clamping tight on her upper arms.

"This isn't your jacket," he said intensely. "This belongs to Charlie."

Grace's eyes widened. Maybe he did have a gifted nose. "He lent it to me. So I wouldn't get chilled while I was looking for you."

Christian dropped his hold and rubbed his palms on his trousers. To her surprise, he appeared vaguely embarrassed. "Of course. That's perfectly sensible. I . . ." He stopped speaking and looked at her. "Grace, I don't think I can say those things in your script."

"Of course you can," she countered, trying to sound steady and businesslike. "You were doing pretty well until Viv and Bonehead threw you."

Christian wagged his head. "I wasn't as good as them."

"You can't expect to be as good as them from the start."

Except he had. The truth flashed across his face almost too quick to see. She knew then, as clearly as if he'd spoken, that Christian Durand was used to excelling at everything.

"You might never be as good as them," she said gently, instinct impelling her to honesty. "If you can't live with that, maybe you should quit."

His shoulders stiffened, his dark eyes sparking with offense. Grace hadn't been trying to provoke this response, but it had her hiding a smile. Viv wasn't the only cast member who was prideful.

"I gave my word," he said.

He pronounced this with unexpected formality, like a knight of yore who lived and died for honor. Grace's cheeks warmed in reaction. She sensed she was seeing a very personal side of him.

"Let me help you keep your word," she said.

Their gazes locked, his pupils swallowing more of his irises. Heated moisture trickled from her sex, dampening her panties. Christian's elegant nostrils flared.

"*Grace*," he said, as harsh as an iron spike dragging on cement.

Grace stepped nervously back from him.

"I have an idea," she said, trying to pretend the moment hadn't happened. "I'm sure I've got extra copies of the script around here somewhere."

Christian crossed his arms, torn between annoyance and frustration over Grace pulling back from him. As she yanked open drawers and dug under couch cushions, her nervousness rode the air like perfume. The scent was as good as fear to the predator that lived inside him. His skin was buzzing, his fangs two hard lengths filling up the front of his mouth. He didn't know why he'd confided in her the way he had, why he'd worried for her safety.

Whoever she was, she had no right to that anymore.

Possibly, his attitude was due to hunger. He'd gone without blood longer when he was on campaigns as a spy, but this was certainly long enough. Not having fed since he'd met her naturally made him want to draw close to her. The read-through hadn't helped, what with those descriptions of him carrying injured heroines. Viv might not stir him, but Grace did. Grace made him want to sink his fangs into all of her juicy spots.

"Aha!" she said, kneeling before the bottom drawer of a tall Chippendale breakfront. "Here's two copies!"

He tore his gaze from her succulent little ass as she rose. She handed him one copy and looked at him hopefully. He probably was glowering. His face felt as if it was.

"Sit," she said, gesturing to the flowered couch with its mismatched Chinese throw pillows. "You can practice saying the lines with me. Nice and easy. Just get them out of your mouth."

He sat, then felt irritated for obeying. "They're still going to sound stupid."

Grace smiled at him and sat, too, her knees mere inches away from his. "Now you're insulting me."

"I didn't mean what you wrote was stupid."

He was frowning, but her smile curved deeper. "You might have, but it doesn't matter. Audiences want to see big emotions. Sometimes you have to be brave enough to gnash the scenery."

"Gnash it?"

She did her own variation of Bonehead's chomping noise, adding a growl and two finger fangs. She looked so adorable, he had to laugh a bit.

"*Chew* the scenery," he said more calmly. "I know that phrase."

"So chew it with me. Have the courage to make a fool of yourself. All the great ones are willing to."

Christian sighed silently. The courage to make a fool of himself. If he'd wanted to be a "great one," as she put it, that argument might carry weight, but she had no idea how reluctantly someone like him relinquished his dignity. Give him a monster, and he would slay it. Ask him to look weak, and he'd rather set his hair on fire.

Not that he hadn't displayed plenty of weakness tonight already, weakness she seemed to inspire every way she turned.

"Come on," she coaxed. "It might not be as bad as you think."

She flipped his script to the page she wanted, then opened the one she held. She wasn't quite as calm as she looked. Her heart was beating too loudly, or—hell—maybe it was his.

"Did you hurt her?" she prompted, Mary's line from the ill-fated boxcar scene.

He thought of all the people he'd hurt: friends he hadn't been able to save in time, enemies he'd taken revenge on, strangers who'd been on the other side of the countless conflicts he'd fought in. He'd made his living as a mercenary before and after his death. His mortal and immortal hands were covered in more blood than Grace could conceive of.

"I stood by," he said, the confession coming out as a rough whisper. "I stood by and let them hurt her."

As if she sensed the underlying truth of his admission, Grace laid her hand on his forearm. Not stopping to think why, Christian moved until his knees bumped hers. Grace's pupils dilated with emotion.

"I need you to believe I can change," he said. "If you have faith in me, maybe I'll find the strength."

"It's in you," Grace assured him, her fingers tightening on his arm. "I'm sure you'd find it even without me."

For one odd second, Christian didn't recognize her response as coming from the script. When he did, he was almost afraid to breathe. He'd forgotten this was make-believe.

"That's good," Grace said, breaking the spell before he could. "You thought about what Joe was feeling. You stepped into his shoes. Trust me, that'll be easier to do with Viv. She has a gift for putting whoever she's acting with in the moment. If you forget she's a brat and just stay relaxed, she can take you there."

Christian stared at her. Grace thought *Viv* would be

more helpful? How could she not remember what she'd been to him?

"Are you okay?" she asked, her human brow furrowing. "Do you want to try that again?"

His control broke with a snap that should have been audible. He hated that she was treating him like he needed hand-holding. Even more, he hated that he'd been acting as if he did. His fangs gave a hard, sharp throb. He wanted to assert his superiority in the most basic way of his kind. That, however, would be giving in to a different weakness. He had better methods for regaining the upper hand.

"I'll tell you what I'd like to try again," he growled.

The shiver that shuddered through her was gratifying. He slid his hands up her ribs to her underarms, using the grip to yank her upward until her mouth hit his.

Grace's body reacted so swiftly it shocked her. Christian rolled his tongue around hers, warmly, wetly, and she melted without a fight. The room tipped sideways. He was under her on the couch. He'd leaned back to pull her up him, and his long, lean body gave hers a delicious hardness to conform to. His thighs, his chest, the rising firmness between his legs, all invited her to squirm. As she did, the broad male hand that banded her waist cruised down to massage her bottom. With the corner of her mind that wasn't riveted on diving into his mouth, she marveled at how his hold tingled through the material of her pants.

She didn't think the effect could be natural. Hands weren't supposed to have electric charges inside of them.

Seemingly unable to help herself, her knees dropped to the couch to either side of his. Grunting, Christian worked one hand between them. When he surrounded her mound and squeezed, she felt like ghostly fingers were pushing inside of her.

Though that wasn't possible, it didn't matter to her body. Grace let out a moan and writhed closer. Her hands clutched his silk-covered shoulders like he was a life raft she was riding through a storm. She wished she could reach more of him, wished her palms were cupping him like he cupped her. She supposed he enjoyed the way she rubbed over him. Gasping, he wrenched his mouth free and brought his lips to her ear.

"Do you remember when you used to do this to me?" he demanded, soft and insidious. The prickling warmth inside her sex strengthened. "Do you remember how I'd beg for the brush of your energy on my cock?"

She had no idea what he meant. In truth, her brain was barely working well enough to be mystified. She liked hearing him say *cock*, though, and the idea of stroking his. She groaned as the sensation of fullness inside her swelled, pressing—or maybe penetrating—the walls of her vagina.

Then, just as she mustered the courage to move her hands, the room around her ceased to exist. Instead of the dripping tap, she heard a crackle like a campfire. Instead of the well-stuffed couch, she felt hard bare earth beneath a rough blanket. Christian's eyes were screwed shut with pleasure, the expression so unfamiliar he seemed a different man. Grace was pushing her fist—which for some reason wasn't solid—down the throbbing length of his erection. His cock was bare and mesmerizing. Its tip was crimson, its hole glittering with a tiny drop of moisture. The him-who-was-not-him threw back his head and sucked air.

Grace was part of this Christian, the edges between their separate bodies blurred. She had no barriers to protect her, not for her skin or her heart. He could break her if he wanted, could disappoint her in ways she'd never recover from. Her throat convulsed with fear at the thought of it.

And then the strange vision or whatever it had been was

gone. Christian was dragging his sexy slash of a mouth up and down her neck, his breath coming hard and hot, his grip like steel compressing the soft folds of her pussy. Her excitement had soaked through the seam of her pedal pushers. Her nerves were a single heartbeat from spasming.

She wanted to stop them, but it wasn't in her power. Something almost real was thrusting slowly in and out of her, brushing those sensitive nerve endings, causing them to wind tighter and start to fire. Nothing should have been able to touch her where he was touching, even if they'd been naked. Helpless, Grace cried out and went over, her body shaking hard against his.

As it did, Christian's hips jerked up and lifted her at the crotch. The pressure felt so good she cried out again.

"Remember," he hissed as if he were angry. "Remember what you did to me."

Grace collapsed on him, panting. To her amazement, he was still hard. He hadn't come when she did. The thickness of his cock was like a branch pushing at her through his nice trousers. She scrambled off him, retreating to the other end of the couch as soon as her trembling limbs would function.

Christian sat up and glared at her. She was really starting to dislike that expression.

"You're crazy," she said, her voice a good bit more breathless than she wanted it to be. "I don't remember you. We've never met before. And I didn't invite you to do that in the first place."

"So I just imagined your tongue shoving down my throat?"

She hated that his face grew cooler as hers flared hot. "I know what I did and I'm sorry. It just isn't a good idea for us to . . . get personal. You need to keep a decent distance from me."

He crossed his arms, not even sweating in his dark silk shirt. "I need to, do I?"

"I'm asking you to." Thankfully, her tone was firmer than before. "I know you have enough self-control not to push yourself where you're not wanted."

His dark eyes rolled. She knew he must be thinking that her not wanting him wasn't the issue. Slowly, his arms unfolded. She held her breath as he rose and looked down at her. Lord, he looked ten feet tall. A part of her wanted him to ignore everything she asked, to take her and take her and professionalism be damned. She could hardly restrain her compulsion to reach for the hump that was pushing out his zipper. The only sign that *he* wasn't in complete control was the way his lips rolled together in a pale line.

"This isn't over," he warned her disdainfully.

Christian got as far the flower bed outside her door, where the intensity of his erection nearly bent him double. He didn't waste time cursing, just unzipped his trousers so he could fist himself. Relief immediately had him gasping. His skin was on fire, his cock so hard it could have been granite. Gladder for his vampire strength than he'd ever been, he tugged a viselike grip from his aching root to his tingling crest. Shaken by the urgent motions of his masturbation, his balls felt tight enough to blow in two seconds.

The things Grace drove him to . . . The things she made him remember . . .

That night in the mercenary camp felt like yesterday. When he'd slept back-to-back with his best friend, Michael. When he hadn't been able to resist begging Grace for help with an orgasm. He hadn't gotten one then, but he got one now. A grunt scraped past his control as tortured bliss seared his sexual nerves.

It wasn't enough. His hips snapped forward, and he rubbed his slippery cock faster. It wouldn't stay slippery long, and he wanted another climax—needed one, if he were honest. More than anything, he longed to be fucking

Grace. In that moment, if he could have killed her with pleasure, he would have.

Furious with himself, he growled low inside his chest. The pressure inside him built: closer, bigger, more impossibly demanding. With his free hand, he squeezed his testicles through the silk lining of his trousers. It should have been her hand, her wet, undulating body pulling out these responses. His growl twisted to a snarl as a second gout of come fired his urethra.

Then he was done if not satisfied. He was still hungry— and still unwilling to feed from anyone but her.

He turned away from her cottage, refusing to look back or wonder if she'd heard what his lust for her had driven him to do. His fangs throbbed, but he ignored them. He wasn't going to force himself to take another woman. If his body only wanted her, so be it.

He'd make Grace pay for that, too, as soon as the chance arose.

His body was preparing to break into a run when he remembered the shattered window and the glass on the floor. Someone had broken into her home. Someone who might return. He looked back and sighed resignedly to himself. He could stand watch till dawn, just this once. She'd never know he was there.

After all, if someone was going to hurt her, it really ought to be him.

Six

Grace wasn't more than half asleep when it happened. The strong LA sun was sneaking tiny rays past the edges of her blackout shades—a necessity when you were expected to get a good night's rest during daylight hours. From the corner of the eye she'd cracked open grumpily, she saw a shape glide into her room, one that was lighter than the dark English furniture. The hairs at the back of her neck stood up.

Last night's intruder must have come back. As she froze, wondering what the hell to do, she heard a familiar voice.

"You can remember if you want to."

Grace bolted up amidst the tangle of her covers. Maybe this wasn't about breaking and entering.

A glowing man in an impeccably cut tuxedo stood calmly at the foot of her bed. He reminded her of William Holden in *Sunset Boulevard*, though in truth he looked nothing like. This man was younger and golden-haired, and his eyes were a bright sky blue. Of course, since this had to be a hallucination, why should who he reminded her of make sense?

"Grace," said the man, nodding politely.

Her lips struggled to form a name for him. She knew it, didn't she? She'd talked to him before.

"Just the other night," he said. "But it's up to you whether you remember. You always have a choice. I simply think you've hidden from yourself long enough."

How could she hide from herself? She, of all people, always knew where she was.

"Who are you?" she demanded in a breathless voice.

"A friend," said her visitor. "A friend to the pair of you."

The mattress shook like they were having an earthquake. Grace braced both hands on it . . . and abruptly awoke.

She wasn't sitting anymore. She was lying down, curled up on her side. She'd tossed and turned for hours last night over what had happened with Christian, her mind spinning round and round as she tried to explain away what he'd done. Considering how little sleep she'd gotten, her alarm clock was ringing too loudly now. The time read five past eleven. She'd been sleeping through the bell for five minutes. Rattled, she slapped the ringer off and shoved her hair from her sweaty face. She willed her heart to stop thudding so rapidly. A second later, the phone rang.

"Jeepers," Grace said and picked up the receiver.

The caller was Viv, whom Grace didn't recall giving her private number to.

"It's me," the actress burbled, laughing and light as air. "I wanted to apologize for being a beast last night."

"You weren't a beast," Grace said sleepily. Not to her anyway.

"I thought I'd take you to lunch to make up for it. Maybe Musso and Frank's? You know they have the best martinis in Hollywood."

Grace grimaced at the thought. She wasn't a fan of the little Forrester's favorite drink. "That's nice of you, Viv, but I have things to do for the film all day. Maybe some other time."

"Sure," Viv said, her voice not quite as bright as before. "We'll call it a rain check."

Grace said goodbye and set the phone in its cradle. For a moment, she simply stared in bemusement at its pink plastic. This was shaping up to be some morning. Who'd have thought a glamorous young actress like Viv Lavelle would want to make friends with her?

Seven

On the night following Christian's latest aggravating experience with Grace, a night he'd spent keeping watch in the bushes outside her house, Nim Wei summoned him for a wardrobe test. Apparently, it wasn't enough that he had new everyday clothes. He had to try on half a clothing store before he'd look "hip" enough for her damned movie.

If Nim Wei hadn't thought he was hip, why had she hired him in the first place?

At least in this case, the clothing store came to them. They met on the studio soundstage *Teen-Age Vampire* had been assigned, a long hangarlike building where the interiors for George Pryor's run-down Victorian mansion were being built. Wade Matthews met them next to the partially constructed set with a motion picture camera and tripod. Wade was going to film how Christian looked when dressed as his character.

As they finished the necessary greetings, a custom that

strained Christian's already short temper, a long rack of leather jackets was rolled in by a human male. No more than thirty, the mortal had a face and form so lovely he could have been asked to model clothes himself.

No one but a vampire would have heard Wade Matthews swallow at his arrival.

"This is Andy Phelps," Nim Wei said to Christian. "Our head of wardrobe. We managed to steal him from Paramount."

Andy Phelps smiled pleasantly and shook Christian's hand. He wore Ben Franklin wire-rimmed glasses over his light brown eyes.

"The pleasure was mine, believe me. Edith Head could be . . . challenging to work for." Turning a bit more, Andy noticed Wade. "Mr. Matthews. Nice to see you again."

The genial cinematographer appeared to have been struck dumb. All he managed was a jerky nod for the younger man, after which he had to poke his horn-rims back up his nose. Christian would have been more entertained by this drama if he hadn't noticed a particular absence then.

"Where's Grace?" he demanded.

"Can't last an hour without her?" his director teased.

Christian gave her his coolest stare. Nim Wei knew he wasn't doing this film for her benefit.

"Oh, all right," she relented. "Grace and Mace"—she paused, grinning, to allow him to admire the coupling of their names—"are out leasing motorcycles for the boys."

"Motorcycles," Christian repeated, trying not to bristle at the thought of Grace alone with the hulking actor.

"Mace used to be a member of a real motorcycle gang— a 'social club,' I think he called it. He's going to teach Bonehead, Growler, and your father to ride half a block without falling off. Which leaves Charlie, Philip, and Matthew to be brought up to speed by you. Grace found an empty parking lot that should be perfect for practicing."

Andy must have been used to working around conversations that didn't include him. He was holding up a jacket for Christian to slide his arms into. If the mortal hadn't been standing close enough to do violence to, Christian might have donned it more forcefully.

"You expect me to train them," he said.

"Just enough so we can get a few shots of them actually riding, even if it's behind a tow car. Consider it a bonding exercise for Joe Pryor and his boys. Or a challenge, if you prefer. Mace has taught people to ride before. You wouldn't want your students to fall short compared to his."

Nim Wei's smirk was deliberately insufferable.

"I'm not twelve years old," he said.

With her lips still curved, she considered the leather jacket he was now wearing. Her littlest finger flicked one feather of short black hair from her white forehead.

"Too many zippers," she and Andy declared in unison.

As they laughed, Christian wasn't certain what irked him more: that his old enemy was enjoying herself this much, or that her human associates were clearly enjoying her.

Possibly, his anger leaked past the walls he'd erected to keep the vampire queen from probing his thoughts. Her laughter ceased, and her head swivelled toward him with the machinelike swiftness *upyr* occasionally employed. Noticing something off, Andy widened his eyes at her.

"Andy," she said gently, "why don't you and Wade have coffee while Christian and I sort out a few matters."

Startled, Andy looked from her to the DP. Blood had risen into the costumer's cheeks, suggesting Wade's fascination with the younger man wasn't one-sided. "Sure. I'll show Mr. Matthews where the break room is. Just holler when you want us back."

Christian was still wearing the idiotic Marlon Brando–from–*The Wild One* jacket. With a restraint that should have earned him a medal, he pulled it off and draped it carefully over the clothing rack.

Watching him, Nim Wei put her tiny hands on her tiny waist, like a miniature superhero from a comic book. "Exactly how long *are* you going to sulk?"

Christian's fury frosted over his face—almost literally; his poreless skin was noticeably chill. "I shouldn't be surprised you have the sand to ask me that."

"You're holding a grudge for something I did five hundred years ago, something that changed your life for the better."

"For the better!"

"You think every *upyr* gets to be transformed by a queen?"

"Oh, that's rich." A dry laugh scraped across the infinitesimal ice crystals on his face. "Tell me, *Naomi*, at what age would I have become a master if I'd been turned by anyone but you? A hundred? Maybe one fifty? If you had your way, would I ever have come into my full power?"

"The idea that elders can prevent their children from becoming masters is a myth."

"In every elder's case but yours, maybe. What percentage of the children you've created reach master level? Two? Three? Compare that to the ten percent of your sire's get who crossed the threshold, and a blind man could see a pattern. Unless you're implying Auriclus was stronger than you?"

Nim Wei turned a look of frigid contempt on him. She'd had daddy issues with her dear departed maker, to say the least. "No one's stronger than me."

"And that's the root of your problem. You need so intensely to believe that. You've never understood there are different forms of strength from the magic or physical. If you keep your people on a choke chain, they're going to resent you."

Though Nim Wei opened her mouth to argue, Christian was far from done. He'd been wanting to lay out these truths to her for some time.

"Frank Hauptmann went mad dog under your leadership. Not Auriclus's. Not Lucius's or Aimery's. You're the one who brought out the psychopath in him and his girlfriend."

"Well, of course you'd blame that on me." Though the queen appeared controlled, she was sufficiently enraged that her objection rode out on a puff of white vapor. "What else would you say, you being so cozy with the shape-changers."

A sudden revelation streaked through his mind like a lightning bolt.

"That's why you chose me for this project. You can't stand that the shapechanging vampires trust me. It isn't just that I slipped out from under your rule. You're jealous that they like me. You're still fixated on Edmund Fitz Clare. Directing me in your movie is your way of stealing me back from him."

It was a sign of how well aimed his thrust had been that her parry was not particularly good. She waved her hand as her top lip curled. "You can throw out all the outlandish theories you please. The fact remains that if it weren't for me, you'd be dead."

"Maybe, maybe not," he said, thinking of Wade and Matthaus and Grace.

"Maybe not! You were mortal, Christian. Even if your father had failed to kill you, you'd have died of old age."

He had no desire to explain himself. "Now I understand what you're playing at with these humans," he said instead. "They can't threaten to turn into rivals like your children. It's safe to gather them around you like pets."

"They're colleagues," she said stiffly. "Friends."

The cracks in her facade were widening, the hint of defiance suggesting even she didn't believe her assertion.

"*Friends*," he scoffed. "How long would that be true if these humans knew who and what you are? Hell, how long would they keep circling your orbit if you didn't hold the key to their livelihood?"

The alabaster serenity that smoothed over Nim Wei's features told him he'd delivered a coup de grace. She'd never admit it, of course. It would have to be enough that he knew.

"Christian," she said, one slender finger tapping his chest lightly. "Training those boys is part of the job you agreed to do. Fulfill it, or break your precious word. Just spare me any more flak."

She spun away and strode off, following the route Andy and Wade had taken across the cavernous soundstage. She wore one of her more piratical looks tonight: a red satin blouse with skinny black trousers and knee-high boots. In the way of the oldest vampires, her pointy heels didn't clack on the concrete floor. They wouldn't unless she focused her power on the sound effect. Christian truly had rattled her cage if she'd forgotten this.

He thrust off the guilt he might otherwise have felt. He had no reason to be ashamed for having injured her in the one spot she was capable of feeling it.

Christian didn't actively dislike humans; he simply counted few of them as friends. Humans were fragile and, in most cases, needed to be lied to. Unlike his queen, he associated neither of those qualities with forming meaningful connections.

As a result, he was less than delighted to be ferrying his mortal students to their lesson in Nim Wei's pink and cream Plymouth. Christian's Thunderbird had arrived from Texas that morning, but the black convertible seated only two, and Grace insisted on operating the pickup that was carrying the bikes. To his added annoyance, Christian's high-spirited passengers seemed intrigued by the novelty of riding in the car Grace customarily drove.

"Grace likes going fast," Charlie informed him from the backseat, where he'd been banished with Philip for chattering. "I mean, she tries to act businesslike, but put her behind the wheel and that girl can burn rubber."

"Grace is a hottie," Philip agreed.

"Too bad her knees are glued together," Matthew put in glumly. The quietest of the trio, he'd earned a seat up front beside Christian. Now he rubbed his arms as if they were prickling, not realizing his comment had sent Christian's energy spiking. It probably didn't bode well for his control that these silly, barely grown humans were riling him. With an effort, he reined in his asinine jealousy.

"I thought you liked Grace," he tried to say calmly.

"We adore her," Charlie assured him, regrettably scooting forward to drape his forearms over the front seat. "Grace is the most. We wouldn't talk like this to her face."

"I don't know what *you're* complaining about," Matthew said to Charlie. "You got Viv to pop her clutch for you."

"A Pyrrhic victory, my friend. The little Forrester is not a fireball in the sack. She lays there like a wet rag."

"Or a fish," Philip interjected with a snicker. "The whole time, I thought she was deciding what color to paint her nails."

Matthew clucked in disgust. "You slept with her, too? You're not any better-looking than I am. Why am I the one the chicks say no to?"

"Must be your cooties," Philip teased, smacking Matthew's head from behind. "Wait until the film comes out. Then maybe you'll get lucky."

"You need to pick your target," Christian said absently, as usual making sense of patterns in human behavior quicker than they could. "Focus on a single girl instead of chasing half a dozen. Females like to think they're the only one on your mind."

"Really?" Matthew rubbed his hair where Philip had slapped it. "That works?"

"It doesn't work all the time," Christian clarified. At

least, it didn't work all the time for humans. "Sometimes a girl simply isn't going to dig you. It's a good place to start, though. Intensity can be as appealing as good looks. Anyway, you're good-looking enough for most girls."

"You think?" Matthew asked with an innocence Christian doubted he'd ever had.

"*You think?*" Philip mimicked before Christian could respond. He turned to Christian with his hands folded girlishly beneath his chin. "Do you think I'm pretty enough, Christian?"

Philip fended off Matthew's retaliatory slap before it landed, turning the right half of the car into a Three Stooges war of blows.

"Cut that out," Christian said quietly.

The two boys froze mid-flurry.

"Whoa!" Charlie let out a peal of giggling laughter. "You're like John Wayne or something!"

"Or something," Christian muttered, wondering just how interminable this lesson was going to be.

The practice spot Grace had selected was an empty elementary school parking lot. Trees shielded it from its neighbors, and the high-intensity lights would help the humans see. The lot's surface was smoothly paved and recently swept. Christian concluded he couldn't have found a better place himself.

He'd have preferred the tension inside his chest not uncoil when Grace drove up. It did, though, as if a missing part of him had slipped into place. The sensation of sudden wholeness unnerved him. His only recourse was to keep his face impassive.

His onetime ghostly lover looked unfairly fetching getting out of the pickup in her casual shirt and jeans— a tomboy rancher's daughter with world-class breasts. The cone-shaped bras females were favoring this decade might have been designed with bodies like hers in mind. He wasn't sure he'd ever seen anything as cute as her red bouncy ponytail. To make matters worse, Grace seemed unconscious of her attractions. When she lowered the door to the pickup's bed, she displayed the confidence of someone who'd done the task before. Christian supposed working for Nim Wei demanded all sorts of skills.

"We'll get that," Charlie cried, rushing over with Philip and Matthew.

Grace smiled, stepped aside, and left setting up the unloading ramp to them. Christian joined her, probably standing too close but unable to help himself. His left side tingled where it faced her.

"You got big-twins," he observed, referring to the three large Harley-Davidsons lying on their sides.

"I know," Grace said, her lips pulling ruefully. "The guy at the lease place said the smaller models are easier to learn on, but these are what Miss Wei will use in the film. Can you teach them to ride on them?"

Her worried eyes turned to his, their clear green beauty pulling heat into his midsection. For a second, he'd have promised her anything. He caught himself at the last moment.

"I can teach them a little. Hopefully enough not to kill themselves."

She laughed, though he didn't think he'd been joking.

"Hey!" he said sharply to Charlie. "Don't try to stand that bike up until I show you how. You've got about six hundred fifty pounds of metal there."

"I know," Charlie said. "My cousin has one. I've ridden with him a couple times."

With a grin that was at least half for Grace, Charlie demonstrated the technique for getting his butt underneath the side of the bike and pushing up with his leg muscles.

"All right," Christian acknowledged, because he'd done it just as he should. "Don't get cocky. And use the hand brake to roll it down the ramp."

Following Charlie's lead, the boys walked the motorcycles with mincing care. They looked trim and athletic in their full riding leathers, more than the average beginners would have. Christian warned himself not to put too much stock in this. Their eyes were sparkling with more excitement than he thought was advisable.

"Prop stands," he barked. After a bit of searching, his pupils found and engaged them.

One by one, he inspected the big machines.

"You can sit on them," he pronounced, once he was satisfied they were in order. At Charlie's whoop, he jabbed his index finger at the freckled boy. "No touching anything. No turning on the ignition. We're going to go over which parts do what."

Christian pointed out the throttle and the clutch and the foot gearshift. He told them how and when to use the front and rear brakes, repeating himself until all three boys rolled their eyes. Fortunately, Christian couldn't have cared less if he was making them impatient.

"Recite it back to me," he ordered.

He couldn't deny the actors were quick, but he needed more than memorization from them.

"Again," he said, "and this time, point out each instrument with your eyes closed."

When they proved they could identify them backward, he handed each of them a safety helmet and moved on to the somewhat involved procedure for starting the engine.

"Jeesh," Charlie said, stealing the curse from Grace. "I told you, I already know this stuff."

"Do I know your cousin?" Christian asked him. "Do I have any reason to believe he's as experienced and responsible as I am?"

Philip and Matthew laughed as Charlie's cheeks reddened.

"You give it a try," Christian said to Matthew.

Matthew stalled the engine on his first two attempts,

but within twenty minutes, all the boys were successfully starting, riding, and stopping in a straight line.

"Can we do turns now?" Charlie pleaded. "Before I die of boredom?"

"Slow, wide turns," Christian conceded. "And no footing."

"*Footing?*" Matthew asked.

"Don't put your foot down to keep your balance. It's not so dangerous when you're going slowly, but it's a bad habit. You only need it for conditions like mud or ice. Otherwise, you'll be more stable if you keep your feet on the pegs or boards."

"Got it," Charlie said, revving his bike loudly. "I will now perform a left turn without footing."

He leaned into the turn perfectly, with the same exaggerated good behavior he'd used to walk the bike down the pickup's ramp.

"Good," Christian said, deciding that—for the moment—he'd take Charlie's compliance any way he could get it.

"Yay, Charlie," Grace called softly, obviously wanting to encourage him.

"Watch—" *the pressure on the front brake,* Christian began to say, but he was too late. With Grace as his admiring audience, Charlie lost his grip of his impulses. He turned the other way, tighter than he had before, and just fast enough for his instincts to tell him the bike might be getting away from him. Wanting to regain control but forgetting how to go about it, he clamped the front brake, ignored the rear, and unintentionally locked the forward tire.

The six-hundred-plus-pound machine slewed out from under him exactly as Christian had warned it would. He had a heartbeat to decide whether to flash to Charlie and rescue him. Would the bike skid farther than Charlie did? Would it land on him? Given the protection Nim Wei had laid on Grace, could Christian thrall the memory from her if she saw him using his powers? His indecision ate up more milliseconds than he had. The next thing Christian knew, Charlie was pinned beneath the chopper and screaming.

This was probably because one of his shin bones had snapped in two places.

Cursing, Christian ran to him faster than he should have and lifted the bike away. To his relief, Charlie stopped screaming.

"Jesus," Matthew said, short of breath from rushing over. "Is his leg supposed to look like that?"

True to their purpose in protecting riders from road scrapes, the leather trousers Charlie wore hadn't torn. That didn't prevent his right lower leg from looking distorted. Christian shifted his vision to examine Charlie's aura, in hopes of pinpointing the damage. Energy as red as blood streaked out from jagged breaks in his fibula, the fracture's edges disturbingly touched with black. Real blood dripped from the bottom of his pants leg onto the asphalt, so the bone must have broken skin. Under other circumstances the blood might have excited him, but for the moment he just felt grim. He wasn't guarding his face well enough. Charlie took one look at his expression and went even pastier.

"Oh, God," he said, beginning to weep. "It's bad, isn't it?"

Christian knelt beside the boy, gently removed his helmet, and took his head in his hands. "Look at me, Charlie. Look at me and be calm."

Charlie was crying too hard to focus. He pounded the asphalt with his right fist. "I can't believe I did this. You told me not to be cocky, and I went ahead anyway. Now I've blown my first big break. Maybe my only one."

"Charlie." Grace's voice rang with compassion. She dropped to her knees beside Christian, one hand tenderly stroking the injured boy's sandy hair. In spite of everything, Christian's fangs gave a little throb as her arm brushed his. She was breathing too quickly, but he could tell she was trying to remain calm. "You'll be all right. Even if you're not well enough for the start of shooting, Miss Wei will cast you again, I swear."

"This was *my* role," Charlie insisted, his passion astounding Christian, considering the pain he was in. "There's no way I wasn't going to shine in it. Christ, every time something good happens for me, I always trip myself up."

He started to fling his forearm over his eyes, but Christian caught it before he could cover them.

"Enough," he said in his firmest tone. "You're going to look at me now."

Charlie looked, allowing Christian to trap his gaze. As his thrall took hold, the mortal boy's pupils swelled. "You're calming now. You're relaxing. The pain is sliding away, breath by breath. You're going to let me help you. You have perfect faith in me."

"Are you hypnotizing him?" Philip asked.

"Shh," Christian said. He scooted down to lay his hands on Charlie's misshapen lower leg. Healing humans wasn't something he often did. To be honest, he wasn't sure he should do it now. Charlie had been warned, and his injury wasn't life threatening. As much as he looked like Christian's lost friend Charles, the spirit inside him was a stranger's. Christian knew that as surely as he'd known Wade Matthews was Matthaus. Christian owed Charlie nothing . . . except maybe sympathy.

Every time something good happens for me, I always trip myself up.

Christian didn't glance up at Grace. He didn't want her to see the redness in the whites of his eyes. He wasn't doing this for her anyway. This time, it was Charlie who'd brought out the idiot in him.

* * *

Grace had been convinced Christian had the boys well in hand. Despite being around the same age as them, and despite her doubts concerning certain aspects of his character, Christian radiated an authority the other males responded to. It hadn't crossed her mind that anything bad was going to happen.

Seeing Charlie go down had been a breath-stealing shock.

I distracted him, she thought. *I should have kept my mouth shut.*

As long as she lived, she wouldn't forget his screams.

"Can you help him?" she asked Christian as he laid his hands atop Charlie's leg. He'd certainly calmed Charlie quickly—as good as a mesmerist.

"I'll try," Christian said.

Instead of looking up, he closed his eyes. Grace couldn't tear her gaze from him. He was so serene, so still, like a Buddha with a Western face. The night seemed to quiet in response to him, the buzz of insects falling silent, the air oddly soft and heavy where it touched her skin. Something flickered at the edge of her vision, drawing her attention down to his hands. Her breath caught. His fingers were glowing as if a fire burned within his bones.

"Jesus," Philip said, evidently seeing it, too.

"What's he doing?" Matthew asked.

"Whatever it is, shut up and let him," Philip urged in a hoarse whisper.

Their instructor didn't seem to be listening. Christian's head fell back, and the glow grew brighter, until his hands were swallowed by golden white balls of light.

"My leg feels warm," Charlie mumbled like he'd been drugged.

Grace's heartbeat tripped in her throat as if a little

hammer were tapping there. She realized she was clutching the sleeve of Charlie's leather jacket harder than she should. From the place she touched, *something* was flowing up her forearm. The sensation tickled, like currents in a bath when you were immersed. Memory pushed for recognition from the underside of her mind.

"Close your eyes," Christian said.

She thought he might be speaking to her.

Would it be better not to see, or should she stay vigilant? Before she could decide, Christian placed one hand on Charlie's knee and the other on his ankle. Gripping each spot firmly, he pushed the holds apart.

Everyone except him winced at the wet cracking sound.

"What the hell?" Matthew gasped.

But whatever Christian had done wasn't painful. Charlie gave out a sigh and relaxed. Though he was still pale enough for his freckles to stand out, his pallor wasn't tinged with green anymore.

With a grace a dancer would have envied, Christian rose to his feet and faced Matthew. His gaze drilled into the other man's. "It was only a strain. Charlie's ankle twisted and popped out of its socket. We'll ice it, and he'll be fine."

Matthew's mouth fell open. To Grace's surprise, he blinked and then nodded.

Philip was more than surprised. "That was no strain," he accused, his cheeks flushing dark with anger. Arms stubbornly crossed, he jerked his head toward the spot where Charlie lay. "Charlie's got a pool of blood underneath his foot. His leg was bent in two places. You're some kind of faith healer."

Christian turned his eyes to him, his head swiveling strangely. As easily as that, Philip also fell quiet. "I promise you I'm not lying. The accident wasn't as bad as you thought." When Philip's arms uncrossed and dropped to his sides, Christian shifted focus to Charlie. "You're extremely lucky. I'm sure you'll be up and walking after a good night's rest."

"I'm sure, too," Charlie agreed, sounding sleepy already. "I'm very lucky I wasn't hurt too bad."

They were acting like zombies, like Christian had put them under a spell. Panic built inside Grace's chest. She felt as if a protective veil were about to be ripped from her, leaving her naked and vulnerable. She couldn't let that happen. She had to keep up her guard.

"Grace," Christian said.

She didn't want to look at him, but she couldn't help it—like he was a car crash on the side of the road. His eyes glowed gold, his thick black lashes casting perfect spiky shadows along his cheeks. His face could have been sculpted from Carrara marble. Each exquisite feature was buffed and polished, each proportion harmonious. The mouth she'd always thought too thin was the color of young roses, delicate and mobile. She literally ached as she gazed at it, as she remembered him kissing her. The veil she'd feared losing had been torn from him.

This was who Christian was. This was the threat to her heart.

No human could be so beautiful. He'd drive other humans mad.

"Don't be afraid," he said softly.

"You . . . you did something," she stammered, trying desperately to throw off the impression of strangeness. "I thought I saw—"

Though she couldn't tell what emotion lay behind his expression, she knew it intensified as she trailed off.

"What do you think you saw?" he prompted.

She felt him waiting, breath suspended, like this was a test she could pass or fail. Philip and Matthew had shaken from their fugues and were helping Charlie up off the ground. Their fellow actor was limping, but that was all. An amoeba-shaped puddle glistened on the asphalt where he had lain. It could have been blood or anything dark and wet. Motor oil from a school bus.

She dragged her eyes reluctantly back to her tormentor. His face was almost normal again.

"Nothing," she said through the lingering tightness in her throat. "I was upset. I must have been seeing things."

Christian gazed at her a moment longer and then nodded.

Though it made no sense, she couldn't help thinking she'd disappointed him.

Christian was aware that Grace had glimpsed beneath his glamour. He didn't think he'd meant to drop it, but he'd seen his own eyes glowing and knew he was no longer hiding his true nature. Apparently, exposing himself to her didn't matter, no more than his inability to thrall her did.

Grace was able to deny the most obvious truth without any help from him.

Eight

~~~~~~~~~~~~~~~~~~~

Grace didn't think waking up with a knot in her gut was good. Normally on the first day of shooting, she'd be as excited as a kid at Christmas.

A kid who wasn't her, of course. Her childhood holidays hadn't been worth stashing in a time capsule. The only thing she'd ever gotten for asking if they could buy a tree was the back of her father's hand. *Money doesn't grow on them,* he'd informed her, after which he'd laughed loudly at his own wit.

"That's over," she told her hollow-eyed reflection in the pink Plymouth's side-view mirror. "You left that life behind years ago."

Despite the pep talk, her hands were trembling as she turned the key in the ignition. She drove the fifty-yard distance between the cottage and the main house with her jaw clenched tight. Luckily, Miss Wei wasn't in her most observant condition when she slid in the other side. Her sunglasses were her darkest, her trademark mile-long scarf pulled close around her face.

"Bloody hell," she swore in the British accent she sometimes slipped into when she hadn't quite woken up. "I abhor early-morning location shoots!"

Grace didn't know a lot about her employer's history. She supposed Miss Wei might have lived in England, or even been born there. No doubt, talking like an American gave her one less difference from the studio system's "old boys" to overcome.

"First day," Grace said, once she thought her voice was steady. "You've got to be looking forward to that."

Miss Wei groaned and sank lower in her seat. "I am. I just don't have the energy to show it."

Grace had plenty of energy—most of it nervous. Her palms were so clammy she wished she were wearing gloves.

Today will be fine, she tried to convince herself. *Busy. Exciting. Everybody chomping at the bit to get out of the starting gate.*

The fact that Grace was revisiting her worst nightmare didn't have to ruin that.

Not unlike an invading army, the crew for *I Was a Teen-Age Vampire* had commandeered a section of a suburb outside LA. Impressed in spite of himself, since he hadn't expected quite so large a production, Christian rubbernecked behind his Ray-Bans as he inched his Thunderbird into the controlled chaos. His path was narrowed by the big trailer trucks that formed a line along one side of the otherwise well-groomed street. The neighborhood was a postcard of the America Americans longed to believe in, everybody with their house and their car and their identically placed palm tree. On this day, lighting equipment, generators, wardrobe, and makeup found places in paradise. The scent of scrambled eggs and coffee wafted out from a mobile kitchen, reminding Christian he hadn't fully addressed his own dietary needs.

Last night, Roy had brought him what he termed a "present" from a community blood bank. *Drink it or I'll tar your heinie,* Roy had threatened. *It's O-negative, just like that gal the queen has been dangling in front of you.* Christian had sucked down the plastic bag's cold contents, grudgingly thanked Roy, then felt compelled to inform him that he didn't give a damn what blood type it was. *Fine then,* Roy had snapped. *Next time I risk life and limb stealing you a pint, it'll come from a rat.*

Christian smiled to himself at the memory. Roy wasn't comfortable with straightforward thanks anyway. Plus, he'd probably bribed someone for the blood.

Spotting an empty stretch of curb ahead, Christian squeezed his black convertible into it. Though he'd put the top up, driving it in daylight wasn't ideal.

"Cool car," said a mortal as Christian left its questionable shelter. Short and stocky, the man was clad in a plaid cotton shirt and jeans. Like many of the humans who were milling purposefully about, he carried a walkie-talkie and clipboard.

He smiled at Christian in a friendly way. "Christian, right? Our Joe Pryor?" Suddenly distracted, he frowned down at his clipboard. "I don't remember seeing you on today's call sheet."

"I'm not here to shoot a scene," he said, feeling oddly cowed by the man's knowledgeable air. "This is my first acting job. I thought I'd get a sense of how things worked."

The man considered him with his head canted to the side. "Evelyn!" he bellowed without warning. "Escort Mr. Durand to the AD so he can watch filming."

A harried young woman bustled over. Shifting her clipboard underneath one arm, she shook his hand briskly.

"Christian, yes? Our Joe Pryor? It's very nice to meet you. I'm a PA. Let me know if you want coffee."

Christian nodded as if this made perfect sense to him. He followed the frazzled woman to the single-story suburban home around which the movie army's actions were centering. A snakelike tangle of electric cords spread across the golf-course green lawn. The cords led to a picture window where three burly men were gingerly removing one pane of glass.

"Reflections," said his female escort. "Miss Wei wants a shot from outside. Can't have the DP showing up on film."

Christian concluded everyone but him understood what was going on around here. He'd finally watched the movies Grace recommended and read a book Roy had picked up along with the blood. The book was by Stanislavski and was called *An Actor Prepares*. The actor might have prepared, but Christian the vampire remained at sea. The movie business was a foreign country, peopled by natives whose positions all seemed to be identified by letters— hardly conducive to calling up "affective memory" as the book advised. Despite the Coppertone Christian had slathered on this morning, his head had begun to spin.

"Christian!" exclaimed a blissfully familiar voice.

"Grace," he responded, so obviously grateful to encounter her that she laughed. Evelyn the PA gave Grace a small salute and left. "Please don't call me 'our Joe Pryor,'" he added. "I'm getting the impression that's my new name."

Smiling, Grace took him by the arm to steer him into the epicenter of the hubbub. To his surprise, her hand was cold and shook just a bit. Annoyed anew that he couldn't read her, he surmised she was feeling awkward over what she'd managed to deny she'd seen him do to Charlie.

If she was, she wasn't going to mention it.

"Crew develop a sense of ownership," she explained. "If the film is a hit, it's a victory for them, too."

"Everyone wants to work on a winner."

"Exactly," she agreed.

They'd reached the living room of the house, which was overrun with people and equipment. Christian took off his Stetson and held it before his chest as he looked around. Most of the furniture had been removed for the sake of space. Two men in earphones sat before some sort of recording console. Christian spotted Wade and Nim Wei and Viv standing together, though only Nim Wei seemed to be talking. Viv was either nervous or getting into character. She was tugging the sleeves of her white sweater over her hands, making her appear even younger than she was. The doorway behind the trio revealed a blindingly bright and colorful kitchen. The silhouettes of more crew moved there.

"We're shooting the breakfast scene," Grace said, leaning closer to his shoulder so he could hear. "The one between Mary and her parents before her first day of school. Miss Wei is reminding Viv what emotional notes she wants her to hit. After the grips finish setting up the lights and booms, she and Wade will run through the blocking. Then, depending on how fresh the boss lady wants everyone to stay, she might have them do a quick rehearsal."

"And she'll do that for my scenes, as well?"

"Absolutely," Grace said. "It's the director's job to make sure the actors are comfortable and know where they are in the story."

Grace must have thought it was *her* job to reassure him.

"Grace, I don't know what Naomi told you to do, but I don't need hand-holding."

"Of course you don't," she said, her attention plainly not on him. For some reason, her gaze had drifted to the fireplace across the room. Christian couldn't see what would have drawn her attention. The hearth was made of beige-painted brick and had a plain wooden mantel. An ugly round mirror hung above it, with a dull gold sunburst raying out from its face. Grace swallowed and touched the pulse beating in her throat.

He couldn't help but notice how rapid her heart rate was. In an instant, he forgot his personal irritations. Worry flooded him so swiftly he stepped around to face her.

"Is something wrong?" he asked. "You've gone ashen."

She looked at him, but he had the sense she was seeing someone else. It took a second before her expression cleared.

"I'm fine," she said with an awkward laugh. "Between you and me, this house gives me the willies."

Grace had no sooner uttered the confession than she regretted it. A deeply incised furrow appeared between Christian's brows, his concern impossible to miss even with his sunglasses on.

"It's nothing," she said. "I'm fine. This house just reminds me of a place I lived as a teenager. It was a long time ago."

Christian bent to peer in her face. "Maybe you need air."

"It's nothing," she reiterated, trying not to sound like she was gasping. She lifted her clipboard with a too-bright smile. "Have to work anyway. Lots of lists to check off. Why don't you take one of those empty chairs? We'll talk more when I have a minute."

She turned away without watching what he did. Her face was as hot as if she were fevered, the channel of her spine beginning to trickle sweat. She'd been dreading this day since the location scout first showed them his Polaroids. The ranch-style house they'd obtained permission to film in was too like the house her father had nearly killed her in. If she hadn't had a job to do here, she'd have run for the literal hills.

Pull yourself together, Grace, she ordered, bracing her shoulder on the wall next to the sound men.

She should have chosen a different spot, but her knees were shaking too much to move. She could see the fireplace clearly from where she leaned, an eerie twin for the one George Gladwell had flung her into when she was seventeen. The brick in their Ohio house had been just that putty color, the wood-plank mantel just as stupidly faux rustic. This one seemed to have a gouge precisely where her head would have hit.

The memory of the long-ago impact slammed back to her: the solidity of the pain in her skull, the flash of light, and then the darkness. She'd died for a couple minutes, lost in that void from which there was no escape. The men from the ambulance her mother called had revived her.

Grace pressed one fist hard between her breasts, telling herself the ache there couldn't be a heart attack, no matter how wildly that organ was galloping. She hadn't been sick a day since she'd come to work for Miss Wei. She was simply anxious and overwhelmed. Too many parts of her life were out of her control right now. The attraction she felt for Christian, the things about him she couldn't explain, even the strange break-in at the cottage increased her feelings of insecurity. The weight of her past was too much to add to that. She couldn't stuff it into its box right now. In fact, if she didn't get out of here in the next two seconds, she was going to scream.

"Grace?" someone said, lightly touching her shoulder. "Does Miss Wei wants us to—"

Grace stared uncomprehending at the female PA, the ringing in her ears drowning out the question Evelyn was asking.

A second later, Grace jerked. Christian had appeared beside her like a conjurer's trick, his battered cowboy hat on his head again. He was surrounding her with his upper body and leading her away, as if he'd read the desperate longing straight from her mind. Despite the relief she felt, she couldn't let him do it.

"I'm okay," she said, feebly shoving at him as he more or less dragged her toward the door. To her dismay, she could hardly hear her own voice. "Christian, I'm okay."

He mustn't have believed her. As soon as they cleared the house, he hooked one arm behind her knees and lifted her off her feet. She clung to him, unable to resist, her face hidden in his neck. God, he felt good. She hadn't imagined how smooth his skin was the other night. It was soothingly cool even in the sunshine, and he smelled mysteriously like the beach. His hold shouldn't have been so comforting, but it was. She dragged her nose up and down his throat.

His face had been steely, but this seemed to amuse him.

"Grace," he said with a groaning laugh. "You truly are determined to drive me mad."

The moment Christian saw the PA approach Grace, he knew he had to act. The symptoms Grace was exhibiting— the dead-white pallor, the sudden sweat and shortness of breath—were similar to those he'd seen in human soldiers he'd had charge of, often long after battles were over. Whatever triggered the attack, she was in no shape to be fielding questions, not if she didn't want her colleagues guessing she was panicked.

He threw his glamour around them to deflect attention and carried her as swiftly as he dared to the wardrobe trailer. Thankfully, it was out of the sun and unoccupied. Andy Phelps must have run an errand. Reluctant to set Grace down, Christian found a fat chintz chair tucked between costume racks. He sat there with her curled up in his lap.

The part of him that was male loved how she snuggled closer. The part of him that had its wits about it noticed she was nattering about Ohio.

His hand slipped upward to stroke her short ponytail, tied today in a jaunty scarf. To his deep satisfaction, her breathing steadied at his caress. The queen might have blocked his ability to calm her with his aura, but he could still do it the old-fashioned way. "We're in California, sweetheart, not Ohio. I can show you the palm trees."

"I know. I was just telling myself that." She wriggled in his lap, causing other male parts of him to stir. "You're very soothing. Would you mind if I held you awhile longer?"

He laughed under his breath, mostly at himself for wanting her where she was. "If you stay, I think you should tell me what upset you."

She sighed and let her head rest on his shoulder. "I died once."

A chill ran across his scalp. "You died?"

"My father . . . It was sort of an accident. I made him angry, and he threw me into the fireplace. He was drunk. I don't suppose he meant to do real damage, but it took the men from the ambulance six minutes to bring me back."

Christian's lips felt cold. His ghostly Grace hadn't said much about the manner in which she died. He'd presumed she hadn't wanted to dwell on it. All he really knew was that her father had caused her death. Unsure where this was leading, he reminded his hand to continue kneading the tightened muscles under her ponytail. A relaxed Grace would be a forthcoming one.

"When did this happen?"

"A little over six years ago. I was seventeen."

Seventeen. The same age his ghostly Grace had been.

"Do you remember—" He had to swallow and begin again. If it were true . . . if she was his Grace, one and the same and not reincarnated . . . "Do you remember anything that happened when you were dead?"

She shook her head, rubbing her face against his collar in the process. He wanted to concentrate on her answer, but the sensual, catlike motion sent distracting twitches through the mechanism that allowed his fangs to erect. "I know some people see tunnels and lights and angels, but I don't recall a thing. The afterlife was a blank to me."

When she shivered, he pressed his lips to her hair. "It might have been more than that. Sometimes people forget things they can't handle remembering."

"You mean like hell?" Her tone was only half teasing.

"No," he said, surprising himself with how serious he was. "I'm sure you didn't go to hell."

Her head drew back so she could look at him. She seemed calm now, almost contemplative, but, God, her green gaze went through him, a thick arrow of heat targeting his groin.

"I'm not who I was then," she said. "I'm not a cowed little girl, afraid to kiss a boy or make a single friend. I'm Grace Michaels. *I* tell people what to do today."

"Yes, you do."

"I left that house. My parents. I never looked back again."

He ran the knuckles of his fingers along her creamy cheek. "You shouldn't look back. You should embrace who you've become."

He hadn't been considering what he was saying, the idiot inside him enjoying the unique pleasure of comforting her. Given how he was acting, he supposed he shouldn't have been surprised when she twisted in his hold and came to her knees. The sudden absence of her weight from his lap made him aware of how stiff and full his erection was, enough that he shifted on his haunches in discomfort. Her knees were wedged in the flowered armchair to either side of his hips, the skirt of her turquoise dress spread out over him. Even with his vampire senses dulled by daylight, he couldn't miss the heat radiating out from her sex.

"I'm not afraid to kiss a boy now," she said.

He sucked in a breath he didn't usually need. Her thumbs stroked the little muscles to either side of his mouth. Beneath her right thumb, the dimple he didn't like admitting he had threatened to turn visible. Slowly, carefully, she slid his sunglasses off. His hat was next, laid aside by slender fingers that couldn't resist fondling it. Vampire though he was, he quivered at the strength of the anticipation that coursed through him.

"If you're going to kiss me, I wish you would," he said.

She bent to him, taking his mouth with a tenderness that

made him ache right down to his soul. He couldn't squash
the reaction. Her kindness, or its semblance, had always
been his downfall. Her tongue was sweet and thorough,
rolling his, sucking his, pulling tingles down his spine and
out the tip of his cock. On and on the oral caresses went.
No one kissed him like this. No one cared enough, not in
five hundred years. When she pulled back, her gentle hands
still framing his face, he wanted to follow her.

"Oh, boy," he said in spite of himself.

Her gaze lowered to the hump rising from his lap.

"I want to touch you," she said, the declaration wonderfully breathless. "I want to run my hands all over you the
way I didn't have the nerve to when you kissed me. I want
to remind myself I survived."

"Again," he said a trifle huskily, "if you're going to, I
wish you would."

He made her smile. Maybe she shouldn't have let him, but
she couldn't help herself. His permission was so heady, like
wine rising to her brain. She slid her hands down his dark
pin-striped shirt to the Western belt buckle at his waist.

Damon from Mattson's definitely hadn't selected that.

"Allow me," he said when she couldn't figure out how to
unlatch the medallion.

His fingers were so graceful they made her shiver. After
the belt was open, he placed his hands back on the chair arms.

"I think you can handle what comes next," he said.

She didn't know if she could, but she wanted to, especially because she sensed he didn't often let women have
control. She took hold of his shirt to pull the tails gently
from his trousers. When she reached around him to free
the back, he lifted his hips to help. He might have gone
higher than he needed. The bulge of his hard-on brushed
her panties. That was a distraction she didn't need, as
was the heated way he watched her. Struggling to ignore

both, Grace unbuttoned him from the bottom, her lip caught between her teeth as she tried to make her fingers work smoothly. When the shirt was free up to his collar, she pushed the halves to either side of his lean, hard chest, framing his tapering gorgeousness in dark cloth.

His beauty was enough to make her forget self-consciousness. His skin wasn't tanned, but more of a pale olive. Smooth as cream, it wrapped his ribs and muscles, drawing her palms and fingers irresistibly across it. As she touched him, he rolled his neck, then stretched his fingers and bunched his thighs—as if it were impossible to stay still with her hands on him.

"You're hot," she marveled, drawing both sets of fingers down his long center line. "Sometimes your skin is cool, but when I touch it, it's fiery."

Suddenly, she understood why the Production Code censored people's navels from being shown on film. Christian's was sexy, a deep, moon-shaped orifice that demanded her longest finger be swirled in it. She thrilled when his stomach muscles tensed in reaction.

He caught her wrists before she could stroke up his chest again. Trapped by the gentle hold, her thumbs came to rest on either side of his erection. The size of it was imposing. Maybe he knew she thought so. Maybe he liked her being afraid. When she glanced up, his dark eyes were molten. He rolled his hips off the chair toward her.

That this was a suggestion soon became clear.

"Unzip me," he said. "Make my cock fiery."

She was certain it was already, but she wasn't going to refuse. This was what she wanted: this feeling that every part of her was alive. With trembling fingers, she unhooked his waistband and found the zipper. His lungs moved faster as she eased the metal tab down the teeth. A moment later, her breath sucked in. Christian wasn't wearing underwear. There was nothing beneath the fine silk-lined wool but him.

"Oh, my God," she breathed as his maleness was released through the parted cloth.

He was lovely, more than she'd expected, almost too perfect to be real. His skin was the pink of a baby's blush, his twisting, engorged veins the blue of lapis lazuli. Once his shaft was free, it rose thick and straight from a nest of surprisingly orderly raven curls. He could have been a naked statue—except statues were never carved this big. His cock was both thick and lengthy, with a ruddy cap whose slit welled with a single diamond of liquid.

Knowing instinctively this was a good thing, Grace's entire body clenched with desire.

"I thought you were going to touch me," he said.

She didn't need more prompting. She wrapped her hand around his base, her palm enclosing no more than half his length. Because it seemed wrong not to appreciate all of him, she pulled her grip to his flaring tip, sweeping the now-trickling wetness off with her thumb. The second she felt him there, she had to keep rubbing. His crest was smoother than anything on earth.

Apparently, it was also very sensitive. Christian's breath rushed out as he fought not to close his eyes. Grace had to fight not close hers, too. She gripped him again and repeated the savoring pull. He was so satiny, so warm and vital, his pulse a strangely slow, hard thudding within her hold. It was as if his body ran in slow motion compared to hers. Fascinated, she spread her second hand over his rippling abdominal muscles and slid her palm up his chest, stopping only when she found a tightened nipple to rub over. His light hair made the friction whisper deliciously.

She didn't see Christian's hands move, but suddenly they were clamped over her buttocks under her skirt. With a forwardness that should have shocked her, his fingers kneaded her panties as a growl rumbled in his chest.

"Grace," he said, his hoarse voice licking fire through her. "I want to take you. I want to be your first."

Heat welled from her, wet and silky, her body ready to surrender before the rest of her was. She felt like she was melting from the inside, like she could simply fall back and fling her legs wide for him. Despite the craving, she found she wanted something else even more. She shoved his shirt over the ball of one broad shoulder, bending to suck that rock-hard muscle against her teeth. His skin was just barely salty here.

"Did you hear me?" Christian demanded, his own face buried against her neck. He sounded angry, but his touch had gentled. The drag of silken lips on her pulse point made her shudder.

"I heard you," she panted, "but I'm not done with you."

"I need you," he insisted, wrenching his sleeves fully off his arms. This new stretch of naked skin invited exploration, especially the bulging firmness of his biceps. "You've no idea how long I've been waiting."

Though his young man's impatience was flattering, it was hard to take seriously. "If you want me to hurry, you shouldn't be so touchable."

She moved her hands to his back to caress him there, her fingertips gently tracing the edge of his shoulder blades. He cursed as she made a tremor run down his spine. His mouth opened on her neck and then—with seeming reluctance—retreated.

"You're lucky it's daytime," he grumbled even as he found the zipper behind her dress. "I wouldn't have the patience to put up with this after dark."

Grace was wondering what he meant when a sudden breeze on her upper body startled her. He'd had time to lower her bodice, but her longline bra was no small item to remove. It had straps and hooks and an elasticized lower portion that shaped her waist snugly, a recommended undergarment for the fitted dress she had worn today. Nonetheless, Christian had it off her too quickly to resist, almost too quickly to be embarrassed.

He looked at the natural shape of what he'd uncovered for all of two seconds.

"Jesus," he groaned and latched his mouth onto her nipple.

The effect of his suckling was as powerful as an electric shock, but far more pleasurable. His lips were wet and clinging, his tongue laving hungrily over and around her peak. He seemed to know when he'd teased her nipple as tight as it would go. With a sigh that moved her almost beyond bearing, he pulled her breast hard into his mouth. The pressure he exerted created an aching line of feeling, one that stretched from her throbbing nipple to deep between her legs. Her clit pulsed like he was squeezing it. Grace's spine arched as her hand knotted in his hair.

"Wait," she moaned as he shifted breasts.

In answer, his hands curved back around her bottom. She could hardly think for what he was doing—his mouth working magic on her other nipple, his fingernails scratching lightly over her soaked panties. Groaning, he pushed the damp cloth deeper into her folds, so close to the nexus of her sensation that she longed to groan back at him.

"Wait," she said again, more weakly.

"Grace," he growled warningly.

"We aren't thinking. What if someone from the crew comes in?"

"I locked the door, Grace. No one's interrupting us."

She hadn't heard him lock it, but he seemed so certain with his gold-sparked gaze blazing into hers. In truth, looking at him, it was hard to remember her objection. The faint flush on his harshly handsome face, the way it darkened his lips and brightened his eyes, was incredibly arousing.

"I want you, Grace," he said. "God help me, but I do. All you have to do is decide if you want me, too. All of me. Deep inside you. Hot and hard and making you feel more alive than you've ever been. That's why you kissed me. That's why you touched me. To remind yourself *you're* in charge of your life."

Though he was more experienced than she was, she hadn't expected this depth of understanding from a man his age. The words he'd spoken were so true tears sprang into her eyes.

Seeing them, his hand lifted to her face. His fingertips feathered the edge of her hair. "Be who you want to be," he said softly.

In that moment, Grace knew exactly who that was.

She wanted to be the woman who'd say yes to him.

He didn't have to read her. He could see the answer in her expression.

"Good," he said and tore her panties right off her.

She gasped, the smallest edge of nervousness in it. Pleased, Christian smoothed his hands over the rounded muscles of her now-bare bottom.

"I like that," he murmured next to her ear, "when you're a little afraid of me."

She shivered, and he loved that, too. Then, as he moved one hand to cup the folds of her mound, her body creamed over him. With a growl of appreciation for her responsiveness, he curved two fingers slowly—one knuckle deep— into her wet, soft heat. A well-aimed pressure on the cushioned wall of her sex made her gasp again.

"I guess we know how *you* feel about being scared," he said.

"I feel too good to care that you're being snide."

He laughed at her tartness, and because she writhed as he worked his fingers to the edge of her barrier. He stopped laughing when her head flung back on a sensual groan. Her lovely neck was completely exposed to him, her pulse so strong he could count it. Daytime or not, his fangs surged completely down, his tongue running across them in stark hunger. He craved this woman for more reasons than sustenance.

He'd barely pressed his lips together before her head tipped back toward him. Her green eyes smoldered as brightly as an *upyr*'s.

"Chris," she whispered, the little nickname that drove him so inexplicably insane. "Show me how to do this with you."

"I'll get you started," he said, too hoarse to hide the change in his voice. "Once you get going, it comes pretty naturally."

"Show me."

She took his cock again in her gentle hands, surrounding it in the human heat that was so attractive to all his kind. His responses were slower than usual, but they were building. His eyes drifted shut with pleasure as she glided her fingers over the shape of him. Nearly overwhelmed with hunger, he clenched his molars hard enough to nick himself with his fangs. The brief taste of blood was another hammer strike to his lust.

"You like when I touch you."

"Yes," he agreed, "and I'll like it even more when we fuck."

He opened his eyes to watch the word make her jerk. She drew her hands back, clutching them at her waist where her bodice had fallen. He'd watched his ghostly Grace make that gesture, knew it like the back of his hand. He couldn't wait any longer. If he didn't sate at least one of his desires, he was liable to lose control in ways that would not serve him. Excitement swamped him with the decision. He slid forward in the soft chintz armchair and put his hands on her narrow hips. Her breath came quick and shallow as his grip lowered her.

"Brace on my shoulders. I want your hands on me."

She blushed and did as he asked. His skin blazed hot where her fingers restlessly kneaded him.

"God, you make me crazy," he growled. "You always made me crazy when you touched me."

"Christian, I never—"

The tip of his erection found her, silencing her denial. Her cheeks turned the most beautiful scarlet.

"Feel this," he said, his eyes holding hers. "Feel me go into you."

He pulled her onto his aching hard-on, only the illusion of control in her hands. Strictly speaking, it wasn't in his, either. The clasp of her outer reaches, the meltingly soft tight heat, was close to making a slave of him. The head of his cock squeezed inward, causing her to squirm and him to gasp at the wet friction.

"It's too big," she said unsurely.

"It isn't," he promised. "You're very wet, and it's very smooth. There might be a little pain, but you'll like my pike staff being all the way inside you."

He pulled her a fraction farther, his spine threatening to melt with bliss. Grace made a small, doubtful sound—half pleasure, half pain, the latter of which he tried to ease by smoothing one hand up the curve of her vertebrae.

"You're really stretching me. I don't remember it being this difficult the first time."

His eyes came slowly open. "What did you say?"

She blinked at him. "I said, is it supposed to be this difficult the first time?"

Sensual overload notwithstanding, he knew those weren't the words she'd used. But maybe she thought they were. She was staring at him in seemingly genuine confusion.

"It's not so bad," she admitted, her pelvis giving another devastating, experimental wriggle. "You don't truly have to stop."

Oh, she brought out the conqueror in him, whether she intended to or not. His eyes were hooded as his gaze slid down her bare torso. Those breasts of hers drove him crazy. His voice came out as soft and dark as smoke.

"Maybe if I touch you where we're connected, it would be better. Maybe you'd beg me to continue."

He thrust his hand underneath her skirt, finding her clitoris by the quicker pulse beating inside it.

Grace jumped, her eyes briefly losing focus as his fingers smoothed around and then directly over their target.

"Yes," she said in a higher, slightly embarrassed voice. "That does seem to be helping."

He didn't ask her to talk after that, simply let her focus on the sensations his extremely practiced fingers were pulling out of her. The changes that came into her expression were his reward: from wariness to surprised enjoyment to pleas she didn't have the nerve to put into words.

Through it all, he rocked his prick into her—steadily, gently, reminding her it was waiting for her to welcome it. Her hold tightened on his shoulders, her fingernails starting to dig in. She was rocking back at him, though not with the full abandon he would have liked.

But maybe she'd have liked more abandon, too. "Oh, God," she cried finally. "Just do it!"

He didn't wait. He drove into her in a long plunge of fiery heat, with a grunt a caveman wouldn't have been ashamed to use. He couldn't help the desperate gratitude of the sound. In that instant, it meant that much to him to claim her.

Treating the motions as extensions of each other, he finished the thrust by carrying them both to the trailer's floor.

His inner marauder exulted at being on top of and inside her. Belatedly, he realized he must have moved at greater than human speed. Her reaction to finding herself beneath him was stunned.

"Are you all right?" he asked, his hand cradling her head. "Was that too rough for you?"

Despite his concern, he couldn't wait for her to answer. He kissed her—crazily, deeply—wanting to thrust the ecstasy he was feeling at full penetration back into her.

She didn't resist him. Her slender arms came around him, and then her legs, and then the heat and wetness in her increased.

He wanted to bite her, to draw her lifeblood into him until they were one again. His body shook with the instinct, his cock stiffening even more as his different urges heightened each other. He thought he'd never been more at the mercy of his vampire nature. If Roy hadn't bullied him to feed, he wouldn't have had the slightest hope of not putting his mark on her.

Grace responded to his urgency, whatever she might interpret as the cause. Her body began to work under his, her undulations moving his cock a few inches in and out of her. That she couldn't restrain herself was obvious. The mewling noises she was making were those of intense desire.

Kissing her in his current state was too big a risk. If he cut her, he'd drink, and if he drank, he'd form a bond he didn't want with her. Knowing it was for the best but regretting it, Christian tore his mouth from hers.

"Let me," he said, one hand steadying her hips. "Let me take us both where we want to go."

The instant he began to thrust in earnest, he was glad it was day. He didn't crash precipitously into climax the way he would have at night, when his perceptions of friction and heat and pressure were their most sensitized. He was able to give her long, controlled lunges, going as deep as she could take him, as hard as she could stand.

Her rising moans said she liked the force he was using. He could tell his aura had healed any hurt he'd done by taking her maidenhead. She went over fast, with a cry of what he thought was surprise for how potent the climax was.

Her energy backwashed over him like flames from a very erotic fire, almost but not quite as drinkable as blood. Though the influx wound his arousal tighter, he slowed to let her enjoy her glow of relaxation. Only when her lashes began to drift did he pick up the pace again, this time adding a rolling motion to his pelvis that strafed his tip against a different sensitive spot on her inner wall.

To judge by Grace's gasp, the spot was a top-notch choice.

He liked it pretty well himself. The change in angle had a new set of his own nerves singing, enough that grunts for the sharply pleasurable sensations escaped him. The trailer floor began to vibrate as he kept vigorously at it, hangers *ching*ing all around them on clothing racks. If he felt this good, he knew Grace wasn't going to hang on long.

He gave the spot she liked a little more pressure.

"Oh," she said, her big green eyes widening. "Oh, oh, *God.*"

She slapped her hands on his ass, under his trousers, as her body arched up to his. Her orgasm clenched him in a slick hot fist for a good long time.

"More?" he growled, knowing the answer even before she bit her lip and nodded.

He felt like a god as he drove her from peak to peak, watching her body go progressively softer, seeing her eyes fill with the gentlest sort of surrender. He could believe she'd loved him when she looked at him like that—at least once upon a time. Her hair spilled around her in a dark red halo, having escaped the bonds of her ponytail. Her lips were bruised from his hard kisses.

Utterly biteable.

Christian shuddered at his compulsion to sink his fangs in her there. He adored fucking her, but his body's frustration was approaching pain. It was becoming obvious that he wasn't going to ejaculate. Not while the sun was up. Not without feeding.

Finally, Grace reached up and clasped his face.

"You," she said. "Christian, you take your pleasure now."

He couldn't bear it. He wanted to do what she said too much, and if he watched her eyes glaze with bliss one more time, he was going to do whatever it took to join in. With a heartfelt groan, he drew his cock from her pussy, hovering above her on shaky knees and elbows. Wet as he was from being inside her, the air was cold on his simmering skin.

"I'm not sure I can," he said ruefully. "I'm really . . . not a day person."

Grace laughed, but in a soft way he couldn't mind. Making love to him had made her bolder. Her hand slid down his lightly perspiring chest, a testimony—had she but known it—to his intense excitement at taking her. Her smile curved deeper as her fingers found his painfully swollen cock. They played along the shape of him—his crest, his flare, the pulsing streams of blue veins. When her thumb and index finger formed a ring around his base and pulled, he couldn't contain his intake of breath.

His rebellious hips tried to follow the tug back down.

"Grace," he murmured to caution her.

"No," she said. "Let *me* see what I can do to help *you*."

Grace didn't know what guided her. Maybe all women had these instincts. All she knew was that she felt like a different person. Each thrust of his beautiful cock inside her had remade her.

She shimmied under him, pressing little kisses to the muscles of his torso. His knees were spread, and she wiggled between them on the trailer's dusty linoleum, barely sparing a thought for what this would do to the already crumpled mess of her dress. Christian was hard, he was lovely, and his body had been trembling for a while now with its need for release.

That was what mattered. Not where her shoes had fallen or how she would comb her hair. She wondered if he'd be able to stay crouched above her while she did what she planned, or if his muscles—like hers—would turn to sunwarmed honey and fail to support him.

Willing to find out, she used the grip she had on his erect penis to tug his hips to her.

"Grace," he groaned as the melting smoothness of his glans slipped into her mouth.

He was sugar candy she could suck, was chocolate and brandy and all things lickable and yummy. She rose to him as he sank to her, his palms slapping down on a new position, his thighs sliding out of the vertical to bring his groin closer. He didn't fall on her even then. He still had control of his weight. He writhed, though, slowly, groaning as if each pull of her warm, wet mouth hurt too good to miss out on. The press and ebb of his hips cast a spell on her. He made her want to draw him deeper, to prove how brave she had become.

"Grace," he groaned as she ran her tongue around him. "God in heaven."

Suddenly noticing something she'd missed before, Grace pulled back and ran her thumb around the edge of his flare. Some extra folds of skin were gathered under there.

"What's this?" she asked.

He couldn't answer. His head was thrown back at an angle that obscured his face. In contrast, the snarl that curled from his throat was unmistakable.

"Am I hurting you?"

"No!" he panted, one hand flying down to keep hers right where it was. "I'm just . . . not circumcised. That's my foreskin. Please play with it like you used— Please play with it any way you like."

"It feels good?" She squeezed the soft little covering, her fingers somehow knowing how to pull it over his crest.

He made a sound like he was choking. "Very good."

She had to use a bit of pressure so it wouldn't retract. Christian certainly didn't mind that. Not only was he writhing again as she twisted it experimentally over him, but the slit in his tip was leaking like she did when she especially wanted him.

He cursed as she curled her tongue out to lick the drops.

"I think it's nice that you taste this good," she said.

He laughed, and groaned, and she realized she maybe wasn't being as focused as he'd like. He hadn't made her wait for her orgasms.

"What if I—" She blushed and forced herself to go on. "What if I took you in my mouth and played with you at the same time? Do you think you could . . . have a release then?"

"Grace," he sighed, a mysterious wealth of meaning in his utterance of her name. "Yes. Please do that."

"Wouldn't you rather be on your back?"

In answer, he rolled them around so neatly her elbows weren't even bumped. She came to rest between the sprawl of his legs.

She looked up at him one more time before she began. His eyes were closed, his lips rolled together, his expression a hypnotizing mix of agony and pleasure. Seeing it, she was overcome by such a strange emotion she hardly knew how to describe it. She wanted to keep him like this forever, wanted to always be making him happy. She smoothed her hands up his powerful thighs, which were still clad in his dark trousers.

"Grace," he said, his eyelids twitching but not lifting. It must have been her imagination, but she thought she saw a gleam of golden light under his lashes. He cleared his throat as if he weren't sure he should ask what he wanted to.

"Tell me," she said. "If I can, I'll do it."

His beautiful fingers forked through her hair, the tension in them fighting with gentleness. "Suck me hard, Grace. Use all the force you have."

* * *

She took him at his word, and he thought he'd die from delight.

"Don't let me choke you," he gasped.

She wrapped his base in one fist, leaving the top of him for her mouth. Just as he'd thought, her full, soft lips were made for this act. She sucked him so hard he felt the edges of her teeth.

"Yes," he groaned, unable to be hurt by this. He was thrashing under her, helpless to stop himself. His neck arched off the floor in frustration. God, he wanted to come.

And then she was digging into his trousers, her left hand warmly surrounding his drawn-up balls. His knees jerked wider at the new pressure. He'd taught her he liked this all those centuries ago, though she'd never used so much force as now. Her fingertips found the stretch behind his testicles that liked extra stimulation. They dug in, and rubbed, and Christian's inner switch *almost* flipped.

"More." The plea was strangled, his hips urging his cock more insistently into her mouth.

Even a human's strength could have overwhelmed her, but she didn't back away or tense. She trusted him. She gave to him, with absolute fearlessness. Her thumb and one finger came into her mouth, playing with his foreskin even as she tongued and drew on his crest. His brain flashed white with immense pleasure.

"Grace," he choked. "Oh, God, I love you."

He came before he could regret what he'd said. The orgasm thundered up his hungry nerves like a speeding train—a train with a thousand cars, apparently. He had to jerk himself from her mouth as he kept spuming. Not only were his responses slower during the daytime, but so was the unraveling of his climax.

His body knew what reward it wanted for his consideration. Quick as thought, he dragged Grace upward, using both hands to make a channel between her breasts that he could thrust into. That channel slicked with his ejaculation as the hard, tight pulses of bliss went on. He used the pads of his thumbs to press pleasure into nipples gone hard as stones. Grace nipped a kiss onto his belly.

Loving that she loved this, he moaned her name like the refrain to his favorite song.

Finally, when his body trembled from emptying, Grace sat up shakily. His hold slipped reluctantly from her gorgeous breasts, the feel of their silken warmth lingering on his palms. Her nipples were cherry red from him thumbing them. Grace looked down at herself, then covered her mouth in shock.

"Jeesh," she said. "Look at me! I must have lost my mind. Everyone's going to know what we've done."

Her words hit him like a slap of ice water.

"And that would be so bad because?"

She gaped at him like he was crazy. "I'm Miss Wei's assistant. You're an *actor*."

"I'd say I'm a good deal more to you than an actor."

"For Heaven's sake," Grace cried, "I barely know you!"

It was the sharpest dagger she could have thrust. He couldn't believe he'd let her do this to him again. He'd seen the caring in her eyes. He'd felt it in her caresses. She had to have heard him say he loved her, and now she *barely knew him*?

"Oh, heck," she said, a different kind of remorse softening her face. "I didn't mean to hurt your feelings. That was . . . You were really wonderful. Amazing. It just doesn't change the fact that us getting involved isn't appropriate."

His throat felt like chilled gravel. "I know you heard what I said."

Her cheeks flushed a shade darker. "I know you didn't mean it. You were about to . . . you know."

"And before you were about to *you know* for the umpteenth time, you didn't notice a bit more going on between us than sexual chemistry? You didn't think it strange that you knew how to do exactly what I like?"

She wasn't going to answer. She pressed her lips together with the truculence of a five-year-old. "If you wouldn't mind," she said, "I could use some help finding my brassiere."

He more than helped her. In spite of his fury with himself and her, he used the tidying powers of his aura to set her to rights again. By the time he'd finished, her dress was crisp, her hair smoothed back into gleaming waves. Only her starry eyes and her heightened color might reveal what she'd been up to.

He wasn't certain he'd have undone that evidence even if he'd been able to.

She paused as she opened the trailer's door. "Thanks," she said. "For everything."

Christian knew his eyes had slitted. "It was as much my pleasure as it was yours."

"Right. I should—" She glanced longingly out into the sunshine and back at him, her desire to escape warring with her damned professionalism. Christian wasn't the least surprised by which won. "We have our first press conference this afternoon. Miss Wei said she'd prepare you for it. If you stay here, she won't be able to find you."

"I'll be sure to touch base with her."

He crossed his arms and waited for her to go. She hesitated, then left without saying more.

Nine

Nim Wei had her own trailer with a section for her secretary and an office for herself. Being a filmmaker required her to work human hours at times. Though she'd learned to adjust, even for her it occasionally was too much. This shiny aluminum Airstream was her retreat—or it ought to have been.

Christian strolled in without knocking as her favorite vampire physician finished injecting her with his nearly pure-iron needle, the only metal capable of piercing an *upyr*'s skin. Resigned to enjoying her "vitamin" booster a little less, Nim Wei rubbed away the burning from the bend of her arm. Since her secretary hadn't objected, she concluded Christian had used an eye lock to get past her.

Irked by the interruption, Rupert removed the rubber tourniquet with a snap. He would have snapped at Christian, too, had the other vampire not flared his aura and poked him. Rupert was almost a century old, but he was no elder. Satisfied that their respective power levels were established, Christian gave the doctor an infinitesimal smile.

"This is a nice tableau," he observed dryly. "What percent solution have you worked yourself up to?"

"No percent," she said, knowing he was referring to injections of cocaine, which kept their kind awake but sometimes led to addiction. "Rupert here has developed a blend of medical-grade caffeine and plasma that we can tolerate. If you're smart, you'll let him give you a shot."

Christian turned measuring eyes to the doctor. "You're a shapechanger."

"Contrary to your belief," Nim Wei informed him, "the furry vampires don't all hate me."

Rupert was smart enough not to comment. He lowered his gaze in the wolflike way some shapechangers had. "I'd be happy to dose you, sir. And if you have any qualms, I can give myself the first half of your injection."

Christian hesitated, then offered up his arm. Nim Wei hid her amusement. Rupert was brilliant, able to treat humans or *upyr*, but his greatest knack was getting people of all species to trust him.

"I hear you've scheduled a press conference," Christian said as Rupert tied off the tourniquet. The rubber tubing held iron shavings, or it wouldn't have done a thing.

"I have," she said. "Pre-publicity. Introduce our cast to the slavering masses. And it doesn't hurt to show our faces while the sun is up. The sort of humans who believe in vampires are generally the easiest to throw off track."

"You honestly think people are going to mistake this movie for something real?"

"I'd be disappointed if a few didn't. I mean, if I can't excite the loonies' imagination, will I really have done my job?"

Christian snorted and shook his head.

"You wait," Nim Wei warned him. "Once this film comes out, teenage girls will be flinging themselves at you with their necks outstretched."

"Teenage boys as well," Rupert joked.

Christian was surprised into laughing at the same time as a knock sounded on the door.

"Miss Wei?" said her secretary through the barrier.

"Come," Nim Wei called, seeing that Rupert had tucked his paraphernalia back into his black bag.

Melody entered before the last of Christian's humor faded, which caused the pretty young mortal to blink at him in a dazzled way. Nim Wei couldn't blame her. Christian Durand smiling was quite a sight—though, until now, she hadn't been certain Melody noticed boys.

"Yes?" Nim Wei prompted. "You have messages for me?"

Melody shook herself. "Messages?"

"That sheaf of pink things in your right hand?"

"Oh, yes. They're from Adam Chelsea. I'm afraid he found out we started shooting, and it upset him."

The bolstering effect of her recent shot allowed Nim Wei to push aside her irritation. In truth, though, she sometimes wished all humans could be as self-directed as Grace was.

"Melody," she said. "You don't have to take messages from Mr. Chelsea. In fact, you have my permission to hang up the next time he calls. He has to know by now that I'm not listening to his complaints."

"But he—"

"No buts. I don't pay you to be harassed. Do we have security for the press conference?"

"The studio is sending some over."

"Good. Make sure they know he's not permitted anywhere near us."

"Who's Adam Chelsea?" Christian asked after the girl had gone.

"No one," she said, true enough as she saw it. "Anyway, I'm glad you barged in. I want to give you your strategy for handling the media."

"*My* strategy."

"Don't worry," she said, a grin breaking free. "When you hear it, you'll wish it was your idea."

Like any business, moviemaking evolved. In this balmy autumn of '56, film productions had to deal with shrinking audiences, expanding screens, and the shake-up of the studio system by the Supreme Court. Jack Warner, the head of Warner Bros., felt so threatened by the growing popularity of television that he forbade any home in any of his movies to contain a TV set. Budgets had to be watched more closely, studios soothed, and audiences seduced with ever-greater creativity. To all these new realities, Naomi Wei responded that challenges added spice to life.

It was one more quality for Grace to admire in her.

Fortunately, Celestial Pictures, the studio who'd picked up *I Was a Teen-Age Vampire*, was a solid player to be working for. In existence since pre-sound days, Celestial operated out of Hollywood not far from Paramount's main lot. Also like Paramount, their entrance was iconic—a baroque, marble-columned arch whose double gate boasted genuine gold leaf on its fleur-de-lis.

To Grace's delight, they were holding their first press conference in front of it.

Preferring to leave the circus barkering to her boss, Grace was watching from behind the elevated platform, her presence further hidden by a banner displaying Celestial's logo of a muscular golden leopard leaping over a rosy cloud—the implication being that Celestial's mascot could swat down MGM's lazy lion with one paw tied. By leaning around the banner, Grace spotted reporters from the major networks and the AP. The *Hollywood Reporter* and *Variety* were represented, plus the usual gawkers. The full-force crowd was probably thanks to Viv Lavelle. The former child star was much beloved.

Grace felt so gratified by the turnout that she barely jumped when Christian laid his cool and heavy hand on her shoulder. The rest of *Teen-Age Vampire*'s young cast was onstage already. Per Miss Wei's instructions, only Christian stayed back with her.

"What are those women doing here?" he asked.

Grace turned her head to him. For a second, time folded back and he was above her again, plunging between her legs on the trailer floor. She could smell his intriguing wet-pavement scent, could feel his cock stretching out her lubricious sex. How much she wanted him was crazy. She couldn't decide which was more insane: that she'd thrown herself at him in the first place, or that she never intended to again. His face changed as she watched, his harsh mouth softening, suggesting he was remembering, too. Before he could speak, she tore her gaze away.

"Some of the girls are here for Viv," she answered. "And some are here for the boys. They've all had small roles in other films. The girls with the fang marks on their necks, however, are definitely here for you."

"Those lipstick things are fang marks?" Christian was appalled. "You'd have to have a mouth the size of a year-old croc to leave holes that size."

"Perhaps they want to be sure you notice them."

"Our esteemed director put them up to this, didn't she?"

Christian's arms were folded, his scowl impossible to miss even with his Stetson and sunglasses. Grace bit her lip to repress a smile. "If they only scream, they might have been paid. If you notice tears and trembling, chances are they're sincere."

"They don't even know who I am."

"They've heard of you," Grace said. "Miss Wei's search for 'our Joe Pryor' made for an epic tale."

"Not you, too," he grumbled.

"Take off your sunglasses," she advised. "Miss Wei is introducing you."

* * *

As he climbed reluctantly onto the platform, Christian resettled the black motorcycle jacket Nim Wei and Andy had finally decided on. It had half the zippers of the first they'd shown him, and had been dragged behind a truck over gravel to simulate being broken in. Christian had been very sternly instructed to wear its collar up. He hadn't been misled about this being the stylish choice. All two dozen of the girls with fang marks broke into squeals when they caught their first glimpse of him.

The tears and trembling didn't start until he removed his Ray-Bans and tucked them, folded, into the neck of his white T-shirt.

Christian didn't understand the furor. He wasn't using his thrall, and his glamour wrapped him as tightly as it would go. He should have looked no more exciting than any reasonably handsome twentyish human male. He was forced to conclude these girls were whipping themselves into a frenzy for their own reasons.

Flashbulbs exploded to capture their reactions.

"Bite me!" one girl cried above the clamor, pointing to her neck. "I'm the yummiest, Christian!"

Well, Christian thought. At least they knew his real name. Not sure he ought to, he leaned down to the microphone, the stand to which was set low for their director.

"Haven't got my fangs in now," he said.

At the sound of his Texas twang, the girl who'd called out to him collapsed. She appeared to have truly fainted. As if he saw such things every day, a member of Celestial's security staff scooped her up and carried her away.

Viv spared him from standing there with his jaw agape by stepping to him and squeezing his arm tight against her side.

"You see how lucky I am!" she cried. "Look who my first grown-up screen kiss gets to be with!

"*Smile,*" she ordered Christian from the side of her mouth.

Christian smiled and shifted his hold to behind her back. Viv nestled affectionately closer—exactly as if she didn't think he was a talentless idiot.

"Viv!" one of the reporters shouted. "Aren't the stars you've been seen around town with going to be jealous?"

Viv let out a merry peal. "What do you think?" she asked coyly.

"What about you, Christian?" called another. "Any pretty little fillies waiting on you back in the Panhandle?"

This was what the media wanted to know? Who each of them was dating? Fearing his response might cause more of their female audience to swoon, Christian bent to the microphone.

"No," he said, employing the one-word answers Nim Wei had told him to stick to.

"Do you feel lucky Miss Wei discovered you?"

He bent again. "Yes," he growled, his manner considerably less convincing than his costar's.

Young-old pro that she was, Viv covered the lapse easily.

"We all feel lucky," his leading lady burbled. "It's an honor to work for a director of Naomi Wei's caliber. Her film *Revenge of the Robots* was a tour de force, one of the best popcorn movies I've ever seen. The teaming of her and cinematographer Wade Matthews is sure to be groundbreaking. Of course, if you really want to know why I signed on to this production, I have to call someone up onstage who you haven't met."

She leaned around Christian, beckoning to where Grace was hiding behind the Celestial Pictures banner.

"Come on," Viv coaxed, keeping at it until Grace gave in and came up.

"She's shy," Viv laughed, tugging Grace by the hand until she stood at Viv's other side. The actress beamed at Nim Wei's assistant with a warmth that seemed genuine. "This is Grace Michaels, the person who convinced me I had to be a part of this film. Her reworking of the script moved me more than I can express. She understands what it is to be a young woman with a yearning heart today."

Since the press had no idea who Grace was, Viv's announcement stirred a small flurry. Another spate of flashbulbs burst, causing Grace to curse underneath her breath. She put her hand over the microphone.

"This is about you," she said when Viv would have urged her forward. "You and the boys and Christian. No one cares who the writer is."

Viv tried to convince her, but Grace managed to extricate herself firmly. With a grimace of a smile and a jerking wave for the reporters, she slipped back off the platform. Christian watched her go, finding it interesting that she seemed more annoyed than shy at having been yanked, however briefly, into the spotlight.

She must have known he wanted to corner her about it. With a dexterity an *upyr* would have been proud of, Grace evaded his attempts to speak to her after the press conference. He was forced to accept Charlie's general invitation to the cast to join him for drinks at the Villa Nova, a restaurant on Sunset whose primary recommendation seemed to be that big stars drank there. Even then, it took Christian twenty minutes to get Grace alone back by the restrooms. Thankfully, the sun had set, and his mental gears were turning more smoothly.

"You're avoiding me," he said, one hand planted beside her head on the dark brick wall.

Since she'd just exited the bathroom, she couldn't claim she had to go in. Her frown said she wanted to—just as she wanted to try ducking away from him.

"I'm faster," he warned, secretly pleased that he could read the urge in her eyes.

"I'm not avoiding you," Grace said crisply. "I simply don't have anything to say. I already told you why what happened earlier can't occur again."

"I don't care about that. All right, I care. Frankly—and,

believe me, this isn't bragging—most women I make love to can't wait to do it again. That, however, isn't what I want to ask you."

Grace gave the impression of rolling her eyes without actually doing it. Happily for his ego, the spots of color on her cheeks told a more flattering story. "Fine. What do you want to know?"

"Why were you so determined not to accept Viv's praise publicly?"

Grace's brows shot up. "*That's* your question?"

"Yes."

Mace's braying laugh rose above the noise in the bar, evidence that Nim Wei's ploy to keep the halves of the gang at odds was not working perfectly. Grace glanced toward the sound and then back at him.

"I'm Miss Wei's assistant, her directorial apprentice. Until I'm ready to direct myself, I'd rather stay in the background."

"And it's nothing to do with your father?"

"My father?"

"You said you ran away from him. What if he saw a picture of you and Viv in a newspaper?"

Her heart gave a little thump. He steadied her shoulders as her balance wavered. Her hands came up to grip his forearms—probably unintentionally.

"I hadn't thought of that. When I first ran away I worried, but . . ." Her eyes were huge as her voice trailed off.

"I'm sorry. I didn't mean to bring back your fears."

She shook her head. "No. You're right. It doesn't hurt to be cautious, though I sincerely doubt my father reads *Variety*. He's never tried to find me that I know of."

"And your mother?"

Grace's face hardened as it hadn't at the mention of her father. "She stood by and watched. For years. And pretended my father was a reasonable man. She liked to say we girls had to make allowances for his temper. If I hadn't nearly died that night . . ." Grace's eyes were cold. "As far as I'm concerned, she couldn't matter less."

Christian's hand slid down Grace's arm as she pulled away. He didn't stop her from leaving, though he also didn't believe her words. Grace's mother mattered. Her example, or lack thereof, had formed Grace's character every bit as surely as her father's abuse. Her mother was the one who'd convinced Grace she only had her own strength to rely on.

His chest felt strange as he watched her offer slightly stiff goodbyes to Charlie and his party. Viv's protests that the night was young didn't sway her. Grace smiled, kissed Charlie's freckled cheek, and waved to the others.

"Don't stay too late," he saw her lips say. "Tomorrow's a working day."

I hurt her, Christian thought. *Made her want to curl up in her old ball, away from people who care for her.* He didn't relish how that made him feel. He knew what it was to be on guard against the whole world.

He also knew what it was to have a mother who wasn't there. He'd lost his to death as a child, but maybe he'd been lucky. His mother's ability to disappoint him had been curtailed.

Waiting a minute for appearance's sake, he went to say his own farewells. Grace wouldn't want to know it, but she wasn't going to be on guard by herself tonight.

Christian's plan to spend another night in Grace's bushes was delayed by his need to make a phone call. Unsure whether Nim Wei had his line at the hotel tapped, he used a booth near Schwab's Drugstore. Charlie would have been devastated to discover both Natalie Wood and Dennis Hopper were eating fries inside. They hadn't spotted a single celebrity where they were.

On the sixth tinny ring, Christian's party picked up.

"It's Christian Durand," he said and gave his identifying code.

"Don't be a spaz," Graham laughed. "I didn't forget your voice just because you left X Section."

Graham Fitz Clare was one of the "furry" vampires Nim Wei had referred to. Unlike Nim Wei's get, they could change into animals—eat like them, too, which some considered morally superior to feeding on humans. Most shapechangers transformed to wolves, but Graham's animal was a tomcat. Considering how devoted Graham was to his wife, Christian found this amusing.

"Right," he said, as always unnerved by Graham's trademark Fitz Clare warmth, especially since it now extended to him. "Seeing as I'm not with X-Section anymore, I'm calling for a favor."

"Ask me how I am," Graham prompted.

"What?"

"You heard me."

"Fine," Christian sighed, realizing Graham wouldn't let him talk business until he observed the formula. "How are you? And Pen? And Sally and her hell spawn?"

"I'm great, Christian. And Pen gets smarter and more gorgeous each time I turn around. This marriage business really is like wow, especially when you can enjoy a swell girl like Pen long-term. You should try it sometime."

"I'll get right on that," Christian said, deadpan.

"Ben and Sally are great, too," Graham went on. "Still in London and still human—if a bit souped-up from Edmund's energy. The hell spawn is at Oxford, studying history like his grandpa. Cutting a swath through the lady scholars, or so I hear."

"That's great," Christian said, then waited in stoic silence to see if Graham was finished with his update.

He was finished. He simply had to laugh his head off awhile longer.

"All right," Graham finally said, probably wiping tears from his eyes over in Charleston. "What's this favor you need from me?"

"I want a deep background check on a woman named Grace Michaels. She's Nim Wei's assistant on the movie I've been roped into starring in."

"We heard about that, though I personally couldn't believe it until Percy told me FC Air flew you to LA. No offense, old chap, but you aren't my idea of a teen idol."

Christian wasn't his idea of one, either, but he had no desire to discuss that now. "Do you need more information before you begin a search?"

"Christian." Graham's tone was gently scolding. "Give your former colleagues some credit. We're already aware of Grace Michaels' existence."

"Care to tell me why that would be?"

The pause on the other end said his sudden coolness took Graham aback. "We're aware of everyone who's been working on Nim Wei's new venture. As you might imagine, we don't want the queen of the city fang gangs causing trouble for the rest of us."

His explanation was perfectly reasonable, so reasonable Christian should have guessed it without asking. He grimaced at his own prickliness. "You probably had the script before me."

"We did," Graham confirmed, "and found it suitably misleading as regards the true facts of vampire life. Thus far, the queen has done nothing we object to . . . unless you know differently?"

"I don't," Christian admitted.

"So maybe she really wants to be a director. Maybe she's having fun."

"Maybe," Christian said doubtfully.

"Well, regardless, we'll put our eyes and ears on your request."

"Appreciate it."

"And we'll see *you* for Christmas," Graham said.

With some dismay, Christian realized he'd just been told what the payment for his favor was.

Ten

With everything else he had to occupy his mind, Christian was only half as nervous as he'd expected for his first official appearance in front of Wade's cameras. The crew was setting up for what everyone was calling a "walk and talk." He (as Joe Pryor) would accompany Viv (as Mary Reed) through the deceptively peaceful suburbs of Haileyville. In the script, Joe had already saved Mary from a group of human bullies on her first day at her new school. Now, because night had fallen, he'd play her guard dog against the threat posed by his father's gang of bloodsuckers.

Christian would also be expected to imitate a teenage boy trying to impress the girl he was falling for.

No one had to tell him which of those personas would present the greater challenge. Regrettably, that had never stopped a human from offering her two cents. Viv confronted him as he exited the makeup trailer, planting herself dead center across his path. She'd been dressed as a schoolgirl, with saddle shoes, plaid flare skirt, plus ponytail and bangs. Wardrobe aside, if her fans had seen the steely glint in her big brown eyes, they'd have known the littlest Forrester had grown up.

"It's time to cowboy up," she announced.

They stood amidst the other trailers in what was colorfully called the circus. For tonight, it was located on an undeveloped plot of land at the edge of the neighborhood they were shooting in. The grass was longer than any suburban lawn was allowed to be and wet beneath Christian's boots. Squaring off on it with his leading lady, he couldn't help but think of *High Noon*. Which one of them was Gary Cooper was up for grabs.

"*Cowboy up?*" he repeated.

"You know what that means," she snapped. "You have rodeos in Texas."

Liking her moxie, he allowed one corner of his smile to show. "You mean you need me to come out of the chute with a good grip on the bronco between my thighs."

"You need a grip and then some. This movie is my chance to reinvent myself. Viv Lavelle isn't going to end up on the heap of once-loved and now-pitied adult child stars. I can act, Christian, and you'd better prove you can, too. So help me, if you drag me down with you . . ."

"Viv," Grace interrupted, appearing from around the end of the next trailer. "I'm not certain threats are the way to bring out the best in your costars."

Grace was smiling, but Viv looked horrified all the same. "Grace, I didn't mean—"

Christian stopped hearing her the instant Grace's gaze turned to him. As it seemed to do too often when she was near, his mouth emitted words without forethought.

"I didn't expect to see you tonight. Thanks for coming."

"There's nothing to thank me for. We're shooting. I'm working. It's my job to be here."

The stubborn set of her jaw dared him to mention her suburbaphobia or any of the other reasons she might not want to be here for him. That she *was* here for him seemed likely when her cheeks took on a more delectable shade of pink. She held her clipboard closer to her chest.

"You're needed in wardrobe," she said. "If you want, I'll run lines with you."

"I can run lines with him," Viv piped up.

Grace's little start of surprise told him she'd forgotten the girl was there. "Oh, Viv, that's good of you, but you're due in makeup now."

"Sure." Viv hesitated. "I *do* want Christian to do well. I only said what I did because this role means so much to me."

"Of course," Grace reassured her. "We all appreciate how passionate you are."

Viv stared at Grace a moment longer, nodded, then turned to ascend the steps of the makeup truck. Her thoughts were locked down as tightly as her expression.

"Ready?" Grace asked Christian.

Her face was lovely in the starlight, innocent without being childish, beautiful without being cold. It seemed impossible that she could be hiding the least intent to do harm. Though her opinion should have meant nothing, he had an urge to prove himself to her.

"I know the dialogue," he said as he fell into step beside her. "It's the feelings that trip me up."

Grace gave a little snort. He lifted his brows at her.

"Sorry. You just don't seem to have any lack of feelings."

He supposed he didn't, seeing as he'd burst out that he loved her in the middle of having sex.

"You're not so different from Joe," she said after a moment's thought. "You're hoping to fall in love, but at the same time, you don't really believe in it."

Christian stopped in his tracks, and she did as well. He wondered if he ought to be insulted that she'd announced this so casually—and never mind her implication that those words he'd accidentally blurted were a delusion. "You think I'm hoping to fall in love?"

"That's how it seems to me." Grace's shoulders hitched in a shrug. "Just imagine feeling that way and then meeting Mary. She's pretty. She's sweet. She needs protecting. You can be a man for her. You can be the opposite of the people you grew up with. You can be for her what you wish your father had been for you. All you need is to let those feelings rise far enough to show."

Christian felt himself gaping. *All* he needed was to let his most painful feelings rise? As if every tragedy in his life had no higher purpose than to help him be an actor? She couldn't know what she was saying. She couldn't be that insensitive. With a conscious effort, he shut his mouth.

"You can do it," Grace said. "The only thing that might hold you back is your fear of looking foolish."

The door to the trailer behind her opened. Andy Phelps, the head of wardrobe, stuck out his head to see if they'd arrived. He must have sensed Christian and Grace were caught up in their conversation, because he didn't call out to them.

"What holds *you* back?" Christian retorted, the openness of his anger surprising him.

Grace jerked her head back from him. "Me? I told you why I can't be with you."

He held her eyes, doubting her, until she wet her lips nervously. "You did tell me. I just didn't believe you."

Christian's parting words weren't what Grace wanted in her head. She clutched her hands together at her waist, one thumb rubbing the knuckle of the other. Her duties taken care of for the moment, she was on the sidelines, behind an array of moonlight-simulating lights. Any discomfort she felt at being back in suburbia was blotted out by hoping Christian would do all right.

She'd upset him too close to shooting. She wasn't totally sure how, only that she had—when the last thing she'd wanted was to throw him off balance. They'd already burned through one take, and Christian looked worryingly stiff as he stood a ways down the glistening asphalt street with Viv.

Just let go, Grace prayed silently. *Whatever I did to bother you, let it go.*

She watched him push his arms out to crack his knuckles. When they fell, Wade signaled that film was rolling.

"Action," Miss Wei called for the second time.

And then the magic happened, what everyone in their crazy business dreamed about. Joe nudged Mary's arm with his elbow as they moved forward, everything but the story falling away. The couple's steps were dawdling, just like they were supposed to be—two young people bumping sides together as their hearts formed a fragile bond.

"That was some tree I caught you staring at back at school," Joe said. "Like somebody spray painted its leaves scarlet."

Mary smiled shyly, darting a sidelong look at her escort. "I l-liked the way that tree made me feel. It was big. And dramatic. Oh, I wish I owned a good camera."

"A camera," Joe repeated, the scorn of a self-styled cool boy warring with interest.

"If I had a camera, I could take pictures, and if I had pictures, I'd never forget when nice things happened."

Joe laughed and began dancing backward in front of her. The move was so natural, so seemingly unaware of the camera being pulled alongside them on the dolly, that tingles swept Grace's scalp. Joe was controlled exuberance in action, a strong young male showing off his grace for a girl.

"You could take pictures of me," he said, flapping his black jacket open. "I'm a nice thing."

"Oh, like I'd take time on a waste like— Crap," Viv said, aware that she'd flubbed her line.

" 'Oh, like I'd waste film on you,' " the script supervisor fed to her.

"Cut," Miss Wei called, patiently enough. "Back to the beginning, kiddies. I'd like this stretch of dialogue to roll as one shot. Christian, you're doing good."

He was better than good. Grace knew that from the way the crew was exchanging glances and perking up. The table read hadn't revealed his unexpected flair for physical acting. Christian had walked like she'd always imagined the character would, preened like him, spun like him, every muscle under his control. If he could keep this up, they'd be cooking.

Christian's gaze found hers as he and Viv returned to their starting marks. Strictly speaking, it was the director's place to offer comments, but Grace couldn't resist giving him an on-the-sly thumbs-up. Hopefully, whatever their differences, he'd accept the encouragement.

She thought she saw the glimmer of a return smile before the next take was slated with the clapper board.

Everyone held their breath for Viv to get through the line she'd messed up before.

"I'll get you a camera," Joe boasted when she did.

Mary shot him a dubious look.

"I wouldn't steal it. I'd buy it with my own money."

Both Christian and Viv remembered to stop as the camera operator panned to Joe's face. Grace wished she could see if Christian was pulling this moment off, but her line of sight wasn't right for it. Though Miss Wei was following the dolly closely enough to judge, Grace couldn't decipher her expression.

"Maybe I'll be a fireman," Joe said. "Or a pilot. I bet I'd be good at that."

"I bet you'd be good at anything," Mary said.

"Let's take that again," Miss Wei interrupted. "Christian, I want more defensiveness from you, more awareness that you're trapped by the fate your father has planned for you. You're saying you could be a fireman, but what you really think is that you're destined to be a killer. Viv, more dreaminess from you."

"Do you want it sappy?" Viv asked. "Mary *is* naive."

"Maybe," Miss Wei said, "but think of it more as her faith being very pure, so pure she can infect Joe with it."

"Still rolling," Wade warned her.

Miss Wei waved for them to proceed.

"Better," she said when they'd gotten through it. "Let's go again and give me more intensity for the stare. You're looking into each other's souls, without the guards you usually put up. This is the moment you realize you could fall in love with each other. If that isn't scary, I don't know what is."

They did two more takes before Miss Wei called a break. Her tiny frown said she wasn't getting what she wanted.

"Ten minutes," she instructed. "Christian, go jump around or something."

Grace knew very well he wasn't going to do that, though he did walk off into the shadows shaking his head. She didn't go after him, not because she didn't want to, but because she suspected Miss Wei didn't truly want him to loosen up. As long as he wasn't boardlike, tense was good for this last exchange. The more Christian's nerves wound up, the more authentically it would play. When Miss Wei had the crew start setting up for a close-up, Grace knew her guess was correct.

"Hit him with both barrels," Grace heard the boss lady say to Viv. "Even if the camera isn't on you, I want you fully engaged for his coverage. Make him feel it's really happening."

"Tears?" Viv offered.

Miss Wei grinned at her. "Go ahead and give him a glimmer. If he's like most males, worrying they'll spill over ought to scare him the right amount."

* * *

That's a wrap, kiddies," Nim Wei called. "Good work, everyone."

A little cheer broke out from the crew, though whether from relief at the night's ordeal being over or actual enthusiasm he couldn't say.

Christian didn't know if he'd been awful or all right, only that he felt terrible. His shoulders were as tight as if an iron brace were screwed to them. The crew was already beginning to break down their equipment, undoubtedly eager to get home. The best Christian could manage was to hang his neck and attempt to wag the kinks from his spinal cord.

His head ached from the unfamiliar task of coordinating his glamour with the application of fake color on his face. This was one more ball he'd needed to juggle while also trying to emote opposite an old pro like Viv. Her eyes had dewed on cue—repeatedly—as if her tear ducts were attached to a bloody switch. Really, if he'd crashed and burned, it was no wonder.

"Grace," Viv said, causing his neck to snap up and look for her.

Excitement flooded him when he found her. Grace resembled a glamorous gal Friday as she walked to them in her narrow knee-length tweed skirt.

"Good job," she said to Viv. "I loved how your eyes welled up at the end."

"Miss Wei liked my idea to do that. She thought—"

Grace laid her hand on the sleeve of Christian's leather jacket. He'd turned toward her as she approached. Only when she touched him did he realize he'd also pressed his palm to his heart. Disconcerted, he forced it back to his side.

"You did good," she said softly. "You kept up with Viv just fine. Wade got some great footage."

Her approval shouldn't have meant so much, but it warmed

him unbearably. *I didn't want to let you down,* he almost said into her beautiful shining eyes.

"Viv!" a crewmember hailed from behind them. "One of your gentlemen callers is pulling up in a white limo."

"Crap," Viv said, causing Grace to laugh.

"Must be hard. Juggling dates with famous movie stars."

"More like famous movie farts," Viv grumbled.

"Well, have fun," Grace said. "You're making all the other ingenues jealous."

Viv left with her bow lips pursed in distaste. Christian and Grace were alone.

"Well," Grace said, beginning to pull away.

Christian succumbed to impulse and caught her hand. "I'll drive you home tonight."

"Miss Wei—"

"—will have no shortage of volunteers to chauffeur her if she decides she can't drive herself." Abruptly happy, and for no better reason than that her fingers were twined with his, he smiled coaxingly. "I survived my first night of filming. I'm officially an actor. Don't you think your boss would approve of you buying me a drink?"

"You want to have a drink with me?"

He wanted a good deal more, but he'd settle for a drink and keeping an eye on her. The corners of his lips curved higher as she regarded him warily.

"One drink," he promised. "Then I'll disappear like the wind."

"No trying to make me change my mind about anything?"

He crossed his heart and grinned outright. He liked knowing she doubted her ability to stand firm.

"Come on, Grace," he said, giving her hand a tug. "I think you deserve to be taken care of for a change."

Eleven

Grace was practically purring as she circled his black T-Bird. When she trailed her hands around the headlamps, Christian's groin tightened. There was no denying she was fondling his car.

"I hear Ford smoothed out the suspension on this year's models."

"And increased the horsepower," he said.

Grace let out a wistful sigh. "I won't ask if I can drive. I wouldn't let me if this were mine."

Rather than contradict her assumption, Christian opened the passenger door. "Milady."

She smiled at his courtliness. "Those girls are right," she said as she scooted in. "You're dreamy when you want to be."

Christian didn't mind the compliment from her. He slid behind the wheel, feeling a decidedly primitive satisfaction at having her in his vehicle. There wasn't much point in trying to fight the reaction. She'd proved she could override a considerable amount of civilization and self-control.

"You might want to hold on to your hair," he said. "This baby gets breezy with the top down."

She laughed and reached over to tug his forelock. "Hold on to your own," she teased.

The look on her face was joyous, her guards forgotten in her enjoyment of his fast car. If he hadn't been in love with her already, he was convinced he'd have fallen then.

Crap, he thought, borrowing Viv's curse. How many times could one man fall for a woman he shouldn't trust?

Unable to answer and unwilling to abandon the pleasure of the moment, Christian started up the car and pulled out of the grassy lot. When Christian drove was when he most felt a part of the modern world.

He didn't get a chance to open up the engine until they were on Mulholland Drive, winding along the ridge of the Santa Monica Mountains. He wished he could have loaned Grace his night vision. Seen in their full range of colors, the twinkling views across the valley were breathtaking.

She made a little sound above the rushing of the wind, one hand holding her wildly flipping dark red hair away from her eyes.

"Too fast?" he shouted, though he knew his lightning-quick reflexes were up to even these sharp turns.

Grace grinned and shook her head.

He slowed a little, helpless to keep from being just a bit protective of her white knuckles. The thought ran through his mind that keeping her safe wouldn't be the worst way to spend his life.

You're an idiot, he told himself. *An absolute, love-struck fool.*

The land dropped away behind the next guardrail, forcing him to slow more. When Grace shot out her arm and clutched his knee, he thought every sexual nerve he had would explode. Neither of them could resist each other. Their private fears and personal agendas had no power against their attraction. As surely as the sun would rise, Christian knew they'd end up in bed again.

He looked at her, smiled at her, not even trying to rein in his emotions. He'd take his victories where he could.

"Christian," said her lips, and then he heard it: a sound a hundred battle missions had seared into his memory banks.

On the slope above them, hidden among the trees, someone was working a rifle bolt.

The vampire version of adrenaline surged in him, narrowing his extra senses down to pinpoints. He probed the mind behind the weapon. As the shooter's finger tightened on the trigger, Grace was in the telescopic sight. Clear as this was, it didn't tell him how to avert disaster. His attention was split between the road and the sniper. Triumph swelled, and it wasn't his.

Left, said a voice that wasn't his, either.

A force seemed to grip his hands, turning the wheel so sharply the car spun in a donut. The closest he'd felt to this was when a more powerful vampire had seized control of his energy. Despite his best efforts, he hadn't been able to regain his volition then. On this night, he barely had time to try. The windshield burst halfway through the dizzying rotation. Christian slammed back into the seat as if a shovel had struck his chest.

The car slewed to a stop a heartbeat later, the sound of the squealing tires echoing in his ears. They were lucky they had this stretch of road to themselves. Christian couldn't have prevented a collision with another car.

"Christian," Grace gasped. "Oh, my God, you're bleeding!"

He shook the shock from his body, grateful to discover his limbs were his to control again. A bullet had penetrated his chest wall, but the slug wasn't iron, and it hadn't gone very deep. Though it hurt like hell, it wasn't going to kill him. Whoever had positioned Grace in his crosshairs wasn't aware of the nature of her companion.

This, of course, didn't mean they could stay where they were. As soon as the sniper realized he'd missed his target, Grace was a sitting duck.

Almost too fast to think, Christian straightened out the idling car and jammed his foot on the gas. He grabbed Grace's nape with the same sense of urgency.

"Down," he ordered, shoving her head between her knees. Windshield glass glittered in her hair.

With a fervor he wouldn't have recognized a month ago, he said a prayer of thanks for the T-Bird's power. He ignored the way Grace was struggling against his hold.

"Christian," she said, her voice muffled by being obliged to speak into the foot well. "Let me up. We have to get you to a hospital."

"Stay *down*," he growled, his hand preventing her from rising.

"But I think you were shot. You shouldn't be driving. You could pass out and kill us both."

He shifted in the seat and winced. He was only bleeding sluggishly but more than he should have. That had been a high-velocity rifle—eight hundred miles per second was his estimate. On top of this, his normal healing powers were hampered by his recent neglect of his nutrition.

Knowing they'd driven far enough that it was no risk, he reluctantly let Grace up.

"Holy smokes," she breathed on seeing the wreckage of the windshield. The laminated glass had mostly held together, its surface crazed like a spiderweb but not shattered. The jagged hole at the point of impact was the exception. He noticed some of his blood had blown back to it. The tiny clinging drops looked like red candy.

"I'm all right," he said gruffly. "You could put pressure on the wound. And shake those splinters out of your hair."

Grace shook, then dug two folded white handkerchiefs out of her little patent-leather purse. He didn't let his pain show as she pressed them to his left pectoral. She was experiencing enough anxiety as it was.

"This is bad," she said.

Christian almost laughed. It wasn't so bad that the beast in him didn't enjoy the way her white teeth worried her lower lip. His fangs were trying to lengthen, his instincts intent on replenishing the blood he'd lost.

"*Teen-Age Vampire* doesn't need this sort of media attention," he said with an inspired flash. "I'll take you home, and you can patch me up."

"I'm not a medic. I can't remove a bullet."

She wasn't going to need to, but he didn't say that.

"I'm taking you home," he insisted.

The pressure of Grace's hand on his chest got harder. "Who would shoot at us? Do you think it was a hunter? Do people hunt deer in the middle of the night?"

He knew her shock was fading, and consequently she was trying to make sense of seemingly nonsensical events.

"I don't think *us* is who they were shooting at," he said.

She fell silent at his emphasis. Maybe she knew she didn't want him to be clearer. He appreciated the quiet, because he might have been a little light-headed after all. She had to remind him which exit to take to Nim Wei's Pacific Palisades estate. Whoever had shot at Grace likely knew she lived there, but now that Christian was fore-warned, they wouldn't take him by surprise again. There was also the added—if dubious—advantage that Nim Wei would be close by. If he had to call on the queen for help, he would. She might be playing games with him, but he couldn't doubt she valued her assistant.

He stopped the Thunderbird in front of Grace's cottage without quite recalling how he'd got there. Grace removed the key from the ignition. The lower half of his once-white

T-shirt was soaked with blood. He stared at it dazedly. He couldn't remember when he'd last bled this much.

"Stay," she said firmly. "I'll come around and help you get out."

"Don't call an ambulance," he cautioned as he leaned a portion of his weight on her. She smelled better to him than he thought was safe. "This isn't as bad as it looks."

"You know you're an idiot, right?"

It wasn't funny, but he laughed. The sound cut off when she lowered him to her flowered couch. He swallowed a groan as she swung his legs up onto the cushions. The bullet was starting to wiggle, his vampire immune system thrusting it out of him. Though it was necessary, the sensation was hideous.

Slamming into his super-hard immortal muscles had flattened the projectile considerably. He didn't want to, but he sat up far enough to shrug off his leather jacket.

"Let's get this off you, too." Grace sat next to him at hip level. She cut the hem of his bloody T-shirt with a pair of nail scissors, then ripped it the rest of the way upward.

Christian couldn't stop her. He was too busy holding his breath with pain. A fresh spurt of wetness ran down his chest, indicating that the misshapen bullet had reached his skin layer.

"*Oh.*" Grace's hands fluttered above his ribs. "It looks like . . . like the bullet is being pushed out of you."

He gasped as it tumbled out, his lungs agreeing to work again. The air in them felt hot and cindery.

"Christian, how did that happen?"

"You know how," he said wearily.

"I swear I don't. Unless the bullet was going slowly and didn't penetrate as far as I thought."

He opened his eyes and looked into her pleading expression. Somewhere inside, buried under that mountain of denial, she remembered exactly who and what he was.

"You know what the wound looked like when we were in the car. Wipe away the blood and see what it looks like now."

"I don't think I should touch it," she refused nervously.

He pulled the ripped shirt out from under him and wiped the wound clean himself. More white showed around Grace's eyes. Even as she watched, the edges of his injury sealed closed.

"That's not— Christian, you shouldn't play tricks on me."

"I don't even need to thrall you, do I? No matter what oddities I show you, you'll explain them away."

She didn't seem to appreciate his dark humor. "Maybe you're delirious. Let me get you some orange juice."

He caught her wrist before she could rise. Both their fingers were bloody. "Orange juice isn't what I need."

"But you've gone pale. I'm sure your blood sugar's dropped."

He wasn't pale; he'd simply lost his hold on his glamour— along with shedding the remnants of his film makeup. Grace was seeing his true face, in all its shining white glory. His fangs were stretching behind his lips, his hunger rising intolerably. Her blood would finish healing him, would make him strong enough to protect her from any threat. The reasoning was seductive. His gaze fell to the pulse that throbbed between her clavicles. She touched the hollow uneasily.

"Christian," she said, but he was unable to lift his eyes from that ever-faster beating temptation. "Tell me what you need. If it's mine to give, I will."

This was more permission than most *upyr* waited for. She stroked his hair from his forehead, and he realized he was panting, because the sound hastened at her touch. His right hand seemed to rise by itself. It cupped the back of her neck, his bloodstained thumb stretching forward to stroke the silken warmth of her skin. He swallowed hard with longing.

"Grace," he said huskily, his palm beginning to exert pressure. "If you're going to pull away from me, do it now . . ."

Grace didn't want to pull away. She wanted to go soft and pliant, to let him do whatever awful act he seemed to have in mind. Her body felt fevered as her elbows braced on the cushions beside his ribs. His head was propped on the couch's upholstered arm. His eyes were glowing, his palm a curve of steel underneath her hair. When he wet his lips, something white and pointy glistened between them.

He wasn't too weak to lift up his head to her. His lips whispered hot and satiny on her neck, and his breath came harder. His tongue curled out, stirring a shiver. As he tasted her, he let out a moan of longing that clenched her sex and filled it with liquid. There was a second when she could have pushed him away. Then he widened his jaw and bit down.

The pain brought tears to her eyes, two sharp spears of it piercing her. She struggled, but his hands were tight on her arms. His lips had formed a seal on her skin. She felt his tongue move between them a moment before his cheeks hollowed.

They both cried out: he against her vein, she with her spine arched so strongly she could have been a contortionist. He was feeding from her, swallowing her blood, and the pleasure was incredible—wave rolling over wave as every cell in her body tried to contract in orgasm. With another cry, he jackknifed up, his arms hugging her closer. Wanting that as much as he did, she clutched him back. The noises he made as he sucked on her were so sexual, so hungry, so unbelievably arousing that she wished she could record them.

The person who could utter those noises really appreciated her.

He was also careful of her. The moment she felt a smid-gen dizzy, he stopped.

"Shh," he said at her sound of protest, one long finger stroking down her cheek. His face was more relaxed than she'd ever seen it, his cheeks flushed, his thin mouth totally sensual.

"You bit me," she said, slurred and dreamy. "You drank my blood."

Golden embers flared in his eyes. "You know you aren't as surprised by that as you ought to be."

She didn't want to talk about that. "Do you feel better now?"

Her hands were resting on his shoulders, partly to caress his amazing skin and partly to keep from keeling over at the aftershocks of pleasure. With his gaze locked to hers, Christian took her right hand and drew it down his bare chest. He slid her fingertips over his navel and the waist-band of his worn jeans. He didn't stop until her palm lay atop the impressive hardness at his crotch. Heat radiated through strained denim as he molded her hand closer.

"I want more," he said, low and rough. "I want to bite you when this is inside you. I want to fill you with my come while I suck your blood into me. That's the ultimate plea-sure for someone like me."

She shuddered with renewed desire, her flesh twitching so strongly she almost came.

"Yes," she managed to get out. "Please do that."

Maybe her perceptions had been distorted by their brush with death. Christian growled with approval as her clothes seemed to fly off her. Her body whirled and she was beneath him on the couch, naked, with her thighs spread for his approach. Kisses stung the peaks of her breasts like fire, and then his velvety smooth erection was sliding into her. The living, pulsing heat of it stole her breath.

"God," she gasped, her hands pressing the muscles at the small of his back.

She guessed he liked this. He snarled and bit her neck and lunged all the way inside her at the same time.

For a second, before he began to thrust, before he drew in a tiny sip, the sensation of the double penetration coiled her nerves up exquisitely. Her anticipation of what was coming was painful.

Fortunately, he didn't wait long to whip up the curtain on the main event. With an urgency that astounded her, he began to move. The feel of his body surging powerfully in and out was even better than him only biting her. Her climax was a nail he was hammering repeatedly. Each time his mouth pulled on her, each time his big blunt tip struck her utmost limit, ecstasy rang through her. She was crazed with pleasure, filling up and filling up and then just as deliciously emptying. He was coming, too, over and over, as if he couldn't get enough of her. She loved how he grunted as he went over, loved how he tried to hitch himself deeper at the ultimate moment. Certainly, there was nothing graceful about how she slung her hips up his cock, or the wetness that ran from her. This was about sensation, about giving—and getting—more of it.

After about ten minutes, he hiked her feet up around his ears. Since he'd stopped biting her, he could speak.

"I dreamed of this," he panted, holding her legs in place with his shoulders. "I fucking wanted this the day you walked into my barn."

Grace couldn't answer. She was coming so hard tears ran from the corners of her eyes. The new position, and his excitement at it, had her nails digging in his back. She suspected he liked the fact that he controlled both their motions. The couch springs squealed like they were about to snap.

"In the dirt," he said, punctuating the image he was creating with a thrust and twist of his hips. "Me in your cunt and you sweating under me." He groaned as her inner muscles tightened, then sped up savagely. "Can you feel how big you make me? God, you fuck me so good."

Grace loved every rough word he said. This was what he was really thinking, no prettying up his language for female ears. It made her feel close to him, made her feel abandon. At that point, if she could have driven herself *into* his body, she would have. Christian gasped at her enthusiasm, one hand clamping on her bottom to keep her in sync with him. His grip was strong but welcome; she couldn't go wrong with it guiding her. In truth, nothing could go wrong with him for a partner.

He nuzzled her like he felt it, too, his mouth opening on the bite he'd left on her throat. The way he licked it, as if he were savoring one last drop, pulled pleasured shudders from inside her.

They came one more time before he eased her legs down. Grace responded to her freedom by digging her heels into the cushions, grabbing the back of the couch, and pushing her pelvis all the way up him.

"Grace," he moaned. "Jesus, honey, that feels good but don't hurt yourself."

His hand stroked her side and hip soothingly. Part of her wanted to keep going, but he *was* more experienced and probably knew better. In any case, what they'd done was almost enough. Physically, it was more than. She let herself go limp beneath him, let her thighs relax and her feet smooth over his bunching calves. Her hands cruised up and down his chest, which was heaving enjoyably.

"You're so *good* at this," she marveled. "I never would have guessed having someone bite me would be that exciting. I suppose my . . . predilections are as unusual as yours."

Grace thought he had a *predilection*? As if drinking blood was a new fetish? Christian had accused her of denying whatever oddities he showed her, but this was ridiculous. She had to have felt his fangs, had to have seen his

glamour-free foreignness. They were in the midst of filming a vampire movie. How could she not jump to conclu-
sions? To his amazement, when he tried to read her, he still
couldn't penetrate that mysterious head of hers. He should
have been able to. He'd done more than the minimum for
forming a blood bond.

Once he'd drunk from Grace, Christian should have been
able to override any compulsion or protection Nim Wei had
put on her. The queen was strong, maybe stronger than he'd
comprehended, but as far as he could tell, she hadn't bitten
Grace. Something else was keeping him out, possibly the
same force that had seized control of his body inside the car.

Struck by the idea, Christian rose uneasily from the
couch. He was naked. He'd torn off his clothes as hastily as
he had Grace's, and they lay in untidy heaps in her living
room. Grace, apparently, wasn't used to nude males. She
rolled onto her side to watch him.

The attention flattered him until she spoke.

"What's wrong?" she asked.

He turned to her and, for a small space of time, got a bit
distracted. Over the centuries, he'd seen plenty of naked
females, but those females weren't Grace. Her human skin
was all cream and roses, especially her nipples . . .

"Christian?"

He dragged his eyes to her face. "Do you ever feel like a
guardian angel is watching over you?"

Grace's laugh was a rush of air through her nose.
"Hardly. Why do you ask?"

*Because someone helped me save you tonight. Because
back when you haunted my mortal life, you spoke of a
heavenly guide.*

Nim Wei had been able to read his mind when he'd
been human, with the exception of thoughts that involved
Grace. He'd never put much stock in Grace's talk of divine
assistance. Despite the faithfulness of the time he'd been

born to, or possibly because of it, hell had been easier to believe in.

Maybe he'd have to reconsider that.

Grace drew his attention by sitting up. Somewhat pointlessly, she pulled a small Chinese pillow into her lap. "You're thinking something very strange, Christian. You should see the expressions crossing your face."

"I hardly know what I'm thinking," he said.

"Well, you should dress," she replied, reluctantly setting aside the pillow as she rose to search out her clothes. "I know I'm as much to blame as you are for what we did tonight, but I'd prefer it if people didn't know you'd been here."

Before Christian could formulate a response, she lifted her blouse from behind a lamp. She stared at it with her mouth open. The white cotton was in shreds, as if an animal had clawed it off her. Christian had enough of her blood in him that he blushed. He'd exercised even less control than he'd thought. He was probably lucky he'd stopped drinking when he did.

Grace blinked and set the tattered blouse aside, one more piece of evidence she was going to ignore. "I hope your clothes are in better shape," she said.

Anger flared inside him. "I don't need them. I'm not leaving you alone."

"You're not staying over."

"Grace, someone shot at you."

"We don't know that."

"*I* know that!" he said. "I read it straight from the shooter's mind!"

"Christian, I see you're taking this Method acting business seriously, staying in character and all, but—"

He cut her off with an infuriated snarl. "I'm not leaving you tonight."

Grace folded her arms underneath her breasts, which did nothing for his already fragmented concentration. "If you're that worried, why not call the police?"

"The police can't protect you as well as I can."

"Christian."

"I'm not leaving. *You* call the police if you want my naked body out of here that badly."

At last, he'd hit on the right riposte. She turned red, huffed in a flustered way, then stomped out of the room. She returned, dressed in pajamas, with a blanket and two pillows.

"You bled on the couch," she said. "You'll just have to lie in it."

Her snit would have been more convincing if her gaze hadn't drifted to his cock and widened. He'd risen again, fully and with fervor. His kind didn't take long to recuperate, particularly after they'd fed.

Grace shoved the bed things at him. "You keep that . . . that *prodigy* away from me, you hear?"

He was grinning as she flounced back into her bedroom and slammed the door. One kiss would have had her sighing for him again, one touch of his practiced fingers.

Some facts of life even Grace Michaels couldn't deny.

Christian's face haunted Grace all night; the rest of him as well, actually. He was beautiful without his clothes on, shining and white and strong. She fell into one dream of him after another, reliving his strange but exciting bite, his forceful movements when they made love, his cries as he found pleasure. The thickness of his cock was a fantasy by itself. Each time she shuddered awake amidst her tangled covers, she verged on coming. How she mustered the strength not to go to him, she would never know.

Despite all this nocturnal drama, she woke as if she'd had the best night's sleep of her life.

It was just past dawn, and she was starving. When she tiptoed into the living room, Christian was sound asleep on her couch. He'd found a second blanket somewhere, and both were pulled up over his head.

He's here! something stupidly girlish inside her sang. *He stayed with me all night.*

A flush she didn't think was arousal swept over her. Her heart and not her lust was rejoicing in his presence. She wanted to crawl under those blankets with him, wanted to snuggle close to him forever.

Then her stomach growled, reminding her ideas like that were neither smart nor practical.

She fixed herself a proper breakfast: not just coffee but eggs and bacon and buttered toast. She mixed some frozen orange juice for good measure and drank down two glasses. None of her clanking around woke Christian, which she might have secretly hoped she'd do.

He didn't stir until she was slipping quietly out the door.

"Hold it right there," he snapped, so much authority in the froggy order that her muscles froze. "You're not going anywhere without me."

"I left a note saying when and where you're working today."

"Screw the bloody note," he growled.

Did Texans say *bloody*? she wondered.

"Wait for me," he said, grabbing his clothes and heading for her bathroom. "I'll be ready in five minutes."

In her experience, attractive men as young as he was took longer to primp than that. The water in her shower turned on, then shut off before it had the slightest chance to warm up. Her medicine cabinet opened and shut, but she held on to her patience. She was glad she had when she discovered Miss Wei hadn't come home last night. Christian's was the only car she had access to.

"Let's go," he said, zipping his motorcycle jacket up his bare chest. Aside from his missing T-shirt, last night might not have happened. He didn't have a scratch on him. Not a scab from being shot or any signs of lingering weakness. If he'd stepped under her icy shower, he'd managed not to dampen his hair. His eyes were sleepy, but the rest of him appeared as hale and hearty as she was.

Oddly, he smelled of the fancy French sun cream she'd treated herself to last summer.

"Where are your sunglasses?" she asked him dazedly.

He pulled them from a pocket and put them on. He looked so handsome with his dark eyes hidden that her mouth watered.

Grace couldn't think of anything else to say until they reached his car. Before her mouth could do more than open, he tossed her the T-Bird's keys. Grace's heart jumped as she caught them.

"You can't hover over me forever," she asserted, aware that her indignation was somewhat tinged with delight.

Christian was already slouched in the passenger seat, his cowboy hat securely planted over his face. "You've got the wheel, little lady. That means I'm just along for the ride."

She knew there were holes in his argument, but she grabbed the chance to drive anyway. They were on the highway, and she was stroking her neck absently, before she realized his bite hadn't left any more mark on her than being shot had on him.

Twelve

One thing Nim Wei knew about making movies: it wasn't a job for those who couldn't stand ups and downs. They'd had a decent final night of shooting at their suburban location, mostly shots of Christian's movie father lurking in the shadows while Joe and Mary said goodbye in front of her parents' home. Because that had gone smoothly, Nim Wei let Grace take over. The girl had done second unit work on *It Came from Venus*, directing less-important scenes that had to get in the can in a tight time frame. Grace could oversee Mary's disapproving mother dragging her daughter up their front walk, away from her new hoodlum friend. The actress who played Delia Reed hadn't appreciated being handed off, but that made no never mind. Delia Reed was supposed to be pinchy-mouthed. Even if Grace got nervous, Wade was behind the camera. The brilliant and kind DP would ensure she kept her footing.

So all that had been lovely. Delia was in a serendipitous foul mood, and Grace was excited, the tension she'd displayed the other day dissolved. Nim Wei congratulated herself for that. Being thrown into taking charge always brought out the best in her assistant. The down to the up came when their location scout stepped into Nim Wei's mobile office with his report.

"You can't be serious," Nim Wei said from behind her Scandinavian-style blond-wood desk. "How difficult can it be to find one big tree with red leaves?"

"Autumn in California can be tricky. I've been looking up in the hills. Hell, I've recruited a network of leaf scouts. So far we haven't struck pay dirt."

"Which means we might have to resort to spray painting one."

The scout shrugged at her. In the not-so-old days, she'd have put the fear of God in him for his failure. Too bad humans didn't work as well as vampires when they were terrified.

"Fine," she said. "Let me know me when you have a good candidate. If we need to, we'll drop everything and go where you are."

The scout gave her a salute.

"I should put the fear of God in Mother Nature," Nim Wei muttered to herself. She noticed Christian coming in as the scout went out. Once again, he'd declined to let her secretary announce him. Since she'd refrained from thralling Melody except in emergencies, his lack of consideration irritated her.

"Lord," Nim Wei said, her bad mood in need of venting. "Next you'll be telling me I have to spray paint you."

Christian raised his eyebrows. He didn't need spray painting. His glamour was in place, and he was a natural human color. "I'd rather speak to you about Grace. I need your help convincing her of something."

His ramrod stiffness told her how intensely he didn't want to ask for her assistance. That, at least, cheered her up.

"Go ahead," she said.

"Grace needs to let me continue staying at her cottage. She's threatening to check into a hotel if I don't stop crowding her."

He needed to *continue* staying at her cottage? Was that the reason for the change she'd noticed in Grace tonight? She'd had a determined, militant gleam to her—as if she'd taken one of Dr. Rupert's vitamin shots. Being bitten did things like that to humans, once they'd gotten over their lassitude. An unexpected discomfort tightened Nim Wei's ribs. She hadn't realized Grace and Christian had reached that stage of intimacy—though she hadn't doubted they would eventually.

All this ran through her mind in a twinkling, the little pang swiftly subsumed by calculations of how to best exploit the development. She folded her hands on the smooth pale wood of her desk.

"Christian, as much as I want you to be a happy member of my cast, I'm not sure I should interfere in Grace's decisions concerning who she sleeps with."

"Someone took a shot at her," he said.

Nim Wei's face went cold. "Took a shot, as in *with a gun*?"

"Yes."

"But who? Grace doesn't have enemies."

Christian's expression was grim even for him. "If I knew who was behind it, they'd be dead already. I'd follow her to any hotel, of course, but I'd rather guard her with you nearby."

This was no small concession, and it was made with no small passion—bottled up though it was. Obviously, she hadn't been paying sufficient attention to the depth of Christian's attachment to her assistant. But better not to comment until her own thoughts about the matter were more ordered.

"I'll speak to her," she said.

"Convince her," Christian insisted, his eyes flaring.

As a rule, Nim Wei didn't tolerate demands. Christian

was her subject and Grace her human to protect; her friend, if she was allowed to flatter herself. Nonetheless, she felt confident the icy-hearted mercenary would lay down his life for her assistant. Which was as it should be, of course.

"I'll convince her," she promised. "Until this threat is negated, you're Grace's new roommate."

Thirteen

❦

Grace was once again behind the wheel of Miss Wei's two-toned pink Plymouth—though Miss Wei wasn't in it this morning. Ever since she'd ordered Grace to let Christian breathe down her neck, Grace's boss had been getting rides to the set from Wade. She claimed it was so she and the cinematographer could go over the day's setups, but Grace knew that wasn't the reason.

Miss Wei realized how furious Grace was and didn't want to be shut up in a car with her.

For one whole week, Christian hadn't left her side long enough to return to his hotel. On the second night he made his bed on her couch, his man Roy came by with a small black bag of "necessities," saying he'd be back when he thought Christian needed more.

Whatever the satchel held, it wasn't clothes. Those Roy had handed over in two brown grocery bags, which Christian—without asking permission—had stashed in her coat closet. If Grace hadn't had the consideration to hang them up, his nice new things would have turned into a solid mass of wrinkles.

She reminded herself it *was* fury she was feeling. Not increased sexual temptation. Not grudging gratitude for Christian's misplaced dedication to her safety. Though he'd been high-handed, he was also patient with her bad temper, never losing his own and not pushing her to be intimate again. No, all he'd done was stare at her with those cold-hot eyes and stroll around her house with his torso bare. The constant glimpses of male muscle made her mouth water. Each time his biceps flexed, she grew more certain he was doing it on purpose.

Her neck was stiff from the effort it took not to glance sideways at him now, and never mind that his shirt was on. She was driving him and his boys—Charlie, Matthew, and Philip—to the studio soundstage. There, they'd film interior scenes set in George Pryor's run-down mansion. If she'd had her way, she'd have stuck Christian in the back; he'd been the last one ready. Sadly, his boys had decided he truly was their leader, and they'd saved the front seat for him.

Christian was his usual laconic morning self, silent and still behind his Ray-Bans and cowboy hat. Also per usual, he reeked of Coppertone. Apparently, he intended to cultivate an authentic vampire pallor.

Grace bit her lip to conceal a smile. His unexpected devotion to his role, after having had to be sold on it, really was amusing.

As if he sensed he wasn't tormenting her enough, Christian looked at her. A wash of heat swallowed her. Thankfully, they were at a stoplight on Sunset, and she didn't crash into the bumper ahead of her. The car behind her only honked once before she noticed the light was green.

"What I'm wondering," Matthew said from the back, continuing a conversation he and Philip had been having about their roles, "is why we're wearing each other's shoes. The script makes such a point about it. We've both got one blue sneaker and one black the first time we're seen onscreen."

"I think we're color blind," Philip said. "We've done it by mistake."

"Or it's an Ibsen thing: there just to be absurd."

"Feet are the symbolic fount of understanding. Maybe it's supposed to mean we have a telepathic bond."

"I don't know how to play telepathic," Matthew said worriedly.

"Oh, please," Christian interrupted. "Your characters aren't telepathic; they're homosexual."

"We are not!" Philip objected.

"You are," Christian said. "You're wearing each other's shoes because it would cause a ruckus if you exchanged jewelry. It's your way of being close to each other."

Philip turned to her to settle the dispute. "Grace, tell him he's wrong."

"Um." Grace squirmed in the front seat. "I'm afraid that was also my impression from the initial script."

Matthew threw his hands in the air. "So then my interpretation is all screwed up!"

"It's not screwed up," Grace soothed his reflection in the rearview mirror. "It just has a new subtext. I'm sure Miss Wei doesn't want you to flounce around. You and Philip are best friends. You love each other that way first."

"Being gay would explain your fondness for playing chess," Charlie put in puckishly.

"Chess isn't gay," Matthew said.

"Chess is extremely gay," Charlie teased. "It's all about capturing the queen."

He must have made some rude gesture, because Matthew smacked the side of his head.

"*Scheisse*," Christian muttered as the three boys started wrestling like twelve-year-olds.

"I'm driving here," Grace reminded, but the tussling only got wilder.

"Hey!" Christian barked in a hard, low tone.

It was as if a master dog trainer had brought out a rolled-up newspaper. All three boys sat up and settled.

"Sorry, Grace," Charlie apologized. His hazel eyes were twinkling, but Grace nodded anyway.

"Just in time," she said, pulling up to Celestial's golden gate. The guard waved at her from his booth, and she drove onto the lot, enjoying the quiet in the car until she reached the warehouselike soundstage they were using. A giant tarp-covered backdrop was being carried by a dozen men through the street ahead. Grace caught a peek at a blazing sunset under the canvas, probably destined for some characters to ride into.

Enchanted by the reminder of the magic they were here to make, she twisted in her seat and smiled at her passengers. "All right, you guys, break a leg today."

"You're not coming with us?" Christian exclaimed.

"I can't," Grace said, her shoulders bracing. "I have an errand to run."

"That is *not* acceptable," Christian said.

From the corner of her eye, Grace saw the boys glance from her to Christian and then at each other. Their brows began to wag as they deduced their relationship must have changed—precisely what Grace hadn't wanted to happen.

"I'll be in public," she said as levelly as she could. "In broad daylight. And Miss Wei knows I'm going."

"Clearly, Miss Wei doesn't take your safety as seriously as I do."

"There hasn't been an incident in a week."

"There was an incident?" Charlie asked.

Christian didn't bother to answer. He was too busy glaring at her from under his Stetson's brim. Even his irritation was sexy. Grace willed her cheeks not to redden.

"I need to do my job. And you need to do yours."

"*Grace*," he warned, a rumble darkening the sound.

"Stop smothering me!" she cried. "I'll run my errand, and I'll come straight here. I won't be more than an hour."

Christian pointed his finger of doom at her. "An hour is all I'm giving you. I'll come after you if you make me."

He swung out of the car before she could come up with a retort. *I'm not a child, you caveman,* didn't hit the right professional note for her. The other boys got out more slowly than Christian had.

"Boy," Charlie said as he shut the door. "Love can be a real pooper."

Grace did her best to ignore Charlie's observation. Yes, she was stupidly attracted to Christian, maybe even romantically addled. That, however, didn't mean she was in love. It wasn't her fault Charlie was too young to tell the difference.

"A total baby," she assured herself as she parked the car across the street from the typing service's glass storefront.

She was here to pick up fresh pages for the movie's climactic scene. Miss Wei had decided Charlie and not Matthew ought to be the friend Christian's father killed, and had asked Grace for a rewrite. Grace had understood her reasoning. Ever since Charlie crashed the motorcycle, Christian had developed a rapport with the smart-mouthed boy. Their star would naturally be more affected by playing out a death scene with him. Unfortunately, this meant Matthew was going to be crushed. He'd been looking forward to expiring cinematically.

True to form, Miss Wei couldn't simply tell everyone. She'd asked Grace to keep the switch a secret, refusing to have her own secretary type the changes for fear of the news leaking. The choice was probably strategic, to keep Charlie from overthinking or Christian from preparing for the shock ahead of time. Miss Wei was no coward, but sometimes she did things too indirectly for Grace's taste. She tended to treat her actors like chess pieces rather than human beings.

But that was her right as the boss. Resigned, Grace pushed through the jingling door to the typing place. The bored, gum-chewing girl behind the counter had her job ready, mimeographs and all. Grace signed for it and tucked the box underneath her arm. Her watch still missing, she glanced at the wall clock before she left. She was finished earlier than anticipated. If she wanted, she could go have coffee; use up the full hour Christian had *allotted* her.

Knowing she wouldn't, she dashed back across the two lanes of traffic, grimacing wryly. Her work ethic was too strong for that sort of childishness.

As she reached the opposite sidewalk, she noticed a tall dark-haired man leaning on the front grill of the Fury. Alarm ran through her in a sharp ripple. The man was Adam Chelsea, *Teen-Age Vampire*'s original screenwriter.

It occurred to her that he had a grudge against her. He could have broken into her cottage, maybe even taken a shot at her. The latter seemed unlikely, though the possibility was sufficient to slow her steps. Sympathy warred with caution inside her gut. Adam Chelsea was an uncomfortable person to be around. Being organized enough to kill someone seemed beyond him, but Grace supposed she shouldn't bet her life on it.

He straightened his rail-thin frame when he spotted her. He looked worse than when she'd last seen him: shaggy hair uncombed, clothing rumpled, big dark circles shadowing his eyes. He smelled like he was still showering, but maybe not this morning. Her grip tightened on the box of script pages.

"Adam," she said gently, her heart as always going out to him. "You know Miss Wei doesn't like it when you talk to me."

"You have to help me," he said in his intense way, as if every word were a matter of life and death. "No one else will return my calls. No one else understands."

Grace wasn't sure why he thought she did, but there

seemed no point in saying that. "I can't change the script back, Adam. Audiences wouldn't have watched it the way it was."

"You took out half the characters! Their story needs to be told. You know they deserve it. You had to have recognized them when you read what I wrote."

Adam's right hand was jammed in the pocket of his frayed sport coat. He was holding something whose tip stuck through the tweed in a silver point. Her heart abruptly in her throat, Grace took a careful step back from him. This side of the street contained a small grassy park, but the only person in it was a little boy and his dog. If she ran down the sidewalk, she was pretty sure Adam would catch her.

When she spoke, her voice shook more than she wanted. "Maybe we should go have coffee. Talk this through like reasonable people."

"No," he growled and lunged forward.

He was strong for a skinny guy, his long arms grabbing and shoving her easily into the backseat of Miss Wei's Fury. Her box of copies fell into the gutter along the way. To her dismay, Adam crowded into the car after her. She didn't have a chance to get out the opposite door.

"Stop that!" she shouted, but not loudly enough. One female pedestrian turned to look, then simply walked faster. Grace's pulse went crazy as Adam pulled out his knife. Though it wasn't huge, it seemed plenty sharp, especially when he pressed it against her neck. When Grace swallowed, she nicked herself on the point.

"*You* stop," he said. "You know what I wrote was true."

"Vampires aren't real, Adam."

"Vampires don't matter!" His expression was as wild as if he were the one cornered. "Hans mattered. And Michael and William. You erased them!"

"I'll put them back," she promised. "Let me go so I can."

For a moment, she thought he might. He sat back a little,

the knife easing off her throat. Tears welled on the lower lids of his eyes. Ridiculously, she saw his lashes were pretty.

"Don't lie to me," he said in a leaden tone. "Those were people I used to love."

I'm not going to drop you," Christian said patiently for the second time.

He and George, his movie father—the slightly washed-up star of black-and-white Westerns—were running through the blocking for their first confrontation scene. Nim Wei thought it would be more dynamic if Joe responded to George's shove by thrusting his father into a chair, which he would then tip onto the ground. As long as George trusted Christian to hold his weight, there'd be no risk of injury.

"We can call your stunt double," Nim Wei offered, but not as if she wanted George to accept.

"I don't need a goddamned stunt double," he blustered. "I've been taking falls since this yahoo was in diapers."

"Then what's the problem?" Nim Wei inquired.

"The problem is you want my son here to get the best of me. It's too early in the story for him to pull that off."

"It's not too early for him to be stronger than you. Kids his age can often overpower their fathers, though I admit Joe doesn't know for certain if he can at this point. What it's too early for him to do is go full-out toe-to-toe with you. That's why, as soon as he has you on the ground, he'll back off, thereby proving he's not ready to depose the corrupt king."

"I don't know . . ." George said, wagging his handsomely silvered head.

Christian took a literal step back from their debate. George had disliked him ever since Christian had nearly barreled him over on his hasty exit from the read-through. Given that this was so, George and Nim Wei would settle the issue quicker without his input.

The pair had lowered their voices, so he wandered toward the wall of the Victorian parlor. In person, the stage set seemed staged: no ceiling, no next room adjoining it, acetate curtains standing in for silk. On film, he'd been assured it would all look real. He supposed he'd find out when he saw it.

He rubbed the back of his neck, aware that a pointless tension was knotting there. Grace wasn't due back yet, and Nim Wei had confirmed she'd sent her on an errand. Christian was an adult. He'd get through a morning of shooting without Grace to cosset him.

Then a flashbulb seemed to go off inside his skull, exploding through his normal guards against intrusion. Before the brilliant light could fade, he saw Grace cowering in the backseat of Nim Wei's car. A man he didn't recognize was looming over her, holding her at knifepoint. Grace was trying to convince him of something as fear-sweat rolled down her face.

Christian was shaking when the strange and too-brief vision snapped away. Without a true blood bond between him and Grace, he doubted he'd see more. To be honest, he was surprised he'd seen as much as he had.

"Where is she?" he demanded hoarsely of Nim Wei. "Where exactly did you send Grace today?"

She told him with a succinctness he appreciated, then began to ask what was wrong.

Christian didn't stop to answer. He barely had the restraint to duck behind the set's fake walls before he sped away. He hoped no one had seen, but that wasn't his first concern. He wasn't going to lose Grace. Not again.

Not ever, if he had his way.

He'd have been faster if it were dark, but Christian still reached Grace within five minutes. The god-awful pink car was parked across the street from the address Nim Wei had given him. Traveling so quickly while the sun was up left him dizzy and panting. Ignoring that, he bounded over and through the traffic. It barely took a second to yank the Fury's street-side door open and haul Grace out to safety.

He doubted her attacker saw more than a smear of color.

"Christian!" Grace exclaimed as he let her settle to her feet in the little palm-dotted park.

Her hands were on his chest, her eyes wide with shock. He couldn't have stopped himself from embracing her. He was going to hold her like this forever, was going to rock her and stroke her and press his trembling lips into the cool red waves of her hair. Grace seemed agreeable with his plan. She hugged him back for a good half minute. She made him glad his jacket was unzipped.

"I knew you'd save me," she said against his white T-shirt. "I wasn't half as afraid as I should have been."

He kissed her temple and let out a little growl. He hated that she'd been afraid at all. "Let me get you away from here. I'll come back and deal with that man."

Grace pushed away from him, her hands covering her mouth. "My copies, Christian! I have to rescue them from the gutter."

Christian tensed as he registered the man who'd threatened Grace coming up behind him. Christian didn't care that he spun too quickly for a human, as long as he shielded Grace. Her attacker was tall and gangly, thirty or thereabouts. He still carried the knife, but as if he'd forgotten what it was for. Grace's hands knotted on the back of Christian's jacket. Christian hoped she'd stay where she was, though the man didn't seem to pose an immediate threat. For a crazed assailant, the dawning wonderment on his face was odd.

"Christian?" he said when he was a few feet away. "What are you doing here?"

Despite the brightness of the day, Christian felt as if he'd been plunged into ice water. Was this *another* soul returned from his past? He racked his mind for which enemy it might be. Timkin, his father's assassin? Lavaux, who'd been good with blades? Or maybe his sire himself had returned again.

"It's me," the man he was facing said. "It's Charles."

Christian was stupefied. This wretched soul was *Charles*? His friend Charles, who'd once been the merriest person he knew? The actor who played Charlie in the movie looked a hundred times more like him—felt a hundred times more like him, for that matter.

"I know," the man said, seeing his doubt. "I'm called Adam now, and I don't look much like I did. You, though . . . my God, you take me back to those days."

"He's Adam Chelsea," Grace whispered behind Christian's shoulder. "He wrote the original screenplay."

Christian didn't have much time to absorb this. Adam frowned at Grace, which caused Christian to bristle. Adam shifted his gaze back to Christian and rubbed his forehead. The gesture would have been innocent if he hadn't used the hand that still held the knife. Christian was wound up like a watch by then. Grace caressed his arm as if she wanted him to calm down.

"She was there, too," Adam said in bewilderment. "She should believe me."

"Let's call the police," Grace murmured. "You don't need to fight him. He ought to be in a hospital."

Christian's heart broke without warning. Maybe Adam was troubled, but he was right. Grace should have believed him. When she'd come to Christian as a spirit all those centuries ago, it had taken her a while to learn to be visible to his friends. Once she had, she and Charles had gotten along. Charles had charmed her with his wit and humor, as he had most females.

Christian didn't think that happened so often now.

"You can help me, can't you?" Adam/Charles asked. "Get the bitch queen to listen? She was there, too, but no one can count on her to be fair. She's trampled so many people I don't think she keeps track of them anymore."

Christian startled himself by laughing. Charles' grasp of Nim Wei's nature was sad and funny at the same time.

"I can help," he said quietly.

"Oh, good," Charles responded. "I really want our friends back in the movie."

The person Charles had become certainly was focused. He looked hopefully up at Christian as Christian took his face in his hands. Touching him was a little shock. Despite the changes in friend, his energy did feel familiar.

"Just be calm," Christian said, "and look straight into my eyes."

Because it was daytime, if Charles had resisted, this might have been difficult. Luckily, his old companion didn't fight the eye lock, but stood passively under it. Christian got the impression Charles had been longing for someone to take control of him for a while.

He schooled his own mind to stillness, ignoring the emotions that wanted to boil up in him. Only if he was tranquil would his thrall have a chance to work.

"It's time to let go," he said. "Your memories of our old life aren't as important as you think they are."

"But they're true," Charles said unsurely.

"It's also true that you're a new person. You need to build a new life. Leave Grace and the movie people alone. Find peace inside yourself."

Charles' mouth had fallen open. "You used to be my friend."

"Trust me, Adam, I'm being your friend now."

Charles stared at Christian. He didn't have the dazed look most humans got when they were caught in an *upyr*'s thrall. Of course, Charles had looked dazed before. Maybe it made sense for him to be clearer now.

"I *think* I could let go," he said slowly. "Maybe I could write about something else. Werewolves are interesting."

Christian smiled and slid his hands to Adam's shoulders. He gave their bony breadth a squeeze. Even in the short time they'd been talking, Adam's aura had strengthened. "Take care of yourself, old friend."

"I will," Adam said, then looked embarrassed. "Could you loan me money for a cab home?"

Christian handed him every bill in his wallet.

"I'm not broke," Adam said, passing half of it back. He leaned a bit around Christian so he could catch Grace's gaze. "Sorry, Grace. I won't . . . bother you again."

They watched Adam walk away, a slender figure in wrinkled clothes, halfway broken but dignified. He flagged down a cab and got into it, turning to look at Christian as it drove off. Christian wondered if he'd see him again. If the thrall had done its job, he might not. He pressed one fist to the hollow spot in his chest. When he turned to Grace, she was swiping a tear from her eye. She'd sensed this moment was sad even if she didn't recall the reason. Maybe she was embarrassed to be seen crying. She dropped her gaze to the grass.

"That was nice of you to say those things to him," she said. "But do you really think it's enough to turn him around?"

"He wasn't the man who shot at you."

True to form, Grace's brows lowered stubbornly. "We don't know anyone shot at me, but Adam still pulled a knife. What if he does something like that again?"

"He'll take care of himself." Christian was positive of this much. "If that means going to a head doctor, he'll do it."

He did wonder at himself for not expunging Adam's memories. Erasing them would have removed the danger once and for all. Was he too attached to the past himself? Had he wanted his old friend to continue remembering him, even if it left Adam unhappy? Christian had never asked himself these questions. Was he wrong to push Grace to reclaim her memories?

"Werewolves," Grace broke into his thoughts with a shaky laugh. "Adam isn't a bad writer. Maybe he'll do better telling stories about them."

Christian caught Grace's arm as she began to walk

toward the car. "Grace, when you first got the script from Adam, were there vampires in it?"

"There were twice as many. Why do you ask?"

He asked because Charles hadn't lived long enough to see Christian change. That being so, why recast Christian's life to include the fanged? It couldn't be a coincidence. Was Adam so sensitive to what lay beyond ordinary reality that he had access to more than the facts of his former life? Maybe more to the point, if he were that sensitive, would he willingly give it up? Was Adam, in his own way, living the life he chose?

"It's nothing," he said, shaking his head. He slid his arm around Grace's back, hugging her to him. "Let's get those copies you dropped, and I'll drive us back to the studio. Nim Wei must be ready to draw and quarter me by now."

Grace handed him the keys without argument.

"Christian?" she asked once they were in motion. "How did you know I was in trouble?"

He supposed it was a sign of progress that she was curious.

"I'll always know," he said, laying his hand gently on her knee. "I'll always know, and I'll always come."

He felt oddly better for saying it, as if—like Adam— he was releasing a burden that weighed on him. Whether Grace felt better for hearing his promise, he truly could not have said.

Fourteen

The first thing Christian did after driving himself and Grace to the studio was have a fight with Nim Wei. She was quite irate that he hadn't told her Grace was in danger.

"I should have known," she said, pacing the soundstage break room with her little hands fisted. Christian was glad he'd pulled her there. Her glamour was fraying, her true face shining out enough to risk exposure. Fairy tales were written for looks like hers: empresses of snow with dangerous ruby lips. Seeming unaware of this, she spun to confront Christian. "How is it that *you* knew she needed help?"

Christian sat back on a bright orange table that was littered with coffee mugs. In spite of the circumstances, he enjoyed watching the queen lose her cool. "Adam nicked her throat. It must have activated our blood bond."

"I should kill that nutcase. I can't believe you just let him go."

"Adam felt compelled to defend the script because he

remembered our former life. He wasn't murderous; he was obsessed."

Nim Wei pulled a dismissive face and strode angrily the other way—too angrily, he guessed. She cursed as the stiletto heel of her right shoe snapped. Judging she was off balance in more ways than one, he decided to see if she'd give him a straight answer. "What was Grace's reaction when she read Adam's version of the script?"

"And how is that your business?" the queen inquired frostily. "Oh, *fine*." She kicked off her second shoe to stand barefoot. "She said his story caught her imagination. She thought if we simplified it, it would catch other people's, too."

"She didn't mention it seemed familiar?"

"So, you're claiming you knew Grace, too? You think she was your medieval laundress, or what have you? I introduced you to her, Durand. She's *my* assistant. You should have told me *she was in trouble!*"

Nim Wei astonished him by grabbing an empty coffee carafe and flinging it at him. Christian was fortunate he ducked. When the glass hit the wall, it didn't shatter; it vaporized.

A heartbeat later, the door opened.

"Everything okay in here?" Grace asked.

Nim Wei was so far from looking human that she had to turn away. "Everything is fine," she said tightly.

Grace shifted her gaze to him. There was no bracing for the effect she had. The moment their eyes met, a gear fell into place inside him. The clockwork of his soul was abruptly turning the way it should: sweetly, smoothly, no more grinding over his fate. It occurred to him that he'd never had a hope of revenging himself on her. This small sign of the link between them was all it took for the half-person he'd been so long to feel whole.

"The crew is set up for the scene," she said softly.

"We'll be out," Christian answered just as gently. "Give us five minutes."

She held his look and nodded. As she shut the door, he realized he'd confirmed an important fact.

Nim Wei had no memory of Grace's life as a ghost. She remained unaware that Grace had witnessed the role she'd played in his friends' murders. When and if Grace retrieved those memories, he suspected they wouldn't be as conveniently fuzzy as Nim Wei's were.

As if their director's surly mood were catching, the actors took forever to settle and hit their marks. Matthew and Philip continued to brood over the black and blue shoe issue, Charlie caught a case of the giggles, and Grace lost track of how many takes they shot for Joe and George's first scuffle. The upside was that, with so much footage, they'd be able to cobble something together in the editing room—or so Wade reminded her when they wrapped. Even he looked weary when he said it.

"I'll see that the boys and Naomi have rides," he told her. "You take care of yourself tonight."

Grace was glad for the favor. This was one of those times she wished Miss Wei would just hire a fleet of drivers. She was running on fumes by the time Christian drove them home.

It disturbed her that she was thinking of it like that— as if this cottage, which didn't belong to her, were her and Christian's honeymooners' nest. She couldn't afford to do that. She knew it didn't pay to count on other people in the long run, no matter how reliable they seemed in the short.

"Grace?" Christian was holding her door open. This would have been more helpful if she'd had the energy to get out of the convertible.

"You know," she said, "it's very annoying that you get more sprightly as the night goes on."

Christian's mouth curved in the gentle smile she'd been seeing lately, the one that made her heart twist recklessly in her breast. With a little bow, he offered his hand. "You should see how annoying you are first thing in the morning."

"We're oil and water," she informed him, to which he replied, "Opposites attract."

He unlocked the cottage door for her, familiar with her keys by now. She knew she shouldn't feel a blossom of warmth at that, but she did anyway. He helped her collapse into a chair at her kitchen table, then began opening cabinets. Was he planning to cook for her? She was extremely touched . . . until she recalled the unpalatable coffee he'd served her at his house. She wasn't sure the box of dried pasta he was pulling out would be safe.

"I'm too tired to eat," she groaned.

Christian leaned into her refrigerator. "I can boil water. You had a fright this morning and a long day. That can tire anyone. Eating will help you recuperate. Don't you have tomato sauce in a jar?"

When he turned to her, his face was worried—boyishly so.

"What is it?" Grace asked.

He pressed his slashing lips together. "I want you," he admitted. "This morning, I was afraid I'd lost you. I've been thinking about being with you all day. I don't know if I can stop myself from seducing you."

In any other man, the suggestion that she wouldn't have had the strength to refuse him would have been egotistical. Coming from him, it made the flesh between her legs ache. A resigned sigh gusted out of her.

"I don't want to hurt you," he said. "What if I can't control my instincts?"

His gaze drifted to her neck, and he wet his lips. Tiredness forgotten, Grace's sex began to pulse harder. She shouldn't encourage him, but—God—she wanted him to take her, in whatever eccentric manner revved his engine.

"We could call for takeout," she said.

His eyes were blazing when they rose to hers, his hands balling into fists. She actually saw the cloth of his zipper rise.

"Grace," he rasped. "If I don't fuck you in the next five minutes, I'm going to die."

Her kitchen wall phone started ringing the instant he took a stride toward her. Grace didn't know whether to laugh or cry.

"Damn it," Christian cursed.

"I'll get it," she said. "It could be Miss Wei."

"Stay," he barked, already picking it up.

His face changed as the person on the other end spoke to him, his eyebrows lifting briefly before his expression went marble still. For a moment, the clean lines of his profile mesmerized her. Then she shook herself.

"Who is it?" she asked.

His long-fingered hand covered the mouthpiece. "Sorry," he said. "It's for me."

Despite her obvious exhaustion, Grace was polite enough to get up and leave the room. Christian waited until he heard her bedroom door close.

"Why are you calling me here?" he asked Graham.

"Roy told me where to reach you. We've got some new anti-tapping technology. No one can listen in."

"O-kay," Christian said, hoping to hasten him along by not answering too much.

Naturally Graham sensed this. "I'm sorry, Christian," he chaffed him. "Am I keeping you from something?"

"Please just tell me what you found out."

"Quite a few things, as it happens. First of all, Grace Michaels' name is really Grace Gladwell. Born in Arizona to George and Helen, after which she moved around a lot."

"Her father's name was George?"

"That mean anything to you?"

Only that she—or Adam—had given her father's name to *his* father in the movie. He forced an unpleasant shiver not to rise up his spine.

"I don't know," he said. "What else?"

"Well, one of her parents—probably George—must be a piece of work. Medical records show a history of hospitalizations for broken bones dating back to Grace's childhood and culminating in her having to be resuscitated from a serious head injury."

"She mentioned that."

"It's worth a mention. Grace Gladwell was absent from the living for six minutes. Her recovery was sufficiently remarkable that the fellow who drove the ambulance still remembers it. To hear him tell it, the medics were surprised by her return from the dead. Evidently, you two have something in common."

Christian didn't laugh. The puzzle pieces snapping together inside his head robbed him of his humor. Six minutes was a long time to cross the Veil, maybe long enough to become a spirit. Did time exist in the afterlife? Did it possibly follow different rules? If Grace had traveled backward, it would explain the strange way she'd sometimes talked, as well as her vagueness concerning her origins. His ghostly Grace might have thought he wouldn't believe she'd come from the future—not on top of everything else.

"Christian?" Graham asked at his long silence.

"Shh," he said and pressed his skull back against the wall.

Maybe when Grace was resuscitated, her spirit had been yanked back to her own time and her own body. Maybe she'd never meant to abandon him. His heart pounded at the possibility. From what he'd seen, most humans weren't like Adam. They forgot their previous incarnations when they were reborn. Could Grace's return have erased her memory in a similar fashion? Did he in truth have nothing to reproach her for?

Did it matter if the answer to that was yes?

He already loved her. He already forgave her.

If he were honest, he owed her that. All those years ago she'd forgiven him. The bitch queen wasn't one to simply change a healthy male into a vampire. She'd made certain Christian enjoyed it. When Grace had read the signs of his perfidy, she'd still sworn to love him forever. He'd believed she'd broken that vow. Now it seemed he'd been wrong.

"Graham," he said, his voice rough with the emotions storming inside of him. Oddly for him, he was glad the other *upyr* was there, even if Christian wasn't listening to Graham's response. Graham was a friend, and this was a big moment. He stared at the plant-filled window above the sink, the side of his fist pressed hard to his mouth. He'd figured it out: how Grace could be the same Grace he'd known. Blinking for the first time in minutes, he let his hand relax.

"Graham," he said, this time very firmly. "Tell me you know where to find her father."

It didn't take more than Christian walking into her room for Grace's heart to speed up. She'd changed into her pajamas while he was on the phone. They were men's style and very modest: light blue cotton with white piping. She wore only panties underneath them, but she was lying on her stomach on the bedcovers. To her mind, nothing too interesting was revealed.

None of this mattered when he sat on the edge of the mattress and stroked her hair. The movement of his graceful hand caused sweat to prickle across her back—and never mind what his touch did to her nipples. She reminded herself she hadn't agreed to sleep with him tonight. He might have assumed she would because of her comment about the takeout, but the word yes hadn't officially left her lips.

Of course, the thought of saying no made her wriggle uncomfortably. One very persuasive part of her didn't understand why she was fighting this.

"Grace," Christian said, rubbing a circle on her back. "I need to ask you something."

The seriousness of his expression said this wasn't about sex. Grace sat up with her pillow hugged to her breasts. "Okay."

His hand shifted to caress the side of her face. He was looking at her mouth, and his lashes cast long shadows down his smooth cheekbones. She hoped he wasn't going to go off on one of his tangents. She'd rather he not be quirky now.

"Sweetheart," he said, "do you know where your father is?"

Grace's head reared back in surprise. "That call you took was about my father?"

A trace of humor slanted his mouth. "You can be quick when you want to. I don't imagine you'll like this, but I had a friend of mine look into your background. I know your name used to be Grace Gladwell. I know your father hurt you more than once. I think he might be behind the sniper who shot at you. That picture of you and Viv at the press conference was picked up by the tabloids."

Perspiration fogged across Grace's back for a new reason. It took some concentration to pick her jaw off the floor. "If your friend knows all that, why can't he tell you where George Gladwell is?"

Her voice was distant and tinny. Christian gathered her hands in his. "Your father dropped out of sight a few years ago. Stopped paying taxes or using his bank accounts."

"Maybe he changed his name."

"Maybe."

Christian's eyes were steady and kind. He'd looked at her caringly before this, but she thought there was something new in his gaze, something patient and accepting. He waited for her to absorb what he'd said.

"My father never paid me much attention, not unless I was right in front of him."

"He paid you enough attention to put you in the hospital seven times."

Had it been so many? Grace supposed she'd been too young to remember.

"Lots of times we didn't go," she admitted reluctantly. "When all I had were bruises. My mother used to say I was lucky I healed so well. Since I couldn't stay out of trouble, I could make up for it with that."

Christian eased the pillow from her grip and pulled her against him. Though his hold was loose, she sensed he wouldn't let go. Her cheek settled onto the stretch of his left shoulder. His plain white T-shirt, which he'd worn for filming, was as soft as swansdown. She noticed he smelled like a rain-swept pavement again.

"I wish I'd been there," he said, his cheek dragging in her hair. "I wish I'd been there for you."

Grace's palms tightened on his back. "I don't think he was the shooter. I think he poured himself into a bottle and never climbed out again."

"For his sake, he'd better hope that's true."

Something in his voice made her sit back. It wasn't anger; whatever darkened his tone ran deeper than that.

"I won't let him hurt you again," he said.

"You wouldn't . . ."

"I'd do whatever it took to stop him."

He sounded like a soldier saying he'd do his job.

"I haven't always been a rancher," he said.

She didn't ask him what else he'd been. She didn't know if he'd tell the truth or spin more fantasies. To her relief, nothing in his manner suggested he'd be rash.

"You shouldn't offer to do a thing like that for me. You could end up in jail."

He didn't argue, just cupped the side of her face, his steady gaze holding hers. In that moment, he seemed far older than his years. "Lie down, Grace. I'm going to sleep here tonight."

"But—"

"I won't push you. I'm just not leaving you alone."

This wasn't precisely what she wanted. Too embarrassed to be clearer, she lay down. Christian arranged himself behind her, grabbed the coverlet from the foot of the bed, then pulled her into the curve of his body. They fit together—maybe too well. She could feel the hard swell of his penis pushing eagerly at his jeans.

"Christian—"

"It's all right. I want you to sleep for now."

He slid his arm beneath her neck, the hardness of its muscles wrapped in the velvet warmth of his skin. Her body couldn't help but relax with him shielding her, though her excitement at being near him didn't completely fade. He seemed to notice her tension.

"If I could carry a tune, I'd sing you a lullaby," he said.

She had the oddest vision of herself humming "Bali Ha'i" from *South Pacific* while *her* body cradled his. This had never happened, but she felt as if it had. His heart beat against her back in a slow rhythm.

"I do . . . care about you," she admitted. "I wouldn't feel this safe in anyone else's arms."

His lungs let out a sigh as the arm he'd draped around her waist tightened.

"Good," he said.

The response was better than if he'd claimed to love her again. Strangely at peace, Grace closed her eyes and let herself drift away.

The swiftness with which Grace dropped off told Christian she'd needed rest. All the same, lying next to her while she slept was difficult. He loved her, and it was night, and all his reactions to her were sharp. *Upyr* weren't designed for abstinence—not when their appetites and affections were engaged. Grace smelled like heaven and warmed him like a fire. His body wanted to take possession of her in every way it could. His fangs were too sharp to grind his teeth together.

He withstood the torture for two hours, then rolled onto his side with his back to her. He'd long since unzipped his jeans to make room for his huge hard-on. He was glad for that as he pushed his hand into the opening. When he wrapped his fingers around his shaft, the compression felt too damn good. He probably should have left the bed. The instant he started tugging, he was going to wake Grace up with his moans.

He might have woken her already. The mattress creaked. She mumbled something and squirmed around, her warm, cushioned body now spooning his. Her little nose found the back of his neck and nuzzled—one advantage to having short hair, he guessed. Aroused by her new position, his cock pulsed crazily in his frozen hand. He tried to resign himself to waiting longer to ease himself, but Grace's touch slid down the arm he'd shoved into his jeans.

Every nerve came alive as her nails strafed his fine arm hairs. A bead of moisture rolled down his erection's tip.

It was immediately replaced by another one.

"Christian," she said sleepily. "Let me help you with this."

Her offer was a spear of delightful agony through his groin. He started to answer, to warn her that if she touched him, doing him by hand wouldn't be enough. The words twisted into groans when she drew a circle with two fingers around his weeping crest. Chills that were somehow hot followed her second circuit. Her third made him shiver, and when she rubbed the indentation from which his pre-ejaculate was seeping, his head stretched back over her shoulder.

"I love that you get wet like I do," she whispered into his ear.

Usually, he was the one who whispered dirty things to her. If this reversal weren't enough to send his temperature soaring, her circling fingertips were soon supplanted by the cup of her palm. The sudden increase in pressure was incredibly powerful.

"Grace," he gasped, sensation spangling through him from scalp to cock. In seconds, even the soles of his feet tingled.

Grace let go and sat up. Material rustled. He turned to find her removing her man's-style pajama top. She hadn't unbuttoned it. She was simply peeling it over her head. Her lush breasts jiggled in the light that shone out through her cracked bathroom door.

"Maybe you shouldn't do this," he said weakly. His tongue swept around his fully erected fangs, his mouth watering violently. Her nipples were as pink and swollen as candy. "You're not really awake. And you never ate dinner."

Without leaving the covers, she began squirming out of her pajama bottoms. They and her panties flew across the room in short order.

"You can't convince me you don't want to," she said.

Because she was right, he moaned, not giving a damn that he tore off his own clothes much too quickly.

"How *do* you—"

His mouth cut off her foolish question by covering hers. He rolled her beneath his weight with a gratitude so deep it didn't seem natural. The kiss was delicious but delicate—a necessity due to the state of his fangs. He had to back off when her enthusiasm threatened to draw her own blood. He didn't want to feed from her when she was so tired.

Other pleasures were too tempting to resist. He kneed her silky thighs apart as her hands found his hips. He loved that they both were naked, skin to skin under her covers.

The gentle curve of her stomach rose and fell with her excitement, intermittently touching his blood-filled cock. From the way her fingers rubbed his hip bones, from the way they slid around and caressed the crease between his thighs and ass, he could tell she liked touching him.

"Wrap your legs around me," he said.

The order was guttural, but she didn't seem to mind. Her heat as she hooked her ankles tentatively behind his butt was something to revel in.

To his mind, her showgirl's legs were exactly where they belonged.

"Like that?" she asked.

"Just like that," he growled.

He didn't have to guide himself. The weighty head of his cock was the most sensitive part of him, born to home in on her wetness. She gasped as he entered her, her hands fluttering to his shoulders where they got a good grip on his muscles. This wasn't the only place she held him securely. Sleep had left her body pliant, but her pussy was slick and tight, and his prick pressed inward only in slow surges. Her calf muscles urged him to ignore the resistance. He bit his own lip when he reached the sweet end of her. ·

When he put a bit of extra push behind his penetration, she had a mini-orgasm.

The added lubrication drew his fingers, and then his fingers found the wild pulsing of her clit. He knew the precise force with which to squeeze and roll this treasure.

"Chris," she cried, her neck arching hard.

At that display, his cock and fangs tried to lengthen. His cock he let have its way. He closed his eyes and began to rock: short jabbing thrusts that had them both gasping with pleasure. This was lucky, because Christian couldn't rein in his reactions. After two hours of lying beside her with a granite-hard cockstand, restraint was too much to ask. Sensation screamed through him as he worked his prick into her pussy. Her heat and tightness did the job he needed. He came in under half a minute, spurting hard and groaning at the sharpness of his relief. He might not have impressed Grace with his control, but he'd had to take the edge off or risk doing things he'd regret.

In any case, he was pretty far from having taken his fill of her.

"Oh," she said, a sound of pleased surprise as he kept on going right afterward. She'd come herself and her sheath was still rippling. Her body was softer than when they'd started, allowing him a fuller range of motion. Her hips gave a squirming wriggle, her telltale request for more.

"Longer strokes?" he offered, his breathing more ragged than hers was.

"Yes," she said, planting her feet firmly on the mattress. "Please."

He could tell she meant to help, which was fine with him. He threw off the covers, wedged one arm underneath her waist, and with the other got a firm grip on her headboard.

She cried out as he began to thrust at a slightly faster-than-human pace. This, evidently, was what she'd been longing for.

The bed frame protested, but neither of them cared. Her hands slid up and down his chest, his lift above her giving her room for it. He wondered if she knew she was a natural sensualist. Her delight in what she was doing was as obvious as it was charming. He choked something wordless when her thumbs searched out the place he was driving in and out of her. The whorled ridges on their pads pressed his shaft as it slid past them, adding friction to nerves already drowning in pleasure. He couldn't go quite as deep with her hands there, but it didn't matter. The idea that she wanted to feel him penetrating her had his blood boiling.

Possibly she mistook the strain on his face. "Is this okay?" she panted, her touch inching unsurely back.

He fought not to grit his teeth. "Yes," he said, determined not to release his hold on either her bottom or the headboard. "I love . . . the feel of your fingers there."

She put them back and got her assurance soon enough. This time, he took five whole minutes to explode. To his delight, she nipped his shoulder as she stiffened and came, too.

Perhaps unwisely, he opened his eyes again. He couldn't regret it, though it did make his fangs sting within his gums. Grace's post-orgasmic beauty was quite a sight. Her very human full-body flush could have unhinged him all by itself. He'd craved this so much when he was mortal, just to *stay* physical with her. Now it was even better. Because he was more than mortal, their energy was blending, each one's pleasure pushing the other's. He doubted he could have a climax without triggering one of hers—reason enough to let himself be greedy.

Happily, Grace was greedy, too. She'd slowed when they came, but she hadn't stopped.

"*God.*" He grunted at how good she felt thrusting back at him. "I could do this all night, every night, with you."

She clutched his waist in hot hands, agreeing with her body. His tension rising, he rolled her on top of him.

"You can do it," he said when her mouth fell open. "It's no harder than sitting on a horse."

"Oh, sure," she said, rolling her eyes and laughing.

The laugh told him she'd be fine. She pushed up tentatively at first but soon was riding him as gamely as any rodeo cowgirl. She hummed with approval as his cock pressed different places inside of her. Her enjoyment was as good as flipping a switch for him, even if her rhythm was uneven. This was going to be the climax that finished him. He could feel that down to his bones. When he saw the way her breasts bounced, he had to jack up his torso and suckle them. Her nipples tightened silkily on his tongue, her areolae compressed between his fangs. Clearly liking this, she tunneled her fingers into his hair, keeping him close to her.

If he hadn't wanted to bite her so badly, he could have stayed like that for a while.

They both made noises of regret when he wrenched his mouth away. Perhaps inspired by the pleasure she'd felt, Grace's hands wandered from his shoulders to his nipples. They were smaller than hers but sharp. Goose bumps broke out across his skin at her firmness in rubbing them.

"You like that, too," she said.

He liked everything she did, which made him ask himself if maybe she felt the same. "Do you trust me, Grace?"

His eyes were starry and not fearful. She nodded with a shyness that every beastly thing inside him found arousing.

"Maybe you shouldn't *always* trust me," he said with a shaky laugh.

"Maybe I won't," she teased breathlessly.

It was as good as a challenge and had him casting off caution. He drove his tongue into her mouth, tweaked her nipples, and slid his fingers into her creamy folds. He painted his hand in her wetness, giving her pleasure even as he prepared himself.

Grace flung her hair back and bit her lip. He nuzzled her throat, then groaned with longing as he licked it.

"You make me shiver when you do that," she said.

He couldn't answer. Still rocking into her as she rode him, he played her clit with the fingers of his left hand. The fingers of his right he moved into place behind her. She tensed but didn't stop him as he pushed his longest into her anus.

She caught her breath, started to speak. He licked up her throat and made her shiver again.

"I know," he said, nose to nose with her. "Most people don't do this. We can do what we like, though. As long as we think it's pleasurable."

He rotated his knuckle inside that nerve-rich passage

and watched her eyes go glassy. Her pussy got wetter, its muscles closing in on his shaft. Caught in that grip, his cock grew so hard it hurt.

"Let me handle thrusting into you," he rasped. "All I want you to do is concentrate on what you're feeling."

It was no trouble for him to lift her and roll them both up onto their knees. Her thighs wrapped his hips as he slid a second finger into her. From that position, he had more leverage, which he took full advantage of. Grace's moans were all the praise he needed. It might have been his imagination; they weren't linked mind to mind, but he thought he sensed a shadow of the delights that ran riot inside of her. All these nerves he stimulated were connected, spreading out and deepening the effect of him fucking her.

He knew the moment she decided it was all right to enjoy what he was doing. Her breasts pressed closer, her bent arms plastered tight around his shoulders.

"Oh," she gasped, wriggling her hips back and forward as if she wanted more penetration everywhere. "Oh, my God, Christian."

He gave her what she seemed to crave: more fingering, more deep, rolling thrusts of his pelvis that increased in speed until her exhalations changed into high thin cries. The only hard part was that he was feeling even more than she was. It was the nature of his nerves to register the smallest sensations.

He clung to the edge for her, his balls practically cramping with desire. If he bit her, she would go over. Her scent was high with sex, with the salty sweat that beaded up on her skin. His face was buried in the crook of her neck, his lips peeled back from his fangs with need.

"Christian," she begged, his desperation catching. "Go harder."

Doing what she wanted pulled a snarl from his throat. His cock was clamped on his ejaculation, coming and not coming at the same time. He couldn't deny his other instincts. His lips locked onto her skin and sucked.

Grace went over with a loud gasp for air.

The flaring of her aura toppled him with her. The climax shot from him, thick and hot. He came until he groaned with it, until his muscles melted with lassitude. Sated, his cock finally softened inside of her.

"Grace," he murmured as she weakly petted his hair. His arms were locked around her, unwilling to let her go.

"My goodness, you *are* a stallion," she said.

"Would that make you my mare?" he teased.

She blushed, which he thought was adorable. To his amazement, he saw he hadn't bitten her, only left a somewhat gruesome hickey on the side of her neck. He kissed it gently better, sending his healing energy into her.

He crooned with pleasure as her discomfort eased.

"Now *you'll* sleep," she said with no small hint of smugness.

He liked seeing her victorious as much as he liked her shy. He smoothed her sweaty hair away from her face, relishing the heat and pulse of her skin.

"I will if you will," he promised her.

Fifteen

"You mean I don't get to die?" Matthew asked plaintively.

When Grace realized Miss Wei still hadn't broken the news about the change in the script, she'd ordered everyone but Matthew out of the makeup trailer. Those replacement pages were slated to shoot that afternoon. Whatever Miss Wei was thinking—if she was thinking at all—she absolutely could not drop this anvil on Matthew in front of the cast and crew.

"I'm sorry," Grace said, giving his gawky arm a squeeze. "Miss Wei decided the scene would pull more from Christian if he played it opposite Charlie."

Matthew had been sitting on the counter looking pole-axed, but now his face twisted bitterly. "That guy gets everything."

"I know it seems that way—"

"It more than seems that way. He gets the girls, the laughs, and now he steals my big death scene."

"Matt." Grace's voice was sharp enough that the actor focused on her. It wasn't possible for Matthew to hide his feelings when surrounded by those brightly lit mirrors. Understandably, his eyes were welling with anger and self-pity. Grace recognized that what she said now might matter for a long time. "You know how crazy this business is. Sometimes one person gets a break; sometimes another does. Charlie is talented. Everyone on this movie is."

"I would have killed that scene," Matthew said.

"I know you would. You think people don't notice you because you're quieter than the others, but I've been watching, and I know someday you're going to be a great actor."

"Someday . . ." Matthew blew a disparaging raspberry. Grace decided not to remind him he was just twenty-one.

"Listen to me. Charlie's smart and funny and has an advantage because he's good at thinking his part through. You, though, you feel things more than he does. You throw caution to the wind, and you've got an instinct for what will come across on camera. When I'm ready to direct, I hope you'll be willing to work with me."

"Really?" Matthew said. "You want to direct?"

Grace laughed. Apparently, she was playing her aspirations closer to her vest than she'd thought. "You could pretend to be flattered that I'd want to direct you."

"Of course I am. I mean—" He stopped and really looked at her. "I bet you'll be good, Grace. Maybe better than Miss Wei."

"Thank you, though you might want to keep that under your hat." She jerked her head toward the trailer door. "Ready to go out and face everyone?"

"I guess." Matthew sounded glum as he scooted off the makeup counter, but he looked calmer—not on the brink of tears anymore. He took a deep breath and stood straighter. "Thanks for telling me, Grace. This was better coming from you."

"I'm glad," she said, feeling better herself.

Now all they had to do was pray that Christian could scale this Matterhorn.

Christian stood in the kitchen set of the Pryor mansion while the gaffer checked his reflective qualities with a handheld light meter—yet another test of Christian's ability to calibrate his glamour.

They were filming a serious scene today, one that took place toward the end of the story. Joe, his boys, and Mary were on the run from Joe's murderous father. Self-preservation said they ought to keep running, but Charlie had remembered the gang's last human victim was still alive. Because they'd decided not to be bad vampires anymore, Charlie had begged them to return to the mansion and save the girl. His desire to play hero would get his friend Matthew killed. The requirements of drama being what they were, George Pryor would foil the rescue by showing up. He'd spear Matthew with a tree branch, then be killed by his son for his villainy.

The emotions of the scene were operatic, to say the least. Christian was trying not to dwell on whether he could drag them out of himself for other people to stare at.

Left with little to do but stand there, he watched the confab Nim Wei was having with Charlie, Viv, and Philip on the edge of the set. Something was going on there. All their body language was strange. Charlie in particular wore a mix of guilt and excitement. Christian searched for Matthew and discovered him leaning with his arms crossed against a scaffold, his attention narrowed on the others. Christian had to frown at his attitude. Matthew should have been "going deep inside himself," or whatever Method acting hoo-ha he'd decided to use for this. A fragment of Matthew's thoughts waved for his notice. The young actor was deeply resenting Charlie . . . and thinking Grace was the nicest, prettiest woman he'd ever met.

Grace was standing a short distance from him, talking to a grip. The means by which Matthew wanted to show his appreciation had Christian's neck hairs bristling—at least until he deciphered what Grace had done to earn his devotion.

"Hell," he said, his possessive anger changing directions.

The gaffer straightened from placing a tape mark on the antique kitchen's convincingly grimy checkerboard tiles. "You can take a break now if you need to."

Christian didn't need a break. He needed an explanation. The gaffer took an instinctive step backward as Christian's jaw tightened. Not wanting to alarm him, Christian patted his shoulder.

"Excuse me," he said. "Just need to clear something up."

Nim Wei's head turned as he strode from the kitchen set and across Soundstage Six to her. She'd have done better to conceal her faint amusement. The cables that snaked over the floor between them tempted him to wind them around her neck. He could study what electrocution did to elderly vampires.

"Christian," she said, once he was close enough. "I suppose you'd like the new pages for today."

He looked at the sheaf she was holding out. They had to be the mimeographs Grace had rescued from the gutter.

"Grace knew about this?" he asked.

Nim Wei pursed her lovely mouth and shrugged. "I ordered her not to spill the beans. It appears she's told Matthew, but I've learned to make allowances for her tender heart."

"You mean as opposed to having no heart at all."

Philip and Charlie widened their eyes at him, but Viv just smiled at her shoes. The actress knew the sort of bitch her director was.

"I don't see why this bothers you," Nim Wei said. "You like Charlie. You should be happy for him. And it's not as if you'll have trouble learning new lines. That quick brain of yours is one of your assets."

"What bothers me," Christian said icily, "is you playing games. Nor do I appreciate you telling Grace to keep important things from me."

Nim Wei knew how to match him in haughtiness. "Grace is my employee. As are you. Or have you forgotten our agreement?"

"You know I haven't."

"Then honor your word. In any case, I played this game for your benefit. Imitating human feelings isn't good enough for this scene. This is *Teen-Age Vampire*'s climax. You need to inhabit Joe Pryor's skin. You need to be imbued with his spirit."

Christian's glare was met by the queen's single raised eyebrow—which threw more coals on his temper. *She* dared to doubt his honor? To use it to twist the facts about which of them was right? The air between them began to vibrate with their warring energy, the effect almost strong enough to be perceived by mortals.

"I won't let you down," Charlie interrupted hesitantly.

It was an effort to break off his staring match with the queen, but as Christian looked into the boy's hazel eyes, he saw Charlie's soul laid bare: how excited he was, how nervous, how badly he felt for Matthew while at the same time being determined to make the most of his chance to shine. Charlie genuinely liked and admired Christian—and wanted Christian to do well for his own sake. He thought Christian would be a solid actor, if he'd let himself loosen up.

Even as this awareness ran through the front of Christian's mind, the back was filled with memories of the real Charles dying on that bridge in Florence. Of all his friends, Charles had been the one who'd seemed too full of life to snuff out. To see him—or rather Adam—the other day, his haunted gaze watching Christian through the taxi window, had been a terrible shock. The Charles he used to know was gone. Nothing could bring him back.

"You can do this," Charlie said softly.

Though it probably hurt Charlie's feelings, Christian had to turn away. His palm was pressed to his stomach, a gesture he should have had too much self-control to use. All these threads winding together from the past and present were making him uneasy.

Joe was in the garage with Mary, settling the injured mortal into the back of a decades-old limousine. They needed to drive the girl to the hospital, to get her a transfusion. Joe's skin was all-over anxiety. Everyone was counting on him to pull this off, and he wasn't sure he could. He was hoping the ancient Rolls would start when an awful cry rang out from the house.

"My father," he breathed to Mary, both their eyes gone round. "He's found us."

"Go," she urged. "I'll watch out for her."

Joe barely took a second to be grateful Mary had strong nerves. He ran at vampire speed through his father's decrepit house. That tortured cry had come from one of his boys, their pain distorting the sound too much to identify who it was. He didn't think he could bear to lose any of them, not when they'd risked their lives to switch allegiances to him.

His immortal heart was beating much too hard when he burst into the unused kitchen. It took a moment for his eyes to make sense of the shambles there. Matthew and Philip lay beneath the wreckage of a butcher block table. At first he feared they were dead, but then he heard faint pulse sounds. A small puppylike whimper drew his gaze toward the pantry door.

Charlie was on his back, sprawled across the pantry threshold amidst the dust and neglect. Joe gasped in disbelief. His friend had been stabbed clear through his sternum with a long tree branch. The thing was pinning him to the floor. Joe's father crouched above him, fangs out, face twisted like a demon's. Even as Joe watched, George shoved the branch deeper. Blood bubbled up in a pool from the entry wound.

"'Bout time you got here," George gloated to his son.

The noise Joe made was a mix of fury and anguish.

"It's all right," Charlie gasped before Joe could rush recklessly over. "It hurts, but he missed my heart."

"Missed it on purpose," his father crowed. "Wouldn't be much fun if my Joe's buddies died too quickly."

Red flashed across Joe's vision, blood and rage rising up in him. He didn't care how much older and stronger his father was. He'd been bullying people too long, and Joe had been letting him. He catapulted himself at George, dragging him up and hurling him off Charlie. Joe and his father wrestled back and forth across the antique kitchen, turning even more of it into kindling. Pans swung on their hooks and clanged. Chairs broke and cabinets splintered. George threw his son into the iron stove with such force that its door buckled.

Temporarily stunned, Joe shook himself, struggled upward, then hunched forward like a linebacker. He barreled toward his father with all his unnatural speed. George crashed backward at the impact, falling beneath him. A broken chair leg lay close at hand. Joe seized it, his biceps bunching in preparation for staking his sire with it.

Despite the blood running down his face, his father began to laugh.

"You can't dust me," he wheezed. "Charlie's dying. I'm the only one whose blood is strong enough to save him."

Doubt assailed Joe, his hand hesitating on the fatal blow. His father was an old vampire, and his blood did have healing powers. All born vampires possessed that gift. The thing was, Joe was a born vampire, too. Maybe he . . .

"Ah-ah-ah," taunted his father. "You won't have the juice to save him for another century."

Joe couldn't tell if the bastard was lying.

"Kill him," Charlie urged, drawing Joe's eyes to where he was fixed gruesomely to the floor. "None of us is safe as long as he's alive."

Joe looked back at his father, reading the truth of this in George's mocking expression. He would kill them—today, tomorrow—whenever Joe or the others let down their guard. George's upper lip curled in a sneer.

"You always were a weakling. Just like your mo—"

Joe set his jaw and plunged the stake down with all his might, the strength of both arms forcing it in. His aim was true. He caught his father right in the heart. For an awful second, nothing happened. They simply stared at each other in horror. Then George's skin sank into his face, his body skeletonizing before Joe's eyes. In moments, Joe was squatting over a pile of ash.

The stake clattered from his hand. He'd done it. After all those years of abuse, he'd killed his father. George Pryor would never hurt anyone again.

Joe was panting from more than exertion.

"Charlie," he said like a dreamer waking.

"Still here," Charlie tried to joke.

Joe rushed to him, only then taking in the full ghast-liness of his impalement. Though Charlie was a vampire, he was a lesser breed than Joe. Considering his injuries, survival seemed improbable. Joe felt wetness run down his face and knew he was crying.

"Just pull it out," Charlie said, the knowledge of what that would do to him evident in his face. "I'm not sorry if it ends this way. At least I . . . did the right thing for once."

Joe wanted to touch Charlie, to comfort him, but didn't know where was safe. He choked back a sob as Mary came to the door. When she saw Charlie, she sucked in her breath sharply. It shouldn't have mattered that Joe was crying, but he swept his cheeks dry with the back of his forearm.

"Is the girl all right?" Charlie asked Mary.

Mary stared at him blankly, then shook herself from the shock. "She's safe for now." She turned her dazed eyes to Joe. "Do you need help? Would drinking my blood help him?"

Joe's love for her welled unstoppably up in him, a wave of emotion like nothing he'd felt before. His human sweetheart was very brave. She knew Charlie's bite might kill her, and still she offered herself. His eyes spilled over at the same time as a tender smile cracked across his face.

"He needs my blood," he said huskily. "I'm just not certain it's strong enough to heal him."

Knowing he had to make the attempt, Joe braced on Charlie's chest and yanked out the branch. More blood welled from the hideous hole, prompting Mary to cry out. Charlie's eyes rolled white, but Christian slapped him awake again. He bit his own wrist until it bled.

"Try," he begged, shoving the gash against Charlie's mouth. "Please try to stay with me."

Grace's heart was pounding as Christian's plea faded.

"Tell me you got that," Miss Wei said to Wade.

The cinematographer beamed angelically. "I'm pretty sure we got it on both cameras."

Getting what they needed had taken a number of time-consuming resets for the various harness stunts, as well as multiple takes—one of which had been spoiled by an overactive blood-delivery device. That said, the confirmation of Christian's star power was indisputably in the can.

Christian hadn't run out of gas. Each take had drawn more emotion from him, as if the story were a spell that was strengthening. Those tears Christian had been crying weren't supplied by makeup. Even better, a couple members of the crew were wiping their eyes, too.

For her part, Grace felt as shaken as if she'd lived through the scene herself. Christian wasn't back yet from his immersion in the role of Joe. He was sitting balanced on his heels with his head hanging. Charlie punched his arm as the actor who played George pushed creakily off the floor. The visual effects department would have fun turning him to dust. For now, he was simply banged up and tired.

"Good work," George said, the praise almost ungrudging. "Both of you."

Charlie's recuperative powers were more youthful. He sprang to his feet with the prosthetic wound plastered to his chest. Andy from wardrobe started freeing him from it.

Matthew had also risen from his unconscious sprawl. He walked a bit unsurely toward his colleague. "I thought you were going to lose it," he said, "when that bladder started squirting blood in Joe's eyes."

"I almost did," Charlie admitted. "I bit my cheek so hard to keep from laughing it's swollen now."

"You owe me a beer," Matthew said.

"I owe the world a beer," he agreed, grinning brilliantly. He clapped Christian's shoulder and offered him a hand up. "Come on, Hamlet. We've got to celebrate your first triumph as a real actor. You, too, Grace. No excuses. Everybody gets drunk tonight."

Not everybody would be celebrating. Someone shouted "wrap" and announced a six A.M. call for crew. Grace forgot to wince at the early hour when Christian's gaze found hers. His eyes were different: still open and soulful from playing Joe. Grace felt mesmerized by what she saw in them.

"You coming?" he asked.

"Wouldn't miss it," she said lightly.

His lean chest went up and down.

"Oh, boy," Charlie said. "I think we need to give the lovebirds a few minutes."

"I'll drive her," Christian said, not looking away from her. "We'll meet you at the Villa Nova, the place we drank in before."

"Be sure you do," Charlie warned. "You're the man of the hour."

Christian's intent expression made Grace nervous— or maybe it was her reaction to it that unsettled her. He always affected her, of course, but tonight a little earthquake seemed to be quivering inside her, a longing so deep it shook her foundations. Christian had exposed himself today, in ways he'd probably spent his whole life avoiding. Every scrap of intuition she possessed said he'd done it for her.

Her feet took a step back from him. "I have to grab my things."

He nodded, his eyes taking on the golden gleam she'd grown too familiar with. It was, without a doubt, his best bedroom look.

She spun away before her sex ran out in a hot puddle. She'd given him enough assurances of her interest. Give him more, and she'd never be safe again.

She told herself she didn't love him as she strode to the store room where she'd left her sweater and purse. The shadows at the back of Stage Six were thick, lights shutting down here and there as crew packed up for the night. Her heels rang out on the cement floor. They reminded her of horses' hooves on cobbles. A clanking like a crazy radiator came from her left.

"Viv?" Grace had lost track of the actress once they'd completed her coverage, though in truth she doubted Viv was making the sound. Light flashed above her head, and Grace looked up.

The ceiling with its struts and catwalks had turned to sky.

She was on a bridge above a river, and her limbs were encased in steel. She gripped a long, gory sword in her right gauntlet. Or, it wasn't *her* gauntlet, it was Christian's. She was in his consciousness, her energy joined to and strengthening his.

How natural this felt was ridiculous.

She—or they—were facing an armored man who looked about nine feet tall.

"Tell me, Lavaux," she and Christian said, "did you really imagine only my father brought allies to this fight?"

The other man was afraid of how strong they were. He took to his heels and ran with a mouselike squeak. Christian wanted to give chase, but there were other, closer threats to counter. Hand-to-hand combat was taking place on every side of them.

Grace shrieked as a weight struck them. It was a severed head in a helmet. It bounced off Christian's stomach and landed at his feet. His friend Charles' wide green eyes stared up through the visor, his irises glazing as Christian gaped.

Charles was dead, not just Philippe and Matthaus. No matter what Christian did, he couldn't save his men. His father and Nim Wei had stacked the odds too high against them. His chest tightened with what he feared this day's end would be. The hope that he could save any of his friends seemed too cruel to cling to. Grace's spirit was knotting inside of him, as if it couldn't abide his dread. At least she was safe from Gregori. Even his sire couldn't kill a ghost.

"Grace," Christian said, shaking her shoulders between his hands.

She was back on the soundstage, but his face wasn't his face when she blinked at it. It was too perfect, too buffed and shining and beautiful—more like a piece of jewelry than living flesh. Christian's eyes were obsidian lit by flames, an effect far more *other* than what he brought to her bedroom. His lips moved and spoke, but they were chiseled from rose marble.

What had he meant when he referred to her as a ghost?

"*Grace*," he repeated. "Why aren't you answering me?"

Was he right to claim she ought to remember him? Were other things he'd hinted at true as well? The chance they were real was a sun she didn't want to stare into.

"I don't feel well," she said numbly. "Please make my excuses to the others. I'm going to grab a cab and go home."

Sixteen

Grace hurried off the studio lot as if Christian were chasing her—which might have been true. He was so protective of her . . . except that now he was the person she needed protection from.

A cab was idling outside the gate, her own mini-miracle.

"Hollywood Bowl," she told the driver.

The Bowl was a natural amphitheater, set among the hills beneath the famous Hollywood sign. They were past the season for summer concerts, and now it served as a park. Grace slipped in the Highland entrance, under the Oscar-like statues of Music, Drama, and Dance. The outdoor theater was blissfully empty. She found a seat that faced the arching bandshell, near the new—and currently silent—reflecting pool and fountain.

It had been two years since she'd come here to think.

When she first arrived in Hollywood, this landmark had drawn her more strongly than any other. More than

Grauman's Chinese Theater. More than Schwab's Drug-store. She'd never known why before.

Tonight she knew everything.

Her imagination had made a fantasy of this place, a little slice of heaven for her spirit to sojourn in when she'd died temporarily. She'd met her angel guide here and had been presented with the opportunity to travel back in time to meet her soul mate. Michael had called Christian the friend she always returned to, the one she cared for life after life.

She'd jumped at the chance to know him, even if she only went as a ghost. A friend was her holy grail. Before Christian, she'd never had the nerve to make one.

She closed her eyes and leaned back in the wooden seat. Tremors ran through her muscles, aftershocks from the earthquake that had begun earlier.

She'd died, and it hadn't ended her existence. She'd been more *herself* as a spirit than she'd been when she was alive. She'd been fearless, for one thing, giving the medieval Christian her heart long before he'd thought to ask for it.

Where is that girl today? she wondered. *How did I become so cautious again?*

She should have remembered Christian the moment she spotted him in his barn. No, she should have remembered him the moment she read the script. All Christian's friends had been in it. All Christian's long-dead Swiss mercenary friends.

He wasn't dead, though. She leaned forward, her hands like claws on her knees, as a new twist in the unfolding maze came clear.

Christian was more than the same spirit; he was the same man. For that matter, so was Miss Wei.

Christian had let Grace's boss do something strange to him.

One hand flew up to her neck, where her skin was warm and unmarred. He'd bitten her. He'd drunk her blood. How on earth had Grace reasoned that away?

Christian was a vampire.

"Jeepers," she said, though perhaps she should have chosen a stronger curse. Christian Durand, their new teen idol, was an actual vampire.

Christian should have moved faster to stop Grace. All he'd wanted after playing that scene was to hold her and close his eyes. Adam and Grace's screenplay had caught the essence of Christian's long-ago losses. Watching Charlie die, being engulfed by those very human emotions, shook his grip on reality. He hadn't trusted how much he wanted Grace's nearness to ground him.

He'd let her slip away because of it, though he knew she wasn't in her right state of mind. When he caught up to her by the store room, she'd acted like she was dreaming with her eyes open. Not for the first time he cursed his inability to read what she was thinking.

Well, ask then, he thought. *Go after her and ask.*

He picked up her personal perfume on Vine Street. That much of a link between them he could rely on. The scent led him toward the freeway and then west. The sound of rustling leaves began to compete with traffic. He'd reached a large city park. There was a stage at its center, with thousands of seats fanning out underneath the stars. His heart gave a leap he couldn't have stopped it from making. Grace was sitting in one of them.

Too eager to wait, he blurred to her. She didn't startle, though he must have seemed to appear from thin air. Abruptly unsure of his welcome, he sat awkwardly. Her gaze remained on the graceful white bandshell in front of her.

"After my accident," she said. "The one where I . . . died. I'd have these dreams, sometimes twice a week. In them, I met an angel here. His name was Michael, and he always wore a tuxedo." She smiled slightly. "Even in my dreams, I was obsessed with Hollywood glamour."

Christian didn't miss the name she'd used, but he also didn't want her to stop talking. Her face was different—more relaxed, as if she'd forgotten to maintain her guard against him.

Her green eyes flicked to him before returning to the stage. "I'd run away from my folks, and I was trying to support myself as a waitress. I took those dreams as a sign I really would be a director. Until I met Miss Wei, they were all I had to cling to."

He covered her hand where it curved over the chair's arm. She turned hers until they were palm to palm.

"I wish I'd known you existed," he said, meaning it with all his heart. Before this, he'd resented what their separation had done to him, but she'd been left alone as well. No protectors. No allies. And he'd been on this earth with her all this time. The thought of what he might have spared her tightened his throat. "I wish I could have made your life easier for you."

She nodded, her profile to him, her lips pressed flat with emotion. "I remember you," she said.

He wasn't prepared for this new bombshell. Heat flashed across his face. He should have felt triumphant. He'd been trying to get her to recall the past ever since they'd met. His fingers curled closer on her hand, but he caught himself before he could hurt her.

"You remember me?" he asked hoarsely.

She turned fully to him, her expression like a painting of a saint who'd just had her first vision. "I remember what happened after I died. I remember being a ghost and going back in time to meet you. I remembered your friends . . . being slaughtered on the Ponte Vecchio. That's what *you* remember, isn't it? You're not going to tell me I'm crazy now."

"That's what I remember. You coming to me. Us falling in love." He looked to where their hands joined together. "There's more, Grace. Things you might have a harder time swallowing."

She flung away from him and stood, her hands squeezing her temples as if they hurt.

"Grace—"

"I know," she said. "About you being a vampire. I know Miss Wei turned you into one. Oh, God, it's all so insane!"

He was on his feet beside her, sliding his palm down her back. She wore a simple outfit, a white-necked gray-knit dress with a coordinating jacketlike sweater. Conservative as it was, she hardly looked like a woman who'd believe in monsters. "I'm afraid I can't make the craziness go away."

"You bit me, Christian. Am I going to turn into a vampire?"

Her face turned up to his. He could tell the thought alarmed her, which hurt to an extent that stunned. Had he truly been hanging so many hopes on her? Preferring not to let her see that he had, he chafed her shoulders. "I'd have to do more than feed from you for that to happen."

"Right," she said, nodding to herself. "I'd have to drink your blood, too. Like in the movie."

He stroked her face with his fingertips, bringing her gaze back to him. "*Not* like in the movie. Nim Wei made certain the film is misleading. That stuff about 'born' and 'made' vampires, about turning humans with an exchange of blood—it's all nonsense."

Her luscious mouth was hanging open, her cushiony lower lip a temptation for his thumb. She closed it and swallowed with a visible effort. "Does Miss Wei know who I am? Does she know the ghost-me saw what she did to you and your friends?"

He tried not to resent that she was thinking about her boss. "I don't think so. On some level, yes, she probably was drawn to hire you because she sensed a tie. I know you admire her, but the queen can be intuitive about exploiting advantages."

"The queen . . ." Grace shook her head.

"She rules the— You don't want to hear about all that now."

"I should want to hear. My head is jangling. I keep getting flashes of what happened in your time. I was so different when I was a spirit. *We* were different."

His heart constricted inside his chest. Did she mean she couldn't love him anymore? "Everyone changes over time," he said carefully.

A look of determination hardened her expression. "Show me your true face. I've caught glimpses of it, I think. You have some sort of disguise."

"You mean my glamour."

"Yes."

Dropping it was harder than he expected. He felt naked without the concealment, especially when Grace went up on her toes to peer in his face. He was glad she didn't seem afraid, but being examined this closely was uncomfortable. He realized he liked passing for human.

At last, she settled back on her heels. "You're so beautiful. No matter how hard I look, I can't find a flaw. You must lure people in without trying."

"I don't hurt them. I've learned not to harm the people I feed from."

Her gaze rose to his. Her cheeks were pinker than they'd been a moment ago. "How often do you need to . . . feed?"

Despite the circumstances, Christian's cock stirred in his jeans. Talking about feeding—and with her—was inherently erotic. "Ideally, every few days. I'm older, so I can go longer."

"You've been going longer since—" She stopped and rolled her soft lips together.

"Yes, since I met you. I haven't bitten anyone but you since you strolled into my barn."

"Your man, Roy, brought something to my house."

"Bagged blood. He bribed someone at the local blood bank."

"But biting a person is more pleasurable."

Christian's prick was thick enough to be stiff. "You know yourself how pleasurable it is."

Her breasts were rising and falling within her modest gray dress, the tightness of her nipples visible even through her bra. Her hand rose, hesitated. "Could I— Are you—"

"Am I what?"

"Are your fangs down now?"

"Peel back my lip and see."

He wasn't sure she'd do it, even though she seemed to want to. His muscles coiled with anticipation. His incisors jutted the last bit longer the instant she touched his mouth.

"Oh," she said, jumping just a little. Christian held his breath, but her interest overcame her alarm. Shifting, she held his lip up with her left hand. The forefinger of her right slid onto his gum, lightly stroking the reddened place where his elongated tooth rooted. The nerves she stimulated were intimately linked to his cock. Its crest, which felt like she was touching it, knocked against his zipper. Though he didn't moan, he couldn't keep his eyelids from growing heavy with enjoyment.

"You like that," she mused.

"You might as well have shoved your hand between my legs and rubbed."

"Oh." Her finger drew slowly back, letting his lip fall. "If this feels so good, why would you give up feeding for me?"

"I've already told you why, Grace." His voice was rough with arousal, with all the strong things he felt for her. She dropped her eyes to his chest. He wouldn't have been surprised if she could see his heart's slow pounding.

"I didn't remember what your fangs were like," she said.

For the moment, Christian allowed himself to be steered in this new direction. "You didn't know me as a vampire for very long. You disappeared soon after I was changed. I have a theory that when the medics revived you, they pulled your spirit back to the life it had been born to."

"You must have thought I'd abandoned you. And after you'd lost your friends." Her face changed as another memory returned, a tinge of horror darkening her dismay. "I left you after you'd killed your father."

Gregori had been renting rooms in Florence, hiding from his son's vengeance. Christian had found and killed him, and then Grace had found Christian. That was when she'd forgiven him for turning to Nim Wei. That last time, she'd stayed physical long enough to make love. Against the wall, as he recalled, with his father's body cooling on the floor.

He guessed he couldn't blame her for being horrified over that.

"I *couldn't* forgive him," Christian said defensively.

Grace stroked the side of his face with her warm fingers. "There's no point regretting that now."

He couldn't tell what was in her eyes—if it were understanding, or if she simply wanted to avoid discussing his murderous impulses.

"God," he swore. "I wish the bitch queen hadn't blocked your thoughts from me."

Grace jerked back, her fingertips leaving cold spots on his cheeks after they were gone.

"Never mind," he said, instantly regretting his words. "I'm sorry. I'll take you home."

"You can read people's thoughts?" She appeared as appalled by this as she'd been about his dead father.

"Not yours. And only when I concentrate."

She mulled this over and then nodded—grimly, it seemed to him. "Where did you park?"

A smile broke across his face. "I didn't drive here, Grace. Some things your movie says about us vampires really are true."

Was it wrong of Grace to be this gratified that he'd come after her? Surely it was inconsistent to be both alarmed by and attracted to him, to be so titillated by his true nature. It was one thing to regret her lost bravery and quite another to have everything inside her yearning to yield to him. A vampire, after all, was no better romantic prospect than a handsome male actor.

In the current instance, Christian was disqualified on both counts. In spite of this, his fangy grin was irresistible. His single dimple was winking out at her.

"Put your arms around my neck," he said.

"What?"

"I'm going to pick you up. You need to hold on."

He scooped her off her feet with no help from her. She had little choice but to put her arms where he'd instructed. His neck felt extremely strong.

"Don't look so nervous," he said. "Or is Charlie wrong about you liking to go fast?"

"I don't—"

His initial upward leap stole both breath and words. At first, she thought he was flying, but he was simply taking the Olympic long jump to eye-popping new levels. He touched down on Highland Avenue, pushed off, and then the wind was streaming through her hair again. The traffic on Hollywood Boulevard didn't put him off. His speed and agility landed them easily between cars. The drivers didn't see him long enough to honk, which Angelenos were never shy about doing.

"Jeesh," Grace breathed. "You're better than Superman."

Christian chuckled beside her ear. "I can't go back in time. You're the one who did that."

His arms tightened around her as they bounded off again. They landed on the pavement in front of Schwab's, leaving foot-shaped cracks in the concrete that Grace expected would be hard to explain. Fortunately, they didn't have to. Their journey became a whirlwind of streets and parks and beautifully landscaped yards. Grace didn't know how to be afraid; it was all too exhilarating. She caught an

aerial view of Santa Monica Bay with the tiny waves glinting by starlight. She supposed Christian couldn't rebound
off water, because he turned as they reached the coast.

He barely jarred her dropping down in front of her cottage.

Her heart was beating too hard to release her tight grip
on him.

"You're chilled," he said as he set her onto her feet. "I'm
sorry. I didn't think."

"At least I didn't drop my purse," she got out between
chattering teeth. "Or let my shoes fall off."

He laughed and hugged her against him. His body was
very hard, but she liked it close anyway. It seemed unfair
not to admit that she'd enjoyed what he'd done.

"Thank you," she said. "That was fun."

"Grace," he murmured against her hair, still not letting
go. His hands slid up and down her back. "I'm afraid it's
easier for you to warm me than vice versa."

Grace wasn't sure about that. His words sent a flush
through her. She tipped her head back and looked at him.
Discovering he was a vampire should have changed her
reactions, but apparently it had not. Something in her expression must have told him what she was thinking.

"Grace," he said, lower and throbbing.

He wasn't hiding how his eyes glowed. His normally dark
irises were fiery gold with desire. When he kissed her, his
fangs were sharp. She curled the tip of her tongue between
them, shivering when he sucked it languorously. After a long
exploratory minute—which Grace thought might have been
the most sensual of her life—he drew back a few inches.

"Still cold?" he asked huskily.

She slid her palms underneath the back of his leather
jacket. He was both more and less of a stranger than she
had known. "If you keep that up, my clothes will catch
fire."

His face transformed. She thought it was relief she saw

cross his features, but it could have been hope as well. He lowered his head and kissed her with no holds barred. She matched him moan for moan as his immeasurably powerful body crowded hers back against the ivy-shrouded door to her home. Her sense of helplessness, of vulnerability, was undeniably delicious. It didn't take much pressure for her to feel how very ready for sex he was.

He broke free, panting, and kissed her neck where her pulse raced wildly. He licked her there and dragged his fangs gently on the spot. She'd felt him do that before and hadn't known what it signified. Now that she did, her lower body began to squirm.

"God," he said, his tone so dark and thrilling it made her wet. "You have no idea how much I want to make love to you. How much I want to slide inside you and have you know who I am."

She spread her hands across the small of his back. "I want that, too, Christian."

"Give me your key. Before I crush your doorknob."

She had to fumble in her purse, but she found it. With one arm, he held her tight against him as he used it, that big male ridge digging into her belly insistently. When he had it open, he lifted her off her feet and walked her inside.

"Your clothes are history," he warned her, kicking the door shut. "I've been waiting to do this for half a millennium. You'll be lucky if you can walk tomorrow."

"I'll be lucky if I can't," she gasped.

He laughed, but the sound was tight. He groaned her name and licked up her neck.

"I love that," she cried, clutching his shoulders. "Oh, God, I love that."

The kitchen telephone rang shrilly.

"No," he growled. "We are not postponing this again."

"What if it's your friend? What if he found my father?"

He cursed more than she was used to and picked it up. As before, the call was for him.

"Slow down, Charlie," he said, his fingers tunneling with frustration into his hair. Grace thought it unfair that he looked sexy doing it. "I don't understand what you're saying about Viv."

"Something happened to Viv?"

He put up a hand to request patience. "Which hospital did they take her to?"

As Grace and Christian rushed out of the cottage, Miss Wei was vaulting—high heels and all—into her pink Fury. Grace felt oddly embarrassed to see her, now that she knew she was a vampire and had been lying to her for years. Her boss looked surprisingly at home behind the wheel.

"You heard?" Miss Wei flung her white silk scarf back around her neck. "I just got off the phone with Philip."

"We heard," Christian said. His hand rubbed Grace's elbow. "Why don't we meet at the hospital?"

Under normal circumstances, Grace would have volunteered to chauffeur her boss. Chances were she still should. Instead, she edged an inch closer to Christian.

Miss Wei furrowed her brow at her. "Are you all right, Grace? You left the set without saying goodbye."

"Yes," she said, sure she sounded unnaturally stiff. "I'm just worried about Viv."

Miss Wei's head tilted like a bird's. "Very well. I'll see you both there."

Christian let her pull out of the curving drive before he started his Thunderbird. For the first few minutes of their journey, he was silent.

Seeming unsure whether he should change that, he rubbed his chin and shot a quick glance at her. "The queen truly cares about you, you know. I don't think she'd hurt you."

"She bit your father's men to make them stronger. She ensured your side wouldn't stand a chance in a fight. And she did this for no better reason than wanting you to be hers."

"I know." Christian's hands shifted on the wheel. "Believe me, I don't like being in the position of defending her."

"Then don't."

"She's changed, Grace. Maybe not completely, but some. God knows she can be ruthless, but neither of us would make the same choices we did then."

Grace looked out the window. She didn't want to be forgiving. The emotions she felt toward Christian might be confused, but one thing she knew for sure: the way Miss Wei had treated him and his friends was wrong. She hadn't been fighting for her country or defending her life; she'd simply wanted to claim someone who'd said no to her.

"We should be focusing on Viv now," she said aloud.

Christian reached out to squeeze her leg. "We can do that," he said.

As Christian and Grace pulled into the hospital parking lot, they spotted half a dozen clustered paparazzi with their big-flashed cameras strung around their necks. Someone must have tipped them off about a passing driver's call for an ambulance. Eighteen-year-old Viv Lavelle being rescued from the roadside, fall-down drunk and beaten up, was big news.

"Shoot," Grace said, shutting the convertible's door behind her. "Why do they have to be such vultures?"

"Nim Wei is with them." Christian took her arm and pointed. "You don't have to worry about them being vultures much longer."

When she looked closer, Grace saw her petite employer had been hidden by the circle of reporters. She appeared to be speaking calmly to each of them—too calmly, actually. There might have been a faint glow around her, like a misty halo. The paparazzi looked to be hanging on every word.

"What's she doing?"

"Thralling them. We can do that to most humans who meet our eyes."

"Well, that *is* like the books and movies." She remembered Charlie's not-so-minor accident with the Harley. "You did that to Charlie and the boys! You made them think he hadn't broken his leg."

"I can't thrall you. Nim Wei blocked my influence."

"But I—"

"You convinced yourself you didn't see what you saw."

"I've been very stupid," Grace said slowly.

"Stubborn," Christian corrected, his lips curving crookedly. "And determined. But at least you know that . . . whatever you feel about me, it's really you feeling it."

They'd stopped at the end of a row of cars. Christian used his gentle hold on her elbow to remind her to continue. As they passed Miss Wei, she acknowledged them with a nod.

Christian leaned down to Grace's ear. "She says she'll wait outside to head off any more reporters."

"She can talk to you telepathically?"

"If I let her," Christian said darkly.

Though she'd been the one to advise it, Grace was having difficulty focusing on their female star.

"Are you afraid of crosses?" she couldn't resist asking as they crossed the hospital lobby.

"No."

"Stakes?"

"Not wooden ones." He steered them onto an elevator.

"I know you go out during the day."

"Hush," he said as two interns joined them.

"Bats?"

"*No*," he said, the corner of his mouth twitching.

Grace shuddered in relief. She didn't think she'd like

it if he turned into one. Then another thought occurred to her. "Bugs?"

His eyebrows shot up. Grace lowered her voice. "Like that fellow Renfield. You wouldn't, um, make your human friends eat spiders?"

Christian's laugh snorted out his nose. Luckily, the elevator doors opened and he nudged her out. "I promise you, Grace, I wouldn't find that any more appealing than you do."

They remembered they shouldn't be amused when a formidable-looking nurse stepped into their path. Her hair was improbably blonde and unconvincingly roller curled. She crossed arms as sturdy as a blacksmith's across her ample chest. The door to what Grace presumed was Viv's room was behind her. Christian's vampire powers must have led him here.

"Who are you two?" the nurse demanded.

"Christian Durand and Grace Michaels," Christian supplied.

"I'm Miss Wei's assistant."

"Her second in command," Christian clarified.

Wade was closer to being that than Grace was, but the nurse nodded, satisfied. Grace glanced at Christian to see if he was using his tricks on her. Unable to tell—possibly the glowing mist effect didn't show under fluorescents—she turned her attention back to the nurse.

She'd planted her hands on her generous hips. "That poor lamb consumed a lot of liquor, then got herself whaled on good. She was crying and raving when she came in here, but she's sobered up some. You can talk to her if she'll see you."

They found Charlie, Philip, and Matthew already inside, having snuck or charmed their way in. Grace couldn't restrain her sympathetic hiss when she caught her first glimpse of Viv. Someone had really lost control with her. Grace didn't remember ever looking this bad after her father had beaten her. The head of the bed was raised, so Viv was sitting. She seemed weak, but she was awake.

"Oh, great," the actress said as if she weren't bruised and purpled all over. "More ghouls to hover over me."

Charlie gave Grace the seat by the bed. Hardly knowing what to do, Grace took it and laid her hand over Viv's bare, mistreated arm. *Defensive injuries,* she thought. Viv fought her attacker. None of her bones were broken, though her left eye was swollen shut. She looked about twelve years old without her makeup. Appearances notwithstanding, Viv seemed determined not to drop her wisecracking attitude.

She cocked her head to indicate Charlie. "Promise me you won't let him use this as an excuse to steal *my* part."

"As if you'd let me," he retorted. "You cling to every line, tooth and nail."

His worried eyes sent a different message. Viv bared her teeth mockingly at him. To Grace, the pair acted more like brother and sister than people who'd once been intimate. Not seeing how their squabbling was useful, Grace smoothed back the actress's hair. Christian was standing behind Grace's chair. The hand he settled on her shoulder made it easier to speak.

"Viv," she said. "What the heck happened?"

"You heard the nurse: I got myself whaled on."

"Come on," Grace said. "That's not a real answer."

Viv pulled a disparaging face, wincing as the movement irritated a tender spot. "I broke up with one of the old farts. His pride couldn't take it. It's no big deal."

"It's a darn big deal," Grace protested. "No one should be allowed to do this to you."

Grace's kindness broke the girl's defenses. Her nose turned pink a second before her eyes spilled over. Viv lifted one arm to wipe the not-so-little Forrester tears away. As she did, Grace spied her missing bracelet watch on Viv's wrist, complete with its unmistakable movie-themed charms.

She drew an automatic breath to exclaim about it, then realized it being there likely meant Viv had stolen it.

Now was not the time to accuse Viv of theft. Unfortunately, Grace didn't hide her reaction soon enough for Viv to miss it.

Viv's resultant smile was both cynical and resigned. "Boys," she said, "why don't you let Grace and I talk girl stuff for a while."

Christian's hand tightened on Grace's shoulder. "I'll stay, too, if you don't mind."

Viv's mouth twisted. "I don't suppose you're giving me a choice. Fine." She waved her hand. "Everybody else: out of here."

Charlie didn't leave as quickly as the others. He stopped at the door to jab one finger toward Christian. "The police couldn't squeeze anything out of her. We're counting on you to get to the bottom of this."

Grace didn't know what to say once they were alone. Viv heaved a bitter sigh.

"Yes, I stole your watch," she said. "I broke into your cottage. That's why I was late to the read-through. I wouldn't let the nurses take it from me when they brought me here."

"But why?"

Viv rolled her eyes at Christian. "I wager he can guess."

If he could, he wasn't sharing. Viv sighed again.

"I thought you were like me, Grace," she said. "You never let the boys get anywhere with you. I wanted a piece of you to carry around. Like Matthew and Philip and their damn shoes."

"Oh," Grace said, the light finally dawning. "I—I didn't know. Viv, I'm sorry."

"Obviously, *sorry* wasn't the reaction I was hoping for."

No eighteen-year-old should have looked as timeworn as Viv did then. She wasn't embarrassed; she was weary of life itself. "Why didn't you tell us not to set you up on those dates?"

"Oh, please," Viv said. "I can't tell people what I am. My career is teetering on oblivion as it is. Being a former child star is too close to being a laughingstock."

"But, Viv, you're really talented."

Viv shook her head. "That won't matter if this gets out."

"Viv," Christian said. "You need to tell us who did this."

"I can't. He's too big a name. He'll retaliate."

"I can find out without your help. You've only been dating three or four actors."

Viv's stare was every bit as cool as his, though Grace suspected the reasons for their icy faces were different. "I'd appreciate it if you didn't. He'll make sure everyone knows there's something wrong with me."

"There's nothing wrong with you." The edge in Christian's voice was abruptly hot. "It's the world that needs to grow up."

Viv turned her head to the wall, away from him. Christian stepped around Grace and braced his hands on her bedrail.

"Sweetie," he said, reminding Grace with that single word that he was not the same age as his costar. "I know you think you're as hard as nails, but you need help handling this."

Viv didn't answer. Christian touched her shoulder.

What happened next was utterly unexpected. Light burst out from his skin and he went board stiff, the illumination bright enough to shine through his clothes.

"Lavaux," he gasped, staggering back a step.

Lavaux was the name of one of his father's men.

"What is it?" Grace stood and put her hand on his arm.

Christian shook himself. Sweat was beading on his forehead, faintly pink with blood. He grimaced as he tried to paste his glamour back where it belonged. Some inner turmoil prevented it. Light continued to flicker across his skin. Curious, Viv turned her pummeled body under the crisp white sheets.

"My God," she said. "What's the matter with his face?"

Grace forced her brain to work fast. "He confiscated one of those reporter's flash things. It must have gone off in his pocket."

"That's not what flashbulbs do."

Christian squeezed Grace's fingers hard. "Sorry," he said, then pushed awkwardly from the room.

"There's something wrong with him," Viv insisted.

Grace didn't have another story to reassure her, even if she'd been inclined to search for it then. "I have to go after him. I'll try to get him to promise not to take action against your attacker unless he talks to you first."

She didn't wait for Viv's response as she hurried into the corridor.

To her relief, she discovered Christian sitting in his car. He must have run there with vampire swiftness, but he hadn't disappeared into the night. He sprawled behind the wheel with his head back and his eyes closed. As she slid in the other side, he opened them and turned.

"God," he said, a shaky laugh in it. "It's ridiculous how happy I am you came after me."

"I felt the same when you followed me to the Bowl."

He rubbed his knuckles across his forehead. "I love you, Grace. I don't think these feelings can go away."

She nodded, because she didn't know what to say. He laughed softly at her response, though she didn't think he really saw it as humorous.

"I wanted you to know me," he said. "But I never planned on you knowing this."

"I wish you'd tell me what 'this' is. If I can, I'd like to make you feel better."

It was Christian's turn to nod.

"She's Lavaux," he said. "Viv is Lavaux reincarnated."

"Your father's man? The one who killed Philippe and Matthaus and maybe tricked Hans into that accident with the boar?"

Christian swallowed, his eyes still a little wild. "I saw it when I touched her. I was feeling— I like Viv, Grace. I admire her talent and her ambition, and I felt bad that she had to watch you . . . that she saw you seem to fall in love with me. Then, with all that . . . sympathy welling up in me, I discovered she was my enemy."

"That was then, Christian." Grace slid her fingers over the fist he'd balled on his thigh.

"Right," he said. "That was then."

Looking at him, she barely recognized his face, and this wasn't just because his glamour was in tatters. There wasn't a sliver of ice in his expression. He was struggling with his emotions, clearly unsure what his conclusion about this situation should be.

"I killed Lavaux," he said. "After you disappeared. He ran away before the battle on the bridge ended, but I tracked him to his home in France. He was barely surviving on his family farm with his younger brother. I guess their parents had died, because no one else was there. I didn't hesitate, Grace. I killed the brother, too, when he tried to defend Lavaux. At the time, considering what Lavaux had done to my friends, it seemed like justice for him to watch his sibling's blood run into the ground. But neither of them could have harmed me. I was a vampire then."

He shook his head, the fist he'd made bunching underneath her hand. "I can still feel Lavaux's flesh giving when I spitted him on my sword."

"So it confused you that you were willing to protect her from her attacker."

"Yes," he said, one deep crease running up his brow.

His eyes pleaded with her to help him make sense of this, or maybe it was absolution he wanted. Grace thought back to her own reaction to discovering the truth about her boss. She drew a slow breath before she spoke.

"I can't tell you killing them was okay, though Lavaux

doesn't seem to be dead now. I guess I understand why you did it. The right and wrong of it is too big for me to judge."

"Do you think I'm a monster?"

"I've never thought that. Do you think you're one?"

Her question took him aback. He sat straighter and stared at her. "No," he admitted. "Maybe I should, but I don't."

They looked at each other through the bars of brightness and shadow cast by the lights in the parking lot.

"Do you still want me?" he asked.

She cupped his face. This was a tiny thing to confess, given the rest of what she probably harbored in her heart. "From the moment we met," she said. "Then and now."

Seventeen

Grace's confession sent a sensual wave rolling over him, one that actually left him weak in the knees. "I'm taking you home," he said. "We're going to finish what we started."

She put her hand on his thigh, high up. "Good," she said. "Please go fast."

He probably broke a land-speed record. Halfway there he had to urge her to cup his cock; his erection was crying out that badly for attention.

"You won't come?" she asked, after which she blushed. "I mean, I know you can finish more than once, but—"

"I'll save all the times for you," he promised, mentally cursing the next stoplight. "I just need you to hold me."

Taking him at his word, she unzipped his jeans and worked her hand inside. Her grip found his base and tugged wonderfully upward. Luckily, the hour was late and traffic was sparse. No cars were near enough to see.

"I do have to drive," he reminded even as his hips rolled greedily off the leather seat.

"You're a vampire. Use your special powers of concentration."

She didn't duck her head down into his lap until they reached the three-quarters mark. He gasped, but he didn't stop her. Those wet, warm pulls of hers felt too good. Eventually, though, their effect was more than he could withstand. He dropped his hand gently to the back of her neck.

"*Grace*," he warned, his fingers stroking beneath her hair.

Heartless or perhaps aware that select parts of him didn't want her to stop, she hummed and continued sucking his stiff and quivering upper half. Needing his hands for driving, he gave up. Maybe gritting his teeth would enable him to hold on. Grace seemed to be counting on it, to judge by the little tricks she tried with her tongue. The Thunderbird's gears ground as he shifted down and turned into Nim Wei's dark estate. The place was empty. Everyone was out or off at the hospital. Pebbles flew out from under the wheels as he fishtailed the car in front of Grace's house.

Those first few seconds of being able to concentrate on the pleasure she was giving him were heaven. The next few reminded him how close he was to shooting everything down her throat.

"We're home," he groaned.

Her lips released him grudgingly as she sat on her heels. Bereft and stimulated to the screaming point, his cock poled straight up and shuddered. Christian wasn't the only one in a wound-up state. Grace was a picture he didn't think he would soon forget. Her deep red hair was tousled, her cheeks and lips flaming pink. She reached behind her and shoved the door open. As she backed out, he saw she'd removed her shoes. The sight of her stockinged feet drove a vicious kick of lust through his groin.

Barefoot equaled prey to the neck-biting beast in him.

Not that Grace was thinking of herself as prey. The way she looked him over made him feel dangerous. Her guard was gone, her eyes like gems set ablaze. When she wet her lips, her desire for him was completely unconcealed.

"Stay where you are," she said throatily.

The beast struggled at her order, but the man loved it. In that moment, he would have given her anything she asked. His life, his ranch, the head of his prick on a silver platter. He watched her, rapt, as she caught the hem of her soft gray dress in both hands and pulled it over her head. Her undergarments were crisp white lace, glowing in the darkness. Over the years, he'd seen many fashions in underthings. With the overkill this decade favored, her bra turned her breasts to rockets while the panties shaped and lifted her in ways her already feminine figure didn't require. His libido didn't mind the exaggeration. Certainly, the messages her stockings and garters sent about the places they *didn't* cover had his blood simmering.

He really had no suaver option than to ogle her. Finding appealing body parts was no problem, but when she ran her hands up her torso, their path magnetized his eyes. His fangs were throbbing, his neglected cock knotted with desire. She cupped her breasts, and his mouth watered. His gaze refused to rise far enough to check if she was smiling.

"We should go inside," he rasped. "We're steps from the door."

"I want you to take me on the hood of your car."

Desire blinded him. If that's what she wanted, that's what she'd get. In a flash, he was out of the car and on her, shoving her forward over the still-warm metal with her arms outspread. The cry Grace gave out was pleased. Satisfied this was what she wanted, he ripped the crotch of her panties and kicked her knees apart.

Her thighs shone white against the black car.

"Keep your hands where they are," he ordered. "It's my turn to touch you."

He went to his knees on the gravel, turning so his back was to the wheel well. He spread her thighs wider with his shoulders.

"What *are* you doing?" Grace asked.

"Warming you up. And you're not to move a muscle."

He slid his fingers inside her first, curving them, massaging her, until her warmth ran over them in the cool night air. She squirmed, of course. She was always responsive to his caresses.

"Stay," he reminded and tipped back his head to lick her.

She gasped at that, not expecting it. Like any oral-fixated creature, he was good with his tongue. Tonight he stroked it like a blade up and down her seam, skimming and teasing her hungry nerves until her little wriggling motions turned into stronger bucks. The scent she gave off was incredible.

"Chris-tian," she said, his name breaking on a groan.

He didn't suppose she meant for him to get up, but he did, folding his full height around her and cupping her in his palm.

"Jeesh," she said as he sank his fingers back into her from the front. Christian smiled at her titillated annoyance. Right then, driving her to orgasm was the last thing he intended.

He dragged his fangs along the soft skin beneath her ear. He knew the languid motions of his hand were frustrating her. "Had enough of going fast tonight?"

She panted before she answered. "Is that a trick question?"

"No." He pushed his cock against the creamy petals of her labia, riding it slowly, luxuriantly, through her wetness as his thumb searched out her clitoris. The little organ was swollen, begging to be rubbed. When he did, not quite firmly enough, a fresh rush of moisture ran out of her.

"I don't—" She twisted her hips in an attempt to drive his teasing fingers deeper. "I don't understand what you're asking."

He nipped her earlobe just enough to draw blood, the tiny taste causing his prick to thump crazily. "In a way, this is our first time. Because you remember me. Because now you know how long I've been missing you. I want it to be big. I want you—us—to come together in one long explosion."

"And?"

"And I can't do that if I rush. I thought, maybe, you'd try to hold back with me."

He bumped her entry with his crown, then eased into her in a single lubricious glide. He filled her a millimeter at a time, his cock pulsing ever harder as she enclosed him. She was snug, but she took him—with a sigh that told him how much she liked being stretched by him. When he was all the way inside her, pressing that rapturous spot at the end of her, she couldn't leave her hands where they were. One came off the hood to grab for his hip.

Ignoring what it was urging, he pushed her up until her feet left the ground. Her bra hooks were there for the popping, so he did away with the stiff garment. Discarding her panties took one more rip. Then her beautiful, female body was naked under him. Well, naked but for the stockings and garters. His cotton T-shirt was soft as silk from his aura. Knowing this and hungry for more contact, he rubbed his chest across her undulating back.

Evidently, doing this out in the open excited her. Her pussy clutched him as she moaned and writhed harder.

"Christian," she said. "I don't—" Her hips nearly took his head off as they twisted. "I don't think I can hold back at all."

"You can," he growled, uncertain he could himself.

He took the hand she'd flung onto his hip and placed it back on the car, manacling both her wrists in one hand.

Stretching them above her head got her going, too. She liked being at his mercy as much as he enjoyed having put her there. Her insides quivered, hot cream flooding over him.

"I want to watch you," she pleaded. "I want to know what this does to you."

"I'll turn you. When we come, you'll be facing me."

She moaned a protest, but he couldn't let her have her way in this. He wanted to be good to her, wanted to be sweet and tender. She hadn't said she still loved him. If he gazed into her eyes . . . If he saw that all she felt was lust . . . He didn't want that knowledge to change how he treated her, but he was afraid it would.

So he pushed into her from behind with her hands held captive and her throat letting out helpless mewls of bliss. Though he was dressed and she was naked, to his heart it seemed the other way around. He squeezed her pubis with his free hand, but only fingered her clit lightly. In and out he moved his penis, pulling, pushing, feeling every inch of each motion on those sensitive vampire nerves. Despite it nearly killing him, he forced himself to be as patient as the ocean under the cliffs nearby.

"Chris," she moaned.

"Grace," he answered, licking the salty bend of her neck.

She shuddered under him, breathing hard.

The top of his head was floating on the edge, the sting of pressure in his balls epic. Her round little ass was both a cushion for his rocking and an ideal means for her to torment him with her squirms. The hold he had on her wrists didn't prevent her hands from clenching.

"Christian," she hissed between her teeth. "If you push into me one more time, I'm going to go."

He believed her. Her energy had that quality of being ready to burst its seams. With a tortured groan, he pulled his hard-on out of her warmth. They both panted for a moment, their aroused bodies adjusting to the denial of what they most wanted.

"Release my hands," Grace whispered.

He released them, bracing his arms on the car. His body temperature was so unnaturally elevated that his palms fogged the black finish. Grace wriggled onto her back within the cage he'd formed. Her eyes went wide when she saw his face.

His wish that he could claim her forever must have been written there.

"I'd chain you to me if I could," he admitted. "I'd never let you slip away again."

She touched the center of his chest where his heart was thudding in slow motion. "I'm here now, Christian."

This was all she could promise, all any lover could. She feathered her fingertips along the sides of his neck, bending her legs until the soles of her feet were supported by the side of the car. He looked at what her white garters framed: the flushed wet beauty that was her sex. It meant the world that she didn't try to hide herself. He saw he'd prepared her well for this finish. Her muscles were twitching, as eager as his to join. Despite that eagerness, her hands were infinitely gentle—always his heart's downfall. Within their lush frame of lashes, her eyes shone like stars. Whatever she felt, it was more than lust. That he'd bet his life on.

He leaned into her, his pulsing tip returning to the sleek welcome of her folds.

"Oh, God," she breathed as he found her opening and gently pushed.

Entering her was like coming home, a paradise designed just for him.

"Don't close your eyes," he said.

She didn't seem able to obey. Her neck arched as he lengthened his penetration, the change in angle changing what she felt. Her hands slapped onto his rear. Little spasms from her sheath rippled up his shaft, causing him to inhale sharply. His fangs ached like they were burning as his cock tried to swell half an inch longer.

"Oh, God," she gasped again.

"Open your eyes, sweetheart."

Her lashes fluttered upward, her knees shifting higher on his ribs. His lips were peeling back in preparation for biting her, an involuntary reflex he couldn't control just then. Grace didn't seem to mind the predatory display, though it dismayed him. Maybe she saw that. Tears glittered in her eyes.

"I'm staying with you," she said. "I'm not going anywhere."

He reached her end and pushed once, hard, the extra pressure causing her to cry out.

"Soon," he snarled, so close he could barely understand himself. "*Soon.*"

He dragged his prick halfway out of her, and then his instincts completely snapped their leash. His head swung down to her neck even as her hands came to cradle it. His jaw widened, saliva flowing. She pushed her pelvis up him, and suddenly his hips were whipping in and out by themselves. The immediate explosion of sharp sensations did them both in. Christian growled and bit her, pulling in one hard swallow as the climax burst. It was as huge as he'd wanted, as long and as mutual.

He couldn't hear Grace's thoughts, but—by God—he could feel her pleasure. It propelled his own to stratospheric heights. His toes curled in his boots, his thigh muscles bunching to sling him even deeper inside of her. He stopped sucking only when her heart gave a tiny skip. He licked the wound closed with a conflicted groan. Her blood had felt like love running down his throat.

"I'm okay," she slurred before he could ask. "Just a bit dizzy."

"I took too much."

"Only what I wanted to give."

He checked her aura. She seemed no more weakened than she ought to be. Her index finger traced the line of his lower lip. "You're a worrier, you are."

"Ha," he said, unsettled by how easily she saw into him. "There had better be food in that fridge of yours."

"Cold pizza," she said as he swung her into his arms. "And, thanks to you, I won't feel guilty eating it."

Grace consumed two slices of pizza and a tall glass of orange juice, but once she'd filled her stomach, she was done in. Seeing Viv laid out in that hospital bed had brought up memories she'd rather have let lie. She visited the bathroom, washed up, and brushed her hair. When she came back to her room, Christian was stretched out on his side on her bed, his head propped casually on his hand— pretty much like he belonged there.

He'd stripped off his white T-shirt, giving her a lovely view of his lean and muscular torso tapering into his jeans. Though his body was at rest, the way his sexual organs filled up the crotch intrigued her.

Unlike her, he didn't look the least bit ready to yawn.

"Shank of the evening for you, I guess," she said.

He smiled and patted the mattress. "I'll watch over you while you sleep."

That sounded so good to her she sighed.

She crawled up, burrowed under the covers, and snuggled into him. His arms came around her as if they belonged, too.

"I won't let go," he said.

Her heart gave a little crack, but it wasn't breaking. It was letting him in. He was her safety, not because nothing bad could happen, but because he truly cared for her.

"I do," she mumbled against the smooth muscles of his chest.

"You do what?"

"I do love you back."

He went very still beneath her, and her lips curved up in a smile. Her heart wasn't cracking now; it was singing. This must be what joy felt like. She thought she'd relish a chance to get used to it.

"I'm glad," he said after a moment, one hand moving to pet her hair.

"Better be," she retorted, then let a wall of sleep tumble over her.

Christian was no more a mystic than his father had been. By now, however, he'd met a ghost, become a vampire, and encountered at least three of his old associates reborn. Four, if he counted the similarities he sometimes saw between Roy and Hans. He wondered who else might have come back without his recognizing them. His doughty comrade, William? His best friend, Michael? Or had Michael switched teams to become the angel who'd guided Grace to him? Michael *had* been a mystic, caring but superstitious, his conscience pricked by his failed attempt to join the priesthood.

Christian found it both odd and warming to think of him watching out for Grace. Why he'd do it mystified him. Grace wasn't Michael's sweetheart; she was Christian's. But maybe that was the point, that your friends' happiness mattered. One thing he knew: immortal life could be peculiar.

Christian shook his head at Grace's ceiling. Moonlight poured in through the panes of the French windows. He'd have to draw the curtains before morning. Spare himself getting drunk or roasted before his lover had breakfast. Though Grace would wake more energetic—and likely starving—for the moment, she lay on his chest like a runner felled by a marathon.

The smile that had been tugging at Christian's mouth

spread across his face. She loved him back. She knew what he was, she knew what he'd done, and she loved him back. He couldn't doubt she knew her own mind. The Grace she'd grown into since returning to her own time was a deliberate soul.

"Peculiar," he said aloud. Life was peculiar and wonderful. His eyelids grew heavy with his relaxation. Maybe he'd sleep with her for a few minutes.

If he hadn't been so dozy, he'd have had more warning. As it was, it wasn't a rush of threatening thoughts that alerted him, but an unpleasant buzzing along his skin. Half a second after his eyes snapped open, an intruder with a machete crashed through the French windows. The man was dressed in a black silk turtleneck and knife-pleat trousers, like Cary Grant playing a cat burglar.

Apparently, this burglar wasn't accustomed to breaking doors. He tripped over the wood he'd cracked, nearly losing his large cleaverlike weapon.

"You'll never hurt her again," the intruder vowed in dramatic tones. "Not when I'm done with you."

His theatrics would have been funny if he hadn't been swinging that blade toward Grace.

Christian caught his arm before the strike could connect, then smashed him back against Grace's large English-style armoire. The crack of his skull on the mahogany was satisfying, as was his cry of pain when Christian squeezed his wrist bones hard enough to cause his fingers to go numb and drop his weapon.

"You're out of your mind," Christian growled, shoving the man again. "Trying to kill your daughter in front of a witness."

"What?" George Gladwell said with his jaw dropping.

"Mmph." This came from Grace, who was struggling up in bed, half asleep.

Christian kept his attention on her attacker. His voice

came out low enough to sound inhuman. "You're the one who's never going to hurt her again."

He had his palm spread flat on her father's slightly concave chest. One push with his vampire strength would snap his miserable sternum. He wanted to do it with a nearly sensual longing.

"Don't!" Grace cried. "That's not my father. It's Montgomery Dare, the star of *The Wild Frontier*."

"Yes," said the man whose heart Christian was on the verge of crushing. "She's the woman who stole Vivian's love from me. She's the woman who left *her* for *you*."

"You're a TV star?" Christian said.

"A movie star," the man corrected with a sniff. "I'm just doing TV temporarily."

Christian slapped his hand over the man's forehead, gripping his temples to prevent him from evading his eye lock. His fury wasn't softened by the man's true identity. He'd have enjoyed hurting Grace's father more, but any man who'd harm her would do. That being the case, he shoved into her attacker's mind with a ruthlessness he rarely exercised. Inside, he found a tangle of pride and fury and delusion. Ironically, the distastefulness of Dare's thoughts was a better deterrent than any plea for mercy. Grimacing, he attempted to paw through the snarl more delicately.

Once he'd identified what was pertinent, he pulled back and shook himself.

"He's the sniper who tried to kill you," he said to Grace. "He learned to sharp-shoot in Korea. And he's the person who beat Viv up."

"She broke up with me," the man exclaimed. "None of the other stars she was dating cared a fig about her. They only cared about looking younger when she was on their arms. I loved her. She should have loved me back."

"So you *beat* her?" Christian said in disgust.

"I told her I was sorry. She left me." He turned to Grace,

who was staring at him with her mouth open. "I know it was because she secretly loves you. She'd rather do unnatural things with a woman than be with her soul mate."

He'd begun to cry, which—in a way—was the most repellent thing he'd done yet. Knees buckling as he sobbed, he slid down the front of Grace's wardrobe. Christian's urge to kill him faded reluctantly. As homicidal maniacs went, this one was pitiful.

That, however, didn't mean he would let him go.

"Loan me some clothesline," he said to Grace.

Bless her, she closed her mouth and went to get it. Dare, by contrast, didn't have the decency to resist when Christian trussed him up in it.

"What are you going to do with him?" Grace asked.

Christian's close-lipped smile made their prisoner shiver. "I'm going to pass him on to your boss. She'll find a way to exact an appropriate consequence *and* keep Viv safe from scandal."

Nim Wei accepted Christian's delivery with aplomb, first thralling Dare to glassy-eyed silence, then sitting him— still tied in Grace's rope—on a little upholstered bench inside her front entryway.

The actor had been disconcertingly pleased to meet her, going so far as to suggest she ought to direct a suspense film pairing him with Kim Novak.

Even the queen didn't have a comeback for that.

Ignoring the now-serene man, she leaned out the door toward Christian.

"I'll take care of him," she promised. "He won't lay a hand on another soul." Her eyes narrowed thoughtfully. "I might even throw in a compulsion to confess his most embarrassing personal habits to the media. Unhinged over-the-hill actors do things like that sometimes. When I'm through, his life will be more hellish than prison."

"Fine," Christian said, satisfied to leave the details to her. He turned to go, but a nagging question tugged him around. "Why are you involved in this craziness?"

Nim Wei's dark almond eyes widened. "He tried to kill Grace. He injured my female lead."

"Not that. Why are you making movies?"

Nim Wei's brows lowered. "I *enjoy* it. Directing is *fun*."

This struck him as disingenuous. The queen he knew was a creature of plots and ploys. Seeing his skepticism, she crossed her arms. "Believe what you like," she said.

He nodded and turned away for a second time. He felt Nim Wei's eyes on his back, no doubt glaring coolly at him. Though he didn't betray his awareness of her attention, he was privately relieved when she slammed the door.

Freed from her scrutiny, he glanced at Grace's cottage. The bond between them was ephemeral but there. He sensed she was calming from her ordeal, thinking about him but not worried by his absence. Because his own nerves needed settling, he walked past Nim Wei's Italian villa–inspired pool toward the overlook. The murmur of the Pacific called to him like the rush of blood through a human heart. Eternal and reassuring. A lullaby for all species.

When he arrived at the drop-off, he tipped his face to the sky. The consciousness he hoped to reach was further off than any he'd tried to contact before.

"I know it was you," he said quietly. "I know you warned me to turn the car when Dare shot at Grace. You're the Michael she called her angel."

No voice responded from the cosmos, no sensation that couldn't have been written off as the brush of the ocean breeze. Maybe the circumstances weren't extreme enough for Michael to answer. Left with no clear reply, Christian wondered if his old friend approved of him relinquishing his grudge against Lavaux, if he'd wanted Christian to refrain from killing Montgomery Dare. After a moment, he let the question go. He couldn't live by someone else's standards, not even an angel's. Christian was at peace with his decisions. That's what had to count for him.

The gentle wind gusted in his face, lifting his hair like the motion of ghostly hands.

"All right, old friend," Christian said to the diamond-bright sparkle of the stars. "Just wanted to say thank you. If you ever decide to come here with the rest of us, I'd be proud to know you again."

As he walked around the house, lights went on in the wing where Charlie and the other boys had their rooms. Christian often felt like an outsider peering through the windows of human life. Tonight he took unexpected comfort in identifying the young actors. There was Charlie laughing at something Matthew said. Here was Philip brushing his teeth. Bonehead was lying on his back in bed, enjoying a daydream about a female extra. For now these mortals were a part of his life, and he was part of theirs. Maybe the ties would break when the movie ended. Maybe they'd last longer. Whether they did had nothing to do with Christian being a vampire. These boys took the same risks with each other.

Regardless of what he'd lost in the past, Christian could make new connections. If he chose to. If he dared to. It would be up to him.

He smiled to himself, lighter in spirit than he'd been in a while. Perhaps not everything in his life was perfect, but it was very good for now.

Eighteen

The next two months flew by like a dream for Grace. She was with Christian, and a stream of happiness bubbled under everything she did, almost frightening in its consistency. Viv had been a trouper, healing quicker than anyone expected. That this might be due to "special" treatment from her director, Grace didn't want to dwell on. It seemed too much like something she might have to think better of her boss for. What mattered was that production on *I Was a Teen-Age Vampire* rolled onward mostly without a hitch.

They'd had one very exciting day racing north to shoot beneath a large scarlet maple before its leaves fell off. Grace was bowled over by her first looks at the developed film rushes, and everyone was buzzing over Montgomery Dare's mysterious compulsion to humiliate himself any time he got within ten feet of a reporter. His sole response to questions about his broken-off romance with Viv was, "She was too good for me."

Viv seemed to sense Miss Wei was behind this, though Grace doubted she attributed Dare's behavior to anything more supernatural than a strong warning to back off.

All in all, despite her estrangement from her employer, Grace was enjoying her job more than ever. It might not be professional, but falling in love with a colleague did add spice to her days. Coming home with Christian was even better. The making-love part was very nice, naturally, but so was the companionship. Christian's company suited her. He was quiet enough that she could work in peace with him there, not that quiet was always what she wanted. She liked the times he'd come out with little stories—events he'd lived through, people he'd known—as if he were testing the concept of sharing his past with her. The anecdotes unfailingly intrigued her. There were aspects of being a vampire that had never occurred to her. History was their playground, which meant it had been Christian's.

Tonight he wasn't sharing stories. Tonight he was sitting with his back propped on the opposite arm of the fat flowered couch from her. He thumbed through her copy of *On Acting* while she double-checked her list of things to do tomorrow. The lamp behind him brought out the blue highlights in his black hair. He was so beautiful she had to mentally pinch herself that he was really there with her. The other night, he'd treated the cast to dinner at the Mocambo. Their waitress must have called every friend she had. When they'd exited the nightclub, at least fifty girls had been waiting, all screaming Christian's name. Though the boys had teased him mercilessly, it had taken everyone by surprise. And Grace knew Christian's star was only going to blaze brighter.

But he was hers tonight, his feet resting familiarly in her lap. They were as graceful as the rest of him, his toenails shining and clear like glass. Grace was tempted to test how ticklish his arches were. Christian giggling was a marvel she'd like to see.

Though he'd sworn he couldn't read her mind, his toes twitched and he looked up.

"You read this, didn't you?" he asked, one palm covering the page he was on. He must have reached a passage she'd underlined.

"I took acting classes as well. It's helpful for directors to understand the cast's point of view."

He considered her, thoughts she wished she could follow moving behind his eyes. In the time they'd spent together, she'd learned just how quick and intelligent he was. Relaxed now, he wasn't keeping up his glamour the way he used to. Sparks of gold swam in his irises, and his pale skin gleamed like a shooting star. Every feature he had was harmonious with the others, the overall effect so pleasing it hypnotized.

Sitting across from him, Grace tried not to feel inadequate. Christian liked her humanity, or so he often said.

"It's interesting," he said at last.

"Directing?"

"The whole business. I was thinking that today when we were in harness and jumping off those platforms with the giant fan blowing back our hair—all so audiences will believe vampires can leap far. The average person has no idea what goes into making a movie."

"Six burly men with a safety mattress?"

He met her teasing smile with a fond one. "I thought this acting thing would bore me, once I'd achieved what I set out to."

Grace lifted her brows at him.

His expression turned serious but not cold. "I wanted to make you remember me. At the time, I believed I wanted to punish you, but I suspect my heart had its own ideas even then."

He'd never said this so openly. Her throat was thick when she responded. "I'm grateful your heart won out."

His smile flashed like sunshine, his single dimple making

an appearance. He nudged her midriff playfully with his toes. "We know what *you* wanted back then: a fling with a younger man."

"Too bad that desire was doomed to disappointment." Grace caught his feet and squeezed them, their marble chill warming in her hold.

"Nim Wei gave you more second unit work to direct today, didn't she?"

Grace's face abruptly grew cooler. "It was no big deal. We took some exterior crane shots of the real mansion Joe Pryor's house is based on. Miss Wei didn't have time to spend on it."

"It looked to me like it was a peace offering."

Grace's snort was acerbic. "That's just another name for a bribe. She realizes I can't warm up to her again now that I know what she is."

"She's a queen, Grace. She doesn't need to court anybody's favor unless they matter to her."

"Why are you pushing me to forgive her!"

Grace would have flung herself off the couch if Christian hadn't leaned forward to take her hands.

"I'm not pushing." He pulled her fists close against his chest. "What you decide is your business. I think, though, that I'm more conscious of how forgiving your heart prefers to be. You forgave me quite a lot, after all."

"That was then," Grace said sullenly, "when I went back in time as a ghost. The petty human parts of me faded. Michael as good as told me I'd turn into an angel if I stayed with him long enough. I guess I'm just meaner now."

Christian kissed her knuckles. "I wouldn't call you *mean*. I admit, I didn't like when Nim Wei suggested I shouldn't hold a grudge, but what the queen did was a long time ago."

"It's that she did it to *you*," Grace burst out. "That's what I can't forgive. I'm sorry if that makes me a small person."

Christian's eyes glowed in earnest. "If you're small, what does that say about me for loving you?"

It was a question she'd asked herself. Not wanting to expose her insecurities, she tried to answer him jokingly. "Probably that you're stupid and have no taste."

Christian crawled up her torso and bared his fangs, eliciting the usual quivers between her legs. "I have plenty of taste," he purred, bending to mouth her neck. "Maybe you need reminding how delicious you are."

He'd coaxed her into smiling—and to wrapping him in her arms as his weight settled onto her. She loved the knowledge that he was wallowing in her warmth.

"Maybe I do need reminding," she admitted, her sex going hot and wet. "But I'm sure I need foreplay first."

Since Christian's idea of foreplay was what other people called intercourse, neither of them could object to that.

As he nuzzled toward her cleavage, Grace told herself this affair would last as long as it lasted. She wasn't going to count the minutes. She was going to enjoy them.

Nineteen

The filming of *Teen-Age Vampire* finished without fanfare. They shot a chase sequence in the artificial woods the crew had created on Soundstage Six, enjoyed a relatively decorous party at Miss Wei's home, and then most everyone melted away to pursue their next projects.

Work on the actual movie, by contrast, was only halfway done.

Grace had already watched the first assembly cut with Miss Wei and Wade. This initial and very raw piecing together of the footage assured them the story was all there. Next, boring bits would be trimmed and performances massaged. Grace had offered her opinion when she was asked, but Miss Wei's vision would dictate what ended up in the cut the studio vetted. Grace had no difficulty trusting her boss with that. Miss Wei's directorial eye was keen.

It was the personal aspect of their association that was giving Grace trouble.

She paused outside the private editing suite in her employer's basement, smoothing her businesslike white blouse and trying to compose herself. Though her boss hadn't confronted her about the change in her behavior, each time they interacted, acting normal became harder.

"For God's sake, don't stand out there all night," Miss Wei called through the door.

Grace turned the knob and entered the darkened room. Miss Wei was by herself, the picture editor having left at dusk. Lengths of celluloid hung in a tidy bin beside the director while she watched the Moviola project a scene.

The images reflected light and color on Miss Wei's face, which was as masklike as it could be. She had an open legal pad propped on her right knee. She was jotting notes rapidly on it.

Looking toward the screen, Grace saw she watched a less rough version of the night scene in the abandoned boxcar, where Mary and Joe's boys had joined up. The footage had been shot after Viv's fight with Dare, and Christian's protectiveness toward her, his affection and his respect, infused everything Joe did. What surprised Grace was how innocent he also managed to appear. Joe, as Christian played him, was a young man caught up in the wonder of falling in love for the first time.

The idea that he might have pulled those emotions from his experience with her made her squirm a little and shake herself.

Just because Christian loved her now didn't mean she'd be enough for him forever.

But that wasn't a worry she needed to pick at. Wade was a genius for capturing the layers of feeling in Christian's eyes, as he was for getting everything else the camera saw to tell to the same story. The air of domesticity was exactly as Grace had hoped, created by Mary's glowing portable radio, by Joe wrapping her in his jacket, by the lovers Philip

and Matthew sprawled in the straw nearby. Charlie stood
apart, fidgeting in the doorway over his moral struggle, but
Wade had used an over-the-shoulder angle from behind Joe
to connect him visually to the rest. Even without scoring or
sound effects, he'd caught the mood they were going for.
The characters looked like a group destiny had bonded, a
little family of misfits.

Admiration for everyone swelled in her. Grace felt so
privileged to have worked with this particular cast and
crew that her vocal cords tightened. Once, she would have
expressed that sense of gratitude to her boss. Tonight, she
wasn't inclined to.

"Did you want something from me?" she asked, willing
herself not to clear her throat.

Miss Wei shut off the projector and turned to her. Her
breath huffed out of her nose. "Something more than this
endless civility, to be sure."

Heat crept up Grace's face. "I'm doing my job."

"Yes, you are," Miss Wei said coolly.

"I can't help it if I feel differently."

Miss Wei pushed up from her canvas director's chair,
the move too graceful to be human. She looked like she
was rising through water. Fearing her breathing would turn
ragged, Grace clutched her hands together in front of her
diaphragm. She guessed they were finally going to have
this out.

Miss Wei's eyes glittered like black stones. "Christian
told you what the pair of us are."

Grace had remembered this for herself, but evidently
her employer remained unaware of that.

"I expect he also told you how we met," Miss Wei continued when Grace said nothing. "Spilled a few stories
about what a cruel old devil I used to be?"

She was trying to lead Grace into explaining, which
Grace had no urge to do.

"What trick did you pull on me?" she asked instead.

"Trick?"

"To keep Christian from being able to read my mind."

"Ah, that." The woman Christian called a queen regarded her thoughtfully. "I put a thrall on you to resist vampiric influence. I didn't think Christian ought to have that advantage over a person I considered to be my friend. The spell keeps me from influencing you as well, and—if I say so myself—I'm legendarily good at them. I can't undo what I've done."

She took a step toward Grace, then stopped when her assistant tensed. "You're not asking me to undo it, of course."

Her certainty was annoying. "You're preventing us from being as close as we could."

Miss Wei laughed without humor. "I know a thing or two about you, Grace. You like to keep your private thoughts private. I'd wager quite a sum that knowing Christian can't get into your noggin makes you more open around him. I did you both a favor. You should thank me."

Grace wanted to tell her not to hold her breath. Then again, since she was a vampire, Miss Wei could hold her breath for a while.

"Is there anything else?" Grace asked politely.

Her employer frowned, the tiny flicker smoothing away so quickly Grace told herself she'd imagined it. Miss Wei was as beautiful as a porcelain doll, incapable of feeling—much less of being hurt.

"No," she said. "Enjoy your evening with your boyfriend."

Grace left . . . but wished her ribs weren't contracting with the suspicion that she might be a teensy bit in the wrong.

Twenty

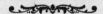

Christian glowered at his reflection in the full-length mirror of his bedroom at the Chateau Marmont. He wore a tuxedo shirt and white dinner jacket with a pale pink bow tie. The manager at Mattson's had informed him this would look rebellious without overdoing it. Despite the excellent cut of the jacket, Christian wiggled his shoulders and wished he were comfortable.

"Got too used to T-shirts," Roy observed from the door.

He wore his own monkey suit, but it was the standard black version. Christian had asked Roy to look out for Grace this evening, since Christian was assigned to take Viv to the premiere. Christian's costar would ride behind him on his Harley, which he'd drive right onto the red carpet. The stunt was Grace's stroke of promotional genius; otherwise he'd have refused it.

He'd much rather have escorted her.

"You want your box now?" Roy offered. "I can hang on to it if you like."

"No," Christian said. "I mean, yes. Or maybe I should just check it."

Roy strode to him grinning, the glossy black Harry Winston box balanced on his palm. "I had 'em give the stone an extra polish before I forked your cash over."

"Great," Christian said, then realized Roy was joking. Exasperated with his own nerves, he blew out his breath.

When he opened the double-hinged lid, the ring was perfect: big and pear-shaped but elegant as well. The softest wash of blue ensured the diamond would complement Grace's hair.

"Marilyn Monroe wouldn't refuse that rock," Roy proclaimed.

Unfortunately, Marilyn wasn't the female he was asking to marry him. Grace was independent, and not in the way this decade's women were painted to be in ads. She wasn't going to stay home cooking her husband dinner on the latest kitchen appliances. That wasn't freedom to her. She had a career. She'd been supporting herself since she was eighteen. She'd rented her own apartment, away from Nim Wei, the day after post-production on *Teen-Age Vampire* wrapped.

Although it was true Christian spent most of his nights at her place, the only expenses she let him cover were prime rib and orange juice. She liked to tease that he benefitted from them as much as she did.

Roy slapped his back and burst out laughing, jarring him from his train of thought. "Son, if you could see how green you look, you'd be shocked."

Christian stifled a sigh. "I ought to feel more sure of myself. We've been together five months now."

"If you were sure, you wouldn't be in love. You've got something at stake with Grace—no pun intended."

He had more at stake than he wanted to think about. He didn't just want Grace to marry him; he hoped she'd share his immortal life. An uncharacteristic sweat prickled under his pink bow tie.

Maybe he should have mentioned his hopes to her earlier. This was a big decision for anyone.

He was relieved when a knock sounded on the door. A distraction was exactly what he needed.

He zipped to open it before Roy could, the visitors he found a surprise. One was a tall, huge-shouldered man with the bluffly handsome face of an English farmer. The other was a rangy, auburn-haired female who reminded him of Katharine Hepburn when she first came to Hollywood. Both were vampires, though the woman was new to it.

"Graham," Christian said. "And Pen. I wasn't expecting you."

Graham grinned and Pen stepped inside to offer him a rib-squeezing hug. New to her powers or not, she was strong, a trait she probably enjoyed. Pen had been a "modern" woman in the 1930s—and a born adventurer. The three of them had worked together to defeat a rather terrible foe.

When Pen finally let Christian push back from her, a smile stretched across his face. He was happier she was here than he'd have thought possible. "I don't think I've seen you since you were changed."

"Five whole years," Pen said, poking his chest with one slim finger.

"You could have sent us an invitation to this shindig," Graham added, "instead of leaving it to the bitch queen."

"Don't call her that," Pen scolded. "At the least, it's not diplomatic. Hey, there, how are you, Roy?"

The pair exchanged greetings while Christian studied Pen. She seemed at ease with her altered nature. Graham had let her live a decent number of human years before transforming her. Grace was only in her twenties, but the thought of waiting twenty more to change her made him itchy. Her father was still out there, and who knew what other dangers. In his opinion, Hollywood wasn't as safe as it should have been.

Pen punched his arm to regain his attention. "We saw

Teen-Age Vampire's billboard. 'He's a vampire with a con-science. She's a helpless human, risking her life for love.' Made me want to stand in line."

"I didn't write that," Christian said in his own defense.

"Speaking of helpless humans," Graham interjected, "where's your young lady?"

"She's hardly helpless," Christian said, though in truth a part of him was thinking precisely that.

"We'd love to meet her." Pen's Southern accent turned the words soothing. "From what Graham tells me, you hold her in high regard."

Christian definitely did that. Whether Grace was pre-pared to be introduced as "his" young lady, he didn't know. The telephone's sudden jangle saved him from responding. When he lifted the receiver, Charlie was on the line.

"Hey, man," he said. "Come join us at Grace's for pre-premiere cocktails."

"Grace's?" Christian tried not to bristle over Charlie inviting him to his lover's home.

"We were going to meet at Naomi's, but she must have been in a mood. She nearly bit my head off when I sug-gested it. Viv's here, too. If you ride your Harley, you can take her straight to Grauman's from Grace's place."

"I have guests."

"The more, the merrier," Charlie said. "I know Grace won't enjoy this half as much without you. You know how uptight she gets at parties."

Grace's uptightness was something Charlie could coax her out of, but Christian appreciated his faith in him.

"We'll be there soon," he said. "Don't let anyone get too drunk."

"I'm on top of that already," Charlie assured him.

Grace couldn't help but notice Charlie had grown up in the last five months. He'd always been confident, but his big break seemed to have made him calmer—maybe even responsible. Tonight, he'd brought his own cocktail-making supplies and was proud of himself for it.

"I'll have you know," he said as he passed Philip a blush-colored champagne flute, "these are authentic Hemingway-style Bellinis, made with Prosecco and peach purée."

He watched as Philip swallowed a cautious sip. "They're good," he said, "but nobody's going to get tipsy drinking them."

"That's the idea, my friends. We're going to have an embarrassment-free premiere."

The younger members of the cast were gathered in Grace's living room, which she'd decorated with brightly colored secondhand furniture. Though the apartment had the advantage of being hers, it was no match for her old cottage on Miss Wei's grounds. The small dimensions of the space made her guests seem like quite a crowd. Luckily, they didn't mind being squished together. Considering how excited and nervous everyone was, it was no wonder they were bubbling more than their Bellinis.

If *Teen-Age Vampire* turned out to be a hit, it could change all their lives.

"Can I talk to you a minute?" Viv asked Grace in an undertone. She was the belle of the ball in her loaned-out diamond necklace and strapless blue satin Dior gown. She'd have to ride Christian's motorcycle sidesaddle, but if anyone could pull that off, it was her. For that matter, if anyone could keep her safe, it was him. Grace's dress was a much less flashy knee-length affair. Its black velvet and close fit satisfied any niggling urge she had to show off.

"Sure," she said, wondering what Viv wanted to talk about. Since part of what she wanted seemed to be privacy, she pushed open the saloon doors to her postage stamp–size kitchen.

Viv preceded her in. She stopped by the sink, where she turned and leaned nervously.

"Here," the actress said, thrusting out a white-lidded box. "It's yours. You never asked for it back."

Inside was the charm watch Miss Wei had given her. Grace remembered how touched she'd been to receive it. Now she wasn't sure she'd ever wear it again. She stroked the coiled silver links and tried to decide what she ought to say.

"I wanted to thank you for being so nice about everything," Viv said.

"I was never mad at you, Viv. You were just—"

"Being an idiot?"

"I was going to say just being eighteen."

Viv looked down at her tangled fingers, then up at Grace again. "I'm seeing someone," she blurted. "A girl someone. We have to keep it quiet, but it's been nice."

"I'm glad for you," Grace said.

"I don't know if it's a forever love affair or anything."

"Does it have to be?"

"No," Viv said, then let a brilliant smile break across her face. "It's been good to finally be myself for a while."

Grace told her heart not to go crazy just because Christian was shouldering into her living room—advice her heart pretty much ignored. Each time she saw him, the love she felt swelled bigger. When he reached her, she had to hug him, and when she hugged him, she had to go to her toes and lay a soft, slow kiss on his lovely mouth. She'd never kissed him in front of people, but celebrating this event seemed to demand it.

A few whistles from the boys were a small price to pay.

The kiss went on until Christian's fangs started to slide down. With a sigh that was half laugh and half reluctance, he pulled his tongue free of hers. Grace quivered inside at how he licked his lips.

"That's quite a welcome," he said, his eyes sparkling with pleasure. "My friends are going to be impressed."

"Your *friends*?"

"They're in the hallway." He held her face and looked fondly down at her. "There's a bit of a crush in here."

"Oh," Grace said. "I'm sorry. I shouldn't have—"

He kissed her lips gently one more time. "You're perfect, sweetheart. And that dress!" He let out a growl that delighted her. "I'll bring you out to them."

She must have grown more sensitive to the signs, because she saw at once that his friends were vampires. She felt a moment's instinctive caution, but it passed as soon as Christian squeezed her hand. No friends of his were going to hurt her.

"Grace, this is Graham Fitz Clare and his wife, Pen."

"I'm so glad you could come," Grace said.

The big man's smile was both sweet and mischievous. "Didn't think I'd ever see old Durand with a real girlfriend."

"Graham!" His wife elbowed him. "We're pleased to meet you, Grace. Any friend of Christian's is a friend of ours."

Grace had caught glimpses of this before—that Christian had led a life between the time she first knew him and the day they met in his barn. The vampire couple's obvious affection for him made her think Christian hadn't told her the whole story of his past. Maybe he didn't know it himself. More people than she had discovered how lovable he was.

Christian's hand slid up her back to rub the nape of her neck underneath her hair. To her surprise, his fingers were trembling. "Grace, do you think I could steal a few minutes with you in private before we have to take off?"

This must have been her evening for tête-a-têtes. "Sure," she said. "Why don't we try the stairwell?"

"You'll be all right?" he asked his friends, his head jerking toward the noise in her living room.

Graham Fitz Clare laughed at him. "Don't you worry. *We* like people."

"They seem nice," Grace said as they entered her building's stairs.

Christian hummed and leaned back to block the metal fire door from opening. She could see his mind wasn't on his friends.

"Is something wrong? You look pale. Paler," she said when he rolled his eyes.

"My glamour's probably thinning." He drew a full breath into his chest—not a common act for him. "Grace, I hope it isn't too soon to ask this, because I don't think I can wait anymore."

"Ask what?" Grace said, her shoulders tightening at his manner.

He held up a finger and dug into his white dinner jacket's right pocket. The black jeweler's box he drew out seemed a good indicator of what this was about.

"Oh, boy," she said, her hand pressed to her suddenly pounding heart.

Her reaction brought Christian's head back up in alarm. "You're surprised. It *is* too soon."

"No." She reached for his arm, not knowing how he could think it. "It's that I told myself not to hope for this."

The stricken look left his face, replaced by one so warm it hiked her temperature. "You can hope for anything from me. In truth, I may be the one hoping for too much."

"How could you— *Ohh*." Her hand flew up to her throat. "You want to change me. You want me to be a vampire like you."

Her voice had risen enough to echo in the cinder block stairwell. Obviously sensitive to her agitation, he stroked back the wave of hair that had fallen over her cheekbone. "It's customary to wait until a mortal's older, but I want you to have my advantages now. I want that even if you don't want to marry me. I want us to walk side by side without—" He paused to search for the right phrasing.

"Without you always protecting me?"

He gripped her shoulders. "Protecting you is my pleasure and my privilege. If you stay with me long enough, you'll absorb some of my powers anyway. You'll be stronger and age more slowly. What I want is for you to have the choice to be with me or not, to have the benefits I can give you without the strings."

He'd struck her speechless. She recalled the night he'd confessed to wanting to chain her to him, and now he was offering this! She had to drop her eyes for a moment to compose herself. He deserved that she take no less care with her words.

"Christian," she said. "The day we first discussed the script at your house, when I drove away afterward, I felt like my heart was breaking. I almost couldn't stop from turning the car around. Everything inside me remembered being in love with you."

He opened his mouth to speak, but she wasn't finished. As gently as she could, she laid her hand on his lips.

"The thing I didn't understand was that you weren't the only loss I was mourning. When I was a spirit, things that used to frighten me began to seem unimportant. What you did didn't matter. I *couldn't* close my heart. Meeting you again reminded me how wonderful that felt. I missed that fearless, loving person you thought was your angel."

"You're her, Grace," Christian assured her. "Everything she was is still inside you. I see it every day."

"I know I'm not as brave as I used to be."

Christian's Adam's apple jerked. "Are you saying you're not brave enough to marry me?"

Grace's heart melted at his vulnerability. "I'm too selfish to refuse you. I adore you too much."

"But?"

She hesitated. She was so lucky he wanted her to be a

part of his life—and as his equal. Honestly, it was more than she'd dreamed he'd ask. Shouldn't she jump at the offer before he changed his mind?

"I want ten more human years," she blurted.

"Ten!"

Touched by his protest, she cupped his cheek. "I'll marry you anytime you want. It's the rest I want to wait on. Believe me, sticking close to you is no hardship, if that's what it takes for you to trust I'll be safe."

"I suppose it *would* be complicated for you to start up as a director if you had to deal with being a vampire, too."

"It would," Grace agreed.

She watched the furrow deepen between his brows. "Very well," he said after he'd mulled it over. "Ten years, and then you're all mine. Now will you take this ring?"

She laughed at his impatience, then gasped as he snapped the black box open. This was no diamond chip he was giving her. "Oh, my . . ."

He took her hand and slid the ring onto her shaking finger. Grace blinked at the huge sparkler. Christian had made certain no Hollywood mogul's wife could outshine her.

"You can kiss me now," he said. "But please forget about being angelic."

His delivery was so deadpan she had to smile. She shouldn't have worried he'd prefer her to be better. Their mouths met and tangled, and she felt her life come together in one warm ball, his arms circling her as tightly as hers did him. What she felt went deeper than happiness. He was her friend, her lover, her inspiration to find the best in herself.

Even if he was an actor.

"Five years," he bargained against her mouth.

"We'll see," she said, laughing. "I should probably mention I've been considering leaving Miss Wei's employ. It's time I discover if I can direct on my own."

"You'll be brilliant," he said.

That he believed this absolutely was obvious. Emotion choked her up as she spoke. "Your faith means the world to me."

"Good," he said, beaming more brightly than any human could. "Now let's go tell those boys you belong to me."

Miss Wei's Fury idled by the curb a few blocks short of Grauman's on Hollywood Boulevard. Grace spotted the petite director behind the wheel, staring straight ahead like a mannequin.

"Hold up," Grace said to the limo driver. "I think I'd better get out and speak to her."

"We'll wait for you," Matthew said.

"You don't have to—"

"We'll wait," Charlie seconded. "Seeing as your *fiancé* is ferrying the little Forrester, you'll need our help protecting your giant rock."

The boys from both of the movie's factions were sharing the big black car. United by their excitement, they grinned and nodded agreeably—which made Grace wonder how much they'd noticed about the cold front between her and her employer.

"Well, thank you," she said. "I'll try to be quick."

Flustered by their support, she exited the limo, thankfully remembering to twist her giant rock around to her palm. She and her boss didn't need to discuss that change in her private life. She slid into the Fury from the passenger side.

Miss Wei's head didn't turn to her.

"You should be driving me tonight," she said. "I bought you a special dress."

"I like the one I bought myself," Grace said.

"Of course you do. And your apartment, too, I presume."

Her tone was cool, but Grace suspected what lay beneath the ice. "You're just nervous about how the film will do."

Miss Wei's bow lips flattened. "Why should I be nervous? I didn't turn a hair when *Revenge of the Robots* opened."

"That project was for fun. This movie means more to you."

"And what does it mean to you?" Miss Wei's profile turned now, her gaze acute but not glowing.

"It means a monster might not be a monster if one person sees good inside his heart."

Her boss's eyes narrowed. Grace couldn't tell if she was offended, though a queen might consider her implication presumptuous. After a silence, during which Grace willed her pulse to stay steady, Miss Wei shifted her gaze to the cacophony of colored neon that glinted off the windshield. All the theaters on Hollywood had their gaudy signs lit tonight.

"I shouldn't have given in to the studio about editing out so much of the blood," Miss Wei said darkly. "Some of our effects have never been pulled off before, and I'm convinced young people have an appetite for gore. Who knows if they'll enjoy a vampire movie this tasteful?"

"The story will stand up. Whatever changes you made, I know you did your best."

"My best wasn't good enough when it came to keeping you as my friend."

"I'm here," Grace said. "We made it to this night together."

"If I'd been honest about what I was when we met . . ."

"I'd have been frightened," Grace admitted. "Or thought you were crazy. Playing 'what if' is pointless."

Miss Wei shook her head. "So sensible for a human." She waved her white fingers toward the window. "You should go. Your limousine is waiting."

Grace hesitated. This wasn't the time to bring up her plan to resign, or to suggest they had a chance to be friends again. The softening in her heart was tentative. Miss Wei wouldn't want Grace to make a promise she couldn't keep—assuming she wanted her promise at all.

"Good luck tonight," she said, then leaned forward to kiss her employer's cool marble cheek. Miss Wei responded with her best basilisk stare. Sending a different message, her hand came up to cover the spot. "I know the movie will do well."

Grace did know. She realized that as she dashed back to the other car. No part of her doubted it. Before she could lift the handle, Charlie opened the door for her.

"Let's get this show on the road!" he chortled. "We are going to wail tonight."

His optimism wasn't misplaced. Celestial's publicity machine had been cranking full out for the last few months. Proving it had paid off, the throng of media and fans slowed traffic to a crawl in front of the theater. Stadium-type seating was set up on the opposite side of the boulevard, and every bench was packed. Day players dressed as vampires tossed Red Hots to excited fans. Because the candy boxes were signed by cast, they were coveted. One girl squealed as she caught one Christian had autographed. Photographers' bulbs went off like supernovas as they recorded her near-hysterical triumph.

"Into the fray," Charlie said.

Like a sextet of glamorous spies, the young actors slid on dark Ray-Bans in unison. Though their tuxedo jackets were a rainbow of pastel hues—with satin lapels, no less—Grace was certain Christian had inspired their choice of eyewear.

His three boys offered their hands to help Grace out of the limousine. Thinking she must be an actress, the photographers went wild as she emerged legs first. When they realized she wasn't anyone important, Grace laughed silently at their frowns. Nothing could dim her enjoyment.

She gazed around at the clamor with the gaudy, lit-up Chinese Theater looming over it.

The turnout for the premiere was stellar. Stars sprinkled the red carpet, each with his or her own cluster of media, from whom they'd wring whatever promotional juice they could. This didn't spark Grace's cynicism. She loved being an insider at the circus. She spied Rock Hudson and Ava Gardner and someone who looked like William Holden but wasn't when he turned around. He winked when he caught her staring, saluting her with two fingers before he melted into the sea of humanity. For a heartbeat, she wondered if he knew her, but there was too much else to look at. To her, everyone was gorgeous, the women's jewels blazing brilliantly in the nonstop flurry of flashbulbs.

Christian and Viv hadn't arrived yet. They were scheduled to roar up at the last, most dramatic instant. Just as the boys were called from her side by reporters, Christian's man Roy appeared. He must have known a few more-than-human tricks. He seemed to have no trouble reaching her through the crush.

With a panache that said he might have been a ladies' man when he was younger, he offered her his elbow.

"I guess it went okay with Christian," he said close against her ear. "Since you've got Gibraltar sparkling on your finger."

"He told you?"

"He more than told me. He's been driving me crazy since he picked out the ring. You're the first mortal he wanted to change, though he's known the secret for two decades."

"I'm the first?" Grace asked, her eyes widening.

"The first, the only, the big, bad anchor of love he's been dragging around all these centuries. Mind you, don't tell him I said that. I expect I'm not supposed to have guessed."

Well, Grace thought, flattered to her toes. No wonder he'd been upset when she wanted to wait ten years!

The press of attendees funneled them between two Ming
Dynasty heaven dogs that guarded the entrance. Just past
the statues, Grauman's lobby was an eye-swirling combination of lucky red columns, dragon carpets, and gilding.
The presence of a big candy counter in the midst of the
glamour—doing brisk business, too—made Grace's exhila-
ration soar all the higher. This was a movie house, *her* movie
house tonight. More red and gold glowed in the theater itself,
which was quickly filling up. Uniformed ushers ensured no
VIPs were insulted, but Grace didn't know if she'd be recognized as one. To her relief, Wade Matthews stood up and
waved.

"Over here," the DP called from the middle row on the
left. "We saved seats for stragglers."

We was Wade and Andy Phelps, the movie's head of
wardrobe. The young man blushed when Grace said hello,
strengthening her suspicion that he and the cinematographer were enjoying a secret romance. There was something
familiar about the chemistry between them, as if—like her
and Christian—their connection had history. She supposed
it wasn't her business, but she liked the idea. They were
nice men. They deserved happiness.

Grace sat next to Wade, who smiled and pushed his horn-
rims back up his nose. She opened her mouth to thank him
when the hairs on her arms prickled. Christian's vampire
friends were squeezing into the row behind them. Grace
had sensed their energy approaching.

"Good heavens, this is exciting," Pen said.

To Grace's amazement, no one around her found the
immortals worth staring at. Even with their disguises up,
the couple was striking.

"Privacy bubble," Graham said to Grace. "Pen's a champ
at building them."

His pride in his wife's accomplishment was sweet, but
the likely reason for it was what twisted Grace around in
her seat. "You have something personal to say to me?"

"Didn't get a chance to before, since Christian yanked you out to propose. It can wait, though, if you don't want to hear it here."

"Just tell her," Pen advised. She met Grace's questioning gaze with kind eyes. "If I were you, I'd want to know right away."

"Go ahead then," Grace said.

Graham put his big hands on either side of her seat back. "Your father's dead."

Grace's mouth fell open as her imagination played out various scenarios of Christian chasing George Gladwell down. Her thoughts were so filled with static she couldn't tell if that troubled her.

"How?" she asked numbly.

"*When* might be more relevant. An associate of ours was able to track your mother, who's been living with her sister in New Mexico. As near as he can figure, a couple years ago there was some weird love triangle going on. Your aunt bumped off your father, and then your mother helped her bury him in the desert behind her house. Our associate told the police where to find the body. I hope that doesn't upset you. It appears your relatives are going to jail."

"Jail," Grace murmured, her brain refusing to move forward on its own.

"I'm afraid those ladies made a poor impression on our man. He wasn't inclined to let them get away with their crime."

Their *man* must have been another vampire, possibly the same who'd dug into Grace's past for Christian. Whatever secrets her aunt and mother had tried to hide, he'd have been able to read. The image of Miss Wei's private physician slid into her mind, but she found it hard to care if the guess was right. Something strange was happening inside her. Her skin was humming and her head felt like it was floating an extra inch above her shoulders. The muscles of her body tightened like rubber bands . . .

With a suddenness that made her jerk in her seat, they loosened all at once.

It's relief, she realized. *Not anything supernatural.* Her reaction wasn't even gloating that her awful family seemed to have met the fates they deserved. A weight had been lifted from her, and the effect of that was profound.

She was finally free of her past. No part of it could hang over her. For that matter, no part of it could hang over Christian. He'd never have to decide if he ought to kill for her.

"Thank you," she said, covering Graham's big cool hand. "I'm glad you didn't wait to tell me."

A cheer from outside the theater said Christian and Viv must be making their grand entrance. In spite of the shock that was reverberating through her, Grace smiled as she pictured it. Viv would eat up the attention much more than Christian, but he was a good sport.

The thought of how to compensate him later widened her smile.

"Oh, boy," Pen murmured in amusement at her expression. "You two really are gone on each other."

Yes, Grace thought. Really, truly, and—just maybe—equally gone. This was such a thrilling prospect that she shivered.

A moment later, the sunburst chandelier in the center of the ceiling began to dim. The audience let out a rippling sigh of anticipation. Down on the stage, the curtain was rising in crimson swags. Grace felt as if she'd dreamed this moment a thousand times. Living it out was better. The enchantment she'd been a part of spinning was about to debut.

A sudden breeze had her hair tickling her cheek. When she turned, Christian sat next to her. He'd snuck to her from whatever seat he'd been assigned to. Grinning, he gathered her hand against his heart and bent closer. His lips whispered along her throat to seal briefly over her racing pulse. Grace's skin warmed under his stroking tongue. When

Christian drew back, a soft gold glow shone out from his eyes.

"I knew Graham was going to tell you about your father," he whispered. "I had to slip back to you. Are you all right with this?"

She nodded. "What about you? Still want to marry me now that I'm out of danger?"

His fingers skated gently around her face. She knew he saw her expression much better than she did his. "I want to marry you because I love you. I want to change you because I've always loved seeing you be strong."

His eyes were glittering, and her own prickled, too. "Chris," she breathed, at a loss for any other words.

His grin flashed white a second before he dropped a quick kiss onto her mouth.

"*Now* I can watch this thing," he said smugly.

Grace's head settled on his shoulder as *Teen-Age Vampire*'s titles began to roll. Behind those wonderful, magic letters—especially the ones that said *story by Adam Chelsea and Grace Michaels*—George Pryor's motorcycle gang was rumbling into Haileyville to torment its shopkeepers. Discordant music swelled, the jazzy orchestration conveying a suitable sense of doom.

Graham sniggered at the first shot of Christian's fangs in close-up. "Hey, Christian, why do your teeth look so much better than the others?"

"*Scheisse*," Christian muttered, but Grace could tell he was laughing on the inside.

As he kissed her hair and put his arm around her, she thought she'd never known a moment this perfect.

Great job, Naomi," the head of Celestial congratulated as the audience shuffled like a big, chattering amoeba back into the lobby. "This flick is sure to pack Joe and Jane America into the drive-ins."

Dick Stewart was a pompous blowhard, but Nim Wei welcomed the vote of confidence all the same. She'd watched the crowd from the back of the theater, with her supposedly icy heart thumping in her throat. The mortals gasped when they were supposed to, laughed and leaned forward in their seats on cue. A few appeared to be teary-eyed as they left, but none of those responses guaranteed a movie would do well at the box office.

She wanted that: the financial bonanza and the critical acclaim. She didn't need either; she *was* a queen—but want it? Oh, yes, indeed she did.

She tensed as Christian and Grace approached her, cozily arm in arm. Christian saw her first and patted Grace to a halt.

"That was darn entertaining," he said in his adopted Texas twang. "I believe I'm proud of myself."

"It was wonderful." Grace's hand tightened on his arm. "You did an amazing job on the final cut."

She meant it, though her body language said she remained braced against her boss. The pale blue diamond that was glittering on her third finger said something even bigger. Nim Wei looked from it to Christian, who jerked his brows and smiled. Grace's mind might be closed to her, but his was letting slip a few things—an incredible amount of contentment being just one.

"Well," she said, "I suppose this means I can't count on Christian working for me again."

Grace looked startled, but Christian didn't bat an eyelash. "Marrying a future director does have its perks. I expect you'll find new actors who excite you. Now that I've seen how the film came out, I'm not convinced you needed to cheat by hiring me anyway."

Maybe she hadn't. Maybe succeeding at this game was closer to her grasp than she'd thought. She turned to watch the pair wend across the lobby with the rest of the crowd.

Grace's face was lifted toward her lover. Curious, Nim Wei tuned her ears to them.

"You'd let me direct you?" Grace was asking in wonderment.

"Maybe," he teased and kissed the tip of her nose. "If I decide I want another break from ranching."

In spite of all she seemed to have lost regarding her protégée, Nim Wei found herself smiling. She suspected Christian had been bitten by the movie bug, and certainly Grace was. At the very least, the three of them would cross paths again.

I'm happy for them, she realized. *It gains me absolutely nothing, but I'm happy.*

That was a development to consider, even for an immortal as old as she.

Twenty-one

❦

"They're vampires," Grace said with an amusing gasp of surprise.

She and Christian were on the tarmac at the private airstrip where she'd first picked him up in LA. The night was misty, but not enough to interfere with their flight. The airline's employees had just finished stowing their luggage— a bit too quickly, apparently.

"FC Air is short for Fitz Clare," Christian explained. "The founder, our pilot, is a cousin of Graham's."

"Well, I'll be," Grace said, absorbing this.

"You two be safe," Roy broke in, having driven them there. "I'll see you crazy kids back in Texas in a couple weeks. Mind you, no wedding planning without me. Neither of you knows squat about throwing a good party."

There was no real reason for Roy to stay behind in California. Christian hadn't asked him to. In his customary no-fuss way, Roy had simply deduced that Christian wanted

Grace and the Two Forks ranch to himself for a little while. Having Grace on his territory, with no one else around, was a pleasure his primal side was looking forward to.

"I'll miss you," Grace said, hugging Roy tightly. "I'll try to look out for Christian as well as you."

Roy seemed startled by her gesture of affection but also pleased. He patted Grace's back awkwardly. "He'd better look out for you, if he knows what's good for him. I'd rather have your pretty mug around any day."

He let her go and shrugged at Christian, who smiled at his bewilderment. With Grace added to the mix, life was going to change from the poky bachelor existence he and Roy were used to.

He clasped the hand Roy stuck out and held it, letting his longtime friend see the fondness that filled his eyes. "Thank you," he said. "For always being there. And don't get into trouble here on your own."

"Ha," Roy snorted even as thoughts Christian had no business reading ran through his mind. "You're the one who's got half the females in the country chasing after him: Mr. Box Office Gold. If you weren't so good at going incognito, you and Grace wouldn't have a hope in hell of being alone."

Christian chuckled as he and Grace climbed the plane's mobile stairs. Roy might pretend to be too old to reel in the ladies, but living with a vampire—and having been one briefly—gave him any extra sparkle he needed to catch their eyes.

"He won't really get into trouble, will he?" Grace asked. "The movie is doing well. What if reporters figure out who he works for?"

Christian squeezed the back of her neck. "Roy can give them the slip. He used to be a spymaster."

"Really? Your Roy?"

Christian loved seeing her intrigued looks when he revealed things like this. He'd never been one to want people to know him, but with her for an audience, being known became a pleasure.

"Roy's a wily coyote," said a familiar voice from inside the plane. Percy Fitz Clare stood inside the cabin, beaming at both of them. His pilot's wings gleamed on his crisp breast pocket, but thankfully he'd overcome his fetish for flight goggles. Given that he'd used to sleep in them, everyone who knew him should have guessed he'd settle on a career that let him wear uniforms.

"You must be Grace," he said with the usual slightly manic glint in his eyes. "I'm delighted to meet you, despite your deplorable taste in men. We've got champagne chilling in a bucket and a steak in the warming drawer. If you need anything beyond that, please tell our stewardess."

He'd stepped back so Grace and Christian would be able to move past him. Before he returned to the cockpit, Christian jabbed a finger at him. "None of your tricks tonight, Fitz Clare."

Percy flashed his fangs playfully. "Not a single loop-de-loop, *Durand*. That is, as long as you promise me an invite to your wedding."

"Get us home right side up, and I'll send you ten."

"Deal," Percy said, sending a wink toward Grace.

Satisfied Percy would keep his word, Christian clapped him on his shoulder and led Grace into the beautifully appointed sitting area. This private prop jet was no puddle jumper. It was outfitted to suit not only its immortal passengers' special requirements, but their most luxurious tastes as well. The cabin could have seated forty, if it had been intended for commercial use. *Commercial* wasn't how it looked now. Rare wood paneling gleamed on the walls, and dark glove leather wrapped the half dozen reclining chairs. The Persian carpets could have graced any tycoon's home. The flight attendant appeared no less sumptuous— probably one of Percy's numerous human pets.

Christian had never met a vampire with as large a harem as Graham's cousin.

"Welcome to FC Air," the woman said in melodious tones. "I'll be in the cockpit with the captain if you need me."

Since she seemed to understand they wouldn't need her, Christian didn't roll his eyes. For her part, Grace was too interested in her surroundings to suspect their stewardess was there to serve their pilot's needs more than theirs.

"This is so *nice*," she cooed, running her palms along the arms of the seat she'd picked for herself. "You bloodsuckers know how to live."

Laughing, Christian settled in beside her and took her hand. Percy was already starting up the engines. Because Fitz Clare Air owned the airstrip, their flights had precedence.

"I think you shocked Roy by hugging him," he observed.

"Oh, I know!" Grace exclaimed, coloring up a delightful bit. "I wasn't thinking. He reminds me of Hans, the older soldier who looked out for you when you were human. I just acted like I would have if I knew him."

Christian touched the warmth that had risen into her cheeks, marveling that he had the right to do this anytime he liked. "He reminds me of Hans as well."

"Do you think he could be the same man come back?"

"I'm not sure it matters. Either way, his loyalty means a lot to me."

Grace bumped his shoulder with hers. "It's more than loyalty. Roy loves you and you love him. You should have warned me this would be a benefit of marrying you."

Not sure what she meant, Christian lifted one brow at her.

"You have a family, Christian, a whole network of people who care for you. Now, maybe, I'll be part of it."

Her tone had turned from teasing to shy, the concept of

family necessarily a tricky one for her. Touched more than he could say, Christian took her face in his hands. If he did have friends the way she believed, he was glad for it because of her, because she'd made him feel part of something, too. He wasn't sure she realized how attached people got to her. There wasn't one of his boys from the movie who wouldn't cross an ocean for her.

"You'll be part of whoever I'm connected to," he said, "whether it be the people of Two Forks or a horde of neck biters. No one who cares for me wouldn't adore you, and everything I have is yours. Every hope you dreamed before you met me, I'll do my best to help it come true."

She started to speak, but stopped as two fat tears rolled out from her eyes. She bit her lower lip and smiled at the same time. "I don't care what Miss Wei did to me. Sometimes I swear you can read my mind."

He kissed her tears away a cheek at a time. "I don't need to, sweetheart. I love you well enough to guess what you're thinking."

"I love you, too, Christian."

He'd never tire of her saying it.

"I'll say it every day," she promised, making him think she might have a gift in the mind-reading direction. "You'll never doubt it even if you can't peek inside my head."

"Good," he said, pulling her closer to his side.

The plane had begun to taxi, pushing them back into soft leather as it accelerated smoothly down the runway. Prodded by an uncharacteristic need to say more, Christian raised his voice above the engine noise.

"I trust how you feel," he said. "Even if you don't say it."

She made a sound like a dove, her hand coming up to caress his face. His body tightened. Her fingers were kind and warm, a perfect reflection of what was inside her. Her lips touched his as they left the ground, causing his heart to leap with the plane. He wanted to match her sweetness, but the kiss turned fierce and deep before he could stop himself. The love he felt for her was savage, the passion that flared as hot as a burning star. She was his for always. She had said yes to him. Groaning with desire, he swung her onto his lap.

At least he wasn't alone in his sudden lust. She was the one who tore his trousers open and pulled his erection free. Her cry of admiration lengthened him, as if being with her made him more of a man in more ways than one. Even as his stiffness thrummed at her snug long strokes, her second hand dug in to cradle his testicles. The heaviness in his groin increased.

"Don't tease me," he said harshly.

"No?" Her fingertips drummed his balls. The gleam in her jewel green eyes challenged him.

He didn't bother to argue, just tumbled her to the floor under him. In her career, she was free to be the boss if she wanted. In this, the lead was his. The carpet was plush, but not half as plush as her body. His eyes glowed hot as he pulled her thighs wide beneath her full-skirted dress. In case she had any doubt where this was going, he licked his lips. Considering that the upper was curling back, she couldn't miss the downward slide of his fangs.

"Christian," she said, her voice shaking on his name.

"You're mine," he said, loving her sensual shudder. "Any way I want you."

She squeaked when he flung up the layers of her skirt, and again when he wrapped his fist in her panties to tear the cloth away.

"Better hold on," he said, his grip like iron on her knees.

There were no more protests as he latched his mouth firmly on her sex, only half-swallowed cries. He had his tongue to play her, and the curve of his fangs. Grace squirmed and sighed and clamped her lovely thighs tight around his ears. Christian massaged their muscles with loving hands.

"You're the only one for me," he growled into her.

To his delight, she didn't have the breath for a snappy comeback. She arched and groaned as he took her clitoris delicately into his mouth, cushioning it on his tongue as he gently sucked. The hardness of his fangs pushed on her but didn't cut, providing an edge of danger he'd learned she liked. For his own sake, he slid his hands up to squeeze her breasts. He couldn't doubt she liked the way he thumbed her nipples. It wasn't long before her pussy quivered on the verge of bliss, her fingers thrust deep into his hair.

They weren't strong enough to stop him when he pulled back from her.

"Bad," she panted, glaring at him. "Leaving me on the edge."

"You'll like it all the more when I'm nice later."

He was crawling up her as he said it, letting her know *later* was coming soon.

"You're setting a bad example," she warned.

He'd have taken this more seriously if her hands hadn't been stroking greedily down his chest. She loved touching him and, Lord knew, he loved her doing it. She found his cock again and fondled it, her knees scissoring auspiciously up his sides. He was congratulating himself that everything was as it should be when a sudden and very interesting pressure on his sexual organs made him grunt and lift at the hips.

She wasn't fondling him now. Her thumb and middle finger had pinched his foreskin together, tugging it past his erection's head. Her other hand enclosed the base of his scrotum, which she pulled lower between his legs. Despite his experience, this wasn't a sensation he was familiar with. The firm two-way stretch created the impression that his dick had grown ten feet long.

To make matters worse, the knuckles of the fist that gripped his sack were pushing on his perineum. By now, Grace knew what this did to the multitude of nerves between his balls and anus. It was no accident when her knuckles rolled harder.

"Grace," he said, more breathless than he was accustomed to. "This isn't a good idea."

"Really? I'm pretty sure it is."

He would have laughed if he could. "You know I don't want to hurt you if my hungers get out of hand."

Apparently unimpressed, she slid her knees farther up his sides. "When has that ever happened, love?"

For all his private claims that he was in charge, he really couldn't resist her boldness. At the least, he couldn't resist the evidence that she wanted him. He groaned as his fingers slid into the cream running through her folds, led onward like magnets to the satiny swell of her clitoris. The frantic beat of its blood enchanted. When he rubbed it inside its slippery hood, Grace flushed but didn't look away.

"All that wetness is for you," she said.

Their gazes held from inches apart, his cock jolting in the stretching grip she still had on it.

"You know what I have for you," he rumbled.

She smiled and guided what he had to her opening, finally releasing the pinch she'd taken on his foreskin. His glans buzzed with sensitivity at its sudden freedom. With equally perfect timing, her fingertips slid down his shaft as he breached her gate. The incredible feelings assailing every part of his cock compelled him to grit his fangs.

"God," he burst out as his big crest squeezed in and throbbed. "I'd like to cram everything I am inside of you here."

Grace arched underneath him, setting off more sweet stabs of sensation. "Remember how when I was a ghost, how I used to push my energy into you?"

He remembered so well his temperature shot up. He grabbed the metal frame that attached the nearest seat to bolts in the floor. He reminded himself not to break it, just use it for leverage. Grace's hips pitched toward him as his cock moved deliciously into her.

"Is that what you want?" he asked, quivering almost as much as she was. "For me to play those tricks back on you?"

She nodded, her earnestness so dear he hardly knew how to reward it. "I want to let you inside me every way I can."

His eyes teared up from the frightening intensity with which he desired her. In some ways his need was worse than before he'd known what it was to lose her, but in others it was better. He appreciated her as his mortal self hadn't known how to. Overcome, he nuzzled her neck. What had he done to deserve a partner as sweet as her?

Sensing the vehemence of his feelings, Grace tugged him back by the hair. "Don't bite me yet," she pleaded. "Try to join us together first."

He told her yes with his eyes. He worked one hand under her bottom, needing the hold to get fully in. He drew one breath to brace himself, then shoved. Pleasure exploded as she engulfed him, nearly driving him past the edge. She must have felt it, too. They both cried out, each heaving toward the other to get closer.

He wasn't in the best state for concentration, but with her warmth clasped tight around the killing ache of his cock, he tried to do as she asked. Sweat beaded on his forehead. He told himself he knew how to penetrate her with his aura. He only had to focus and want to. Grace licked his throat and kissed her way up his jaw. The gentle nip she gave his chin was precisely the kind of foreplay *upyr* were fond of. The distraction proved unexpectedly useful. Christian's instincts took over from his brain. When he caught her mouth and drove his tongue into it, his energy smashed over hers in a wave.

She wasn't lying about wanting to let him in. His skin

prickled with the flimsiest resistance before he pierced the veil between them.

Christian lost his breath. Their auras wove together in sinuous liquid currents, as warm as fire but less solid. Over and around their bodies the streams twisted, stroking them inside and out. The places the energy brushed were outrageously erotic.

"Ohh," Grace sighed, her hands sliding up his back to stir long tingles. "Oh, God, Christian."

He couldn't hear her thoughts even then, but he felt the part of her that lay beneath them, the essence of who she was as a human being. He wasn't certain words could have described her, though his mind did try. She was sweet. She was stubborn. She was a little frightened of the world but courageous in spite of it. She was everything he wanted in a woman. Someone to need him. Someone he could trust enough to let himself need her.

The bond was close to the one required to change a mortal, except their flesh hadn't yet dissolved. By that measure, they were still very physical. Their bodies undulated with increasing fervor, craving a culmination for their sensual torment. Christian thrust longer, harder, with a deliberation of movement that converted every stroke into sheer delight. Vowing to give her everything she wanted, he tightened his grip on the chair, his other hand covering her bottom. His spine stretched, lengthening the range of his hips' fulcrum. Noises of longing broke from her throat. The force he was using pleased her. His energy was making her stronger.

This was the shadow of what she'd be when she was *upyr*.

He adored it, both the differences between them and the similarities. Maybe the ten years she wanted to stay human would have their perks. Her fingers dug into the muscles of his shoulders as she matched the impetus of his drives. She was growling with her need for him, as much of an animal as he was.

The only limit on their lovemaking was not shaking the plane from the sky.

"Chris," she panted, the little nickname that drove him crazy. Her legs climbed higher, muscles bunching, feet bracing on his butt to pull every millimeter of his cock into her. She was so open he could have cried.

When he hit the deep spot that she liked best, her graceful neck arched back. That last display of surrender was it for him. His climax spumed as he punched his fangs into her and fed.

Her blood was a drug that saved and destroyed him, sparking down his nerves until every one caught fire.

Naturally, the pleasure hit her at the same time. She clutched him with all her strength, coming helplessly around him, her own aura bursting bright and hot through his. His hair stood on end as the orgasm went on and on, a shared bombardment of ecstasy. Messages flew at him from all directions, from prick and pussy, from balls and clit, from sweating skin that longed to rub itself against every inch of her. As if she could indeed read his mind, Grace drove one finger into him from behind. Shards of bliss rained outward from this new spot of stimulation. When she rubbed it, just as he'd once done to her, pleasure flung his head back from drinking her. Compelled by needs he couldn't control, his hips drove inward for one last plunge.

The brutality of the union was what they'd both wanted. Christian echoed Grace's gasp for oxygen, his scrotum tightening as he spilled into her one more time from some reservoir he hadn't known he had. The flood ran out of her in a hot torrent, too copious to contain.

For a long sweet time, neither of them could speak.

He did manage to roll until she lay above him, her body relaxed and warm and—to his amazement—still substantially clothed. She sighed as she exhaled, the sound incredibly comforting. He'd pleasured her as deeply as she had him.

"Wow," she said at last, breathlessly. "Is this what I can expect from the next two weeks at your ranch?"

Christian stroked the tousled waves of her deep red hair. "The next two centuries, if you wish."

Grace's mouth curved coyly against his chest. At some point during their mutual madness, *she'd* torn his shirt open. Now her fingers drew a teasing trail around one nipple.

"You know what I think?" she said. "I think ten years of being human will have its perks."

Great minds certainly thought alike. He laughed until his chest shook, until she pushed upward onto her elbows and quirked her brows at him. Even then, he couldn't contain his joy.

Christian Durand was finally, fully glad he was a vampire.

I Was a Teen-Age
Vampire

I WAS A TEEN-AGE VAMPIRE

story by
Adam R. Chelsea and Grace Michaels

CHARACTERS

GEORGE PRYOR: Vampire. Current head of a violent motorcycle gang. This power-obsessed patriarch feels threatened by his son's approaching manhood.

JOE PRYOR: George's teenage son. Like his father, Joe is a "born" or hereditary vampire. Unlike his father, he wants to lead a normal life—go to high school, have a girlfriend, not follow in his father's footsteps terrorizing a town.

MARY REED: Shy and pretty human Mary Reed recently moved to Haileyville, where her pompous, ineffectual father has taken over a drugstore. Mary now attends Joe's school. Her self-involved mother uses migraines as an excuse to shirk taking care of her family. As a result, Mary has no strong adult role models. She must decide how she should grow up.

DELIA and GREGORY REED: Mary's parents.

THE FANGS: The members of the Fangs are all "made" vampires, which is less prestigious than being "born." Made vampires burn in the sun. Born ones can go out in it. Under George's leadership, the Fangs extort protection money from businesses in town. They divide into: PHILIP, MATTHEW, and CHARLIE (who are friends to Joe) and BONEHEAD, GROWLER, and MACE (who are George's sycophants).

UNCONSCIOUS GIRL: The Fangs' victim

Various STUDENTS, POLICE, TOWNSPEOPLE, and TEACHERS

TITLES RUN as the MOTORCYCLE GANG roars into the old-fashioned town of HAILEYVILLE. A huge full moon illuminates beefy GEORGE PRYOR, riding lead with his goggles on. His maniacal fangy grin instantly says what sort of villain he is. The gang surrounds a SHOPKEEPER who is taking out the trash in his ALLEY. The bikes circle him in the confined space as if he's a calf they're herding. Through pantomime from George and the gang, we conclude the man is behind on his protection payments. No dialogue is heard during the confrontation, only the growling of the motorcycles and dissonant jazz-type music. The shopkeeper offers money but not enough. Incensed but also eager to do violence, the gang begins to beat up the man. Effects underscore the vampires' unnatural strength and speed. As the thrashing intensifies, JOE seems to be urging the others to rein in their aggression. He isn't particularly successful, though close-ups on the various gang members' expressions show who might be for or against him. The shopkeeper collapses in the alley behind his store, his face battered monstrously. A bite mark with two punctures shows on his forearm. Joe offers him a hand up, but the victim recoils in terror. Some of the gang members mock Joe for his softness. Clearly torn, Joe turns his bike and reluctantly rejoins them.

We return to JOE the next morning, following an establishing shot of the PRYORS' HILLTOP MANSION. This tree-shrouded Gothic house looks both threatening and run-down. Its windows are boarded up and its grounds overgrown.

Inside, the GANG is sleeping in the large LIVING ROOM PARLOR on an assortment of decrepit Victorian furniture. Multiple layers of moth-eaten blankets protect them from the sun. The gang members remind us of dead bodies—which in truth they are. Two of the bodies share a single couch, though the blankets that wrap them are separate. Their feet stick out at the bottom, revealing that they're wearing each other's shoes. PHILIP has one blue and one black sneaker, while MATTHEW has one black and one blue. GEORGE PRYOR sprawls on what looks like a medieval throne, a half-consumed glass of liquor balanced on his chest. Unlike the others, he is uncovered. He sneers as his son, JOE, stuffs his schoolbooks into a backpack. When that fails to get a rise, George derides Joe for wanting to waste his time with humans. Joe keeps preparing. George rises, confronts him physically. Joe fends him off, then grabs his motorcycle jacket and slips away. Left without a target for his anger, George yanks the blanket off CHARLIE. A second later Charlie begins to smoke. He wakes, drags the blanket back, and saves himself. None of the others stir, but George laughs hysterically. However powerful his nature, we see he's no better than a bully.

Next we see Mary Reed's surroundings, a new SUBURBAN SUBDIVISION outside of Haileyville. All the houses are the same, all the trees, all the mowed patterns on the grass.

Inside, the REEDS' KITCHEN looks straight out of a magazine, every surface perfect and colorful. Mary's parents, GREGORY and DELIA, seem perfect, too, from Delia's cheery apron to Gregory's avuncular shopkeeper trousers and cardigan. As MARY picks at her breakfast, Delia scolds her not to be shy at her new school, like she was at her last. Delia brags about how popular she was when she was Mary's age, a claim her husband substantiates. Their tone is as artificial as characters in a play—no new-style Method acting for them. Mary is near tears by the time she escapes the house, though her parents seem not to notice. Delia exclaims that worrying about "that girl" gives her a headache. Gregory pats her hand and advises her to lie down.

We join up again with MARY, now outside HAILEY-VILLE HIGH SCHOOL. The school is part of the town, with a similar old-fashioned appearance. STUDENTS in cliques loiter on the grounds. We see JOCKS, GREASERS, STUDENT COUNCIL TYPES. They are a gauntlet Mary the new girl will have to pass. The Greasers particularly eye her. Looking frightened, Mary clutches her books tighter to her breasts. She is a buxom little lamb thrown among the wolves. She has just enough courage to climb the steps, where the Greasers begin to make apelike noises and paw at her. The other students watch with varying reactions but aren't going to help her. Mary's fear rises. She might be in real trouble.

From inside the HIGH SCHOOL, JOE spots MARY's dilemma. There's a brief trick of light, a glow around Mary's head almost like a halo. Joe blinks, then shoves through the doors to rescue her.

The GREASERS back off without a single punch being thrown. They're afraid of JOE because of his father's gang. Plus, they sense the predator inside him. Where their toughness is somewhat put on, his is the real McCoy. Joe's intervention leaves MARY grateful and starry-eyed. Her father has none of this natural authority. Joe plays it cool, leaving Mary behind as soon as he knows she's safe. Still, there's something in his manner, in the way he glances back at her one last time, that lets us know he's intrigued by the new girl.

We see a montage of MARY and JOE in SCHOOL, both outsiders in different ways. In the classes they share, Joe sneaks looks at the self-conscious Mary. Whenever Mary looks back, he has turned away.

Inside HAILEYVILLE HIGH SCHOOL LUNCH-ROOM, a prissy FEMALE STUDENT COUNCIL TYPE warns MARY to avoid Joe. He's bad news, she says: a member of the dreaded Fangs. He's the only Fang who hasn't dropped out of school, but he's just as wild as the rest. In fact, he might be more dangerous, because he still pretends to be nice sometimes. Good girls get hurt when they hang out with boys like him. Across the lunchroom, JOE eavesdrops with his super-sharp vampire hearing. His reaction shifts between injured pride and scorn for the "squares." He doesn't realize the student council girl's warning comes too late for Mary. She's already half-smitten.

Dusk falls, an ominous time for a town harassed by vampires. OUTSIDE THE HIGH SCHOOL, the STU-DENTS' spirits are more subdued than in the morning. They hurry away to home and safety. Unfamiliar with the danger, a dawdling MARY crosses the grounds alone. She appears tired from her first day at her new school, her shoulders slumped, her eyes older than her years. A beautiful SCARLET MAPLE catches her attention. She stares up into its spreading branches, touched—at least for the moment—by childlike wonder. A smile ghosts across her face, not an expression she often wears. Though she's isolated and vulnerable, we sense she'd rather be here than home. She shrieks as JOE drops down from the branches, seemingly out of nowhere. A young man's belligerence radiates from him. "You're afraid of me now," he sneers. "Just like that girl warned you to be." "Do you think I believe everything I hear?" Mary retorts. "People say things about me, too." "What would they say about you? They barely know a mouse like you is alive." The truth of this stings Mary, who turns jerkily and walks away. Joe watches her for a second, guilt on his face, before trotting after her.

They progress down Haileyville's deceptively bucolic STREETS. "I'll walk you home," JOE says. "Make sure you get there all right." MARY lets him, though her trust is uncertain. Joe breaks the awkward silence by mentioning the tree she was staring at. He agrees it was pretty. Mary says she wishes she owned a good camera. If she had pictures, she'd never forget when nice things happened. Joe dances backward ahead of her, showing off his fine male form. "You could take pictures of me," he says. "I'm a nice thing." Mary laughs and teases that she wouldn't waste film on him, even if she had it. "I'll get you a camera," Joe boasts. Mary gives him a look. "I wouldn't steal it," he says. "I'd buy it with my own money." We see his awareness that his money comes to him through his father's life of crime, from which there seems to be no escape. "Maybe I'll be a fireman," he says. "Or a pilot. I bet I'd be good at that." Joe thinks this is a pipe dream, and Mary might also, but, "I bet you'd be good at anything," she says gently. They exchange their most open looks up till now. This is the moment they start to fall in love.

It is fully dark now. Streetlights form circles on the tidy suburban street in front of MARY'S HOUSE. JOE stops with MARY at the end of the walk. He knows a boy like him isn't welcome to come closer. MARY'S MOTHER, wearing a housecoat, emerges from the house to eye the juvenile delinquent standing next to her daughter. Mary hurries up the walk as she is berated. We don't need to hear what her mother says. Their gestures make it apparent to us—and to Joe—what the exchange entails. Mary resists a little as her shrewish mother tugs her inside. Mary's sympathies are fully with Joe now. To her, he's the sort of boy grown-ups always misunderstand. Joe leaves, his hands shoved in his pockets, looking resentful. The camera pulls back to reveal JOE'S FATHER spying on him from the dark yard across the street. His expression is calculating and narrow.

A short while later, GEORGE PRYOR has gathered the FANGS around the MANSION'S DINING ROOM table. In the background, almost concealed by shadows, an UNCONSCIOUS GIRL can be seen. She's poorly dressed, maybe a runaway. She sags in ropes that bind her to hooks screwed into peeling wallpaper. The gang ignores her as George speaks. He announces the arrival of a new shopkeeper in Haileyville, one who needs to be set straight about how things work. Worry flickers across JOE's face. Mary is new in town. Could this have something to do with her? The gang—especially BONEHEAD, GROWLER, and MACE—express enthusiasm for dropping in on the newcomer. First, though, George suggests that they have a snack, unless any of them objects to that? From his tone and the tightening of Joe's jaw, we realize this is an ongoing point of contention. Joe's allies—PHILIP, MATTHEW, and CHARLIE—glance at him for guidance. "We're leaving too many victims," Joe says. "News of what we're doing could reach beyond Haileyville. Even you can't thrall the whole state." George scoffs at the idea that anyone can stop him. The vampires are a superior race, and surely even Joe is tired of being a Goody Two-shoes. "We don't *have* to kill," Joe says, the true heart of his argument. "Killing is what we're born for," George shoots back. A natural sensualist, Charlie joins in on feeding from the young woman. Philip and Matthew are shamed into it when Bonehead and Growler suggest they can't get their fangs to come down for a pretty girl. In the end, only Joe holds

back from feeding. We see that watching excites him, but
he fights his hunger.

Inside the REED HOUSE, MARY is pulling on a white
sweater in preparation for leaving. "Don't give your father
trouble," DELIA orders from off camera. The music tells
us going out isn't a good idea.

Outside the MANSION, the GANG prepares to mount up.
Drawn slightly apart from the others, JOE and CHARLIE
speak quietly. "Why do you always butt heads with him?"
Charlie asks. "Because he wants us to be monsters," Joe
replies. "We are monsters," Charlie says. "Only if we choose
to be," Joe avers. Charlie's eyes widen. Joe is making him
consider an idea he hasn't entertained before. "That girl
had parents," Joe reminds him. "Just like you used to." "I'd
be dead if it weren't for your father," Charlie counters. "I
was dying when he turned me." "Yeah," Joe says, "but you
hadn't killed anyone." From too far away to hear their low
conversation, GEORGE PRYOR glowers suspiciously at
them.

An overhead shot of HAILEYVILLE'S MAIN
STREET reveals someone's car driving hastily away with
a squeal of tires. Only one shop's windows shine into the
dark. A nocturnal bird abruptly falls silent.

MARY'S FATHER appears to be alone in REED'S
DRUGSTORE, his aisles and soda counter utterly empty.
He hasn't gotten the memo that Haileyville rolls up its
sidewalks at sunset. His head comes up at the sound of
a distant rumble. Fear fills his eyes, but he dismisses it.
MARY, his free labor, walks out from the back, drying
her hands on a dishtowel. "What's that noise?" she asks.
"Nothing," says her father, as if she's foolish for noticing.
"This town is dead."

We cut to the GANG roaring closer, glimpsing worry
or anticipation on the different vampires' faces. GEORGE
PRYOR is exultant. He's looking forward to his son's
reaction to what's coming.

MARY'S FATHER gasps as the sound of motorcycles rises. "Stay in the back," he orders his daughter. MARY obeys mere seconds before the GANG drives their Harleys straight into the STORE. "You hoodlums can't be in here," Mary's father blusters. "I'm calling the police." GROWLER sneers at him. "Try it and see what happens, old man." CHARLIE spots an attractive watch in a case. He mimes to JOE that they could steal it. Joe tells him not to with a tiny shake of his head. JOE'S FATHER doesn't like this. His son isn't the boss here. He grabs Gregory Reed by the neck, drawing everyone's attention to himself. His vampire strength allows him to dangle the other man off the ground. "You want us to leave?" he says. "Pay our fee." Joe spies Mary peeking in horror around the storeroom door. He jerks his gaze away at once, faint pink sweat shining on his face. If the gang discovers her presence, she'll be in grave danger. Mary's father reaches for the phone. BONEHEAD yanks it away. "Mary!" George cries, effectively betraying her. "Call for help from the back!"

We see all hell break loose from MARY'S point of view in the STOREROOM. The vampires turn fangy, though it's JOE'S altered face she focuses on. The truth of what he is stuns her, though we can't tell what she's feeling beyond that.

Knowing JOE'S FATHER will want to catch and hurt Mary, JOE preemptively rushes him. Their epic battle rages through the DRUGSTORE. Still refusing to confront the reality of his situation, GREGORY REED insists THE GANG will have to pay for the damage . . . even as he cowers behind the counter. The gang's two factions square off, each gleefully attacking the other in defense of their leaders. CHARLIE takes a moment to grab the watch he likes from a broken case. Because his father's cohorts are occupied, when Joe gains a temporary advantage, he's able to grab MARY and flee with her.

Sirens wail in the distance as JOE and MARY reach the ALLEY.

A series of shots shows the small HAILEYVILLE POLICE FORCE finally rousing itself. As officers rush into their patrol cars, we see they're armed.

JOE and MARY are on the run. The WOODS outside of Haileyville provide their escape route. Mary stumbles, not for the first time, to judge by the bloody scratches all over her. Without slowing, Joe picks her up and carries her in his arms. His fangs are down, his face tormented. The longing glances he gives Mary's wounds suggest more than stress from the fight is behind this. He licks his lips uncomfortably, reminding us he didn't share in the other's snack.

JOE and MARY climb into a BOXCAR that has been abandoned on an old siding. "You're a vampire, aren't you?" Mary says breathlessly, making the confession a bit easier on him. "I am," he says, "but I'm trying to be a good man." He explains the facts of vampire life to her—the difference between born and made ones, the fact that they don't have to kill when they feed. "But everyone is so terrified of you," Mary says. Joe's face twists bitterly. He explains that this is his father's doing. George Pryor likes to catch one victim for the whole gang, in which case, the person's blood can be drained. "There was a girl tonight," he begins, but can't go further. He's too afraid Mary will hate him. "Did you hurt her?" Mary asks, just as afraid to hear the answer. "I stood by," Joe cries. "Oh, God, I stood by!" Mary touches him, and Joe stares into her eyes. "I need you to believe I can change," he says fervently. "If you have faith in me, maybe I'll find the strength." "It's in you," Mary assures him. "I'm sure you'd find it even without me." Both well up, though only Mary's tears spill over. Joe clutches her to him and kisses her. Gratitude turns to arousal, which—at least on Joe's part—becomes a more dangerous hunger. "I trust you," Mary says as he nuzzles her neck with his fangs. She seems to be implying that he can bite her. Joe pulls back and looks at her, finding only acceptance in her expression. Joe's heart is truly lost. We see he'll do anything for her now.

We cut to GANG MEMBERS we can't identify running through the WOODS. POLICE with flashlights are shouting and chasing them. The vampires leap over obstacles like gazelles.

Back in the BOXCAR, JOE and MARY are kissing even more passionately than before. They break apart as Joe's buddies, CHARLIE, PHILIP, and MATTHEW, scramble breathlessly through the boxcar's door. So full of themselves they're bursting, the trio boasts how they deliberately made so much noise the police couldn't resist chasing them. [Shots of what they're describing intercut as they speak.] Naturally, George's men also pursued the trio. They couldn't let Joe's faction get away with their mutiny. Charlie, Philip, and Matthew maneuvered both parties together, then—*whoosh*—disappeared at the last moment by jumping into the trees. "The police had silver crosses," Charlie explains. "They arrested your father and his poopheads." Joe is amazed and humbled by this tale. His friends have made him their new leader, essentially burning their bridges with George Pryor.

At the POLICE STATION, the CAPTURED FANGS are herded by POLICE with crosses into a holding cell. The police seem not to have observed the vampires up close before. "Look at them," one nervous YOUNG OFFICER exclaims at their distorted faces. "They're like animals." "They are animals," says ANOTHER OFFICER, "and it's about time this town put them in cages." GEORGE PRYOR is the last to be backed in. As the cell door clangs shut, his glowing eyes make him look more demonic than beastly. Even with the bars between them, the police flinch back from his rabid snarl.

Meanwhile, MARY, JOE, and JOE'S FRIENDS have settled down inside the BOXCAR. An air of domesticity

surrounds them. A portable radio plays the Platters or something similarly soft and romantic. A lantern has been lit for
Mary, who snuggles close to Joe. Joe unzips his motorcycle
jacket so it wraps both of them. PHILIP and MATTHEW
sprawl near the couple, more relaxed than we've seen them
yet. Philip picks a leaf out of Matthew's hair, then gently
strokes it smooth. Matthew is sharing a story about how
when he was human, he wished he could ride the train.
"My father hated me," he says, "and my mother was always
on me about something. Every night I'd dream about
jumping on a train up to Canada, how the snow would
fall like feathers, and it'd be so quiet I could finally think
for myself." "Too bad *this* train isn't going anywhere,"
CHARLIE not quite jokes. He's standing guard by the
boxcar's slightly open door. He fiddles with the watch he
stole from Mary's father, some internal pressure nudging
him. Finally, the pressure bursts. He turns toward the
others. "We have to go back," he says. "That girl tonight.
She was still breathing when we left her." We see on Joe's
face that part of him isn't happy to hear this. He wants to
keep Mary safe, not risk their lives rescuing some stranger.
"Your father's in jail," Charlie points out. "And if the
police come looking for us at the mansion, we'll outrun
them just like before." Philip glances at Matthew, both of
them unsure. "Dawn isn't that far away," Philip cautions.
Hoping for support, Charlie gazes pleadingly at Joe. He
knows the decision is up to Joe, but Charlie wants this
chance to redeem himself. "You said it yourself," Charlie
reminds him. "That girl has a family just like we did. And
maybe hers loves her. We should try to save her before we
skip town for good." Charlie has never expressed a heroic
impulse before. This helps Joe make up his mind. He rises
and slaps Charlie's shoulder, man-to-man. Mary gazes up
at him proudly. "All right," Joe says. "The least we can do
is try."

Back at the JAIL, sunlight begins to stream through

the holding cell's window. BONEHEAD, GROWLER, and MACE try to shrink back but are caught in the beams and go up like torches. TWO POLICEMEN—one young, one older—arrive in time to see this. They shield their faces, expecting JOE'S FATHER also will ignite. Instead, with a berserker's growl of rage, he grabs the bars and rips them out of the wall. Swatting the police aside like flies, he escapes the jail. "I thought he'd burn," the YOUNG POLICEMAN cries. "Why didn't he burn, too?"

The camera shows JOE'S FATHER in the street OUTSIDE THE JAIL. Though he's lost his men, he looks crazed enough to overcome anything. He searches his surroundings and appears to catch a scent on the air. When he takes off, we know he's going after our heroes.

MARY, JOE, and JOE'S FRIENDS reach the PRYOR MANSION under cover of the trees. Only Mary is cracking twigs underfoot. Though the made vampires are looking sleepy, they glide into the house silently. They're armed with sticks they've sharpened. Joe leads them as if he's been in command all his life.

Inside, they find the UNCONSCIOUS GIRL hanging from the hooks in the DINING ROOM. CHARLIE rushes to her. She's still alive! He takes her down tenderly. The girl's eyelids flutter. "You," she murmurs, not as frightened as she should be. Somehow, there is a connection between these two. "Shh," Charlie soothes. "We'll get you to a hospital." He looks at MARY and JOE, the only ones who can brave the sun. "Yes," Joe says. "We'll take her." He accepts the weakened girl from Charlie. Joe's fangs slide out at the blood. "Will you be all right?" Mary asks. "I can stand it," he says. "You three watch out for each other," he tells his men. "Find someplace safe to sleep. We'll meet in the woods by the train depot at sunset."

In the PRYOR MANSION GARAGE, JOE and MARY settle the GIRL into the backseat of a limousine that has to be decades old. Joe finds an old chauffeur's cap, making

Mary laugh by putting it on backward. Suddenly, a terrible cry rings out. "My father's here," Joe cries and rushes back to the house.

JOE comes upon an awful scene in the KITCHEN. MATTHEW and PHILIP lie unconscious amidst the dust and neglect, but CHARLIE'S state is worse. JOE'S FATHER has stabbed him through the chest with a long tree branch. George is crouched above Charlie, both hands wrapped around the impromptu spear, shoving it farther in. He laughs when Joe skids to a halt at the threshold. "It's all right," Charlie gasps through his pain. "He missed my heart." "Missed it on purpose," George crows. "Wouldn't be much fun if my Joe's buddies died too quickly." Joe growls and attacks him. Father and son wrestle back and forth, turning more of the kitchen into kindling. Joe gets the upper hand, grabs a broken chair leg, and prepares to stake his father. "You can't dust me," his father taunts. "Charlie's dying. I'm the only one whose blood is strong enough to save him." Doubt shadows Joe's face as he and his father struggle for control of the stake. "Kill him," Charlie urges, seeing Joe having second thoughts. "None of us is safe as long as he's alive." Joe's father opens his mouth to mock him some more. Joe sets his jaw and plunges the stake deep into his heart. Effects show the body skeletonize and then turn to ash. Joe runs to Charlie, now only taking in the full horror of his impalement. Vampire or not, it seems impossible that he can survive. "Just pull it out," Charlie says. "I'm not sorry if it ends this way. At least I . . . did the right thing for once." MARY appears at the door and gasps. "Is the girl all right?" Charlie asks. "Yes," Mary says, blank with shock. Then she shakes herself and addresses Joe. "Do you need help? Would drinking my blood help him?" In spite of everything, Joe smiles at her with great love. "He needs my blood. I'm just not certain it's strong enough to heal him." Knowing he has to try, Joe braces Charlie down with his weight and yanks out the branch.

Charlie groans. Mary's face reflects how hideous the injury is. Joe bites his wrist and offers it to Charlie. Weak at first, Charlie latches on hungrily. Joe's expression is open to interpretation—maybe pain, maybe pleasure. Whatever his feelings, it's clear the experience is intense. He opens his eyes to look at Mary, and his muscles relax. We see that knowing her has brought peace to his troubled soul.

MARY and JOE wait together in the HALL outside the girl's hospital room. Joe asks Mary if she's sure she wants to leave town with him and his boys. The police are searching for them, and they can't stay. He swears he'll protect her if she joins them, but if she stays in Haileyville, she could still have a normal life. "From the moment I was born, I was meant to love you," she says. "Nothing will ever feel as right to me as that." Joe is temporarily struck speechless. "How can I deserve to be loved by you?" he chokes out. "Love me back," Mary teases. Joe flings his arms around her. "I do," he promises throatily. "I'll love you forever."

FINAL CREDITS roll over scenes of the young people's happiness. They are living in a cozy Craftsman-style house somewhere. It is night and snow is heaped on the windowsills. Framed photographs of the Olympic Mountains, presumably taken by Mary, suggest they have made it to Canada, just as Matthew dreamed. A fire crackles in the hearth while JOE and MARY cuddle together in a big chair. CHARLIE chases the now CONSCIOUS GIRL over and around the furniture while she giggles. We see she's not only recovered from her ordeal but happy. MATTHEW and PHILIP are playing chess. They exchange grins at the new couple's silliness. Joe gives Mary a subtly suggestive look. They rise, hand in hand, while the others hide their smiles and pretend not to notice them leaving. Joe backs Mary against the frame of a bedroom door. "Are you ready?" we see but don't hear him ask. Mary smiles and nods shyly. He leans to her.

Kisses her neck. We expect him to bite her, but then he nicks his own throat with a silver knife. Mary wets her lips, hesitates, and then sucks the cut he made. This time, there's no mistaking Joe's pleasure. His fangs slide out. Mary's eyes begin to glow like his as she feeds from him, and we understand that he's turning her. Romantic music swells beautifully. Their love truly will last forever now.

Turn the page for a preview of the next book
by Michelle Rowen

NIGHTSHADE

Available February 2011 from Berkley Sensation!

One

Life as I knew it ended at half past eleven on a Tuesday morning.

There were currently thirty minutes left.

"What's your poison?" I asked my friend and co-worker Stacy on my way out of the office on a coffee break.

She looked up at me from a spreadsheet on her computer screen, her eyes practically crossed from crunching numbers all morning. "You're a serious lifesaver, Jill, you know that?"

"Well aware." I grinned at her, then shifted my purse to my other shoulder and took the five-dollar-bill she thrust at me.

"I'll take a latte, extra foam. And one of those divine white chocolate chunk cookies. My stomach's growling happily just thinking about it."

Stacy didn't normally go for the cookie action. "No diet today?"

"Fuck diets."

"Can I quote you?"

She laughed. "I'll have it printed on a T-shirt. Hey, Steve! Jill's headed to the coffee shop. You want anything?"

I groaned inwardly. I hadn't wanted to make a big production out of it since I hated making change. Unlike Stacy, math was not my friend.

Finally, I made it out of the office, a yellow sticky note clenched in my fist scrawled with four different coffee orders.

Twenty minutes left.

The line-up at Starbucks was, as usual, ridiculous. I waited. I ordered. I waited some more. I juggled my wallet and my purse along with the bag of pastries and take-out tray of steaming caffeine and finally left the shop, passing an electronics store on my way back. It had a bunch of televisions in the window set to CNN. Some plane crash in Europe was blazing. No survivors. I shivered despite the heat of the day and continued walking.

Five minutes left.

I returned to my office building, which not only housed Lambert Capital, the investment and financial analysis company where I currently temped, but also several other multinational businesses, including a small pharmaceutical research company, a marketing firm, and a modeling agency.

"Hold the elevator," I called out as I crossed the expansive lobby. My heels clicked against the shiny black marble floor. Despite my request, the elevator was *not* held. The doors closed when I was only a couple of steps away from it, a look of bemusement on the sole occupant's face who hadn't done me the honor of waiting.

Jerk.

I wished I wasn't laden down with multiple coffees—all large—as well as my mondo-sized purse that currently gaped open, offering a glimpse at my cluttered life inside. My feet ached from my new shoes.

One minute left.

I nudged the up button with my elbow and waited, watching as the number above the doors stopped at the tenth floor, ISB Pharmaceuticals, paused for what felt like an eternity, and then slowly descended back to the lobby. The other elevator seemed eternally stuck at the fifteenth.

Finally, the doors slid open to reveal a man who wore a white lab coat and a security badge that bore his name: Carl Anderson. His eyes were shifty and there was a noticeable sheen of sweat on his brow. My gaze dropped to his right hand in which he tightly held a syringe—the sharp needle uncapped.

That was definitely a safety hazard I wasn't getting anywhere close to. What the hell was he thinking, carrying something like that around?

Glaring at him, I waited for him to get out of the elevator so I could get on, but he didn't budge an inch.

Behind thick glasses, his eyes were steadily widening with what looked like fear—and totally focused on something behind me. Curious about what would earn this dramatic reaction, I turned to see another man swiftly entering the lobby. He was tall, had a black patch over his left eye, and wasn't smiling. Aside from that, I noticed the gun he held. The big gun. The one he had trained on the man in the elevator.

"Leaving so soon, Anderson? Why am I not surprised?" the man with the gun growled. "No more of your fucking games. Give it to me right now."

I gasped as Carl Anderson suddenly clamped his arm around my neck. The tray of coffees went flying as I clawed at him, but my struggling did nothing. I couldn't even scream; he held me so tightly that it cut off my breath.

"Why are you here?" Anderson demanded. "*I* was supposed to be the one to make contact."

The gunman's icy gaze never wavered. "Let go of the woman."

My eyes watered. I couldn't breathe. My larynx was being crushed.

"But she's the only thing standing between me and your direct orders right now, isn't she?"

"And why would you think I care if you grab some random hostage?" the gunman growled.

Random hostage?

Panic swelled further inside of me. I scanned the lobby to see that this altercation hadn't gone unnoticed. Several people with shocked looks on their faces had cell phones pressed to their ears. Were they calling 911? Where was security? No guards approached with guns drawn.

Fear coursed through me, closing my throat. My hands, which gripped Anderson's arm, were shaking.

"We can talk about this," Anderson said.

"It's too late for negotiations. There's more at risk than the life of one civilian."

"I know. Too bad, really. Thought we were supposed to be working together."

"Sure. Until you decided to sell elsewhere. Hand over the formula."

"I destroyed the rest." Anderson's voice trembled. "One prototype is all that's left."

"That was a mistake." The gunman's tone was flat, but still deadly.

"It was a mistake creating it in the first place. It's dangerous."

"Isn't that the whole point?"

"You'd defend something that would just as easily kill *you*, Declan? Even though you can walk in the sunlight, you're not much better than the other bloodsuckers." The man who held me prone sounded disgusted. And scared shitless—almost as scared as I felt.

Bloodsuckers? What the hell was he talking about? How did I get in the middle of this? I'd only gone out for coffee—coffee that was now splattered all over the clean lobby floor. It was just a normal workday—a normal Tuesday.

More people had gathered around us, moving backward toward the walls and door, away from this unexpected standoff, hands held to their mouths in shock at what they were witnessing. Suddenly I saw someone to my left from the office—it was Stacy with an armful of file folders, her eyes wide as saucers as she looked at me. She took a step closer, mouthing my name.

I tried to shake my head. *No, please don't come any closer*, I thought frantically. *Don't get hurt.*

Where the hell was security?

A shriek escaped my lips when I felt a painful jab at my throat.

"Don't do that," the man with the gun, Declan, snapped.

"You know what will happen if I inject her with this, don't you?" Anderson's voice held an edge of something— panic, fear, desperation. I didn't have to be the helpless hostage in this situation to realize that was a really bad mix.

He had the syringe up against my throat, the sharp tip of the needle stabbing deep into my flesh. I stopped struggling and tried not to move, tried not to breathe. My vision was blurred with tears as I waited for the man with the gun to do something to save me. He was my only hope.

"I don't give a shit about her," my only hope said evenly. "All I care about is that formula. Now hand it over and maybe you get to live."

The gunman's face was oddly emotionless considering this situation. He wore black jeans and a black T-shirt, which bared thick, sinewy biceps. His face didn't have an ounce of humanity to it. Around the black eye patch, scar tissue branched out like a spider web up over his forehead and down his left cheek, all the way to his neck. He was as scary-looking as he was ugly.

"I knew they'd send you to retrieve this, Declan." Anderson's mouth was so close to my ear that I could feel his hot breath. His voice, while shaky, held a mocking edge. "Who better for this job?"

"I'll give you five seconds to release the woman and hand over that syringe with its contents intact," Declan said. "Or I'll kill both of you where you stand. Five . . . four . . ."

"Think about this, will you?" Anderson dug the needle further into my flesh, prompting another wheeze of a shriek from me. "You need to open your fucking eyes and see the truth before it's too late. I'm trying to stop this the only way I can. It's wrong. All of it's wrong. You're just as brainwashed as the rest of them, aren't you?"

With his chest pressed against my back, I could feel his erratic heartbeat. He was afraid for his life. A mental flash of memories of my family, my friends, sped past my eyes. I didn't want to die—not like this.

"Three . . . two . . ." Declan continued, undeterred. The laser sighter from his gun shone a bright, unwavering red dot onto the center of my blue shirt.

Several onlookers ran for the glass doors, and screams sounded out.

"You want the abomination I created that goddamned much?" Anderson yelled. "Here! You can have it!"

A second later, I felt a burning pain, hot as fire, as he injected me with the syringe's contents. It was a worse pain than the stabbing itself. Then he raggedly ripped the needle out and pushed me away hard enough that I went sprawling to the floor. I clamped my hand against the side of my neck and started to scream my head off.

The sound of a gunshot, even louder than my screams, pierced my eardrums. I turned to look at the man who'd injected me. He now lay sprawled out on the marble floor, his eyes open and glassy. There was a large hole in Anderson's forehead, red and wet and sickening. He had a gun in his left hand, which he must have pulled from his lab coat when he let go of me. The empty syringe lay next to him.

Declan went directly to him, gun still trained on the dead man for another moment before he tucked it away, squatted, and then silently and methodically began going through the pockets of the white coat.

My entire body shook, but otherwise I was frozen in place. There were more screams now, from the others who'd witnessed the shooting as they ran in all directions.

After a moment, Declan swore under his breath and then turned to look directly at me for the very first time. The iris of his right eye was pale gray and soulless, and the look he gave me froze my insides.

My throat felt like it had been slit wide open, but I was still breathing. Still thinking. A quick, erratic scan of the lobby showed where I'd dropped my purse and the coffees and pastries six feet to my right. Most of the people in the lobby were now running for the doors to escape to the street outside. A security alarm finally began to wail, adding to the surrounding chaos.

"You—" Declan rose fluidly to his feet. He was easily a full foot taller than my five-four. "—come here."

Like hell I would.

A moment later, the elevator to the left of me opened and a man pushing an empty mail cart got off. The murderer's attention went to it briefly. I took it as the only chance I might ever get. I scrambled to my feet and ran.

"Jill!" I heard Stacy yell, but it didn't slow me down. I had to get away, far away from the office. My mind had switched into survival mode. Stacy couldn't get close to me right now; it would only put her in danger, too.

I left my purse behind—the contents of my life scattered on the smooth, cold floor next to the spilled coffee and spreading pool of blood. I pushed through the front doors, fully expecting Declan to shoot me in my back. But he didn't.

Yanking my hand from my wounded neck, I saw that it was covered in blood. My stomach lurched and I almost vomited. What was in that syringe? It continued to burn like lava sliding through my veins.

I was badly hurt. Jesus, I'd been stabbed in the throat with a needle by a stranger. If I wasn't in such pain, I'd think I was having a nightmare.

This *was* a nightmare—a waking one.

A look behind me confirmed that Declan, whoever the hell he was, had exited the office building. He looked along one side of the street before honing in on me.

I clutched at a few people's arms as I stumbled past them. They recoiled from my touch, faceless strangers who weren't willing to help a strange woman with a bleeding neck wound.

My heart slammed against my rib cage as I tried to run. I found I couldn't manage more than a stagger. I wanted to pass out. The world was blurry and shifting around me.

The burning pain slowly began to spread from my neck down to my chest and along my arms and legs. I could feel it like a living thing, burrowing deeper and deeper inside me.

It didn't take long before I felt Declan's hand clamp around my upper arm. He nearly pulled me off my feet as he dragged me around the corner and into an alley.

"Let go of me," I snarled, attempting to hit him. He effortlessly grabbed my other arm. I blinked against my tears.

"Stay still."

"Go to hell." The next moment, the pain inside me cut off any further words as I convulsed. Only his unrelenting grip kept me from crumpling to the ground. He pushed me up against the wall and held my head firmly in place as he looked into my eyes. His scars were even uglier up close. A shudder of revulsion rippled through me.

Then he wrenched my head to the left and roughly pulled my long blond hair aside to inspect the neck would. His expression never wavered. There was no pity or anger or disdain in his gaze—nothing but emptiness in his single gray eye as he looked me over.

Holding me with one hand tightly around my throat so I could barely breathe, he held a cell phone to his ear.

"It's me," he said after a moment. "There's been a complication."

A pause.

"Anderson administered the prototype to a civilian before attempting to shoot me and escape. I killed him." Another pause. "It's a woman. Should I kill her, too?"

I gasped. He sounded so blasé about it, so emotionless, as if he was discussing bringing home a pizza after work rather than seeking permission for my murder.

His one-eyed gaze narrowed. While talking on the phone he hadn't looked anywhere but my face. "I know, I was followed here. I don't have long." Then finally, "Understood."

He ended the call.

"What are you going to do to me?" I demanded through my fear.

"That's not up to me." Declan loosened his hold on my neck so he could tuck the phone back into the pocket of his black jeans. It was enough to let me sink my teeth into his arm. He pushed me back so hard I whacked my head against the wall and fell to the ground. I'd managed to draw blood on his forearm, which was already riddled with other scars. It was oddly satisfying.

I scrambled up to my feet, adrenaline coursing through my body. I was ready to do whatever I had to in order to fight for my life, but another curtain of agony descended over me.

"What's happening to me?" I managed to say through clenched teeth. "What the hell was in that syringe?"

Declan grabbed me by the front of my shirt and brought me very close to his scarred face. "Poison."

My eyes widened. "Oh my God. What kind of poison?"

"The kind that will kill you," he said simply. "Which is why you have to come with me."

I shook my head erratically. "I have to get to a hospital."

"No." He grabbed me tighter. "Death now or death later. That's your only choice."

It was a choice I didn't want to make. It was one I wouldn't have to make. More pain erupted inside of me and the world went totally and completely black.

Kissing Midnight

THE FIRST BOOK IN THE FITZ CLARE CHRONICLES
BY *USA TODAY* BESTSELLING AUTHOR

EMMA HOLLY

Edmund Fitz Clare has been keeping secrets he can't afford to expose. Not to the orphans he's adopted. Not to the lovely young woman he's been yearning after for years, Estelle Berenger. He's an *upyr*—a shape-shifting vampire—desperate to redeem past misdeeds.

But deep in the heart of London a vampire war is brewing, a conflict that threatens to throw Edmund and Estelle together—and to turn his beloved human family against him…

penguin.com

DON'T MISS THE SECOND BOOK IN THE
FITZ CLARE CHRONICLES TRILOGY
BY *USA TODAY* BESTSELLING AUTHOR

Emma Holly

BREAKING
MIDNIGHT

Edmund Fitz Clare has been kidnapped
by rebellious *upyr* who are determined to
create a new world order. It's up to his
family and his lover to find him.

penguin.com

Discover Romance

berkleyjoveauthors.com

See what's coming up next from your
favorite romance authors and explore all
the latest Berkley, Jove, and Sensation
selections.

See what's new

~

Find author appearances

~

Win fantastic prizes

~

Get reading recommendations

~

Chat with authors and other fans

~

Read interviews with authors you love

berkleyjoveauthors.com